HIS

Wicked

WAYS

THE WICKEDS: DARK KNIGHTS AT BAYSIDE

MELISSA FOSTER

Cover Design: Elizabeth Mackey Designs
Cover Photography: Wander Pedro Aguiar

WORLD LITERARY PRESS
PRINTED IN THE UNITED STATES OF AMERICA

A Note to Readers

Several years ago, when I first met Blaine Wicked on the page, I thought I knew exactly who he was. Boy was I wrong. I've since learned much more about our fiercely loyal, charming-in-his-own-way, too-pushy, and incredibly demanding hero, the heartache he's endured, and the depth of his love. He still took me by surprise at every turn while I was writing this story. I don't know if anyone is prepared for the *real* Blaine Wicked, but it's clear that his heroine, Reese Wilder, certainly wasn't. Reese is a forensic scientist, several years younger than Blaine, but she's not a spineless girl who bends to his will. Reese has had a rough life, and the last thing she needs is a pushy biker telling her what to do. Their story is not an easy one, but it's worth every minute of their struggle. I fell hard for Reese and Blaine, and I hope you will, too. If this is your first Melissa Foster book, all Love in Bloom stories are written to stand alone and may also be enjoyed as part of the larger series, so dive in and enjoy the fun, sexy ride.

Be sure to sign up for my newsletter so you don't miss sales or new releases.
www.MelissaFoster.com/News

If you prefer sweet romance with no explicit scenes or graphic language, please try the Sweet with Heat series written under my pen name, Addison Cole.

Happy reading!
~ Melissa

About the Love in Bloom World

Love in Bloom is the overarching romance collection name for several family series whose worlds sometimes interconnect.

Where to Start

All Love in Bloom books can be enjoyed as stand-alone novels or as part of the larger series. You can start with any book or series without feeling a step behind, and Melissa's newest release is the perfect place to jump in. If you enjoy Melissa's storytelling, you can then decide if you want to read the rest of that series, try another of her family series, or if you enjoy longer series, you can start with the very first Love in Bloom novel, *Sisters in Love*, and then read through all of the series in the collection in publication order. Melissa offers free downloadable series checklists, publication schedules, and family trees on her website. A paperback series guide for the first thirty-six books in the series is available at most retailers and provides pertinent details for each book as well as places for you to take notes about the characters and stories. You can find those items and more at the links below.

See the Entire Love in Bloom Collection
www.MelissaFoster.com/love-bloom-series

Download Series Checklists, Family Trees, and Publication Schedules
www.MelissaFoster.com/reader-goodies

Download Free First-in-Series eBooks
www.MelissaFoster.com/free-ebooks

Playlist

"Fast Car" by Luke Combs

"Heaven" by Niall Horan

"Just Pretend" by Bad Omens

"Come & Get It" by Selena Gomez

"Haven't You Ever Been in Love Before?" by Lewis Capaldi

"Made You Look" by Meghan Trainor

"Trustfall" by Pink

"Nonsense" by Sabrina Carpenter with Coi Leray

"Walk Me Home" by Pink

"Red Flags" by Mimi Webb

"Waffle House" by the Jonas Brothers

"Eyes Closed" by Ed Sheeran

"Something to Someone" by Dermot Kennedy

"Better Man" by Pearl Jam

"Fictional" by Khloe Rose

"Anti-Hero" by Taylor Swift

"Favorite Kind of High" by Kelly Clarkson

"Stolen" by Dashboard Confessional

"We All Need Someone" by the Strumbellas

"Breathe You In" by Dierks Bentley

"Till You're Ready" by Navvy

"Let Em Go" by Matt Hansen

Chapter One

BLAINE WICKED WOULD rather be anywhere other than biding his time at a bachelor party as drunk guys pawed after a half-dozen scantily clad strippers in a posh Boston hotel suite.

At thirty-four, he was well past the thrill of strippers and drunken shenanigans, but he and the buddy who had dragged his ass there, Cameron "Cuffs" Revere, had gone to high school with the man of honor, Jay Harris. Blaine could barely stomach the guy back then, and based on how Jay had decided to celebrate his impending marriage, it was obvious he hadn't outgrown being a dick.

Most of the women looked as if it was just another day on the job, stripping off barely there outfits and giving lap dances in G-strings, but Blaine's focus was on an awkward leggy blonde. Her breasts threatened to break free from a faux-leather halter top, and her minuscule matching skirt stretched tight over thick hips. She wasn't tanned or perfectly made-up like the other girls. Her hair was about a dozen shades of blond, falling in messy waves to her shoulders, as if she'd run into the party late from another appointment. She couldn't dance worth shit, either, but that awkwardness was strangely enticing, as was her flirtatious laugh, which hung in the air like a sound refusing to be forgotten.

A guy reached for her, and she coyly kept her distance, waggling her finger, purring, "*Naughty boy*," and turning away. Her eyes caught on Blaine and widened a little, as if he'd surprised her, and *damn*, she sure surprised him. She had a girl-next-door vibe going on, with a heart-shaped face, thick dark brows above big blue eyes that screamed of innocence and somehow also held a warning not to mess with her, pouty lips perfect for all sorts of dirty things, and an adorable dimple in her chin. She tried hard to mask a hint of trepidation, but while the other assholes were too drunk to notice or care about anything other than getting off, Blaine never missed a thing. He'd been raised in a biker family. Protecting women was in his blood. He told himself to let it go. She was hired to strip, after all, and must have known what she was getting into.

So why do you look like a bunny trapped in a lion's den?

Jay came up behind her, putting his hand on her back. She nearly jumped out of her skin and spun around. *Fuck. Why do I want to break his hand?* Blondie schooled her expression, smiling as she danced around him, but Blaine saw through that tough facade to the weariness she was trying hard to hide. He tried to shake off the itch to figure her out and turned to Cuffs. "Why did I let you talk me into this bullshit?"

"Because you owed me one." Cuffs tipped his glass to his lips. He was a cop, whether he was in or out of uniform, and a fellow member of the Dark Knights motorcycle club. "I told you Jay's an attorney now, and I have to interact with him professionally. Besides, what were you going to do tonight? Now that Marly is with Dante, it isn't like you've got any hope of scoring with her. Not that you ever did." He snickered.

Marly Bowers was a gorgeous brunette and close friend who

Blaine had hooked up with for a while. They'd always flirted and were close, but they'd kept their no-strings arrangement under the radar from their friends and families because neither had wanted more and they didn't want to deal with the hassles of friends pressuring them. When Marly started dating Dante Dubois, the guitarist for Carnal Beat, a local band, she and Blaine had ended their arrangement, and they'd both moved on.

"*Shit.*" Blaine shook his head. "You know there's plenty of women waiting in the wings."

"Speaking of…" Cuffs nodded to a petite brunette dancing toward them with her eyes locked on Blaine.

She flashed a sultry smile. "Anyone ever tell you you're a dead ringer for James Marsden?"

Only every woman I've ever met.

He didn't bother answering. She didn't seem to care as she danced seductively up and down his body, but his attention was drawn back to the leggy blonde across the room, who was now trying to evade Jay.

The brunette dragged her finger down the center of Blaine's chest. "How about a lap dance, *James?*"

"I'm good, thanks," he said without taking his eyes off the blonde as Jay cornered her by the bedroom. Blaine's eyes narrowed, his jaw clenching. He was no saint. He went after what he wanted, and he could be a persistent asshole, too, but he'd never force himself on anyone, and at least he was a loyal motherfucker. Unlike Jay, whose fiancée probably thought he was kicking it old-school with his buddies, not trying to bang the entertainers.

Jay leaned closer to the blonde, saying something that made her laugh, but her eyes darted nervously around the room, connecting with Blaine's for only a few seconds before Jay slid his arm around her and pulled her against him. Her smile faltered, but she was quick to put it back in place. She put her hand on Jay's chest, shaking her head.

"Cuffs, you seeing this?" Blaine lifted his chin in their direction.

"Yeah. She's still smiling, and she's a stripper," Cuffs reminded him. "We have no idea what else she's been paid to do."

"Right." Blaine gritted his teeth against that truth. He didn't judge people. Everyone needed to make a living, but what a way to do it. These girls put their safety on the line with every job.

She started dancing again, inching away from Jay and turning her attention to another guy. Jay grabbed her wrist, tugging her against him. Blaine's hands fisted as Jay backed her into the bedroom and closed the door. He told himself to mind his own business, but every iota of his being told him to get the hell in there. He'd never ignored his instincts before, and damn it to hell, he wasn't about to start. "Fuck this."

REESE WALKED BACKWARD, her heart slamming against her ribs as the smarmy guy closed in on her. This was *not* what she signed up for. Then again, she hadn't asked to take care of her teenage sister, to put her mother through rehab, or to pay off her mother's freaking drug debt, either. But this was her life, and now she was stuck in borrowed clothes, pretending to be something she wasn't, and this asshat was just another stumbling block. All she had to do was hold it together long enough to make it through the party and collect her cash.

"Aren't you the guy who's getting married?" She hoped she sounded lighthearted.

"That's right. I'll be off the market soon, but you lucked out. You'll get *all* of me tonight."

He reached for her, but she ducked and darted for the door. "That's a nice offer, but I really need to get back to the party." He grabbed her and shoved her toward the bed. She landed with her hands on the mattress.

He grabbed her hips. "I'm gonna fuck you so good—"

The heck you are. She jerked upright, throwing her head back, and slammed it into his face.

"You *bitch*. You want it rough? I'll give it to you rough." He latched on to her arm with a death grip and threw her onto the bed just as the door opened and the guy with the messy dark hair and piercing ice-blue eyes walked in.

"What's going on in here?" His assessing gaze moved between them as he closed the door and stepped closer. He was at least six foot two or three, with an air of dominance.

Oh God. Was he there to join the fun? Panic burned in her chest. What had she gotten herself into? She scrambled to her feet.

"What do you *think* is going on?" Smarmy Guy fumed. "Close the door on your way out."

The other guy's eyes hardened like cold steel, his jaw ticking, shoulders rolling back, like a beast readying for battle. "She doesn't look like a willing party to your plan."

"I'm *fine*. I was just leaving." Reese went for the door, glowering at the bastard who had dragged her into the room.

He stepped in front of her, blocking her path. "We're not done yet."

"*She's* done, which means *you're* done," the other guy

seethed, the threat in his icy tone clear.

Reese held her breath, tension mounting in the room like a volcano ready to erupt.

"We paid good money for this bitch, and I'm getting my shar—"

The other guy's fist connected with his jaw with a *crack* so loud, Reese was sure he broke it. The smarmy guy stumbled backward, cursing, and the dark-haired guy hit him again. "Remember this the next time you get the urge to manhandle a woman, you piece of shit." He cocked his arm to hit him a third time, but the door flew open again, and the clean-cut tatted guy he'd been with earlier ran over and grabbed his arm.

"Blaine, *stop*! You don't need to end up in jail tonight. Get her outta here. I'll take care of this asshole."

As Blaine turned away, the smarmy guy said, "I'll sue your ass."

Blaine spun around, punching him in the gut so hard, he doubled over, wheezing. Blaine grabbed him by the hair, getting right in his face. "Go ahead and sue. Judges don't take trying to rape women lightly. And you can guarantee your fiancée will hear about this." He shoved the jerk away.

His buddy pinned the guy against the wall as Blaine put his arm around her, shielding her like a bodyguard, ushering her through the crowd that had gathered at the door and through the suite. Reese's mind reeled as they hurried down the hall toward the elevator. She shrugged out from under his grasp.

"You okay?" He hit the button for the elevator.

I nearly got raped by some jerk, and now I don't have the money to pay my mother's dealer. How the heck do you think I am? "I'm *fine*."

"You're trembling."

"It's a basic physiological reaction to stress. I'm fine, and I could have handled that guy myself." She wasn't sure she could have, but she was not, and had never been, a damsel in distress, and she hated being treated like one.

His eyes narrowed. "Sure didn't look that way."

"What do you know about how it looked? You don't know me." Her head was all over the place. She didn't know why she was snapping at *him*.

His jaw clenched. "Would you rather I'd left you with that fucker? You should really press charges."

"No." She huffed out a breath. "I just want to get out of here and forget this night ever happened. Look, I know you think you're helping, and I appreciate that, but I *needed* the money from that job."

"Bad enough to get raped?"

That word hit hard, bringing the harsh reality of what could have happened. She could have ended up just like her mother. Fighting tears of frustration, she bit her tongue, staring ahead, and crossed her arms to try to stop trembling. *Breathe, just breathe.*

The elevator arrived, and they rode down to the lobby in silence. She stole a glance at Blaine, sizing him up. She'd been caught off guard when she'd first seen him at the party with his dark dress shirt rolled up to his elbows, leather bracelets around one wrist, silver ones on the other, drink in hand, and those mesmerizing blue eyes trained on her. He'd looked hot and harmless, but *holy shit*. The guy must be unhinged the way he'd flipped a switch back there.

He followed her out of the hotel. When he continued following her down the street, she stopped in her tracks, holding his stare. "Why are you following me?"

"I'm making sure you get to your car safely."

"I don't need a babysitter. Besides, you were at that party. How do I know you're not just like him?"

"Did I try to hurt you?"

"*No*, but that doesn't mean you won't."

"Get over yourself, sweetheart," he said gruffly. "I'm not that kind of guy, and I have plenty of willing women to fuck."

She scoffed, uttering "Asshat" under her breath.

His jaw remained tight. "Just being honest."

"So was I." She didn't have time for his arrogance. "I appreciate your concern, but that's my car." She pointed to her decade-old Civic. "I'm *safe*. You can go." She stalked to her car without looking back, climbed in, and locked the doors. She tried to start the car, and it made a clicking sound. She tried again and heard the same lifeless click. "*Nonono*. Come *on*." She took a deep breath, throwing a silent prayer out to the engine gods, and tried one last time. *Click.*

Noooo. She pounded on the steering wheel. *This can't be happening.* She folded her arms over the steering wheel and lowered her face to them as the tears she'd been holding back trickled free.

A knock at the window startled her upright. She swiped at her tears.

Blaine peered in at her. "Need a jump?"

She nodded and said, "Yes, *please*," through the window.

"I'll get my truck." He pointed his finger at her. "Stay in your car."

She hated being told what to do so much, she had half a mind to get out just to defy him, but after the night she'd had, she wasn't about to leave her safe haven.

A few minutes later, he parked a big double-cab black truck

with CAPE STONE on the door in front of her car. He hooked it up and tried to jump it. But it still wouldn't start.

"It sounds like your starter's bad."

"*Great.* Now I have to get it towed back to the Cape." At her breaking point, she looked up at the sky and shouted, "*Eff my life!*"

"Feel better?"

She gave him a deadpan look.

"It could be worse." He pulled out his phone. "I've got a buddy who can take care of your car."

"You don't have to do that. I can handle it."

Ignoring her, he spoke into the phone. "Tobias, hey, man. I need a favor."

As he relayed the situation, their location, and the description of her car, she said, "I'm paying for this."

He made no indication that he'd heard her and continued talking. When he ended the call, he pocketed his phone. "Do you have anything in the car that you need?"

"Just my bag." She opened the door and leaned across the driver's seat to grab it. Her freaking skirt hiked up her thighs. She tugged it down and closed the door.

He held out his hand. "Give me your car key."

"I don't even know you. I'm grateful for your help, but the way my night is going, you'll probably steal my car." She didn't believe he'd steal her car any more than she believed he'd try to hurt her. He'd had plenty of opportunities to do that already, but she was incapable of thinking rationally at the moment. She was overwhelmed and seriously worried about how she was going to pay to fix her car *and* keep her mother's dealer off her back and still have money for food and school loans.

He lifted his brows, amusement sneaking into those serious

eyes as he offered his hand. "Blaine Wicked."

"Reese." She looked at his hand but didn't shake it. "Wilder."

"Well, Reese Wilder, I hate to break your run of bad luck, but I'm not going to steal your car. I just want to get you home safely and make sure your car gets fixed."

She didn't have the energy to fight and relinquished the key. "Thank you, but I'm paying for it. Where is it being towed?"

He tucked the key into the tailpipe and took a picture of the car. As he thumbed something out on his phone, he said, "Come on. I'll give you a ride home."

She wondered if he hadn't heard her question, but she had a feeling he'd simply ignored it. "You've done enough. I can call for an Uber."

"If you think I'll let you get into some stranger's car after the night you've had, you're dead wrong. Let's go." He opened the back passenger door and pulled out a duffel bag.

"Is that where you keep your duct tape and torture devices?"

"Nah. Duct tape is messy. I prefer cable ties." He cracked a smile, which softened his sharp edges. "Unless you mean in the bedroom. Then leather or silk will do."

She rolled her eyes but couldn't help smiling as sarcasm oozed from her mouth. "That's original."

"There's that smile I saw earlier." He held out a black sweatshirt. "Put this on."

"Why?"

"You've been exposed enough tonight. Just put the damn thing on. I don't want you to be uncomfortable in my truck."

How could she argue with that? "Thanks." She took it from him. It was soft, like an old favorite, and had DARK KNIGHTS printed above a skull with dark eyes, sharp brows, and a mouth full of jagged fangs, and BAYSIDE printed below it. She'd heard of the Dark Knights but hadn't ever paid attention to who or what they were. "Are you part of a gang?"

"*Yeah*," he said sarcastically. "Get in."

She narrowed her eyes, hesitating.

"It's a motorcycle club, not a gang. There's a difference." He must have seen the skepticism in her eyes, because he said, "I'm not going to lie and say I've never done sketchy shit. I protect people, and sometimes bad people get hurt. But I'm not going to hurt *you*, so get in the truck, tell me where you live, and I'll drive you home."

"Hold on." She took a picture of his truck from the side, went around the rear, took one of his license plate, and then she snapped a picture of him.

He arched a brow. "Did you just take my picture?"

"Yes. I'm sending it to my friend who's a cop. If I go missing, they'll hunt you down." She sent them to her younger sister, Colette, thumbing out, *My car broke down and this guy is driving me home. If I'm not home by midnight give the cops these pics. He said his name is Blaine Wicked.*

"My buddy, Cuffs, the guy who helped me in the hotel, is a cop. You want me to give you his number, too?"

She thought about the way Cuffs had known how to handle the situation and warned Blaine about going to jail, and her worries eased a little more. "No. I'm good." She climbed into the truck, and he stood with his hand on the door, as if he was waiting for something. "What?"

"Put your seat belt on."

"I never would have guessed you to be such a Boy Scout." She snapped her seat belt.

"Whatever you need to believe."

He closed her door and stalked around to the driver's seat, as if he hadn't just shattered the modicum of comfort she'd found.

Chapter Two

ON THE WAY back to the Cape, Blaine couldn't shake the need to figure out what was up with Reese Wilder. If that was even her real name. Fear lingered in her baby blues alongside something else he couldn't pinpoint that made him want to get inside her head and see what she was hiding. She'd stuffed her heels into her bag, tucked her legs beside her on the passenger seat, pink toenails peeking out from beneath his baggy sweatshirt, and was staring out the window, messy golden waves shielding her face. She looked so damn young. Like she belonged on a college campus, laughing it up with pretty preppy boys. It was hard to believe two hours ago she'd been working a bachelor party.

She checked her phone for the umpteenth time and huffed out a breath, furiously thumbing out a text.

"Problem?" Blaine asked.

"No. I just can't reach my sister."

"How old is she?"

She was quiet for a minute, as if considering the question. "Fifteen."

Shit. If her sister was only fifteen, how old could Reese be? He'd guessed early twenties, but now he wondered if she was much younger, in which case he *really* had no business thinking about her pouty lips the way he was. "It's pretty late. Shouldn't she be home with your parents?"

Without answering, she stared out the window again.

"Are your parents around?"

"That's none of your business."

I'll take that as a no. "Reese, if she's home alone and you can't reach her, I *need* to know."

"No, you don't," she said sharply. "She's not your concern."

If only it were that easy. He didn't know how to turn off worries once they seated themselves in his mind. "We're still about forty minutes from West Yarmouth. How about I send one of my brothers to check on her?"

Angry eyes glowered at him. "Definitely *not.* I'm not sending some guy I don't know to check on my little sister."

"Then do you have a friend or neighbor who can look in on her?"

"No, but I'm sure she's fine. She just hates when I check up on her, like any other fifteen-year-old."

She had a point, but he drove a little faster and tried to gain more intel about the feisty blonde. "So, is that what you do for a living? Strip?"

"*No.* That was the first time I tried it."

"I figured as much. You were pretty awkward."

Her brows furrowed. "That's not very nice."

He laughed. "All I'm saying is that you looked like a fish out of water."

She rolled her eyes. "Sorry I'm not up to your stripper standards."

"I don't have stripper standards."

"You obviously do, if I didn't make the cut."

"All I meant..." He gritted his teeth, not wanting to get any deeper into *that* conversation. "We're not talking about me. If you don't strip, what do you do?"

"What is this, an interview?"

"Just trying to figure out why a beautiful young girl like you would turn to stripping."

Her eyes narrowed. "Maybe I *like* it."

He scoffed. "Try again."

She turned away again.

"Hey, no judgment here. Everyone's got to earn a living, but if you want to earn it that way, you might want to practice dancing in those heels and learn how to get yourself out of bad situations. Or even better, bring a guy to watch out for you so nobody tries shit like that again. Do you have a guy friend you can bring along?"

"*Ohmygod*," she said exasperatedly. "I'm never doing that again, so it doesn't matter."

"How much money did you lose?"

"A lot."

He eyed her questioningly.

She sighed. "Eight hundred dollars."

"Jesus. What did you need it for?"

"That's none of your business. How about *you* answer some questions? Why are you friends with that jerk?"

"I'm not. I knew him in high school, and he still works with Cuffs sometimes, so I went as a favor to my buddy. We weren't planning on staying long, but I'm glad I was there to help you."

"I could've—"

"I get it. You think you could have handled him, but I'm glad you didn't have to. Nobody should be put in that situation."

Her expression softened. "Thank you for helping me."

He nodded curtly. "What else do you want to know?"

"Your truck says Cape Stone. What is that? Do you work there?"

"It's a stone distribution and masonry company, and yes, I work there." He didn't bother telling her that he and his brother Justin, who went by the road name Maverick owned it. "What about you? What do you do for work?"

"I'm a forensic scientist. I work in a crime lab."

"No shit?" he said more to himself than to her. Why the hell was a forensic scientist working as a stripper?

"Don't tell me you're one of those guys who think a blonde can't have brains."

"I wasn't thinking that. Do you work in Hyannis or Bourne?"

"Hyannis. *Shoot.* Why did I tell you that? And why do you know where the local crime labs are?" Her eyes narrowed, and she sat up straighter, leaning closer to the door.

"I grew up on the Cape. I know the area well."

"I've lived here forever, and if I wasn't working in the field, I wouldn't know where the crime labs were. Crime labs aren't like fast food restaurants. It's strange that you know. You said you've done some sketchy stuff. What kind of sketchy things?"

"Nothing you have to worry about."

"Maybe I've run your DNA."

"You haven't." They drove in silence until he turned off the highway, heading for her place. "If your sister is fifteen, how old are you?"

"How old are *you*?"

He smiled. "A lot older than you."

"How do you know?"

"Because you can't be more than twenty-two or -three."

"I'm twenty-*six*, thank you very much."

At least he didn't feel like such a letch now, unless… "Are you really twenty-six? Because you look a lot younger."

"People have been telling me that my whole life. Why would I lie?"

He shrugged. "I don't pretend to know why women do anything."

"I could say the same for men."

He turned off the paved road onto the gravel lane where she lived, passing a few cottages. They drove by a long stretch of woods without any homes. As they neared a dead end, he saw it was packed with cars in front of a small cottage that had seen better days. The mess of a yard gave it an abandoned feel. There were people drinking and making out in the grass, on the deck, and in the open doorway, where the screen door was hanging off its top hinges.

Reese moved to the edge of her seat. "What the heck?"

"Looks like little sis is having a party."

"I'm going to kill her."

He stopped the truck, and she threw her door open and ran to the cottage barefoot, clutching her bag. *Fuck.* He parked and went after her. Music blared from inside the house as he strode through the yard, snagged a beer bottle from a kid who looked about sixteen, and growled, "Party's over." Then, louder, to the other teenagers who were drinking on the lawn, "Party's over. Get outta here."

They hightailed it toward the vehicles and he headed inside. There must have been thirty kids packed into the tiny living room and kitchen, drinking beer, smoking, making out, and ignoring Reese, who was hollering over the music blaring from the television. "Everyone, get out! Colette? Colette, where are you?"

Blaine grabbed the remote and turned off the TV. "Party's over. Get the fuck out. *Now.*" As teenagers scrambled to their feet, he grabbed a scruffy guy who looked to be a few years older than most of the other kids. "Where's Colette?"

"I don't know, man. Check the bedroom."

He scanned the room and saw Reese heading through a door in the hall.

"Colette!" Reese shouted. "What the hell are you doing?"

Blaine got to her just in time to see a dark-haired girl who looked too fucking young to be in a bedroom with any guy, jumping up from the bed, tugging at a crop top that clung to her chest, and a scrawny guy grabbing his shirt from the floor. Blaine's blood boiled. As Colette hollered at Reese for barging in, Blaine grabbed the guy by the scruff of the neck, dragging his ass out of the bedroom.

"What're you doing? Get the fuck off me," the kid hollered.

Blaine dragged him out the front door onto the deck. "How old are you?"

"Eighteen," he spat.

"She's *fifteen*, under the age of consent in Massachusetts. You want to go to jail?"

"No. Shit, man. I had no idea. I swear."

"Then stay the fuck away from her." He threw him off the deck, and the guy bolted toward the last car left in front of the house. Blaine went back inside and heard the girls arguing in the bedroom.

"I work my ass off to keep our heads above water, and this is how you thank me?" Anger and hurt warred in Reese's voice.

"Why would I thank you? I don't even want you here."

"Do you think *I* want to be in this house?"

"Then *leave*," Colette fumed. "Go home!"

"You'd love that, wouldn't you? So you can screw your life up? I'm not leaving you, Lettie. I love you, but if this is going to work, I have to be able to trust you, and I can't if you pull this nonsense…"

The emotion in Reese's voice tugged at something deep inside Blaine, her words bringing out his worst fears. Did their parents leave them? How did she end up in this position, and where was *her* home, if not there? He looked around the cottage, which was in shit shape, and not just from the beer cans and cigarette butts from the party, but in general. The walls were dirty and the blinds, broken. There were missing moldings, a broken windowsill, and about a dozen other things that needed repair. There was no dead bolt locking mechanism on the front door. He made a mental note to check the window locks. This was the last thing Reese needed after the night she'd had.

He knew better than to get in the middle of the nightmare with her sister, but at least he could help clean up the mess. He went to the kitchen and found a box of trash bags under the sink. He went around the house picking up beer cans and bottles, food trash, cigarette butts, joint remnants, and other shit. He found several past-due bills strewn across the living room floor and tried not to think too hard about how they were making ends meet. When he finished cleaning up, he tied off the garbage bag and tossed it out onto the deck. He gathered the dirty dishes and was washing them when the girls' voices escalated.

"You can't tell me what to do!" Colette shouted.

"The heck I can't," Reese seethed. "You're *fifteen*. I'm responsible for you, and you'll ..."

Colette stalked into the kitchen a few minutes later. She was tall and thin, wearing too much makeup and radiating attitude like a rattlesnake shakes its rattle. She sneered at him as she tugged open the fridge. "Are you fucking kidding me?" she said as Reese walked in, red faced, breathing hard, and shaking, either on the verge of tears or a blowup. "You texted saying you were worried about this guy killing you, and then you bring him *home*? Real smart, Reese." She slammed the refrigerator door and stormed back toward her bedroom.

Reese startled when the bedroom door slammed. She crossed her arms and her shoulders rounded forward, as if she were giving herself a hug, which made him want to gather her in his arms and take the pain and irritation away. She eyed him. "Why are you still here?"

"I'm helping you clean up this mess."

"You don't have to do that. I can handle it."

"You're not very good at accepting help, are you?" *Why?* was what he wanted to know, along with about a dozen other things. But she didn't need another inquisition.

"Not many people offer," she said flatly. "Really, you've done enough. You can go. You must have something better to do than hang around here cleaning up."

"I'll leave when it's done. I found some bills on the floor in the other room and put them on the coffee table."

"Thank you. I'll do the dishes." She reached for the sponge.

He pulled it out of reach, and despite his worries, he tried to smile to ease her frustrations. "I'm almost done. Why don't you take a minute to breathe."

"I'm not sure I know what that means anymore."

"It's been a night." He lowered his voice. "Is your sister

okay? That guy was eighteen. Did he...?"

She shook her head. "She said they were only in there a few minutes before we got here, and she *wanted* to be in there with him."

"Has she done anything like this before?"

"I honestly don't know, but not with me." She sounded exhausted and leaned against the counter.

That could mean many things, but he went with the most obvious. "How long have your parents been gone?"

"Oh, they're not dead. Well, I guess my father might as well be. He left a few months before Colette was born, but my mom didn't leave us. I kind of wish she had. I think it would be easier."

The new grief in her voice had him grinding his teeth. He didn't like the direction this was heading. "I'm sorry about your old man."

"It's okay. It was a long time ago."

"That still doesn't make it okay. I take it your mom isn't the most nurturing?"

"You could say that." She glanced toward Colette's bedroom, swallowing hard.

He finished the dishes and dried his hands on a towel. "Why don't you get some shoes on and come outside with me while I pick up the yard?"

"You really don't—"

"I'll meet you outside." He grabbed a couple of garbage bags and headed out the front door. When he got into the yard, he gave the place a quick once-over. There were missing and broken cedar shingles, a cracked window, and a gutter hanging off one side. The deck was missing a railing on the steps, and that screen door needed to be secured. The yard was overgrown and weedy, littered with beer cans and bottles and other party remnants.

He was picking up trash when Reese came out the front door wearing yellow-and-white polka-dot rain boots, looking too damn cute with his sweatshirt hanging down her thighs.

She began picking up trash. "I really appreciate your help."

"I'm happy to do it. I would like to know what the deal is with your mom. Why she's not around."

She studied his face for a minute. "It's embarrassing. She's a mess."

"If she is, that's not a reflection of you. We don't pick our parents. People go through all sorts of bad situations, and everyone handles them differently. You clearly try to do right by your sister, which had to come from somewhere."

"She wasn't always a mess," she said softly, but he wasn't sure he believed her. "But she's in rehab now, and hopefully she'll pull herself together and be the mom Colette needs."

"How about the mom *you* need?"

She shrugged. "I'm fine."

"Yeah, you keep saying that." *But you're hanging on by a thread.* He dumped half a beer into the grass and put the empty bottle in the trash bag. "What is she in rehab for? Drugs? Alcohol?"

"She's not choosy about how she self-medicates."

"Sounds like you've been dealing with this for a while."

She went quiet again, picking up trash and tossing it in the bag.

"Is this her first time in rehab?"

She shook her head. "She's tried before but never stuck with it."

"How long has she been in this time?"

"Three weeks. Only fourteen more to go. My fingers and toes are crossed that this time will be different."

Then the real work begins. Rehab wasn't a magic pill. It was the start of a new lifestyle. A daily struggle to keep the demons at bay. Every scent, sound, and person could serve as a reminder or a draw to past habits. But Reese didn't need to hear that. "Did your mom take medical leave to cover expenses while she's in there?"

A laugh tumbled out. "She doesn't even have health insurance. She works for a few months, gets fired, and tricks someone else into hiring her."

"How'd she pay for the house and rehab?"

"This was my grandmother's house. She left it to my mom when she passed away, and we took out a home equity loan to pay for rehab."

He didn't bother asking what would happen when her mother got out of rehab and didn't make the payments. The answer was staring him in the face. When her mother dropped the ball, Reese picked it up and did her best to run with it. "I take it you moved back home to take care of Colette while your mom is in rehab?"

"You don't miss a thing, do you?"

"You guys were arguing pretty loudly," he said as they went around the side of the house and began picking up more trash. "Are you still paying rent on your own place, or did you give it up?"

"I couldn't get out of my lease."

That explained some of the unpaid bills, but he'd seen some that were long overdue. Her desperate attempt to make money was making more sense. He watched her picking up the yard, and his heart went out to her. She was too sweet to have all this on her shoulders, and he was determined to help her find her way without any more desperate or dangerous attempts.

She looked up, catching him studying her, and smiled bashfully. "What?"

"You're a brave woman, Reese Wilder." He cocked a brow. "If that really is your name."

"It *is*," she said with a softer laugh than he'd heard at the party. This laugh was a little shy, with only a hint of flirtation, which seemed more like *her*—natural, real, and though he didn't understand the thought, *special*—making it even more unforgettable.

He shouldn't like that laugh as much as he did. He tried to distract himself from the growing attraction and tied off the trash bag. "Why don't you give me your number, and I'll let you know when your car is ready?"

She drew her shoulders back, holding his gaze, and probably thought she looked tough, but in his sweatshirt, with those polka-dot boots, she looked anything but. "Can you just give me the number of the shop where it was towed?"

"It's not at a shop. My sister's boyfriend used to work as a mechanic. He's going to work on it at their place." He pulled out his phone, wanting to put her mind at ease and earn her trust. "Want me to text you his number?"

"No." She pulled out her phone. "You can just read it off for me."

He nodded curtly, impressed with her resolve to remain in control, and gave her Tobias's name and number. "Take mine, too, just in case you need anything."

She put his number in her phone. "Thanks. Can I ask you something?"

"Sure." He grabbed the other trash bag from the deck and

tossed them in the back of his truck.

"Never mind," she said softly, and looked down at the grass.

He stepped closer, but she didn't meet his gaze. He lifted her chin, and her worried eyes stirred that unfamiliar sensation deep inside his chest again. He'd helped hundreds of people over the years, and he'd never felt such an intense stirring. Unable to resist, he brushed his thumb over the dimple in her chin before dropping his hand. "What do you want to know?"

"Why are you really helping me? What are you hoping to get out of it?"

"Nothing." He wondered how many men had abused her trust and had the strange urge to track them all down and make them pay for it. "I'm helping you because I was raised to do the right thing, and you don't owe me a damn thing for any of it, if that's what you're worried about."

"So, you just go around saving women from bad men on the weekends?"

"No. I just live my life, but keeping people safe is what the Dark Knights do."

"I think you mean what the *white* knights do." She smiled, and it *almost* took away the worry in her eyes. "That's a complex, you know. You can get help for it."

"I don't have a savior complex," he said with a laugh. "I ride a motorcycle, not a horse, and a pretty little thing like you shouldn't worry about why I do things."

She narrowed her eyes. "I'm not a *pretty little* thing."

"I think I know a pretty little thing when I see one."

"I'm a grown woman with a fully functioning brain."

"A'right. Don't worry your beautiful womanly mind about why I do things. Is that better?"

She crossed her arms, stifling a grin, easing the ire in her eyes. "It may not seem like it, but I'm not a damsel in distress. I appreciate your help, but I don't need saving, or—"

"*Stop*. I don't think of you like that. I think you're brave and strong, and you just got yourself into a bad situation earlier. Now you're out of it, and that's all that matters." He lifted his chin in the direction of the house. "Be sure to lock your doors tonight."

"I always do."

He nodded, and she headed up to the deck.

As she reached for the door, she glanced over her shoulder. "Aren't you going to leave?"

"Once you're safely inside and behind that locked door."

She pressed her lips together, like she was thinking about something. "Tell your parents I said thank you."

"For?"

"Raising a nice guy. I hope the rest of your weekend is easier." She headed inside and closed the door.

He had a feeling the information he'd learned tonight only scratched the surface of the shitload of chaos Reese Wilder was dealing with. If she thought she was done with him, she was sorely mistaken.

Chapter Three

REESE SAT AT the kitchen table Sunday morning with an untouched cup of black coffee, which tasted like tar because she'd forgotten to get milk, and a stack of unpaid bills, trying to figure out what she and Colette could go without. She'd depleted her savings making the first three five-hundred-dollar installments to her mother's dealer, and she still owed him forty-five hundred dollars. He was coming to collect the next installment this week, and she was terrified about what he'd do when she didn't have it.

She took a deep breath. *Nobody is coming to save you. Figure out a solution and make it happen. Colette needs you to be strong and smart.* She'd been giving herself the same silent pep talk since she was twelve years old, which was when she'd realized the mother she'd known might be lost forever to the depressed, drug-addicted shell of a woman who lived in their house.

After going through the bills again, she came up with a plan. Tomorrow she'd turn off the utilities at her apartment and ask her landlord if he'd let her pay her rent late for the next three months if she paid interest. She'd contact the student loan company to see if she could buy time there, too. Maybe they'd forgive a few months for extenuating circumstances. Someone had to cut her some slack, for Pete's sake. It wasn't like *she* was the addict.

If she could pull all that off, it would be a start, but her mother's utilities had already been sixty days past due when she'd gone into rehab. She had to pay something or they'd cut them off. She'd pay what she could, but there was no avoiding the reality of her situation. Even if she got approval to pay all her bills late, she would be in the same predicament next week and the week after, continuously digging herself deeper into debt. She silently counted to ten, trying to tamp down the anger she felt toward her mother.

Reese needed a real ongoing solution, not a bandage, and she wasn't going to make the same mistake she'd made last night. She'd answered a job posting on Craigslist for a bachelor party hostess. She should've known there would be more to the job than hostessing.

She pushed her glasses to the bridge of her nose and picked up her phone to search for a part-time job, telling herself not to look at the picture of Blaine she'd taken in the parking lot. She'd stared at the darn thing so long last night, she was sure his distractingly handsome face was etched into her mind, and don't even get her started on his all-seeing eyes. Every time he looked at her, butterflies swarmed in her chest and her body heated up. Part of that heat was caused by annoyance, she was sure, since he was so darn pushy. But the other part? The spine-tingling, butterfly- and heat-inducing part? *That* was the reason she kept staring at the picture. Looking at him was like taking a dopamine and norepinephrine cocktail, eliciting new and exciting feelings. Feelings she should *not* be so intrigued by, considering she had far more important things to do than think about the hot pushy guy who saved her from potentially ending up as a victim giving DNA samples for other forensic scientists to analyze.

That thought hit as hard as it had yesterday, driving her to navigate to a browser, and search, *How to make cash fast.*

Twenty minutes later, she'd skimmed several threads on Reddit and discovered the top three ways to make money fast were opening an account on OnlyFans, selling her used underwear, or selling pictures of her feet. The thought of doing any of those things made her sick.

She went farther down the list and began researching DoorDash and Uber, both of which seemed to be good options and would work around her schedule. She looked up when her sister strolled into the kitchen, wearing her old, ratty sleeping shirt and shorts, just like Reese was. The fact that they usually chose similar clothes to sleep in had always given Reese a mild sense of comfort. She tried so hard to be a good sister and role model—with the exception of last night's bachelor party debacle—but it was hard to connect when the only things they had in common were their mother and their choice of sleep-wear.

Colette grabbed a box of cereal from the pantry and shoved her hand into it, looking at Reese with an annoyed expression. "So, you can have sleepovers and I can't?"

Reese didn't have the energy for a fight this morning, and Colette always seemed armed and ready for battle. "What are you talking about?"

"You don't have to hide it." She shoved a handful of cereal into her mouth, speaking around the mouthful. "I know your boyfriend came back. I got up at two to use the bathroom and saw his truck out front, and it's still out there, so…"

"*What?* He wasn't with *me*, and he's not my boyfriend."

Reese jumped to her feet and ran to the front window.

Colette followed, and they peered out. "So he's some kind of creepy stalker?"

"*No*," she said emphatically, and realized how stupid she was for thinking she could make that declaration. "I don't know, but I'm going to find out. Stay here." She shoved her feet into her rain boots and stalked out to his truck to set him straight.

He was sitting behind the wheel, all big and broad, flashing a painfully sexy smile, his gaze raking down her body. "What's up, buttercup?"

Her pebbling nipples reminded her that she wasn't wearing a bra. She crossed her arms and narrowed her eyes. Hating that he was even hotter in the daylight. "Don't *buttercup* me. Why are you stalking me?"

"Stalking?" He arched a brow.

"You're not a very smart creeper. Colette saw you out here at two in the morning."

He laughed. "Maybe because I'm not a creeper." His expression turned serious. "Colette was wrong. I was here well before two. I only left to grab some coffee."

I knew you were too good to be true. "That is not working in your favor."

"Do you want to call your cop friend and have me arrested? Oh, *wait*, your alleged cop friend was really your little sister."

She'd forgotten about saying that. "You need to leave."

He glanced at the dashboard. "I didn't realize it was so late. I do have to go. I've got a big ride today with the guys. I just wanted to make sure nobody from the party came back to stir up trouble."

The honesty in his voice gave her pause. "You stood guard out here all night for us?"

"Well, technically I sat, but yes. Did Detective Colette also report that I left half an hour ago for a few minutes?" He held a bag out the window. "I noticed you had no milk in the fridge and thought you might need it this morning. There are also a few doughnuts in there. I don't know what kind you girls like, so I got jelly filled, cream filled, chocolate covered, and glazed. I figured one of those might hit the spot."

Her thoughts stumbled, and she opened her mouth to thank him as she took the bag but couldn't find her voice.

"Do either of you need a ride anywhere today?"

She shook her head as the fog of disbelief lifted. "No. Thanks though…for everything. I'm sorry I called you a creeper. I'll pay you back for these."

"No need. Seeing you in those sexy specs is thanks enough."

Her cheeks warmed, and she absently touched the chic frames she'd splurged on after getting a raise last winter. They were blue tortoiseshell on top, heather on the bottom, with a slight cat-eye shape. Her sister made fun of them, but rectangular frames didn't look good with Reese's round cheeks.

He started up his truck. "See you around, buttercup. Try not to get into any trouble today." He winked and drove away.

She stared after him, wondering if any man could be that kind without expecting something in return. He was either a unicorn or playing her. Despite not wanting or needing a man in her life, it sure felt good to have someone else notice their needs for a change.

"Way to give him hell," Colette said sarcastically, drawing Reese's attention.

She headed across the lawn. "He was watching out for us."

"Uh-huh. I bet that's what all the creepers say."

Reese put her hand on the railing as she climbed the steps to the deck, then stopped cold. The railing had been missing for as long as she could remember.

"What's in the bag?"

Reese was still stuck on the new railing. "He brought us doughnuts and milk."

"Seriously?" Colette grabbed the bag from her. "Best creeper *ever*!" She pulled open the screen door and hurried inside.

Reese stared at the screen door, holding it open with one hand. It had been broken for months. She glanced down the street, wondering how she'd slept through Blaine fixing the railing *and* the door—and why he'd go to so much trouble for someone he'd only just met.

She tried to set aside those confusing thoughts as they sat down to eat the doughnuts. Colette had already snagged the jelly doughnut and the glazed one, leaving Reese her favorites. This was one instance in which she was glad she and her sister differed. Maybe the doughnuts would soften the blow of the conversation Reese had stewed over all night.

"Lettie, we need to talk about last night. What you did was irresponsible and unsafe. Did you even know all those kids?"

Colette rolled her eyes.

"I'm not kidding, Lettie. That guy you were with was *eighteen*."

"So?" She bit into her doughnut.

"He's too old for you. He could go to jail for messing around with you."

"No, he couldn't. I wanted to be with him."

"Yes, he could. How do you even *know* him?"

She looked at her doughnut, turning it, as if searching for the best part. "He came with Jeanette."

Jeanette had been Colette's friend since elementary school,

but for the last few years she'd been all about the boys. Jean-ette's demeanor had slowly gone from a fun-loving kid to girl-on-the-prowl. Even her eyes had changed from clear and open to deep pools of secrets and manipulations. "You mean you didn't even know him before last night?"

Colette shrugged. "So? You didn't know the creeper."

"He *helped* me, and I wasn't fooling around with him." Since their mother had never prepared Reese for dating or having sex, much less anything else in life, Reese tried to be there in that way for Colette. Not that she was comfortable talking about sex or had vast knowledge in that area, but she had enough to keep her sister safe...if she would listen. "Remember that conversation we had about birth control? You agreed to come to me when you thought you were ready."

"I'm not having sex."

"When you bring an eighteen-year-old into your bedroom the first time you meet him, you're giving him a pretty strong signal that you're going to." She thought about the bachelor party and how she'd dressed and danced and realized with a sinking feeling that some might say she'd given the wrong signals, too. Even so, she knew it wouldn't have mattered what she was wearing or how she'd danced. That jerk wouldn't have taken no for an answer anyway, but now wasn't the time to get lost in that nightmare. "Guys have expectations, and we can't control that. But we can control what signals we're giving off and how we keep our boundaries in check."

"Just because you're a prude doesn't mean I have to be one."

"The fact that I don't sleep around doesn't make me a prude. It makes me smart." It wasn't like she was a virgin. She'd lost her virginity in high school to a boy she'd dated for a few months, and she'd had two relationships since then. "Guys aren't my priority. You and Mom and my career are."

Colette rolled her eyes again. "Did you even hear me? I *wanted* to be with him. I wanted him to like me."

Her heart broke every time Colette said anything about wanting to be liked. Reese felt guilty, too, because while their mother had never been nurturing, at least she was *nice enough* to Reese, but she treated Colette like she was unwanted. It didn't take a therapist to know their mother's attitude had caused her sister's insecurities. Reese feared Colette would spend her whole life looking for love in all the wrong places. She tried to make up for their mother's inabilities by being there for Colette and letting her know how much she loved her. But she also knew firsthand how longing for a mother they might never have could leave them feeling unworthy and empty. She'd battled it for years, and she wasn't going to let it ruin either of their lives.

"Lettie, you're smart and you're beautiful, and when you're not pissed off at the world, you're a nice person. You don't need to use your body to make friends. People will like you for you."

"Whatever." She finished her doughnut and grabbed the other one.

"Don't you see? If you don't respect yourself, how can you expect anyone else to?"

Colette ignored her, eyes trained on her doughnut as she ate.

"I'm worried about you, Lettie. Can't you see that? You could get hurt, or pregnant, or contract an STD. I think we should make an appointment to get you birth control."

"I don't *need* it," she snapped. "*God*, you're such a pain. I won't take boys into my room anymore, okay?"

"That's good, but I need to know you won't have parties or have boys over when I'm not home."

"But you won't let me go out when you're not here," she complained, her voice escalating. "Am I a prisoner now?"

Colette didn't know about their mother's debt to the dealer, and Reese was determined to keep it that way. Thankfully, the first time Ice, the dealer, had shown up looking for money, Reese had seen the strange vehicle parked in front of the house and had gone outside to investigate. She'd been shocked and terrified to learn how far their mother had gone to get her fixes. It sickened her to have that man anywhere near Colette. Reese had threatened to call the police, but Ice had threatened her and Colette in return, and she couldn't take that risk. At least she'd convinced him to meet her at a local park on Monday nights from then on instead of at the house. She wanted him as far away from Colette as possible. After he'd left that night, Colette had asked Reese why she was talking to their mother's *boyfriend*, which told Reese exactly how their mother had handled that situation.

"You're not a prisoner. I just need to know that you're safe, and until I can trust that you'll take care of yourself, I can't loosen the reins."

Colette glowered at her. "You suck."

"Yeah, well, I love you, and if that's what it takes to make sure you're safe, then I'll continue to suck." They ate in silence for a minute. "How's that essay coming? Do you need any help?"

"What essay?"

Reese told herself to keep calm. Colette was always forgetting her assignments. Her grades had never been good, but at least she was passing her classes. "The one about *The Outsiders*? It's due Friday."

"Oh. I'll get to it in a day or two. I have time."

"I know, but I'm home all day. I can help you get a head start. I loved that book. Did you?"

Colette averted her eyes and shrugged.

"You didn't read it, did you?"

"I hate reading, but I'll look up the gist of it and my essay will be fine."

"But without reading it, you'll miss out on all the nuances of the story, and that's what—"

"Would you *stop*? You're not my mother, so stop trying to be." She stormed out of the room.

Reese put down her doughnut and buried her face in her hands, hating her mother for what she was doing to Colette and feeling guilty for hating her.

AFTER A QUICK cat nap and shower, Blaine dressed in jeans and a black Henley and threw on his cut, a black leather vest with Dark Knights' patches on the back, hoping a day of wind therapy would clear thoughts of Reese from his head. He hadn't been able to stop thinking about the terrified look in her eyes when he'd found her on her back in that hotel room with Jay hulking over her, or how utterly exhausted she'd looked after arguing with her sister. But she'd put up a strong front, which intrigued him even more. As the oldest of five siblings, he knew the mark of an eldest when he saw it. The telltale resilience one could gain only from a lifetime spent looking out for younger siblings. He loved each and every member of the Dark Knights' brotherhood like family, and he'd give his life for any of them, but there was something about the trust and responsibility bestowed upon eldest children that felt bigger, deeper, and *weightier* than protecting others.

He put on his helmet and climbed onto his motorcycle, his thoughts returning to Reese as he drove away from his house. Her baby blues flashed in his mind. First as determined and angry as they'd been when she'd stomped out to his truck, then softer, mildly perplexed, as they'd appeared before he'd left. That mix of strength and innocent curiosity had stoked a fire he hadn't felt in a long time, sparking a hell of a lot more than just the urge to help her. If he wasn't careful, the urge to satiate her innocent curiosity would get him in trouble.

The fact that she had sweet curves and wore her emotions on her sleeve wasn't helping.

He had no business wanting a woman who was eight years younger than him, much less someone as innocent as Reese. Sure, he was charming when he wanted to be, and he knew how to play the game at work, wearing button-downs or polo shirts that covered his tattoos, so as not to set him apart from his conservative clientele. But there was no taking the biker out of the man. He did things *his* way. In and out of the bedroom.

In the bedroom was what worried him where Blue Eyes was concerned. He fucked hard and took his fill. With consent, of course. He wasn't a player, but he knew his sexual proclivities were too much for some women, which was why he only allowed those he knew could handle it into that part of his life. On the rare occasion he misjudged or they changed their mind, he showed them the door.

There was no question about where Reese Wilder would land in that department.

That sweet blond bunny had no place in *his* lion's den.

Gritting his teeth against that reality, he opened the throttle and sped down the road.

WHEN BLAINE ARRIVED at his cousin Tank's house, the driveway was packed with motorcycles and one pink Vespa, which belonged to his spitfire younger sister, Madigan. She, along with their mother, and Tank's wife, Leah, were hosting a baby shower today for his brother Maverick's wife, Chloe. As he took off his helmet, he realized Reese was only a year older than his *baby* sister. Only Madigan wasn't a child anymore. Blaine had had trouble with that reality when she'd gotten together with her boyfriend, Tobias Riggs, last year. Their relationship was still healing from those growing pains.

Tank's yard was swarming with Dark Knights, and the sight loosened some of the knots in Blaine's chest. Nothing centered him like spending time with the men who understood the complexities and loyalties of the club and lived by the same creed. Blaine's and Tank's fathers, who went by the road names Preacher and Con, had founded the Bayside chapter of the club more than thirty years ago. Blaine and his brothers, Maverick, Zeke, and Zander, and their cousins Tank, Baz, and Gunner were all members. He spotted them in the yard as he looked for Cuffs and Tobias. Tobias wasn't a member of the club, but he worked with their father and Zeke and Zander at their family's renovation business. He was joining them on their ride today.

"Blaine!"

He turned to see four-and-a-half-year-old Rosie, one of Tank's adopted daughters, running toward him. Her thick brown curls, a shade darker than her skin, bounced around her adorable face. Her older sister, Junie, sprinted behind her, doing her best to catch up. Zeke and Baz followed, keeping an eye on the girls.

"Rosie, *wait!*" Junie hollered. She was opposite from Rosie in just about every way, from her red ringlets and fair skin to her careful nature and need to understand every little thing. She'd recently learned to pronounce her *R*'s, and Blaine missed hearing her call her sister *Wosie*, but it was just one of many positive changes he'd noticed since she and Rosie had come into Tank's life.

He scooped Rosie up, and she threw her arms around his neck, pressing a sticky kiss to his cheek as Junie barreled into his legs. He laughed and ruffled Junie's hair. "How're my girls?"

"Gweat!" Rosie exclaimed. "Guess what?"

Before he could respond, Junie said, "Uncle Zeke is taking us on an adventure after your ride!"

"Is that right?" He lifted his chin in greeting as Zeke and Baz joined them.

"Uh-huh!" Rosie said.

"We're going to watch the herring swim upstream!" Junie explained.

"Sounds like a great time." Blaine looked at his brother, who was four years younger than him. Like Blaine and Zander, Zeke had inherited their father's six-foot-plus stature, dark hair, and blue eyes. Maverick was adopted, but also shared those traits, as if he were always meant to be a Wicked.

"Remember how much we loved that place as kids?" Zeke was the most patient of their siblings. He had a special relationship with the girls, as he did with most kids.

"Still do," Blaine said, remembering how he and Tank, as the two oldest, had been tasked with watching over and chasing down their siblings when they'd run off. "You girls are going to love it." He tickled Rosie's belly, and reached down to tickle

Junie's ribs, earning sweet giggles that never failed to get him all twisted up inside.

"Are you taking Zan with you?" Baz asked with a tease in his eye. With his shaggy dirty-blond hair, bronze tan, and easygoing demeanor, he looked more like a surfer than a biker or a veterinarian.

Blaine stifled a laugh. Zander had always been a jokester and good at getting into trouble. When they were younger, he'd used those mischievous ways to distract others from his dyslexia. Zeke had become his tutor and had also taken it upon himself to keep Zander in line. Zander used to go to the edge of the brook just so he could trick Zeke into coming after him, and then he'd push him in.

Their relationship hadn't changed much.

Zeke shook his head. "I'm not a masochist."

"I wanna bring Zander!" Rosie said.

"We can't, Rosie. He doesn't listen good," Junie said, and the guys laughed.

Rosie wiggled out of Blaine's arms. "I'm gonna tell Zander you said that!" She ran toward Zander, and Junie took off after her.

Zeke hollered, "Zan!" When their brother looked over, Zeke pointed toward the girls, and Zander nodded in acknowledgment that he was now on girl patrol. Zander might fuck around when it was just about himself, but he was as responsible as the rest of them where those little girls were concerned. "I swear Rosie has a little Zan in her."

"That's okay," Blaine said. "She's got enough of us to look after her."

"Hell, Junie's got that covered," Baz said as they headed into the yard.

"I've got to talk with Gunner," Zeke said. "I'll catch up with you later."

As he walked away, Baz said, "We missed you at the Hog last night." His parents owned the Salty Hog restaurant and bar. "I heard the bachelor party was a shitshow."

"I guess you talked to Cuffs." Blaine had spoken to him last night and had told him that Reese didn't want to press charges. That was probably for the best. Getting a conviction for longer than six months would be tough and wouldn't be worth the emotional trauma for Reese. But Blaine would make sure that fucker never so much as thought about hurting another woman.

"Yeah. Is the girl okay? Cuffs said she didn't look like she belonged there."

"She's got a lot going on, but she'll be fine, and he's right. She had no business being there, but sometimes you've got to do what you've got to do." Now that he knew why she was trying to earn extra money, he was determined to find out exactly how she'd ended up at that party, so he could make sure she never made that mistake again.

Baz studied him. "What am I picking up on? Interest or trouble?"

"A little too much of one, which will cause a lot of the other if I'm not careful."

"Damn. I've been there before." Baz clapped him on the back. "Act wisely, brother."

"I'm trying. I need to find Tobias. You know where he is?"

"Yeah, up by the house."

Blaine headed across the grass and spotted Tobias at the bottom of the porch steps as Madigan walked out the front door, nuzzling Tank and Leah's baby, Leo. His sister's mahogany hair swept over her narrow shoulders. Tobias was watching her with so much love in his eyes, Blaine could feel it from twenty feet away. Madigan had been right to stand up to him to fight for her relationship with Tobias, just as Tobias had. He was a good man, and Blaine knew he would protect Madigan with everything he had.

Madigan looked up, smiling at Tobias. Her gaze shifted to Blaine, and her face lit up. She hurried down the stairs as he closed in on them. "I'm so glad you're here! I want to know about the girl you're helping."

Blaine arched a brow at her brawny brown-haired beau.

"Sorry, man," Tobias said. "She asked, and you know I won't lie to her."

"I used to like that about you. Has Reese called you?"

"Yeah, a little while ago. I can't get the part until tomorrow, but I can probably have her car ready tomorrow night." Tobias rubbed his jaw. "I know you said you wanted to take care of the cost, but when I told her not to worry about it, she very clearly told me that she didn't need any favors and that she'd be paying in full."

"That sounds like her, but that's *not* happening," Blaine said firmly. "You can tell her the parts were thirty bucks or something, but please, man, don't take more than that. Would you mind checking the fluids and brakes, too? Just give it a good once-over and fix whatever it needs. I'll pay whatever it takes, and I'll handle her."

"Did you just say you'll *handle* her?" Madigan asked with annoyance.

"Yeah. So?" Blaine snapped.

"I swear, you'll never learn. You don't *handle* women," she insisted. "We are capable of handling ourselves. Who is this girl, anyway?"

"Just someone who needed her car fixed," Blaine said.

Madigan nuzzled the baby. "Do you hear that, Leo? That's what Blaine sounds like when he's lying."

"*Mads*," he warned, and ran his finger down Leo's cheek. He was the cutest little guy, with skin a shade lighter than Rosie's, a broad nose, like Leah's, and pitch-black hair like his daddy. "Don't listen to her, buddy. She's making shit up."

"Lie number two. Want to go for three?" Madigan smirked. "Cuffs said you broke Jay's nose for touching her, which means she was at the party, and you left with her."

"Sounds like you already know more than you need to."

"No, I don't," Madigan insisted. "The guys said you didn't show up at the Hog last night, and Cuffs did. Were you with her? She must be pretty important for you to pay for her car repairs. The last time a guy paid for mine, we fell in love."

Blaine gritted his teeth. "Not a chance."

"Come here, blue eyes." Tobias slid his arm around her waist and kissed her.

But Madigan was like a dog with a bone and came at Blaine again. "So...? What's she like?"

"What's who like?" their cousin Gunner, a stocky former marine, with closely shorn blond hair, asked as he, Maverick, and Zander joined them.

"Blaine's new girl he met at the bachelor party," Madigan said.

"A new chick?" Zander raked a hand through his longish brown hair, flashing a troublemaking grin. "Is she hot? Does she have a sister?"

"You're not going anywhere near her sister," Blaine said evenly.

"Dude, that's harsh," Zander complained.

Blaine leveled him with a dark stare. "She's *fifteen*."

"Oh, fuck." Zander held his hands up and laughed. "Hands off that baby carriage. How old's your chick?"

"She's not *mine*. I just helped her get out of a bad situation, and she's older than Mads," Blaine said.

"*Ohmygod.* Am *I* your age-gap guideline?" Madigan asked with disgust, and the guys chuckled.

Blaine shook his head.

"That's a pretty safe guideline if you ask me," Zander said.

"*Ew.* I don't want to be anywhere near your thoughts when you're thinking of women," Madigan said.

Maverick eyed Blaine. "What's really going on?" He was closest to Blaine's age and had been through hell before being fostered and later adopted. He and Maverick had gone head-to-head when he'd first joined the family, but all it had taken was one guy talking shit about Maverick for Blaine's loyalty to kick in.

"Nothing. I helped her out of a bad situation, and she's got a lot on her plate. I'm going to see what I can do to make things easier for her."

"Need a hand with any of it?" Maverick asked.

Blaine didn't even know exactly what he was dealing with yet. "No, man. I'm good. Thanks."

"You know, a dog or cat can bring a lot of comfort to people going through a hard time," Gunner said. He and his fiancée, Sidney, ran Wicked Animal Rescue, and they were always looking for good homes for the animals.

"Trust me, if a dog could fix their issues, I'd get them one," Blaine said, earning a curious glance from Maverick that translated to, *Is there more to this?*

"What are you helping her with besides her car?" Madigan asked.

"None of your business."

"You're my brother. It's my business because you're family. Why was she at the bachelor party, anyway?" Madigan gasped. "Is she a stripper?"

"Dude, does she have any stripper friends?" Zander asked.

"*Jesus.* Both of you, cut the shit," Blaine gritted out.

"What's the matter?" Madigan asked. "You don't like being asked a hundred questions? It's uncomfortable, isn't it? Do you feel like you're facing a firing squad? Welcome to my life."

He could do little more than utter, "Shit," because she was right. "That's different. No woman's going to hurt me the way a man could hurt you."

She stepped closer, staring up at him from chest level with a serious expression. "Then hopefully she has an older brother who can warn her away from you."

"Whoa, Mads," Gunner said. "Blaine's a great guy."

"As loyal as they come," Zander added.

"I know he's loyal, and yeah, he's a good, honest guy, but he's also overprotective, possessive, and stubborn." She said it sharply, and then she smiled at Leo and tickled his chin, speaking in a sweet, melodic voice. "Shall I go on?"

"As if you're not stubborn, Mads?" Maverick said. "Blaine just needs the right woman to wrangle him in."

"What the…? I don't need *wrangling*," Blaine snapped. He was used to watching out for others and getting in their business, not being on the other side of it, and he didn't like it one bit.

"You know what I mean," Maverick said. "Chloe wrangled me, Sid wrangled Gunner, Mads wrangled Tobias, and Tank got triple wrangled by Leah and the girls, and we couldn't be happier."

"Chloe wrangled you, my ass. *You* wrangled *her*," Zander reminded him. "It took you forever to win her over."

"And now she's got my last name and is knocked up with my baby." Maverick threw his shoulders back proudly.

"Well, I for one *love* when Sid wrangles me." Gunner waggled his brows. "I'll gladly supply the rope."

"I'd say the same about Mads, but I don't need you all crawling up my ass for it," Tobias said.

Blaine glowered at him.

"*Aw.* I love you." Madigan went up onto her toes and kissed Tobias. "I give your wrangling five stars." She looked at Blaine. "But you're so pushy, you'll probably get a bad review."

"I never get a bad review, and if anyone's wielding rope, it'll be me, and she'll *enjoy* being tied up," he barked. *What the fuck am I doing?* "But that's *not* happening."

"Not with that bossy bug up your butt," Madigan said. "Maybe you could get a girl to hang around longer than a night if you *asked* her if she wanted to get tied up instead of just doing it."

"What the fuck are you...? I don't even want to know. This conversation is *over*. Where's Tank? Isn't it time to go yet?" Blaine said as Tank came around the side yard with Junie riding piggyback and Rosie clinging to his front like a monkey. At six four, burly, bearded, and tatted from neck to fingers and ankles, with jet-black hair and piercings in his nostril and ears, his cousin was an intimidating motherfucker, but around his girls, he was a giant teddy bear.

"Hell yeah, it's time to go," Tank said.

"Papa Tank said *hell!*" Rosie exclaimed.

"Rosie! You can't say that word," Junie, ever the rule follower, chided.

"I was telling on Papa Tank!" Rosie insisted. "He said hell, so I said hell."

"Papa Tank!" Junie complained.

"I've got her. Come here, squirt." Gunner pried Rosie off Tank's body and held her above his head. "What should we do with her, Zan?"

"Feed her to the bears," Zander said, making her giggle wildly.

"No!" Rosie shrieked. "Papa Tank! Save me!"

Tank's deep laughter rose around them. "Guess you won't say bad words anymore." He reached for Leo. "Let me say goodbye to my little man."

"Fine." Madigan nuzzled the baby one more time before relinquishing him.

Tank looked at Blaine. "You ready, dude?"

"More than you know."

His brows slanted, and he eyed the others. "What did I miss?"

"Not a damn thing." Blaine turned to address the other guys milling about on the lawn. "Let's get ready to ride!"

As they made their way toward the bikes, Blaine watched Tank ushering his girls inside with a dozen hugs and kisses and Tobias loving on Madigan. He'd put money on the fact that the texts Maverick and Gunner were thumbing out were to Chloe and Sidney, and hell if his thoughts didn't go straight back to the blonde he was trying to stop thinking about.

Chapter Four

REESE BOBBED HER head to the beat, singing along to the music blaring from her phone as she attacked a stubborn weed with the rusted garden hoe. She blew at a strand of hair that came loose from her ponytail. It fell into her eyes for the umpteenth time, and she used the back of her gloved hand to push it away, accidentally knocking her glasses off-balance. Righting them, she wacked at the weed again. Gardening was her chosen form of therapy, and after the day she'd had, she needed it. She'd spent the morning cleaning the house, dodging Colette's attitude, and trying *not* to look at the picture of Blaine.

If he knew what she was really dealing with, he'd probably run the other way.

Her mind tiptoed back to last night and the way he'd handled that guy at the party without hesitation or fear. She reconsidered her previous thought. Maybe he wouldn't run, which was even more nerve-racking. She didn't want her mother's mess to take anyone else down with them.

Her afternoon hadn't been much better than her morning. She'd spent far too much of it angry at her mother for the situation she'd put her and Colette in and had gotten so worked up, she hadn't been able to think straight. She'd come outside to find some relief. She always felt better after spending a few hours in the garden. At least at her place where she actually *had* gardens, she did. But she knew today's hard work would pay off with the same beauty once the garden was finished and the flowers she was going to plant had bloomed.

She hadn't yet figured out how she'd afford flowers for the garden, but she'd get there eventually.

If only she could get the world's most annoying weed out of the ground so the flower bed would be ready for planting. But the darn weed wouldn't budge. She put her hand on her hip, glowering at the weed. "It's you or me, Mr. Weed, and I'm not going down." She tossed the hoe into the grass, which was more like a jungle, picked up the hand shovel, and knelt in the dirt. "Time to kiss your roots goodbye."

She felt a tug in her chest and looked around the yard, thinking about her own lost roots and the grandmother and gorgeous gardens that had once brought that house to life. She could still see her grandmother meticulously caring for her *beauties*, which was what she'd called her plants and flowers, and remembered the many hours she'd spent working side by side with the woman who had never given up on their mother. *Your mom will come around. She just needs to want it bad enough.*

It had been fifteen years.

Reese swallowed against a lump in her throat. Maybe her mother would stick it out this time and the third time really would be the charm. She wanted to hold on to that hope. Or at least she *wanted* to *want* to hold on to it. But she knew better. Hope was a double-edged sword that left deep, painful wounds. She'd spent half her life bandaging those wounds and finding ways to move forward without bleeding out. She wasn't sure she could handle much more, especially with Colette's rebellion. That reality added another load of guilt to her already overburdened shoulders.

Why was she thinking about her mother again?

She'd come outside to *stop* thinking about her mother's mess, and darn it, she was *not* going to let it ruin her garden therapy. Working hard to push those thoughts aside, she took out her frustrations on the monstrous weed, digging and tugging, refusing to let it win. She dug around the roots, swearing there were trolls underground playing tug-of-war with her, and cranked up the music on her phone, singing along to "Karma" by Taylor Swift as she wrestled with the deep-rooted villain. Even *she* didn't know who the real villain was, the weed or her mother, but eventually those difficult thoughts gave way to heartfelt lyrics and happy melodies, and her mood lifted.

Determined to bring some beauty back to their lives, she sat on her heels, grabbed the weed with both hands, and yanked as hard as she could. *Once. Twice.* She dug her heels into the dirt, using all of her body weight as she yanked again. The roots broke free, sending her falling onto her back. Laughing as she pushed up to her knees, she held up the scraggly weed. "That'll teach you to mess with me."

Elated, and ridiculously proud of herself for conquering *something*, she tossed the weed into the wheelbarrow and stood up to survey her work. She'd chosen the perfect spot, where the sun came through the surrounding trees. It wouldn't be a huge garden, but it was a start. Now all she had to do was smooth out the dirt and pretend she didn't have to traipse through the jungle to get to it. She grabbed the hoe and began filling in the hole she'd made. When "Come and Get It" by Selena Gomez came on, she used the hoe like a microphone and belted out the lyrics, shaking her butt and bobbing her head to the beat.

"Damn, buttercup. Is that an open invitation?"

She spun around, cheeks burning, taking in Blaine's black leather vest worn over a long-sleeve shirt, low-slung jeans that left no question about the heat he was packing, and black biker boots. He looked like he'd walked right out of an episode of *Sons of Anarchy*. Only hotter and so very *real*. His piercing blue eyes danced with amusement and that ever-present hint of something darker, setting those butterflies aflutter again.

His gaze slid down the length of her, a slow grin shifting into place. "Aren't you a sight for sore eyes?"

His deep voice brought hot prickles to her skin, and she remembered she was wearing her too-big, stained and comfy gardening shorts, a ratty old flannel shirt, and polka-dot rain boots. Her hair was pulled back in a ponytail, and—*oh God*—she looked down, cringing at the dirt on her knees. She quickly gathered her wits. She wasn't out to impress him, and why was he there, anyway? "Where'd you come from?"

"Well, my mom and dad got frisky, and—"

"Not *that*." She laughed softly but forced herself to school her expression, because who just showed up at someone's house like that? "What are you doing here?"

"Fixing the locks on your door and windows. I didn't have time to eat after we got back from riding, so I brought pizza. I hope you're hungry."

She'd been so thrown off by *him*, she hadn't noticed the extra-large pizza box or the bag and toolbox he was holding. "You don't need to feed or take care of us. We're not poor or incapable."

"I didn't think you were either. It's just pizza and a few locks."

"Thank you, but we don't need them."

"If you don't want pizza that's fine, but you need the locks, and I'm not leaving until they're installed."

She swallowed hard, embarrassed. "I can't pay for the locks."

"They're a gift."

What was with this guy? "You already fixed the screen door and the railing on the steps, which I truly appreciate, although I have no idea how you did it without waking us up."

That coy smile reached his eyes. "I'm stealthy and good with my hands."

Her stomach flip-flopped at the thought of those big, strong hands on *her*. She crossed her arms, trying not to think of how often she'd thought about *that* last night. She barely knew him. She needed to figure out his motives, not contemplate his sexual talents. "If you think I'm going to put out because you're helping us, you're wrong."

He closed the distance between them, his brows slanting. "What did I tell you last night?"

He smelled like man and musk and bad decisions waiting to happen, all of which made it hard to think. Did he really expect her to recall a conversation from one of the most frantic nights of her life?

"You don't owe me a damn thing, Reese. Not now and not ever. Got it?" He spoke authoritatively, leaving no room for question.

"I hear you, but I don't get it. You don't *know* me, and you showed up here with pizza, offering to help like we're friends."

"I'm a pretty good friend to have around. Just go with it," he said firmly and kindly. "I'm not going to hurt you or Colette. I just want to make sure you're safe."

The back door opened, and Colette's voice preceded her. "I'm starved. What's for—" She stepped outside, her brows knitting. "You're back?"

"You Wilder girls really know how to make a guy feel welcome."

Colette planted a hand on her jeans-clad hip, eyes narrowing. "Do you have a thing for my sister or something?"

"Colette!" Reese wanted to shrivel up and fade away.

"*What?* He keeps coming back. He's obviously into you."

"Ohmygosh. Seriously, Lettie? Can you *not* do this right now?"

"It's okay. She reminds me of my younger sister." He turned to Colette. "Reese is obviously gorgeous, but more importantly, she's trying her best to give you a good life, and I'm just here to fix the locks. Are you hungry?"

Colette eyed her hopefully, but Reese was struck momentarily speechless. She couldn't remember the last time anyone had acknowledged how hard she tried to do right by Colette. That hit even harder than him calling her gorgeous, which in and of itself was unbelievable.

She studied Blaine, trying to make sense of him. Was he playing her, or was he really a nice guy who believed in helping others? There should be a test for that, like the tests she ran in the lab. *Let me prick your finger and take a little blood to see if you're a lying, manipulative ass or a nice guy.*

"Reese?" Colette was practically drooling over the idea of eating pizza.

Even though Reese knew better than to make decisions based on a hope and a prayer, she couldn't help but want to believe he wasn't lying. "It's okay. He can stay."

BLAINE GAVE COLETTE the pizza box without taking his eyes off Reese, adorably sexy in baggy shorts with dirty knees and dirt smudges on her cheek. When he heard the door close behind Colette, he said, "Smart move."

"Why do you say that?"

"Because you weren't going to get rid of me that easily. You saved us some back-and-forth, which I would've won anyway."

"You *are* particularly pushy." She said it a little playfully, but with an edge, as if she wasn't sure she should let her guard down too much.

That was a smart move, given the way he was fighting the urge to get closer to her. He wanted to wipe that smudge from her cheek just so he could see that bashful smile again and watch it turn to determination. Why did that fuck with his head so much?

"So I've heard." He nodded to the patch of dirt behind her. "What's going on back there?"

"I'm making a garden. Believe it or not, this place used to look like a fairy tale, with beautiful gardens that bloomed in every season."

"What happened?"

"Life. Or rather, *death*," she said thoughtfully. "My grandmother loved gardening and spent hours making them beautiful."

"Did you garden with her?"

"Yes, every chance I got. She's the reason I love gardening. It's like therapy for me. You should see the gardens I made for my landlord. They're gorgeous." Her eyes, and everything around her, brightened with her smile, but just as he thought he'd like to see it more often, it faded. "But my grandmother passed away when I was thirteen. I tried to keep up with the gardens, but it was too much with everything else that was going on."

His chest tightened, memories of losing his own grandmother rushing in. "I'm sorry to hear that. I assume you mean because your mom was in bad shape?"

"Yeah," she said softly.

"I can only imagine how tough that must have been at that age, trying to keep up with school and take care of Colette, who was what? Two?"

"Mm-hm."

"What about your old man? I know you said he left, but didn't he help out?"

She shook her head. "Once he left, he was gone for good."

He'd like to give both her parents hell. It was no wonder she was so untrusting. "Well, that's his loss, isn't it? Why don't you get cleaned up so we can eat, and I'll put your tools in the shed."

"I can get them."

"I know you can, but the pizza is getting cold, and your sister looked awfully hungry. I have a feeling there might not be much left once you get in there. Go on. I've got this."

She lifted her chin defiantly. "You said you were hungry. Why don't *you* go eat, and I'll put my tools away."

She stepped in that direction, and he gently grabbed her wrist. She let out a soft gasp, her eyes widening with only a hint of trepidation buried beneath a sea of desire and curiosity, sending an electrical charge scorching through him. That sound, and that look, brought images he had no business entertaining of Reese lying naked beneath him, wrists pinned above her head, hungry eyes staring up at him from behind those damn glasses, which, for some reason, turned him on even more.

Fuuck. "Are you going to fight me on everything?"

"Are you going to keep telling me what to do?"

He cocked a grin. "Probably."

"Then we have a problem, don't we?" Her lips curved up.

A bigger problem than you know. He released her wrist. "Get your pretty little—" He cursed. "Get your ass inside."

She arched a brow.

Jesus. You're going to be the death of me. "*Please* get your ass inside."

"Fine, but only because you said please." She turned to go inside. "I left a bucket in the grass."

"I'll get it."

"There's a rake out there, too."

"*Reese.* I've got this."

"Right, of course." She reached for the door. "Don't forget to lock the shed."

"And people think I'm a control freak?"

She glanced over her shoulder, flashing that sky-brightening smile, but she only gifted him a glimpse before disappearing behind the door. She was good at making him crave things he shouldn't, and he added that damn smile to the list.

Chapter Five

BLAINE SPOTTED AN old lawn mower buried beneath a bunch of crap in the shed and considered hauling it out to cut the grass, but he had a feeling it would only piss off Reese more than he already had. He decided to leave well enough alone. He grabbed his tools and the bag of locks and headed inside through the back door.

Reese was standing at the sink, adding water to a glass filled with ice. She'd changed into a blue sweatshirt, which made her eyes even more vibrant, and cutoffs that showed off her lusciously thick thighs. One bare foot was resting on the other. Her pink toenails reminded him of how scared she'd been last night, though she'd tried hard to hide it. He was protective by nature, but Reese brought out something deep and primal in him that usually remained at bay unless a threat was imminent. He struggled to rein it in, but it was like trying to stop a speeding train.

"Thanks for putting away the tools," she said sweetly, and began filling a second glass.

He put down his toolbox and set the bag of locks on the counter. "No problem."

"Did you remember to lock the shed?"

"Did you ask me to?"

She wrinkled her nose. "*Sorry.* I'm used to making sure things get done."

"You're preaching to the choir. It comes with being the oldest." He glanced at the open pizza box on the table. There were three slices missing. "I guess I missed Colette."

"She usually eats in her room."

Why did it bother him that they each ate alone? As much as he wanted to sit at the table with Reese, he had a feeling if he didn't keep his hands busy, they might wander. "Grab the pizza box. We'll eat while I fix the locks."

They headed into the living room. She set the pizza on the table and went back for their drinks as he put the toolbox and locks by the front door. When she returned, she said, "Are you sure you don't mind doing this?"

He gave her a *what do you think* look, picked up a piece of pizza and held it up, as if toasting. "Here's to dirty knees and cute shorts." He bit off half the slice.

"*Hey.* I washed my knees," she said with a laugh, immediately inspecting her knees.

"That wasn't a complaint. I like a woman who's not afraid to get dirty."

Her cheeks flamed. "*Blaine.*"

She was finally allowing herself to call him by his name, and damn, he liked the way it sounded rolling off her tongue. "Someone's got a dirty mind. I was talking about dirt from the garden." He took another bite, loving the crimson spreading down her neck.

"You were *not.*"

"Either way, that blush looks good on you."

She rolled her eyes and took a bite of pizza.

He finished his slice, fished out his tools, and began removing the old dead bolt.

"You mentioned a big ride this morning. Was it with your motorcycle club? Is that why you're wearing that vest with the scary skull patch?"

"This vest is called a *cut*, and I don't know about scary, but yeah. We went to see the guys in the Harborside chapter."

"Harborside? That's a long ride."

"Yeah, but a good one. There's nothing like the freedom of the open road to clear your head, and it's always great to ride with my brothers." He put the old lock in the bag and grabbed another slice of pizza.

"How many brothers do you have?"

"Three, but—"

"*Three?* And a sister? I have trouble keeping up with one sibling, but it must be nice to have a big family. What are they like? Are you close to all of them?"

"We're all pretty tight. Maverick and I are closest in age. We work together, and he's a hell of a sculptor. He and his wife, Chloe, are expecting their first baby in June. In fact, the girls threw her a baby shower today."

"That's *so* nice. Will that be your first niece or nephew?"

He finished his slice and went back to work. "Yeah, but I'm like an uncle to my cousin Tank's kids."

"Wait. Maverick and Tank? Are those their real names?"

"No, they're road names, or biker names. Justin and Benson are their real names."

She took another bite and sat on the couch, watching him work. "Do you have a road name?"

"Nope. I've always gone by my middle name."

"Really? What's your first name?"

"Robert, after my old man."

"I like that." She was quiet for a minute as she ate. "How do you *get* a road name?"

"Usually the other members give it to you, but Madigan gave Maverick his when we were kids."

"Why didn't she give you one?"

"You'd have to ask Madigan that. But she picked the right one for him."

"Why do you say that?"

As he removed the old strike plate, he said, "Because Mads has a heart about as big as the sky."

"But you said Colette reminded you of her, and Colette has a wicked attitude toward you."

"So does Mads." He glanced at her on the couch with her feet tucked beside her, looking at him like he was a puzzle. Did she have any idea that she was a puzzle to him, too? "Your sister is just trying to deal with a tough situation at a difficult age. I'm sure she's got a good heart since you basically raised her. It's just bruised and confused at the moment."

Reese was quiet for a few seconds, her brow furrowed in concentration. "So how did Justin's road name come about?" she asked *too* animatedly. "Did your sister watch *Top Gun*?"

He made a mental note about her dodging the topic of her past and went along with the subject change. "Maverick is what they call unbranded cattle that aren't part of a herd, and Justin came to our family through the foster system when he was eleven. Mads was only four, but she'd been enthralled with cows for months, and she knew what a maverick was. She even named her stuffed cow Maverick." He opened the new lock to check the alignment. "Having grown up with all of us and around the other club families, all she knew was that families were big and kept her safe. When she realized Justin had nobody else in his life but us, she gave him her stuffed cow and said he'd never be alone again, because now there were two Mavericks. A few years later my parents adopted him, and when he became a Dark Knight, the name stuck."

"I love that. How old were you when Maverick came to live with you?"

"Twelve."

"Talk about a tough age. What was that like for you?"

"My parents had fostered a lot of kids, so I was used to them coming and going."

"Did they adopt any others?"

"Nope."

"So what was it like knowing he was staying and becoming part of your family?"

Blaine steeled himself against the memories of those early days. "It wasn't easy. I was used to being the oldest and taking charge. My other brothers listened to me for the most part, but Justin had a huge chip on his shoulder. He didn't listen to a damn thing, and he ran away all the time. Rightly so. I mean he was used to basically being on his own and answering to no one, and he'd had a shitty upbringing, but I didn't understand that as a kid. So it was rough for a while."

"It sounds like maybe you had a chip on your shoulder, too. Rightly so," she parroted as she got off the couch and came to his side, "since you were suddenly given another brother to watch over. But you work with him now, so you must get along. How did you get through it?"

"With a lot of fights."

"I assumed as much, but what changed?"

He stopped working to answer her. "When we were kids,

my buddy Cameron—Cuffs, the guy who was with me at the party—said some shit about Justin, and something inside me snapped."

Those expressive eyes widened again. "You hit him?"

"I took his ass down. Justin was living under our roof. He'd already become family, no matter how much we were at each other's throats, and Wickeds are the most loyal motherfuckers you'll ever meet. My loyalty to family, which then included Justin, was stronger than my grievances with him."

"But Cuffs was your friend."

He shrugged one shoulder. "That's how we roll."

"Beating up friends? That's not very nice."

"Cameron's old man was a Dark Knight, too. He grew up in the club, like we did. He knew the score, and he would've done the same to me if I talked shit about his family."

"And you remained friends even after that?"

"Hell yeah. Bruises fade. Brotherhood doesn't."

"Wow." She shook her head. "That's a whole lifestyle I know nothing about."

"Sure you do. Look at what you did to keep food on the table for your sister."

"Thanks for reminding me," she said sarcastically. "But I didn't hurt anyone."

"Yes, you did. Look in the mirror, baby girl." The endearment came out before he could think to stop it.

Her eyes flashed with annoyance for only a second before she lowered them.

Blaine lifted her chin, ready to apologize for letting the endearment slip. But there was no annoyance in her eyes, only a deep-seated loneliness he wanted to quell, and he knew his mirror statement had hit home. Fighting the urge to pull her into his arms, he brushed his thumb over her cheek. "What you did was dangerous but admirable. I have no doubt you'd take a bullet for your sister, just like I would for my siblings."

She inhaled deeply. "I would."

"Of course you would." Their gazes held, the air between them pulsing like a heartbeat.

"Enough about me," she said nervously, taking a step back. "What are your other brothers like? Do they have road names and work with their hands, too?"

"Asks the girl who doesn't like inquisitions but apparently enjoys giving them," he teased.

"You're all about safety. Don't you think I should know something about the man who keeps popping into my life? I want the down-low on these brothers of yours, so spill, Mr. Fix It."

He laughed. "A'right, let's see. Zeke and Zander go by their nicknames, not road names. Their names are Ezekial and Alexander, and they work with our father at our family's renovation business."

"Are they married?"

"You looking for a date?" Trying to ignore the stab of jealousy that brought, he didn't wait for an answer. "They're single, but you're not getting within a hundred feet of Zander."

"*Geez.* You say that like I'm out trolling the streets looking for guys."

"No. I said it like I know my brother. He'll take one look at you and charm your panties off."

She crossed her arms. "You obviously don't know me very well. I don't fall prey to charming players. Besides, I have too much going on for that."

"I've heard that before."

"Is he really *that* bad? Or…that *good*?"

He glowered at her. "He's a good man, but he gets around." He didn't want to think about her with Zander or any other guy, so he went for his own subject change. "But when I said I liked riding with my brothers, I meant it in a more general sense. The club is like a family, and the guys are a brotherhood. We have each other's backs and watch out for each other's families. If any of us needs anything, we're all there to help."

"And you beat each other up," she teased, grabbing another slice of pizza. She handed it to him and picked one up for herself. "How many members are there?"

"A few dozen in our chapter, but there are chapters all over the map." He took a bite.

"Wow, that's a lot. I can't imagine having that many people watching out for me. How did your family get involved with them?"

"We were basically raised in the club. My great-grandfather founded the original chapter in Peaceful Harbor, Maryland, and my old man and my uncle founded our chapter more than thirty years ago."

"You've *always* had that many people watching out for you? When you said Mads knew families were big and kept her safe, I didn't realize you meant family in the bigger sense. I'd have given anything to have had one-tenth of that when I was growing up."

"I wish you could have. If the club had ever gotten wind of what you were going through, you would have had more help than you could've ever wanted." He held her gaze, the urge to take her in his arms hitting hard again. He shoved the rest of his pizza into his mouth and turned back to the task at hand. "The club is a blessing, but as a kid, it was also a curse. A good curse from a safety standpoint, but a curse nonetheless."

"Why a curse?"

"Because there were all these families who were loyal to the club keeping their eyes on us and reporting back to our father to keep us in line."

Her eyes sparked with curiosity. "Were you a bad boy growing up?"

"That oldest-kid-responsibility thing is hard to shake, but I was no saint. I never got away with much, though. As a kid, we never knew who was watching, but we found out pretty quickly that someone always was."

She finished her pizza and licked sauce off her fingers, completely oblivious to the dirty thoughts she induced. "I'd still take that over not having anyone."

The longing in her voice kicked thoughts of her mouth on his body to the curb. "Well, you've got me now."

"No, I don't," she said with a laugh.

"You think I'd turn my back on you or Colette knowing what you're going through, or what you've been through?"

"I don't know." Her brows knitted. "But how can you say that so emphatically when you barely know us?"

"I know enough to say it, but you're right. I should get to know you better, and we can start by you telling me how you ended up at that party."

"If you must know, I answered an ad for a bachelor party hostess, and *yes*, I know how stupid that was. But it was either that or selling my used underwear or pictures of my feet."

"You're not doing *either* of those things."

"No kidding," she said sarcastically.

"How could those things be your only options?"

"I needed fast money. *Cash.* It wasn't like I could wait for interviews and get a safer part-time job. But I think I found a better way to earn money anyway."

He arched a brow. "Pole dancing?"

"No, smarty-pants." She drew her shoulders back with a playful sexy-as-sin look in her eyes. "OnlyFans."

"*Fuck that.* You want a fan? *Great.* Sign me up, because you're not doing that shit publicly. Moving on. What other ideas do you have?"

She laughed. "I was only kidding, but look at you going all big brother on me."

My thoughts are anything but brotherly. "Next option? And it better not include your body."

"Everything I do includes my body," she said with amusement. "I can't stand here without my body, right?"

"Cut the shit, Wilder."

She laughed. "*Fine.* I'm going to apply to be an Uber driver or a delivery person."

"The hell you are."

"Excuse me?" she said incredulously.

"It's not safe for you to take strangers in your car or deliver things to their houses. I'm not letting you do that shit."

"You're not *letting* me? Who do you think you are?"

"Think about it, Reese," he said firmly, knowing he had no right to tell her what to do. But that wasn't going to stop him from making sure she didn't do it. "What happens to Colette if you get attacked by some asshole? Do you really want her going into the system while your mom is in rehab? What if your mother doesn't stick with the program? Then Colette is in the system until she's eighteen, when she'll get booted. What happens to her then?"

She opened her mouth as if she was going to fight him on it, but then her shoulders sank, her bravado draining right before his eyes. "Well, when you put it that way, it makes sense, but I really need to earn extra money fast."

"What about your job? Do they pay overtime?"

She shook her head. "I'm salaried."

Fuck. He'd happily hand her whatever she needed just to keep her safe, but he knew she wouldn't accept a handout. Thinking fast, an idea came to him. "I think I can help you out. We're short-staffed, and we just picked up a new client who wants stonework done and a garden made. If you're interested, I'm handling the stonework, so you'd have to put up with me."

"That'd be a chore," she teased. "Seriously, though. I don't have any experience. Your boss probably wouldn't hire me."

"You just told me you made gorgeous gardens for your landlord, and I'm tight with the big guy. Don't worry about him."

"Do you really think...? *Wait.* Forget it. I need something that'll work around my hours at the lab, and I'm sure you guys start early."

"What hours do you work?"

"Seven to three usually, but there are times when I have to stay later."

"I think we can work around that. How much do you need to earn?"

"Ideally, five hundred a week, but I'll take anything I can get. How much do you think they'd pay per hour?"

He wasn't going to split hairs with Little Miss Independent. "We pay by the job, not by the hour. You'll clear that much as long as you're not a slacker."

"I'm *not* a slacker. You can ask my boss. I rarely take lunch breaks, and I'm always willing to work late to get the job done."

"I was kidding, Reese. I'll talk to the boss and let you know."

"You're serious?" She fidgeted nervously with the hem of her shorts.

"Yeah. No big deal."

"It's a *very* big deal. Even if it doesn't work out, I appreciate you trying to help." She bit her lower lip, looking at him tentatively. "I feel like I should hug you or something."

He told himself not to move, but the draw was too strong, and he opened his arms. She stepped forward, and he hauled her into an embrace. The feel of her lush curves against him reignited that electric charge he'd felt earlier, crackling between them like live wires. She tilted her face up with a too-damn-enticing mix of interest and innocence. Her lips were *right there* for the taking, and *fuck*, he wanted to *give* and *take* until she couldn't remember her own name or her troubles. He wanted to stake claim, to protect her from, *and* ruin her for, any other man. To put her on the back of his bike and ride around the fucking town so everyone knew she was off-limits. It made no sense. He'd never once had that urge.

She licked her lips, her eyes darkening.

He'd probably go straight to hell for it, but his mind hit the gutter. He imagined fisting his hands in those gorgeous golden locks when she was on her knees before him, her tongue sliding along the length of his cock as she wrapped her plump lips around it and he fucked her mouth.

Yup. Straight to hell.

It took everything he had to release her and take a step back.

PLATINUM, GOLD, MERCURY...

It had been twenty minutes since they'd embraced, and Reese had done everything she could to distract herself from the heat that had consumed her. She'd stupidly thought if she asked him to show her how to install a window lock, she'd be too busy to overthink what she'd felt. But she hadn't expected him to stand so close. He was right behind her, his chest brushing against her back, and his body heat was like a whirlpool sucking her into its vortex and scrambling her brain. Even reciting the periodic table for a second time couldn't distract her from the desire simmering inside her.

"Earth to Reese," Blaine said in her ear, startling her from her thoughts.

"Huh? What?"

"You didn't hear a word I said, did you?"

"Yes, I did. You said..." *Shootshootshoot.* "Something about locks."

He laughed. "Nice try. I asked if you had extra light bulbs so I could change the ones that are blown in the ceiling fan."

"Oh... *Whoops.*"

They both laughed.

"You did a nice job on that lock." He took the screwdriver from her, tightened each of the screws, and moved beside her. "What were you so caught up in just now?"

"Nothing. I was just thinking about work."

"Really?" He arched a brow. "What do you do at the crime lab?"

Work was the perfect distraction. "My specialty is DNA analysis, but I do whatever they need me to."

"That's very cool, but there's not that much crime on the Cape, is there?"

"No, but we handle cases in Barnstable, Plymouth, and Bristol Counties."

"That makes sense. Are you working on any big cases?"

"I think all of our cases are big, even when they seem small on the surface, because crime never touches only the victim. It's like a disease that spreads through families and friends and eats away at foundations people spent their lives building." She was getting a little close to home and stopped before she said too much.

"The club deals with a lot of bad people, and you're right about it affecting a wide range of people. It must be rewarding to help catch criminals."

"It is, but it can also be devastating if we don't get a big enough sample or it gets tainted and we can't pin it on them."

"Yeah. I can imagine. How'd you get into that line of work? Have you always been into science?"

She'd wanted to work with plants for as long as she could remember, but after her mother was raped, their lives had fallen apart, and everything had changed. She wasn't about to lay any of that on him. "Science, math, history, English. I pretty much loved it all, but especially science."

"You sound like Zeke. He used to be a special education teacher."

"Why did he stop?"

"Some asshole made nasty comments about the kids, and he got into an altercation that got him fired. He still tutors kids at the community center."

"Wow. Did he fight in front of the kids or something?"

"No. He'd never do that."

She thought about that as he checked the lock again. "Do all of you rely on violence to solve your issues?"

"No. We prefer not to use violence, but when a situation calls for it, we're not afraid to use it. Let's not get lost in all that. I want to know more about you. We should get started on the kitchen door."

"There's no dead bolt on that one."

"There will be." He grabbed his tools, and they went into the kitchen. He eyed her as she leaned against the counter by the fridge. "What're you doing over there?"

"Watching."

"Get over here. I'm going to make a handywoman out of you yet."

The idea of working that closely with him again had her heart racing. "It's okay. I'll just watch."

"Get your ass over here, Wilder."

"You're such a caveman, you seem like the type that wants a woman to rely on you."

"There's nothing wrong with relying on someone, but a real man empowers his woman so she's not helpless."

"*A*, I'm not your woman, and *B*, I'm far from helpless."

"No shit." He motioned with his head. "Get over here."

"You're a pain, you know that?"

"So you've said." He held up a black plastic piece he'd used on the other door. "This is the template. You need to know the size of your hole before you start screwing."

She blinked at him, trying not to laugh.

"Shit." He laughed, which made her laugh, too.

"So you're saying size matters?" she asked cheekily, not knowing where that boldness had come from.

"Fuck yeah, size matters."

"You're such a guy. That's a myth, you know."

"Says a woman who's never been with me."

"*Ohmygosh.* Forget I said anything."

"Not likely, but okay." He showed her how to check the size of the template and lock and screwed the template to the door. "Now we'll take the drill bit off and put the hole saw on." He showed her how to do both and handed her the drill.

"It's heavier than I thought it would be."

"I've heard that before."

She rolled her eyes.

"You walked right into that one. Line up the saw with the hole in the template and drill the hole for the lock."

"Gee, really?" she said sarcastically. "I thought I'd just drill a random hole in the door."

"Smart-ass. Hold the drill firmly so it doesn't slip."

"No slippage. Got it." She lined it up, and he stood beside her, holding the door still. "Don't let go."

"I'd never leave you hanging, baby."

God, this guy… "That's what they all say."

"Yeah, but I mean it."

"I've heard that before." She began drilling the hole.

"So you loved school, huh?"

"I did. It was an escape. The one place I was in control. It didn't matter if my dad was gone and my mom was falling apart. If I worked hard, I got rewarded with good grades, and I learned pretty quickly that good grades opened doors." She finished drilling the hole and turned to look at him. He was right there, his chest brushing hers. His expression was intense but not sexual, drawing out the rest of her confession. "My teachers paid more attention to me and encouraged me to work hard so I could get scholarships and go to college. As ridiculous as it sounds, I needed their praise."

"That doesn't sound ridiculous. It makes sense. Every kid

needs love, and when you can't get it at home, you try to get it elsewhere. Love comes in all forms, and your teachers filled that gap."

It was strange hearing him talk about what he deemed as acceptable violence one minute and kids needing love the next. She'd never met anyone like him. He seemed genuinely interested in what she had to say, and she liked that he was teaching her how to fix the lock herself, but he also gave her butterflies and made her want more of that naughty banter. She was used to understanding people and the reasons they did things, but she hadn't figured out why he was bothering with her, and that made her cautious.

He took the hole saw off the drill and showed her how to put on the drill bit. "Now put the drill in reverse and remove the screws in the template." He handed her the drill and waited for her to do that. "Now slide the dead bolt into the hole."

She stifled a grin.

"You *do* have a dirty mind."

"Shush. You're just trying to make everything sound sexual."

"Sorry, sweetheart, but that's all in your head."

Oh God. Was it? If it was, it was his fault. She'd never been like that.

They worked through a few more steps, and as she prepared to drill the hole in the doorframe, he said, "Don't be shy. You want to go deep so the bolt can fully extend."

She gave him a deadpan look, and they both laughed.

As they worked together, making jokes and small talk, she wanted to trust that the help he was giving them was well intentioned. But how could she trust a guy she'd only just met when she'd been let down by not only the two people who were supposed to love and protect her but every guy she'd let into her life, too? His takes on love and violence were also still nagging at her. She watched him, solely focused as he chiseled-out part of the door for the strike plate.

"Spit it out, Wilder," he said, as if he'd read her mind.

"Spit what out?"

"Whatever that analytic brain of yours is picking apart."

"How do you know I'm picking something apart? You're not even looking at me."

"I can feel it."

He glanced at her, and she swore his all-seeing eyes could *see* her every thought.

Holy cow. Seriously? "You cannot feel anything. It's not like you have Spidey senses."

"Don't I? I know you weren't thinking about work when we were installing the window lock."

He'd felt *that*, too? Mortified, she averted her eyes. "Yes, I was."

"Bet you can't look me in the eye and say that."

She was determined to do it, but he was smirking, and she felt silly trying to lie, and they both laughed.

"It's called having a connection."

"I wasn't…We don't…"

He arched a brow.

She clamped her mouth shut but couldn't hold in her thoughts. "I don't know if the fact that you know I'm thinking about something is creepy or intriguing."

He tossed her a wink, stirring those butterflies to life again. "You know I'm not creepy. You might as well tell me what you're trying so vehemently not to."

She crossed her arms, feeling far too seen. But she wasn't

afraid to admit he was right. She just didn't like it. "Okay, Mr. Know-It-All. I think it's weird that you talk about violence like it's okay, and in the next breath you're talking about kids needing love. Those two things are very far apart, and I don't know what to make of it."

He stopped working, giving her his full attention, his expression thoughtful. "I don't think violence is okay. I said there are times when it's necessary, and I stand behind that. Listen, I live by the club creed, which means believing in love, loyalty, and respect for all, and I stand behind that, too, until a person proves they don't deserve it. And as far as kids go, they don't ask to be on this earth, and they can't fight for themselves or demand respect. Look at your own family. You didn't ask for your mother to have a problem with drugs and alcohol or your father to leave. You didn't ask to be a mother to your baby sister when you were just a kid. I've seen much worse shit happen to kids, adults, and even animals, and I will fight for what's right for those who can't until the day they bury me six feet under. So when I say I won't turn my back on you and Colette, I mean it."

Her pulse quickened. He was so passionate and vehement, everything about him screamed honesty. "And the club instilled that in you?"

"The club and my parents, and if I ever have kids, I'll teach them the same thing." He lifted his chin, his eyes serious. "What else would that analytical brain of yours like me to clarify?"

"I don't know. You're a complicated guy."

"And you're a complicated woman." He focused on the area for the strike plate again.

"No, I'm *not*. I'm a simple girl who's just trying to keep her head above water."

He shook his head. "Does that work for you?"

"What?"

"Lying to yourself."

She swallowed hard, and the truth slipped out. "Sometimes it's the only way to survive."

He looked at her then, and the intensity of his stare told her he not only knew what she meant, but he had firsthand knowledge of doing that himself, which made her even more curious about him. But neither said anything else about that topic as they finished installing the lock.

"Okay, Wilder. Into the bedroom."

"What?" Her eyes widened.

His brow furrowed. "To check the locks…?"

"I know what you meant," she lied. "They're fine. None of them are broken."

He cocked a knowing grin. "Are you afraid to walk into a bedroom with me?"

"No." She crossed her arms, leaning her butt against the counter.

He stepped closer, searching her eyes. "You're safe with me, Reese. We could sleep in the same bed, and I wouldn't touch you unless you wanted me to."

Her mouth went dry at the thought of sharing a bed with him. "I was just—"

"Thinking of the locks. I know. But I want you to know you can trust me." He went back to gathering his tools, like he hadn't just stolen the air from her lungs, and picked up the toolbox. "I guess I'll get out of your hair."

His eyes said, *Unless you want me to stay.* She had the unfamiliar urge to throw caution to the wind, but he made her want things she hadn't wanted in a long time, and although she was starting to trust him, she wasn't sure she trusted herself. She had a feeling he was like the baking soda to her vinegar and water in her sixth-grade science experiment. One little shake and she'd never be the same.

"I really appreciate your help, but I have some things I need to take care of." She walked him to the front door.

"Okay. I'll give you a ride to work tomorrow morning and let you know what my boss says."

"I can take an Uber."

"You're trying to earn extra money. You don't have to spend forty bucks on a ride to work. I'll be here at six thirty, and when you get off work, I'll take you to pick up your car. If it's not ready, I'll give you a ride home."

"You sure you don't mind?"

"I wouldn't offer if I did. Does Colette need a ride to school?"

"No. She takes the bus after I leave."

He glanced toward the hall. "She's been in there all night. You sure she's okay?"

"Yeah. It's her age."

"Okay." He glanced toward the hall again. "If you need anything tonight, call me."

"This place is like Fort Knox now. We'll be fine."

"A'right, buttercup."

"Why do you call me that? Buttercups are poisonous. People don't usually realize that because if they try to eat them, they get blisters and other sores, so they don't ingest them and die. But they're toxic. Oh *God*. You think I'm toxic, don't you? Is that why you keep coming around? Because you're afraid Colette isn't safe?"

"Hell no." He laughed incredulously. "I keep coming around because I want to be sure you're safe, and…that scientific brain of yours is intriguing."

She didn't know what to make of that. "Then why do you call me *buttercup* if not because they're poisonous?"

"When I was a kid, my brothers and I would dare each other to eat plants and bark and shit. Buttercups always drew me in because they were bright and beautiful, but they were one of the things our parents had forbidden us to eat." He opened the door. "See you tomorrow, buttercup. Lock this door behind me."

She watched him walk away, her mind slowly putting together the pieces of what he'd said, turning those butterflies into bees. Thoughts of him tasting her forbidden fruit tiptoed in. That should make her run the other way. Instead, it had her wishing she could run to her apartment and dig out her vibrator.

Chapter Six

A KNOCK SOUNDED at the front door at six twenty-five Monday morning, and Reese's pulse skyrocketed. She peered out the window and saw Blaine's truck in the driveway. She hadn't expected him to knock. She gave herself a quick once-over in the mirror. She'd changed her clothes three times and had finally chosen a blue blouse with a sweetheart neckline that made her eyes *pop* and offered a hint of cleavage and black slacks that hugged her hips. She might not be climbing on the Blaine Train, but she was a healthy young woman, and she liked his attention and their flirtatious banter.

She hurried down the hall, calling out, "I'm leaving," as she passed Colette's bedroom. She grabbed her bag from the kitchen counter and went to open the door. She was greeted with striking blue eyes drinking her in from head to toe and a gravelly "Morning, buttercup. You look nice" that gave her goose bumps.

"Thanks. So do you." He wore a black Cape Stone polo, jeans, and work boots. "You didn't have to come to the door."

"This is for Colette." He held up a bag from the doughnut shop, not even bothering to respond to what she'd said.

"You brought her doughnuts?"

"No, just a muffin. I figured it might put her in a good mood."

"That's so nice of you. I'll give it to her. Be back in a sec." Flabbergasted, she hurried down the hall and knocked on her sister's door.

"What?" Colette snapped.

"Blaine brought you a muffin."

Her door opened, and she looked confused. "Why?"

"I don't know. He's just nice, but I have to go." She handed her the bag. "You should say thank you."

As she hurried back down the hall, Colette hollered, "Thank you," and closed her bedroom door.

"Sorry about that." Reese stepped outside and closed the front door behind her, struck again by the working screen door and the railing on the deck. "I appreciate you bringing her a muffin, but you really didn't have to."

He didn't say anything and opened the passenger door to his truck.

"Thanks." She climbed in, unable to remember another time a man had opened a door for her. Well, other than when Blaine had on Saturday night, but she'd been so frazzled, it had barely registered. She watched him walk around to the driver's side. A shiver of heat trickled down her spine. He moved like a panther. Alert, confident, *powerful*.

He climbed behind the wheel and nodded to the to-go cups in the beverage holders. "One of those is for you. Your muffin and cream and sugar are in the bag."

She followed his gaze to a bag on the seat between them. "With service like this, I might never call an Uber again."

He grinned as he pulled out of the driveway, and she peeked into the bag, relieved to see there were two muffins. She took one out, leaving the other for him. "Do you make a habit of spoiling women?" She tore off a piece of the muffin top and popped it into her mouth.

"A muffin and coffee are hardly spoiling, but to answer your question, *no*."

"Why don't I believe that?"

"Because you feel the need to challenge everything I say and do. I talked to my boss, and you've got the job if you want it. He's fine with paying you under the table, too."

"Really?"

He nodded. "You can start tomorrow if you'd like and work a few hours each day after you get off from the lab."

"I'd love to. Just tell me where and when and I'll be there."

"Send me a text so I have your number, and I'll text you the details. I'll make sure you're home before dark for Colette."

"Thank you." She pulled out her phone, thumbed out, *Thank you!* and sent the text. "You have no idea how much of a relief this is."

She usually mentally prepared for her day on the way to work, but as they ate their muffins and talked about the job she'd be working on, there was no room for thoughts of anything else. The drive flew by, and when he pulled into the parking lot, she was bummed it was over.

He pulled up to the front door and got out of the truck. Confused, she sat there like an idiot wondering where he was going, until she realized he was opening the door for her. He offered his hand and helped her down to the pavement.

"What are you doing for lunch?" he asked as he reached into the truck for her coffee and handed it to her.

"I brought my lunch."

"A'right. Then I'll be back at three."

"Are you sure you don't mind? I can get a ride."

"I'll be in the area anyway, and if your car is ready, we'll swing by and pick it up."

"You really don't have to go to all that trouble."

Ignoring her comment, as he'd done the other night, he said, "See you at three, Reese. Have a great day."

REESE HIT SEND on the report she was filling out and glanced at the clock, anxiously awaiting the end of her workday. It was *2:45*. She'd been on a nervous high thinking about Blaine since he'd dropped her off.

"I think Romeo is waiting for you in the lobby," her raven-haired coworker, Joy Zhang, five foot six of leggy, feisty attitude, said as she walked into the room.

"Stop calling him that. I told you he's just a friend who gave me a ride." Reese had worked with Joy for two and a half years, and she adored her, even if she was as nosy as the day was long and made a habit of twisting tidbits into tales.

"A friend who left you starry-eyed all day." She smiled.

"I'm *not* starry-eyed." She'd loved starting her day seeing Blaine, and the fact that he'd thought of Colette meant the world to her. When Tobias had texted to say her car wouldn't be ready until after six, she'd messaged Blaine to let him know he didn't have to take her to pick it up since it was going to be so late. He'd insisted it wasn't a problem. No surprise there. What girl wouldn't be a little starry-eyed by a man like him? But she wasn't about to admit it.

"Uh-huh. And I don't love my wife." Joy rolled her eyes and

went to her desk. "He's not anything like what I thought your type was."

"I don't have a type." Reese peered out the window, and her heart nearly stopped at the sight of Ice's black Escalade. Panic flared in her chest. How did he find out where she worked? They always met at the park on Monday nights, when all she had to worry about was telling Colette she was running out to the store. She wasn't prepared for *this*. She didn't even have any cash with her. "I'll be right back."

She hurried out of the office, struggling to remain calm as she passed her coworkers in the hall. She caught a concerned look from Terry, the sweet middle-aged receptionist, and saw Ice standing by the doors. He was the very definition of a stone-faced thug at six-plus feet tall with the coldest black eyes she'd ever seen and tattoos covering every inch of skin from his shaved head to his fingers. He wore a black T-shirt and two thick gold chains around his neck.

Her chest felt like it was going to explode, but she refused to show him any weakness. It took every bit of her strength to force a smile and not look away from those dead eyes. "Hi. I wasn't expecting you. Let's talk outside." She blew through the doors, silently praying he wouldn't make a scene, and hurried to the far side of the parking lot, hopefully away from prying eyes, and turned on him. "What are you doing here?"

"Collecting my money."

"Why here? Why now? I don't have it with me." She thought they had a deal, but obviously he wasn't the kind of guy she could make deals with.

"Then let's take a ride to an ATM."

"I can't leave work," she argued. "You're going to get me fired, and then I won't be able to pay you anything."

"I don't give a fuck if you get fired. If you can't pay with cash, you'll pay with your body. Or maybe that little sister of yours would be worth more."

Fury cut through her, charging out. "You go anywhere near her, and I will have you arrested so fast you won't know what hit you."

"I'll take care of that big mouth of yours right now, bitch." He stepped closer.

She stepped back and saw Blaine's truck pull into the parking lot and head straight for them, heightening her panic. She didn't want Blaine getting involved in her mother's mess. "I'll get your money. I promise. I'll get you six hundred tonight if you'll just leave now. *Please*." Her gaze shot to Blaine climbing out of his truck, eyes trained on Ice as he strode over.

Ice's jaw clenched.

"Hey, babe, what's going on?" Blaine's voice was dead calm, serious eyes never leaving Ice's as he put a hand on her back, tension mounting between the two men.

"Nothing," she said before Ice could respond, sure Blaine could feel her trembling. "This is my mom's boyfriend. She owed him some money, and I forgot to go to the bank." After everything Blaine had done for her, lying to him made her feel as low as her mother, but what choice did she have?

"How much?" Blaine asked.

"Five hundred," she answered.

"*Six*," Ice said sternly.

"Right, sorry." *Shoot. Me and my big mouth.*

"No problem." Blaine reached into his back pocket and pulled out a wad of cash that had Reese wondering if he was a drug dealer, too. He counted out six hundred dollars and handed it to Ice. "Is she square now?"

"*Yes*," she reassured him, hoping Ice wouldn't say anything.

But Blaine ignored her, eyes still locked on Ice. "I *said*, is she square?"

"Yeah, she's good." His cold eyes shifted to her for only a second before he strode off.

Blaine's hand remained on her back as he watched Ice's every move until he drove out of the parking lot and disappeared down the street. He pulled Reese against his chest and wrapped his strong arms around her. "You okay?"

He felt so safe, she was tempted to say *no* and admit she hadn't been okay in so long, she wasn't sure what it even meant anymore. But she wasn't going to get him mixed up in this any more than she already had. Mustering all her courage, she stepped out of his arms, instantly missing the safety of them. "I'm fine. My mom told me she owed him money and he'd be coming by, but with everything that's been going on, I forgot." He was studying her, and she knew he was weighing her response.

"If you're in trouble, you can tell me, Reese."

"I'm *not*." The lie tasted horrific. She was in deep trouble. Things with Ice were escalating, and she was so far out of her realm, she had no idea how to stop them. But no matter what, she wasn't going to drag Blaine into it.

"Was that all your mother owed, or should I be worried about this guy coming around again?"

"That was it. It was a onetime thing. It's not a big deal. She owed her boyfriend money, and I paid him. I don't know why you're so worried."

"Because I didn't like the looks of that guy. You're being straight with me?"

He was looking at her with so much concern, she almost

caved, but then she remembered his wad of cash and felt stupid for almost letting her guard down. "*Yes*, but what about you? Where'd you get that much cash?"

"It's the money that asshole owed you for the party." He pulled out the rest and handed it to her.

She stared at it with disbelief. "You went and got it from him?"

Without answering, he glanced in the direction Ice had gone, his jaw ticking. He pulled out his phone and thumbed out a text. He pocketed his phone, putting his hand on her back again. "You about ready to go?"

"Blaine. Is this money really from the party? Because I can't take it if it's not."

"It's *yours*," he said gruffly. "Let's get your stuff and hit the road."

He waited in the lobby as she went to collect her things, heart thundering.

Joy hurried over to her. "Who were those two guys? Which one is Romeo?"

"Were you watching us?"

"Of course! I haven't had this much excitement in my life since Willa brought home that new coffee maker with the frothy milk thing." Willa was her wife.

"You mean the latte maker?"

"Yeah. That thing is *great*. Anyway, I thought those two guys were going to fight over you."

"It's not what you think. The bald guy was my mom's boy-friend."

"So the hot one is yours? Damn, girl. You've been holding out on me."

Reese rolled her eyes and gathered her things. "He's not my

boyfriend. He's just a guy I met at a party who offered to give me a ride."

"I bet he did." She waggled her brows.

"Not like *that*. I've got to go."

"Okay, but tomorrow I want all the details on that party you conveniently failed to mention."

"Goodbye, Joy," she called over her shoulder as she left the office.

"There she is," Terry said, brown eyes dancing with intrigue. "Blaine was just telling me how you two met at a party in Boston over the weekend."

Reese's stomach sank. "He did, did he?" She tried to sound lighthearted but heard the tension in her voice.

"Yes, and I was so happy to hear it," Terry said. "I've been worried about you working so hard and taking care of your sister while your mother is on vacation. It's about time you got out and had some fun. I can't believe you met in Boston and you both live here on the Cape. Sounds like fate to me."

"It's not like that," Reese said. "We're just friends, but we have to get going. I'll see you tomorrow."

"It was a pleasure meeting you, Terry." Blaine pushed the door open and held it for Reese.

As they walked out, his hand landed on her back again. "Did you have to tell her about the party?"

"It's where we met. I didn't say it was a bachelor party. Would you rather I was a dick to her and didn't say two words, like your mother's boyfriend? She asked me about him."

Could this day get any worse? "What did you tell her?"

"That he was picking up something he'd left at your mother's house." He opened the passenger door for her. "She thinks your mom is on vacation?"

"Yes. I don't like people at work knowing my business." She climbed into the truck, feeling like a yo-yo on a string. She couldn't blame him for asking questions. He'd saved her...*again.* "I'm sorry. I didn't mean to be a jerk, and I definitely don't want you to be one. It's just been a stressful afternoon."

He put his hands on the roof of the truck, leaning in. "Then how about we make it a little better?"

Maybe she *was* weak, because she wanted to be in his arms again and pretend like her problems didn't exist. Heck, she wanted to lean up and kiss him until the real world faded away.

Pushing those ridiculous thoughts away, she said, "What do you have in mind?"

He cocked a grin. "How much time do you have?"

"How much time do I need?"

"You do like to challenge me." He shook his head. "Should you be home when Colette gets there?"

"No. She'll text to let me know she's home. But how long do you think we'll need?"

"What I have in mind is more about what you *want* than what we *need,* so I guess we'll see."

He winked and closed the door, sending her heart into a full-on sprint.

He eyed her as he pulled out of the parking lot. "Don't look so nervous."

"I'm not used to guys talking about wants and needs."

"Then you're hanging out with the wrong guys, because your wants and needs should be at the top of any man's priority list when you're with them."

"*Please.* Guys aren't like that. They might start out that way, but when they realize you have more important things to do than cater to them, they change."

The muscles in his jaw jumped. "Like I said, you're hanging with the wrong guys. Is that why you don't have a boyfriend?"

"What makes you think I don't?"

"Because if you did, you'd have called him Saturday night instead of getting a ride with me."

"What if he's out of town?"

"You'd still touch base with him, because that's what people do. They turn to the person they're closest to when they're in a tough situation, and you, buttercup, wanted to handle everything yourself."

She couldn't deny that. "Why don't you have a girlfriend?"

"What makes you think I don't?"

"Because you wouldn't spend all this time with me if you did."

He turned onto another road and glanced at her. "I don't do girlfriends."

"So you're a player like Zander?" she challenged.

"Not even close."

She waited to see if he'd say more, but he offered nothing. "Let me get this straight. You don't do girlfriends, but you're not a player. If you think I believe you don't get around, you're wrong."

He stopped at a red light, giving her his full attention. "What do you want me to say? I don't consider myself a player. If I'm hooking up with a woman, I'm only hooking up with her, and I expect her to do the same."

"Isn't that a girlfriend?"

"No. You think about a girlfriend all the time. What she needs, what she wants, if she's okay. You take a girlfriend out and go the extra mile for her."

"I have a feeling you go the extra mile for everyone."

"Not everyone."

He said it so seriously, her nerves caught fire. What did that mean? Was he helping her because she was special, or did he not consider what he was doing for her as going the extra mile? She couldn't dissect *that* right now, but maybe she could get other answers. "So you don't do relationships, and you use women for sex and expect exclusivity?"

"I don't *use* women," he said gruffly. "The women I'm with know the deal and aren't looking for more. We have mutual respect, and we're both in it for mutual pleasure. Clear enough?" The light changed, and he drove through the intersection.

"Yeah. It's just so different from anything I would ever do, I don't understand it."

"Don't even try to. You're not cut out for it."

No kidding. "How long do you hook up with them?"

"However long we want to. Sometimes it's a night or two, and other times it's a few months."

"A few *months*? That's a relationship, not a hookup. Are you telling me you can sleep with a girl for a few months and not feel something more?"

"We don't *sleep*. It's just sex."

"Don't you develop feelings for them anyway?"

"Sure, sometimes, if it goes on long enough, but not romantic feelings. Just like a friend." He glanced over with a glimmer of cockiness. "With benefits."

She was way out of her league and utterly confused by the mixed signals he'd been sending her. He looked completely unfazed by their conversation, while her thoughts were spinning. Did he think she wanted to be his friend with benefits? He was right that she wasn't cut out for it, so was he just messing with her head? What she'd just learned should end her attraction to him, but it only made her more curious.

A little while later he pulled into the Wholesale Garden Center and said, "Here we are," like they hadn't had that weird conversation.

"What are we doing here?"

"I thought you might want to pick out the plants and flowers for the gardens." He parked the truck.

"Me? Your client didn't specify what they wanted?"

"Nope."

"But I'm not a horticulturist."

"I'm pretty good at that, but I trust you. I have a feeling you've got a great eye." He took off his seat belt and grabbed a set of plans from behind the seat. "Scoot over here, and I'll show you what he's got in mind."

She moved closer, her nerves flaming again as he unrolled the plans. His rugged scent infiltrated her senses like a leader waving a flag, drawing her attention to their close proximity. *Attention, hormones! We have thighs and shoulders touching, and don't miss those muscular forearms!* She tried not to think about all that, or about his hookups, as he showed her the layout of the yard, patios, and existing gardens.

"The land slopes gently toward the water. He wants a sitting area here." His arm brushed the side of her breast, causing prickles of awareness. "I was thinking of making two stone knee walls with a path between them that leads down to the water, and you can create gardens here and here."

Gardens. Focus on the gardens. "And he wants them those sizes and shapes?"

"That was just an idea. You can use your creativity."

She looked at him like he'd lost his mind. "Blaine, I don't have this kind of experience. I can't make those decisions for someone else."

"I think you have more experience than you realize, and if not, then it's time you gained it."

"What if I mess up?"

"You won't. You pulled it off for your landlord. This is no different."

"You haven't seen those gardens. Just because my landlord and I love them doesn't mean your client would like my choices."

"Stop fighting it, Wilder. You know you can do this."

The only place she was used to someone having unwavering confidence in her was at work. Like school, it was her escape. In her heart, she knew she could do him proud with the gardens, and she sure hoped she was right. Determined to do her absolute best, she said, "Do you have pictures of his current gardens so I can get a sense of his style?"

"Yeah. I have some from last summer when they were in bloom."

He pulled out his phone and showed her pictures of stunning gardens. Ideas came to her, one after another, excitement bubbling up inside her, taking her nerves down a notch.

He rolled up the plans. "What do you say, Wilder? Are you up to the challenge?"

"I hope so."

"That's not what I want to hear."

"*Yes.* I'm up to the challenge. I'll look up any plants I'm not one hundred percent sure about, and I'll make sure they're tasteful and not overdone. I won't let you down."

"With that smile, you couldn't let me down if you tried."

Chapter Seven

THEY SPENT THE next two hours walking through the garden center, picking out plants and flowers and talking about ideas. Blaine hadn't been to the garden center in years. He'd gone often when he and Maverick had first opened Cape Stone, handling landscaping and hardscaping. Their reputation had quickly taken off, and they'd shifted their focus to the areas they were most passionate about, stone distribution and hardscaping, and had contracted out most of the landscaping. But he'd gladly do this every damn day and spend every penny he had just to hear the excitement in Reese's voice as she rattled off facts about soil and sunlight and natural ecosystems. She was wicked smart, bordering on what some people might consider nerdy. But Blaine was drawn to her intelligence and found himself getting lost in the things she said and thinking about the things she didn't.

"The daylilies are going to be perfect for the slope of the yard. Did you remember to write down red valerian and dahlias?" she asked excitedly.

"I got them both, and lilacs."

"I love the way lilacs smell." She leaned closer, looking over their list. "I'm a little worried about the peonies. They can be finicky, but I haven't had any die on me, and I think they're worth the risk. They symbolize all the things people should surround themselves with: love, happiness, romance, beauty. I'm eventually going to plant some in my mom's gardens, too. Hopefully they'll survive."

"They'll make it."

"What makes you so sure?"

"What plant would dare to defy you?"

She laughed softly, and they headed down the aisle. "I like our plan. We chose a good mix of flowers, seasonal plants, and shrubs. They'll have color for most of every season, and they should be low maintenance. The red valerian and basket-of-gold will give the border a pop of color, and there's something romantic about roses climbing over the top of stone walls. That whole area will look great."

She hadn't stopped smiling since they'd arrived, and it felt good to be the one to bring that happiness into her life. Especially after what he'd witnessed today. Even though the guy had said Reese was square, Blaine's gut told him that guy was bad news. He'd sent his license plate to Cuffs, but he was still waiting to hear back from him.

"I'm sure you're good at your job, but I think you missed your calling. You have a great eye, and your excitement is contagious. I've been entrenched in hardscaping for so long, I had forgotten what it was like to be on the other side, putting thought into how plants could bring a place to life."

"So you usually don't do landscaping?"

"I'm all about hardscape, but we do landscape for a few special clients."

"So this is a special client we'll be working for?"

Shit. He fucking hated lies. He'd lost count of the number of times his father had told him that lies were an evil type of darkness that had the ability to shatter a person's light. He'd always lived by those words. Hell, his relationship with Madigan had been damaged because he believed so strongly in honesty. But he'd rather lie than have Reese take an unsafe job. "That's right."

"Well, thank you for trusting me. I love being around flowers. If I'm in a bad mood, a walk through a garden always cheers me up." They walked by a display of stone fountains. "Too bad he doesn't want one of these. They're gorgeous."

"You should see ours." Catching himself, he said, "The ones Cape Stone sells."

"Do you and Maverick make them?"

"I do some fountain work, but not sculpting. That's Maverick's domain. He makes some on special order, but as an artist, he makes what he feels, not the same thing over and over."

"That's awesome. I'd love to see his work and fountains you've made some time."

He'd have to figure out how to manage that without blowing his cover. Before she could ask more questions about his work, he put a hand on her back, guiding her toward the front of the store. "I think we should sit on this list until tomorrow, when you see the property, in case you want to make changes."

"Good idea, but it shouldn't take more than a day to get the beds ready for planting. Do you think they'll deliver by Wednesday?"

"Yeah, no problem. Do you want to swing by home and check on Colette before we pick up your car?"

"No. She'll just get annoyed. She's supposed to be working on an essay, and I'm sure she's procrastinating. But if I see her procrastinating, I'll have to argue with her about doing it, and

I'm having too much fun to ruin my good mood with an argument." They headed out of the store. "I really appreciate you bringing me with you today. I haven't been this excited over anything other than work in years. I needed this."

He draped an arm over her shoulder. "Why do you think we're here, Wilder?"

She looked at him curiously.

He could practically see the gears in her mind churning as they headed over to his truck. He opened the passenger door. "Stop overthinking and get your fine ass in the truck."

"Wait, what did you mean by that?"

He wasn't about to step in that snare. "Get in, Reese."

"Just answer me."

"*Reese*," he warned, *this close* to shutting her up with his mouth.

She crossed her arms. "Why are we here if not to get your client's plants? Did you come here just for me? I'm not moving until you—"

He grabbed her by the waist, lifted her up, and plunked her down in the passenger seat.

"*Blaine!*"

"That'll teach you to listen."

"You can't just pick up a woman and put her where you want her."

He leaned into the truck, bringing those pouty lips within biting distance, and the truth rolled out. "It was either that or kiss the fuck out of you to shut you up."

She opened her mouth, then clamped it shut again, brows slanting. "You're infuriating. You can't just kiss a girl, either."

He arched a brow.

She rolled her eyes, but there was no masking the amusement, or the heat, in them.

"Put your seat belt on."

"You're such a Neanderthal." She reached for her seat belt.

"Careful, or I'll drag you into my cave."

REESE DIDN'T WANT to think about kissing Blaine, much less what his Neanderthal *cave* was like, but it was all she could think about as they drove to his sister's house to pick up her car. Should she want to kiss him? *No.* Did she want to kiss him? *Yes.* So badly she'd dreamed about doing it and much more last night and had woken up all hot and sweaty. But the real question was, given the opportunity, *would* she kiss him? That was a hard-and-fast no.

I think.

Or at least I'm pretty sure I wouldn't.

No. I definitely wouldn't. I don't want to be one of his bed bunnies.

He pulled up to the curb in front of a cute cottage. Her car was in the driveway, and a guy was wiping down the hood.

Blaine turned his hawk eyes on her. "You have something you want to say?"

"No."

"Spill it, Wilder. I can feel your tension, and unless I'm mistaken, I know of only one surefire way to get rid of *that* kind of tension."

"It's not...I'm not..." She huffed out a breath. "I'm not going to become one of your friends with benefits."

"Did I ask you to?"

"No, but you said you almost kissed me."

"To shut you up," he said firmly. "Trust me, buttercup, if I kissed you, talking would be the last thing on your mind."

"*Ugh!* Why do men exaggerate everything?" She threw open her door.

"Is that a challenge?" He smirked.

"No, you fool," she said with a laugh. He was infuriatingly fun when he wasn't being so pushy.

"Just checking." He climbed out of the truck, and as they headed up the driveway, he leaned closer, speaking low. "I still feel that tension."

"Shut up."

"You know you're thinking about kissing me."

"Ohmygosh. *Stop*," she said as the man who was wiping down the hood of her car turned around. He was big, like Blaine, but thicker chested, with brown hair and brooding eyes.

Blaine put his hand on Reese's back. "How's it going, Tobias?"

"Great. She's all done." He wiped his hands and shoved the rag in his back pocket.

"Reese, this is Tobias Riggs, Madigan's boyfriend."

"Hi. Thanks so much for fixing my car. How much do I owe you?"

Tobias glanced at Blaine before answering. "Just thirty bucks for the part."

"Okay, what about your time?" She pulled the money Blaine had given her out of her pocket.

"It's on the house," Tobias answered.

"No, you don't even know me. I need to pay you for your time."

"I can't take your money. We don't work that way with

friends," Tobias said firmly.

Her eyes implored Blaine. "You guys are going to make me feel guilty."

"Nope," Tobias and Blaine said in unison.

"Fine." She paid Tobias thirty dollars. "I can't thank you enough. This was above and beyond what I had hoped for or expected."

"No worries. I also topped off your fluids and checked your brakes. You're in good shape."

"You didn't have to do all of that. Let me give you more money."

"No need," Tobias said. "Happy to do it for a friend of Blaine's."

"Thanks, man," Blaine said.

The side door of the cottage swung open, and a petite mahogany-haired girl ran out, wearing a cute black top, skinny jeans, and boots. *"Wait!* I want to meet Reese!"

"Chill, Mads. We're not going anywhere," Blaine said.

"Good." A smile bloomed on her gorgeous face. "Hi. I'm Madigan, and I have not heard enough about you!" She went in for a hug, surprising Reese, but Reese went with it. "My brother has been tight-lipped about his new *friend*."

"Mads," Blaine warned.

"What? I never get to meet your *friends*."

The way she emphasized *friends* had Reese's alarms going off. "It's not like that. We're just regular friends, not friends with benefits."

"Oh." Madigan glanced at Blaine, amused. "Well, not that I'm suggesting you sleep with my brother, but I highly recommend the friends-with-benefits route. That's pretty much how Tobias and I started." She smiled up at him. "Right?"

Tobias chuckled. "That's right, babe." He leaned down and kissed her.

"Overshare much?" Blaine gritted out.

Madigan's eyes sparked with mischief. "Reese, did Blaine tell you that he almost broke us up?"

Reese knew she was trying to get her brother's goat, but she was curious about what he'd done. "*No.* Why would he do that?"

"Because my brother doesn't know the first thing about boundaries."

"Really? I hadn't noticed," Reese said sarcastically, smiling at Blaine. She liked his spunky sister.

"He's the worst," Madigan said.

"I'm standing right here. I can hear you, you know," Blaine said.

Madigan was probably trying to look stern, but her adoration for her brother shined through. "You are the worst, but it's only because you have a big heart and don't know what to do with all that love."

Reese softened at that. "Did you really try to break them up?"

"No. Well, sort of." Blaine glanced at Tobias, and Reese couldn't read the silent message passing between them.

"I was in prison before coming here, and Blaine found out before I told Mads. He was protecting her," Tobias explained.

Prison? Reese tried to hide her shock. "Oh…"

"I went off on him without knowing the full story," Blaine explained. "Tobias is a good man. He landed in prison because he was protecting *his* sister."

"Protectiveness must run in the water around here," Reese said.

"Heck yeah, it does," Madigan said. "We were just about to throw burgers on the grill. Stay for dinner, and we can get to know each other."

"I don't want to impose, and Blaine just spent all afternoon with me," Reese said. "I'm sure he has better things to do."

"I'm all yours tonight," Blaine said.

She had expected him to jump at the excuse to leave, and his calling himself *hers* stirred those flutters in her chest again. "Okay, let me just text Colette and let her know I'll be a little late."

"Want me to swing by and get her?" Blaine asked.

Wow, really? Just like that? "No, thanks. She won't want to come." She texted Colette to say she'd be a little late and reminded her to work on her essay. Colette replied, *Whatever.*

As they headed into the backyard, Madigan looped her arm through Reese's like they were old friends. "I'm so glad you're staying. Is Colette your sister?"

"Yes. She's fifteen, and all teenage attitude." It was second nature to cover for her mother and keep that part of her life hidden. But prison was worse than rehab, and knowing Blaine and Madigan had accepted Tobias had her considering telling Madigan the truth. But she just couldn't. "I'm watching her for a few weeks while my mother is away."

"Her sister reminds me of you, Mads," Blaine chimed in.

"She must be pretty awesome." Madigan flashed a cheesy smile. "Come on, Reese. Let's make a salad while the guys cook the burgers."

Reese followed her into the kitchen.

Madigan took salad fixings out of the fridge and started washing them. "There are cutting boards in the cabinet to your left, and knives are in the drawer to your right. I'd love to know more about you. Blaine won't tell me anything."

Reese set the cutting boards and knives on the counter. "There's not much to tell. I'm just a girl who works in a lab."

"Are you a scientist?" She handed Reese two tomatoes and a cucumber.

Reese began slicing the tomatoes. "I'm a forensic analyst."

Madigan's eyes widened. "Wow, that's impressive. Maybe you can find a cure for my overprotective big brothers."

She laughed. "I don't think so. But if they commit a crime, I might be able to track their DNA."

"That'll never happen. They're the good kind of bad boys, not the bad kind."

"I got that impression from what Blaine has told me about the club. What was it like growing up around a motorcycle club?"

"I'm not going to lie. It could be stifling at times. It was like having dozens of uncles who were as protective as all the males in my family are. But it was also really great, because I had all these people who felt like family, and still do. I think about how my life was different from other kids' at school a lot, and I honestly wouldn't have wanted it any other way."

Reese was in awe of what they had. "Blaine told me that you gave Maverick his road name. How come you never gave Blaine one?"

"I wasn't trying to give one to Justin. I was only four. He just needed us so much, the name fit. But Blaine has never needed anyone."

"Everyone needs someone." *I needed my grandmother.*

"Not Blaine. He's been a confident, in-control lone wolf for as long as I can remember. I mean, the guys have his back, but as far as I know, he's never asked anyone for a darn thing. The only fitting road name I can think of for him would be Knight, because he's always watching out for everyone else. I swear he should have a white horse."

"I think Bulldozer would be more fitting," Reese said softly.

"Yes!" Madigan laughed. "That's perfect. His road name should totally be Bulldozer. You really do know him."

"Don't tell him I said that." Reese finished slicing the tomatoes and began skinning a cucumber as Madigan sliced carrots. "He's done so much to help me. I just wish I knew why."

"Are you worried he has an ulterior motive?"

"I hate to say it, but yes. I want to trust him, but I've been burned before."

"Haven't we all? You can trust Blaine. He doesn't play games. If he's helping you, it's because he wants to, not for some other gain."

"That's good to know. I've never met anyone like him. He's always there."

Madigan glanced at her. "Was he with you last night?"

"Yeah. He showed up out of the blue with pizza and replaced our broken locks. Why?"

"Because he took off after the guys got back from their ride instead of hanging out with everyone. I thought he might have gone to see you."

Reese wondered if that bothered her. "I don't want to keep him from your family and friends."

"No, this is a good thing." Madigan leaned against the counter with a thoughtful smile. "I'm glad he was with you, and if you two really aren't messing around, then it says a lot."

"It does?" She focused on slicing the cucumber instead of on her racing heart.

"Mm-hm. Blaine is a guy's guy. I don't mean that in a sexist way, but he doesn't really hang out with women unless we're all together in a group. Not that I know all about his personal life, but word gets around. I've never heard anything about him going out of his way to spend time alone with women he's not messing around with. To be honest, I was sure he'd hightail it out of here when I suggested you stay for dinner. I'm glad he didn't."

"Me too. You put my mind at ease about him. I appreciate that. It sounded like you and Blaine have had your fair share of going head-to-head."

"We have. He's a bulldozer for sure, but I'm pretty stubborn, too." Madigan looked out the kitchen window at the guys talking by the grill. "I never thought I'd see the day those two were friends. But beneath that arrogant bulldozer is a heart of gold. Blaine would burn down the world for the people he loves."

Reese couldn't help but wonder what it would be like to be loved that much. It was a little frightening, but the only thing scary about Blaine was the fact that their worlds were very far apart, as were their views on relationships. But she was overthinking anyway. He'd made it clear that he hadn't wanted to kiss her. He'd only wanted to shut her up.

But then he'd flirted again.

It was all too confusing.

They finished making the salad and started setting the table. "I don't know what to make of that, but I don't doubt it. I'm just grateful he's been there for us, even if I fight every little thing he does."

"Oh my God, do you really?" Madigan asked as she poured two glasses of wine.

"I can't help it. It's a reflex. I'm not used to anyone helping us."

"That's sad." Madigan grinned. "But I bet you drive him crazy."

"I do. I can't figure out why he's sticking around."

"Because he *likes* you, and I don't mean that he has an ulterior motive. My brothers aren't the kind of guys who beat around the bush. If all he wanted was sex, you'd know. He's obviously attracted to you. Anyone can see that by the way he looks at you. But I think Blaine likes you for you, and if I'm right, he probably has no idea what to do with those feelings."

That makes two of us.

Madigan handed her a wineglass. "Here's to new friends."

Reese couldn't remember the last time she'd had a drink *or* a friend she could talk to like this. As they clinked glasses and sipped their wine, she hoped this might be the start of a real friendship.

Tobias came through the door carrying a plate of burgers, and Blaine followed him in. His piercing blue eyes zeroed in on her, his powerful legs eating up the space between them, making her heart race. He put his hand on her back like it was the most natural thing in the world. "Has my sister told you all the awful things I've ever done?"

"Ha!" Madigan exclaimed. "I'd need about a week for that."

"Only a week?" Tobias joked, handing Blaine a beer.

"I was being nice," Madigan said.

"Careful, Mads. I've got more than a handful of stories about you, too," Blaine said.

An hour later, they'd finished eating dinner, and Reese had learned that Madigan had a multifaceted career as a puppeteer, a musical storyteller, and the creator of her own line of greeting cards called the Mad Truth About Love and that in addition to working with Blaine's father and brothers, Tobias also taught women's self-defense classes, which Blaine tried to talk her into taking.

Madigan had them in hysterics with stories about what it was like growing up with four brothers. "Every year on the first day of school, Blaine walked me into my classroom, and he'd stare down the boys until I swear they were trembling."

"I wanted them to know not to mess with you," Blaine said seriously, but he'd been laughing right along with the rest of them, and Reese loved seeing this lighter side of him.

"I was in *elementary* school." Madigan sipped her wine, eyes dancing with amusement. "And you did it until I graduated from high school."

"Blaine!" Reese laughed. "You have to admit, that's a little over the top."

"The hell it is. She's my baby sister."

"I bet dating was fun with you around," Reese said.

"All the guys were afraid of him," Madigan said. "When a boy finally asked me out, *all* of my brothers were waiting on the front porch when he came to pick me up. Blaine and Maverick didn't even live at home at the time. They scared the daylights out of him."

"That's horrible. That poor boy." As ridiculously overprotective as Blaine and her other brothers were, Reese was a little envious that she had them.

"You don't know the half of it," Madigan said. "Any time I went on a date, one of my brothers would show up. I had to *lie* to get any freedom."

Blaine's jaw ticked. "What're you talking about?"

"That's right, big brother. You didn't know all my secrets." Madigan wiggled her shoulders. "Some of the times you thought I was sleeping at a friend's house or going to a movie with Ashley or someone else, I was out on dates. Only Mom knew where I really was."

"My girl is resourceful," Tobias said with a wink.

"Not resourceful enough," Blaine said. "You think we didn't have eyes on you, Mads?"

Madigan's eyes narrowed. "I *know* you didn't."

He smirked. "Why do you think there was a fire alarm the first time Robby kissed you in the movie theater? And Ryan's flat tire at the fair? That was a good one. Shall I go on?"

Madigan's jaw dropped. "How...?"

Blaine took a drink of his beer.

"Wow," Reese said just above a whisper. *He'd burn down the world for the people he loves.* She turned to Tobias. "Are you sure he doesn't have your house bugged?"

"I did a sweep before moving in." Tobias covered Madigan's hand with his, looking at her like she was his whole world. "Mads is worth whatever they put me through."

"*Aw.* I love you," Madigan said, leaning in to kiss him.

"Love you, too, blue eyes." Tobias was a man of few words, but the way he looked at Madigan said more than words ever could.

Reese felt a stab of jealousy over their relationship as they kissed for the millionth time. She glanced at Blaine and found him watching her intently. Madigan's voice whispered through her mind. *He's obviously attracted to you. Anyone can see that by the way he looks at you.* Her pulse quickened.

"Hate me yet?" Blaine asked in a low voice.

Beneath that arrogant bulldozer is a heart of gold. "Not yet."

He glanced at Madigan and Tobias, who were talking among themselves, and leaned closer, whispering, "You're lucky

I wasn't around when you were in high school."

"You wouldn't have had many guys to scare away," she whispered. "Taking care of Colette kept the few who were interested from sticking around."

"They were idiots. Those sexy glasses would've kept me around," he rasped in her ear, sending her heart into overdrive.

"What are you whispering that's making her blush?" Madigan asked.

"Nothing." Reese downed her wine, while Blaine chuckled beside her. She couldn't figure him out. One minute he was flirting, and the next he was acting like they were just friends.

"Blaine, Reese thought up the perfect road name for you," Madigan said. "Bulldozer."

He and Tobias barked out laughs. Blaine's happy eyes held Reese's. That was a look she wasn't used to, and *wow*, it took her breath away.

"Dude, you can't even deny that one," Tobias said.

"No, I can't. That's a name that would stick." Blaine stretched his arm across the back of Reese's chair, his fingers curling around her shoulder, sending shivers of heat through her as he pulled her closer and said, "Nice one, Wilder."

BLAINE HADN'T KNOWN what to expect when Madigan had invited them to stay for dinner, but he had a feeling Reese didn't have many friends. Even though his sister could be a pain in the ass to him, she was a good person and could be a loyal friend for Reese.

They helped clean up and hung out for another hour.

Madigan showed Reese her greeting cards. He loved seeing Reese giggling and chatting, as they poked fun at him and Tobias. Seeing her so happy made him crave more smiles, more time with her, more answers.

Just fucking *more*.

He knew he needed to back off, but just being around her was a bigger high than being on his bike with nothing but miles of open road ahead of him.

When they finally got ready to leave, Blaine was glad they'd stayed.

"I know you don't have much free time, but I hope you'll consider joining our book club, and I'd love to get together sometime. Just us girls." Madigan hugged Reese goodbye.

"I'd like that." Reese smiled at Tobias. "Thank you again for fixing my car."

"Anytime you need it checked out, just let Mads know."

"Thank you."

Madigan hugged Blaine, whispering, "I love her. Don't scare her off," and backed away with a twinkle in her eye.

"Thanks for dinner, guys. I'll see you around." They walked out, and Blaine didn't think as he draped an arm over Reese's shoulder. It felt so natural, it took a moment for him to realize it probably shouldn't. But after the afternoon and evening they'd had, he went with it. "A'right, Wilder, I'll follow you home."

"You don't have to do that."

"There was a party going on there the other night. I'd like to make sure Colette's okay."

"She texted a little while ago and seemed fine. If she was having a party, she wouldn't text."

"Okay, you caught me. I want to make sure you get home

safely."

She smiled. "Do you do that for all your friends you aren't hooking up with?"

"I don't do that for the women I do hook up with. They go their way. I go mine."

"Oh." Her innocent eyes bloomed wide. "Then why follow *me?*"

Hell if he could explain it, so he didn't even try. "I'll be right behind you."

He opened her car door, and she looked like she wanted to say something, but she climbed in, and he headed to his truck. It smelled like her, intoxicating and like warm honey and oranges. *Fuck.* Since when did he notice things like that?

He followed her toward her house and saw her glancing at him in the rearview mirror several times. *That's right, buttercup. I've got your back. And I'd like to have a hell of a lot more than that.*

When they got to her house, he was out of his truck and opening her car door before she even cut the engine. "How does she run?"

"Perfect." She climbed out, looking a little nervous. "Thank you again for taking me to the garden center, and for tonight. I had a great time. You're really lucky. Madigan and Tobias are wonderful."

"Yeah, I am lucky." He wanted her to have people in her life that she could count on, too. "Come on, I'll walk you up." He put his hand on her back, another move that felt natural.

"You don't have to walk me to my door."

"When are you going to stop telling me what I don't have to do? If a man doesn't walk you to your door, he's not worth your time."

"What is this, free dating tips from Blaine Wicked, the man who doesn't believe in relationships? You could give a girl whiplash."

"I prefer to give a good tongue-lashing."

Her brows knitted. "Tongue-lashing? You want to yell at me?"

"Wrong type of tongue-lashing, buttercup."

"What—*oh…*" Her cheeks flamed, and her devastatingly sexy, innocent eyes drew him in, making him want her even more. "*See?* That's what I mean! One minute you're telling me you don't do girlfriends, and the next you talk about kissing me, but only to shut me up, and then you flirt with me. You took me to the garden center, which made me happier than I've been in forever, and you allude to doing it for me, but you won't *say* you did it for me. Then your sister says you don't hang out with girls you aren't screwing, but you're with *me* every night. So forgive me for being confused, but I'm a science girl. I deal with facts, and I like to understand things. Maybe I'm way off base, and if so, I'm embarrassing myself beyond salvation, but I have to know what this is, and you have me totally conf—"

He crushed his lips to hers, knowing he'd be damned for doing it, but he couldn't take her being as tortured as he was or thinking he didn't want her. He expected her to pull away or slap him, but her lips parted for him. He told himself to hold back, but that was impossible when he'd been thinking about her hot, willing mouth every minute of the fucking day since they'd met. He pulled her closer, pushing his hands into her hair, taking the kiss deeper. She went up on her toes. *That's it. Take what you want.* He intensified his efforts, his tongue sweeping hard and deep, stretching her mouth wide as he took his fill. She made a sensual sound that rocketed straight to his cock. He swept one arm around her, holding her tight, letting her feel what she did to him. His hand slid to her ass, and he grabbed hold. She inhaled sharply, and he felt himself teetering over the edge, wanting to devour every inch of her, but then he remembered they were in her front yard, and her sister could be watching.

Fuuck.

He forced himself to pull back, taking that pouty lower lip between his teeth and tugging, earning a shocked gasp. *So fucking innocent.* He dragged his tongue along her lip. "Open your eyes."

Her eyes fluttered open. Deep pools of desire stared back at him. Something inside him snapped, and he reclaimed her lips, kissing her like he'd never kissed another woman. Slowly, sensually, *protectively.* She went soft in his arms, and it was hell knowing he couldn't continue kissing her until her legs gave out and she begged for more. He brushed his lips over hers, heart racing like a fucking schoolboy as he whispered, "You give me whiplash, too."

She stood wide-eyed, touching her lips. "What...? *Um...?*"

"It's called a kiss." He lifted his chin in the direction of the door. "Get inside so I know you're safe."

He stepped back, and she stared at him for a beat, cheeks flushed, fingertips still touching her lips. When she headed up to the door, she glanced over her shoulder, eyes still hazy with lust.

"Sweet dreams, Wilder. See you tomorrow."

He watched her go inside, then headed back to his truck sporting a big-ass grin. At least he knew he wouldn't be the only one dreaming about the two of them naked tonight. As he pulled away from the curb, he called Cuffs.

"Hey, Blaine, sorry, man. I've had a hell of a day."

"No worries. What'd you find out?"

"Your instincts were right. He's a dealer, but he usually sticks to the Upper Cape. I don't know how your girl's mother got mixed up with him, but chances are slim that it happened in our area."

The club had always taken a stand against drugs, but after losing his cousin Ashley to an accidental overdose several years ago, they'd gone on the warpath to keep their communities clean. A dealer would have to have a death wish to encroach on Dark Knights' territory.

"I fucking knew it. He said Reese was square, but I'm going to track his ass down and warn him to stay the hell away from her and Colette."

"Dude, take a breath. You can't go after this guy half-cocked. If you take a bullet, you'll be of no use to her, and if she's square, she's not in imminent danger. Give me a day to have this asshole followed and see what kind of crew we're dealing with."

Blaine gritted his teeth, wondering if Reese knew he was a dealer, or if she really thought he was her mother's boyfriend. He couldn't fucking ask her, because if she didn't know, he'd scare the piss out of her. He turned his truck around. "Let me know as soon as you have the lowdown."

"I will. You want me to have one of the guys watch her house tonight?"

Blaine pulled up to the curb down the street from Reese's house. "I'm already on it."

HOURS LATER, BLAINE was still thinking about that kiss when his phone chimed with a text.

Reese: *What was that?*

Blaine: *A kiss.*

Reese: *What did it mean?*

Blaine: *That I wanted to kiss you.*

Reese: *Blaine!* An angry emoji appeared.

Blaine: *Yes, buttercup?*

Reese: *Seriously? This is how you're going to leave things?*

Blaine: *I'm happy to come over and give you that tongue-lashing.* He sent an overheated-face emoji.

Three little dots appeared, like she was typing, but they disappeared as quickly as they'd come. A minute later, they reappeared, then vanished again.

Blaine: *That's what I thought. See you on the job tomorrow afternoon. Sweet dreams.*

Chapter Eight

BLAINE FINISHED LAYING out the yard tools and headed up toward the house when he saw Reese pull into his driveway. He'd taken off before she'd left for work so as not to freak her out. She had enough on her mind without knowing he was making sure a drug dealer didn't have eyes on her or Colette. He was still waiting on word from Cuffs, which was hell, since he wanted nothing more than to make sure that asshole never went near Reese again.

Making his way to the driveway, he watched her climb out of her car. She was adorably sexy in a long-sleeve shirt and cutoffs with her hair pinned up in a ponytail, a few blond strands framing those glasses that drove him crazy. He could still feel her silky hair tangled around his fingers, still taste her lustful mouth. He clenched his jaw to tamp down that hunger as she gazed up at his house. He'd gotten the four-bedroom contemporary home for a steal a decade ago and had renovated it from top to bottom.

"Hey, buttercup."

She looked over, and her cheeks flamed. That blush did him in every damn time. She squared her shoulders, lifted her dimpled chin, and strode determinedly toward him carrying a pair of garden gloves. She stopped about six feet from him and planted a hand on her hip. "Hi."

"How's it going? Did you have a good day at the lab?" He'd swung by a few times to make sure that asshole hadn't stopped by, and it had killed him not to text Reese, but he knew she needed to process their kiss.

"Yes, thank you. But before we get started, I just want to put something out there."

He cocked a brow. "You want to put out?" It was cruel, but he couldn't help it. A flustered Reese was about the sexiest thing on earth.

"What? *No!* I want to say something."

"Sorry. You're a little riled up. I thought you might want me to take the edge off."

Her eyes widened, and her jaw dropped.

"Might want to close that mouth. It's looking like an invitation."

"You need to stop talking *right now*."

He held up his hands in surrender but couldn't stop his grin.

"Don't smile like that."

"Like what?"

"All hot and sexy. I'm here for *work*. I can't afford to lose this job, and I don't know if your company has rules against fraternization, so if you could please not kiss me again, I would appreciate it."

That kiss must have opened a floodgate, because he couldn't hold back from letting his intentions be known. He stepped closer. "You sure you want that?"

"I'm serious. There will be *no* kissing. Just work."

The fact that she didn't say she was sure did not go unnoticed. "Work now, play later. Got it."

"*Blaine*," she said vehemently. "I don't want to be one of your friends with benefits."

The desire in her eyes told him otherwise. "How can you know for sure if you haven't tested the benefits?"

"Because it's not about the benefits. I'm sure your benefits are…" Her cheeks flamed again, and she made a frustrated sound. "It doesn't matter how good they are. I'm not wired that way."

"They're not good, buttercup. They're leg-shaking, mind-blowing, forget-your-own-fucking-name *phenomenal*, and rewiring that pretty mind of yours could be fun."

She blinked several times, and then those big blue eyes narrowed. "*No*. There will be *no* rewiring. I could never be comfortable being someone's temporary sex buddy. I wouldn't be able to relax."

"You relaxed pretty damn fast when I kissed you last night."

"Yeah, well." She scoffed. "I didn't really have a choice, did I?"

"You *always* have a choice. You didn't have to kiss me back. You could have said no or pulled away, but you didn't, because you wanted that kiss."

She threw her hands up. "Who wouldn't? You're all bad-boy cocky and playfully charming, and you couldn't be hotter. But you already know that. You have confidence oozing out your pores."

"All good points. But you're the only one I want to kiss." He slid his arm around her waist, pulling her closer but not so hard that she couldn't stop him if she wanted to. "Tell me you don't want me to kiss you and I'll never bring it up again."

Desire swam in her eyes, and she licked her lips. "If you kiss me right now, I won't be able to concentrate on work, and I need the money."

That was not a rebuttal. It was simply a delay in gratification, and he was cool with that. He leaned in so close, her breathing hitched. *That's right, buttercup. You want me as badly as I want you.* "Fair enough." He brushed his lips over the dimple in her chin and released her. "Let's get to work, Wilder." He started to walk along the path through the garden to the backyard and realized she hadn't moved. "Are you coming?"

Her eyes narrowed. "Oh, you'd like that, wouldn't you?" She stalked past him.

AN HOUR LATER they were both hard at work. Blaine glanced at her wiping her brow with her forearm. She knocked her glasses off-kilter and wrinkled her nose as she pushed them to the bridge of it. *So fucking cute.* She went right back to digging up the grass, using a spade like a pro. She'd refused Blaine's help, as he'd known she would. *I've got this. You get the ground ready for your work, and I'll get it ready for mine.*

Most women would have taken him up on his offer, but not Little Miss Autonomous. She'd been left to hold the reins and she took that seriously, but she'd been pretty cagey with him. He wanted to know more about what she'd been through, and he wanted the down-low on the mother who had put her daughters in danger.

"Hey, Reese, how's your mom doing in rehab?"

"I don't know. She told us not to call or visit. The facility offers family counseling, which I thought would be a good idea, but she wanted no part of it."

"That's harsh. I'm sorry."

"I expected it. She wasn't thrilled about going in."

"At least she's making the effort to get clean. That's something."

She planted the spade in the ground and met his gaze with a steely one. "She had no choice. She got a DUI, and it was either that or jail."

"Oh, shit. What about the other times? You said this isn't her first time in rehab."

"She went once when I was eighteen and checked herself out after two weeks, then again when I was twenty-two. That lasted almost three weeks." She started digging again.

"Maybe the DUI will be enough to keep her in this time." He sure hoped so, for Reese's and Colette's sakes. "You said she wasn't always a mess. What was she like before? What changed?"

She was quiet for a few minutes. "Another interrogation?"

"Sorry. I didn't mean to pry. I'm just trying to understand what you've been through."

She stabbed at the ground with the spade. "It's not pretty."

"I assumed as much. You know, nothing you say will shock me or change how I think about you or Colette. I've got buddies who have been through rehab and have dealt with parents who never should have had children. There's not much I haven't seen, dealt with, or helped people through."

"After meeting Madigan and Tobias and learning that he was in prison, I believe you," she said softly.

"I believe in second and even third chances when they're warranted. I might be pushy, but you can trust me, Reese. I'm not looking for dirt on you."

"It's not that, but it will change how you see me. There's no way it can't." She glanced at him pensively. "Colette doesn't know the truth. Nobody who's around anymore does except me and my mom." She continued stabbing at the ground.

Talk about an ominous statement. He continued working so she didn't feel like she was under a microscope. "You have my word that I won't tell her anything you share with me."

Her brows knitted. She focused on the grass she was cutting out and sighed heavily. "I don't think my mom ever should have had kids. She was never the kind of mom who baked cookies or did my hair, but she tried to be nice and she made sure I had a roof over my head and food on the table. But she and my dad liked to party."

He steeled himself for whatever came next, knowing it would be dark.

"Most of the time if they went out, it was during the day, since my father worked at night, and some kid from the neighborhood would babysit me. But my mother would also go out at night sometimes, and I remember waking up to an empty house."

He stopped working, unable to concentrate on anything but her as she tore out a patch of grass. "How old were you when you were left alone?"

"Six? Eight? Ten?" She shrugged. "All of the above on and off."

"Jesus." His hands fisted at the thought of her as a frightened little girl, all alone. "What about your grandmother? Couldn't she look after you?"

"I don't think she even knew, and I wasn't about to tattle on my parents and get into trouble."

He clenched his teeth. "No kid should wake up to an empty house."

"It made me stronger. I learned to believe in myself."

Stop looking for the silver lining. Just say it sucked. "You shouldn't have had to."

"But I did, so I locked my bedroom door and hid under my covers. After you do that enough, you get to a point when you feel like, *the heck with this*, and you no longer need to hide. One night when my dad was off work, they got into an argument, which wasn't unusual, but she stormed out without him. Their arguing woke me up hours later. They argued a lot, but it was usually short-lived. This time it was *bad*. It went on and on. My mom was crying, and my father called her horrible things. It was one of those fights where your blood runs cold from just hearing it." She stilled, holding the spade, staring absently at the ground like the scene was unfolding before her.

Fuck this. He needed to be near her.

He set down his tools and went to her side.

"I went to see what was going on," she said softly. "I remember my mom's face was bloody and bruised, and her clothes were torn. My father was yelling about her *asking for it*. I didn't know what he meant, but I knew sometimes when they'd fight, he'd get physical, so I tried to get between them, thinking he'd hurt her. But it was like they didn't even see me or know I was there. They just kept yelling, and I couldn't understand what was happening. I couldn't put the pieces together. That was the first time I remember hearing the word *rape* come out of my mother's mouth, and I knew it was bad, but I didn't know what it meant."

Blaine's chest constricted, imagining her as a little girl witnessing that horror. "Your mother was raped? By your father?"

She nodded. "Yes, but not by my father. It happened when she was out, and I guess he blamed her."

"That's a shitty thing to do. No woman *asks* to be raped."

"Apparently my father believed otherwise. That was the start of my life imploding. Months passed in a blur of arguments, my father hardly being around, and my mother being high or drunk just about all the time. I was too little to understand that she was depressed and self-medicating. At some point I realized she was pregnant because she was showing. Then my father left, and after Colette was born, it was clear that my mother didn't want her. I didn't even know what to do with that. I mean, I knew what it was like to feel *forgotten* or ignored in my own home, but not *hated*." Her eyes dampened. "From the minute Colette was born, that was all she got from our mother."

His protective urges surged, not just for Reese but also for the child her mother didn't want. "Then why the fuck did she have her?"

"I asked my grandmother that, and things finally started to make sense, but they were also confusing. She explained that my mother was raped and told me exactly what that meant. She said my mother didn't know she was pregnant until it was too late to choose not to have the baby. My grandmother tried to convince her to go to the police right after it happened, but my mother never saw the guy's face, so she didn't report it. I do remember my grandmother begging her to get help, to talk to someone, but she wouldn't."

"Jesus, Reese."

"I know. It sucks. We did our best to shield Colette from my mother's hatred, but after my grandmother passed away, it was just me, and my mother held *nothing* back. I was only thirteen, and it wasn't like I had parents to show me what life should be like or anyone to turn to. All I knew was that our family was different from the way other girls my age talked about theirs, and I already felt like an outcast because of the shame I carried. I wasn't about to confide in someone whose life was so perfect they couldn't understand."

"I wish I had known you then. I'd have been there for you."

A small smile appeared. "I'm glad you weren't. It was awful. I was all Lettie had. I moved her into my room, fed her, bathed her, changed her, held her when she was scared, which was often." She spoke a little softer, as if she were reliving a memory. "On really hard nights, I'd gather leaves and put them by her bed and tell her stories about a chipmunk who was afraid of the dark and lived in a magical forest. I'd say, *as long as she slept in the forest, nothing could ever hurt her.*" She cleared her throat, her voice strong again. "When I was at school, I was terrified of the things my mother would say to her while I was gone. I worried about whether she'd be changed and fed. So I'd prepare juice and snacks and lunch and taught Colette, as a toddler, where to get it. Eventually I set alarms so she'd know when to eat her lunch and taught her how to turn it off. My mother hated everything I did. Thinking about it now, it was crazy, leaving her with a mother who was so awful."

"You had no choice. You did the best you could."

She nodded. "I tried. Once Lettie was old enough to go to school, I signed her up, packed her lunches, and made sure she went every day and got her schoolwork done."

"You still do that," he gritted out. *But who's there for you?* He pictured her back then. Her foundation had crumbled and her life had come tumbling down around her. Yet there she stood, a tiny blond pillar of strength, holding an umbrella made of sheer will in one hand and her baby sister in the other.

"Of course I am. Like I said, I'm all she's got. Lettie didn't move out of my room until she was ten. She was more my child than my mom's. She was, *is*, a part of me. I don't know why my mother didn't give her up for adoption, but by the time I was old enough to realize that had been an option and ask, I couldn't imagine my life without her. I know Lettie can be a pain, but she's my baby sister."

Tears streaked her cheeks as Blaine pulled her into his arms. "You don't have to explain that to me. That's love, baby, as it should be." Knowing what she and Colette had been dealing with killed him. It was a wonder Reese was still standing.

She tried to push away. "I'm okay."

"Just accept my hug, Reese." He held her tighter, wishing he could absorb her pain to rid her of it. "I want to go back in time and save you both from that nightmare. Colette is lucky to have you."

"I think taking care of her is what got me through those years after my grandmother died. We were close when she was little, but she's resented me for the past several years, and I don't blame her. Our mother treats her like crap. She's not super nice to me because I pretty much hate her, but she's nicer to me than she is to Lettie. I was losing my mind, trying to figure out how to make things better for Lettie without going to social services. I couldn't risk them not giving me custody. That's why I moved out six months ago. I thought our mother would ease up on her if I wasn't around. But she never did. I didn't *want* to leave her, but our mother wouldn't let me take her with me. I don't know if she was punishing me or Lettie."

She swallowed hard, visibly battling whatever memories she'd stirred. "The day I moved out, I asked Lettie if she wanted to come with me anyway, but she acted like she hated me. I checked on her every day and texted every night to see if she needed anything. She ignored my texts most of the time. You've seen how she is. I'm pretty sure she resents me even more for leaving, despite the fact that I tried to get her to come with me. I wish I'd never left."

He physically ached for her and took her face between his hands, wiping her tears, gazing into her sad eyes. "She'll outgrow the resentment, Reese. You just have to continue to show her she's loved and wanted." *You're wanted, too*, was on the tip of his tongue, but he held it back, worried she'd think he meant only sexually.

"That's the plan," she said with a strained smile. She stepped out of his reach and exhaled loudly. "Sorry for dumping all my crap on you." She picked up the spade and went back to work, putting on a brave face like she'd been hoarding her hurt and shoving it down deep her whole life.

He was going to break her of that lonely habit no matter how long it took.

"Hey." He touched her arm, bringing her eyes to his. "You didn't *dump*. You shared, and I'm glad you trust me enough to do so. Suddenly your career is making more sense."

"*Ding, ding, ding*. You get bonus points. You said I missed my calling yesterday, but I think I have two callings. Before my grandmother passed away, all I wanted was to work in gardens. I thought I'd grow up and do this for a living. Then my circumstances changed, and I wanted to help catch criminals."

"Criminals or your mother's rapist?"

"Honestly? Both. But I'm not allowed to run my family's DNA through the database, and anyone else would need a police report to run it through. I finally convinced my mom to file one before she went into rehab. I told her if they knew she'd suffered emotional trauma that led to her life spinning out of control, maybe they'd take pity on her and give her a lighter sentence. But she didn't tell them about Colette, so they have no evidence to link the attacker to the rape. It's considered a cold case, and I can't bring myself to tell the police about Colette. She already has one parent who doesn't want her. I don't think she's strong enough to handle the truth right now. But I also feel guilty about *not* doing it, because he might still be out there hurting other women."

"That's a tough call."

She sighed heavily. "I've spilled enough of my dirty laundry. I think I earned some garden therapy."

Fuck garden therapy. He wanted to take her out on his bike or his boat, so she could let it all go and just breathe for a little while. But this was one time he knew better than to push.

"Then get to work, Wilder." He swatted her ass to make her smile and headed back to his area.

"You're a pain," she said with a real smile, then went to work cutting out another patch of grass. A few minutes later she said, "Hey, Wicked?"

He looked over.

"Thanks for listening. I've never shared that with anyone, and as bad as it feels to say it out loud, it feels good to get it off my chest."

"Anytime." He went for another smile. "If you want to get anything else off your chest, I'm here for it. Including that shirt."

She laughed. "Fat chance."

"That's better than a slim one."

She rolled her eyes, but her smile remained.

REESE HAD WORKED hard for the last couple of hours. The gardens were ready for planting, they made final decisions on the flowers and plants, and Blaine had placed the order. She was tired and dirty, but she felt better and *lighter* than she had in a long time. Sharing her past with Blaine had taken the edge off. She hadn't realized how stressful it was holding it all in. She didn't like lying to him about Ice, but with all he was doing for her, the least she could do was protect him from that mess.

After telling him the truth about most of her life, she'd expected him to pull away, but he wasn't trying to put distance between them. He'd been talking and joking around as usual. If anything, he was paying even closer attention to her.

She stepped back and wiped her brow, gazing up at the house. She wondered what type of people lived here. It was like something out of a magazine, full of contemporary New England character, with stone-and-cedar walls and massive windows. They must have a beautiful view all the way down to the water, where a boat was docked. They'd walked along a stone path through gorgeous gardens on the side of the house that snaked into the backyard and surrounded the patios. She wondered if Blaine had made the stone patios. The larger one had a built-in barbecue and curved around a smaller, circular patio that had a firepit in the middle. The place was already a veritable paradise, and the work they were doing would make it even more magnificent.

She set her tools in the grass by Blaine's and took off her gloves. "They have their own private oasis here."

"It's pretty nice." He looked out at the water.

"I can't believe they have a boat. I've always wanted to go on one. I can't imagine what their life must be like. Do you think they'd mind if I brought a sleeping bag and camped out for a while? It would be so nice sleeping under the stars, listening to the water kiss the shore."

"Not at all. Let's try it out." He lay on his back in the grass, tucking one hand behind his head, looking completely comfortable as he patted the space beside him. "Come on, Wilder. Get your ass down here."

"What if they come home?" She looked around.

"The owner's out of town, and I'm sure he wouldn't mind."

She lowered herself beside him, her pulse quickening at their close proximity. The grass tickled her legs as she gazed up at the early-evening sky. "If my life was different, I'd make a point of doing this once a day."

"Why not make time now?"

"Because I can't breathe around my mother's house. But I don't want to talk about her anymore." She glanced at him, admiring his strong jaw covered in thick scruff, perfect lips slightly parted, and deep-set eyes squinting at the sky. He was the most beautiful man she'd ever seen, and after last night's toe-curling kisses, she was sure he was also the best kisser on the planet. She was dying for more of those delicious kisses, but she was also curious about his life.

He turned, catching her staring, and his lips quirked. "What's up, buttercup?"

"I was just thinking about how you have a way of always getting me to talk, and I want to know about you. What are your parents like?"

"A lot different from yours. You sure you want to hear this?"

"*Yes.* Stop stalling, and don't even try to turn this conversation back on me."

"A'right. My mother is from a biker family, so she's tough and knows how to handle people, but she's also warm and loving. It takes a lot to put her in a bad mood, and she has a knack for knowing what you need before you do."

"It must be nice to have a mom who knows you that well."

"It is. She used to come into my room at night, sit on the bed, and ask about my day. But she wasn't just checking off a parental box, you know? If I gave her a half-assed answer, she'd find a way to get me talking."

"That must be where you learned it from. She sounds incredible."

"Is that your sly way of saying that *I'm* incredible?" He cocked a grin.

She laughed softly. "As if your ego needs a boost. Tell me about your dad."

"He's a biker through and through. Tough, tatted, and fearless."

"Sounds like the apple didn't fall far from the tree."

"That's about the biggest compliment you could give me. If I'm half the man he is, I consider myself lucky, and it'd be a testament to him."

"That says a lot. You said he's tough. Was he tough on you guys?"

"He's always expected a lot from us, but at the same time, his love runs so deep, you can feel it from miles away. When I was growing up, he took every opportunity to dole out life lessons, and he wasn't always subtle about it, so I guess you can say he's tough."

"Okay, first, *wow*. I can't imagine being loved like that."

"That's how you love Colette."

"Yeah, I do," she said softly, deeply touched that he'd noticed. "But our mother never prepared us for anything, so being given life lessons, subtly or not, sounds good to me. Did it bother you?"

"Depends on the lesson. And just because it might have bothered me doesn't mean I didn't appreciate it. Like the year Justin came to live with us was a rough one. I'm sure I bitched more than I didn't. He ran away all the time and never got in trouble for it. My parents just told him how much he was loved and wanted in our family. Now I know they did it because he'd never been loved unconditionally, and he needed to see that no matter what he did, they wouldn't stop loving him. But at the time, it pissed me off, because we were the ones chasing after him and dragging his ass back home."

"That's understandable."

"Yeah, but that's where the life lesson came in. One afternoon my father had a truckload of stones delivered to the house so we could build a wall in the yard, and he made me carry them all out back. I worked until I could barely walk, and you know what he said?"

"That sounds like torture. I hope he said good job."

"Not even close. He said, 'Now you know what the burden Justin is carrying around feels like.'" His lips curved up. "He was right, and that lesson made more of an impact on me than anything else probably would have."

"Justin must've gone through a lot."

"He did. His mom adored him, but she took her own life when he was just a kid, and his father was a thief and a real bastard toward him. And there I was, safe every night with food on the table and warm hugs waiting around every corner, bitching about making sure a kid who had been severely neglected and didn't trust or understand what it meant to be loved wasn't running toward trouble." His jaw tightened. "I'm not proud of that."

She got chills as realization hit about the caring bulldozer of a man who confused her as much as he helped her. "That's why you're not running from us. You understand what Colette and I have gone through, and it doesn't scare you."

He rolled onto his side and leaned on his elbow, eyes serious. "What you *are* going through, buttercup. Nothing scares me except the idea of you two getting hurt even more."

Her heart stumbled. Could he mean that? She searched his eyes, looking for the answer, and the sincerity in them took her breath away.

He brushed the backs of his fingers down her cheek, sending tingles through her. "You and Colette deserve a hell of a lot better life."

She expected the knee-jerk reaction of pulling away or telling him they were *fine*, but neither came. She was drawn to him, and that made her ramble nervously. "Then let me live vicariously through yours. What was your life like as a kid? Was it like dinner at your sister's? Fun, with lots of teasing?"

Something about his coy smile told her he knew she was nervous. "It was loud and chaotic, and a hell of a lot of fun for the most part, but we had our moments when we couldn't stand each other for one reason or another. As the president of the club, my old man would have to take off at night sometimes to handle situations. If I heard him take off on his bike, I'd go on instant alert, like I suddenly became the man of the house."

"How old were you?"

"I don't know. It probably started when I was six or seven."

"It really is in your blood to take care of people."

"It's how I was raised. We spent a lot of time with my cousins, too, so we had big family dinners, and we hung out at the Salty Hog a lot."

"The restaurant? Isn't there a biker bar upstairs?" *Duh. He is a biker.* "Which, I guess makes sense."

"Yeah, my aunt Ginger and my uncle Conroy own it. We'd all have dinner there, and then our parents would hang out in the bar with other club members, and Tank and I would watch over all the kids outside."

"That sounds like a handful."

"You're telling me. It's pretty much still like that, only now we hang out in the bar with them. In fact, we're having my father's birthday celebration at the Salty Hog next weekend. You and Colette should come. It'll be fun."

She looked at him like he was crazy. "I'm not going to crash your father's birthday party."

"It's not crashing when you're invited."

"Still."

He gazed down at her with a lazy smile that should ease her nerves, but the heat in his eyes kept her heart racing. "You and Colette could use some fun, and if you're worried about her, there'll be plenty of us to keep an eye on her."

"I'm not. She'll never go."

"Maybe I can convince her to." He traced her collarbone with his index finger.

Her body flamed at his intimate touch, her nipples tightening to needy peaks.

"It'd be good for both of you to get to know some nice people."

His concern for her sister made her want him even more. "Won't that be weird if we just show up?"

"You'd show up with me, and there's nothing weird about it. We bring friends all the time."

Ever since Madigan had said *friends* like she knew about

Blaine's friends-with-benefits situations, the word made her sweat. "But do you bring *regular* friends?" She felt silly for asking, especially since she was dying to kiss him. But wanting to kiss him and wanting to be his friend with benefits were vastly different.

"You're really hung up on what I said, aren't you?"

"I'm just..." She was too nervous to deny it. "Yes. I guess I am. You *kissed* me. Remember?"

His eyes flamed. "That's not something I could ever forget." He cupped her cheek, gazing into her eyes, his thumb stroking her skin in a mesmerizing rhythm. "If you're worried that everyone will think you're my new plaything, don't be. I don't bring women I'm hooking up with to club or family functions."

"*Oh.*" Now she was *really* confused. She couldn't be reading him wrong. Not with the way he was looking at her. *Could I?* That sent her stomach into a tizzy.

"I really want to bring you to the party."

"You do?"

"Yes. I'm into you, buttercup, so stop being so damn cute and giving me those doe eyes." His eyes never left hers. "I want to kiss you so fucking bad right now."

"*Okay*" came out as breathy and needy as she felt, rational brain be damned. But as his mouth neared hers, her rational side charged out. "*Wait.* I want to kiss you, but I don't want to be your no-strings-attached plaything. I'll get hurt, and jealous, and..." She shook her head. "I don't want that."

His gaze softened. "I don't want that either. You've had my strings all knotted up since the day I met you."

"I have?"

"Hell yeah. Your wide-eyed innocence and stubborn inde-pendence fucks with me like nothing ever has." He grabbed her hip, *tight.* "I want my hands and mouth on every inch of you, but I'm not going to make promises I can't keep. So it's your choice. Can we enjoy each other and see where this takes us without labeling it, or do you want me to back off?"

Chapter Nine

REESE'S HEART RACED. Could she relax enough to enjoy being with Blaine without any kind of commitment beyond seeing where it went? Maybe a better question was, could she live with herself if she didn't? That intense and thrilling hum of electricity that seemed to live between them was beckoning her, and something deeper that she couldn't pinpoint but felt important and *real* was drawing her in like metal to magnet. She couldn't afford to get sidetracked from her responsibilities, but when had she ever done something just for herself? Even her career was based on doing the right thing. Not that Blaine was the wrong thing, but he definitely lived in some type of naughty-temptation and chivalrous middle ground. Oh, how she wanted to explore that playground.

"Don't overthink it, buttercup. It's simple. You either want to be with me or you don't."

A nervous laugh bubbled out. For once she took his advice and decided not to overthink. She took off her glasses and held his gaze. "I think you know my answer."

"Hell yeah, I do, because this thing between us is inescapable."

All at once his mouth came down hungrily over hers and his

fingers pushed into her hair, cupping the back of her head, holding it exactly where he wanted her, taking control as he had last night, his tongue delving, sweeping, *consuming*, setting her entire body aflame. His roughness electrified her, unleashing white-hot passion she didn't know she possessed. She arched against his hard chest, grasping at him, moaning, and kissing him back with everything she had. He growled against her mouth, pressing his erection against her thigh, sending spirals of desire to the far reaches of her limbs. It burned in her chest and coiled hot and tight low in her belly. Last night's kisses had thrown her for a loop, but *this*? This was a kiss right out of her dirtiest dreams, a metaphysical experience. He was luring her deeper into him, into *them*, with every masterful swipe of his tongue, every press and grind of his hard body.

He tore his mouth away, and a needy sound escaped before she could stop it. His eyes were as dark as midnight, as ravenous as a panther. "This pretty mouth has fucked with my head for days. Now it's *mine*."

His voice was raw, possessive, and shockingly enticing. Her body screamed *yes*, but her mind uttered, *what?* "You think about my mouth?"

"All the damn time."

Her pulse spiked. "Why? What do you think about it?"

A wicked grin crawled across his face. "You're not ready to hear that, baby girl."

Her breath hitched, dark, dirty thrills skating through her. But she didn't have time to think as his mouth came down over hers in another merciless kiss, dragging her into a fiery darkness that had her *wanting* like she never had before. His hand covered her breast, caressing and groping through her shirt. She moaned and whimpered, arching into his hand.

"Keep making those noises, and I'm going to take you right here."

Her entire body shuddered with that deliciously dangerous image.

She had a fleeting thought about where they were and not wanting to be his plaything, but those thoughts were obliterated by a kiss so deep and sensual, it was all she could do to remember how to breathe. His hand pushed beneath her shirt, unclasping the front of her bra. *Yes. Touch me.* He must have read her mind, because his big, rough hand groped and caressed her breasts. He squeezed her nipple, sending a jolt of exquisite pleasure and pain between her legs, making her damp. "*Yes*" came out greedily.

His teeth and tongue blazed down her neck as he pushed up her shirt and squeezed her nipple again. She gasped as titillating sensations consumed her. "You're fucking killing me with those sexy noises, buttercup." His eyes swept over her bare breasts. "*Mm.* So damn beautiful." He slicked his tongue over her nipple, and she closed her eyes, inhaling sharply as tingles skittered over her skin. "Eyes on *me*," he demanded. Her eyes flew open, meeting his piercing gaze as he dragged the tip of his tongue around her nipple. She fisted her hands in the grass.

"Get those hands on *me*, Wilder. I want to *feel* your need as I drive you out of your brilliant mind."

His demand sent rivers of heat down her core.

His eyes drilled into her as that wicked tongue teased and taunted her, until her entire body was trembling, and her breathing came in hard, sporadic bursts. He lowered his mouth over her nipple, sucking hard. "*Ohgod—*" She bowed off the ground, digging her nails into his flesh, moaning loudly and shamelessly. He continued licking, sucking, and grazing his teeth over the sensitive peaks, electrifying her from the top of her head to the tips of her toes. He sealed his mouth over the swell of her breast, sucking so hard, a loud indiscernible sound shot from her lungs.

"I want to hear *my name*, baby girl," he growled against her flesh.

"Just don't *stop*," she said breathlessly, her cheeks burning as the demand rolled off her tongue. His eyes went volcanic, and in the next breath, he was all teeth and tongue, devouring her breasts with fervor, shattering her ability to think at all. She rocked and moaned, clawing at his arms, squeezing her thighs together as need stacked up inside her. She'd never had an orgasm with a man, much less without being touched *down there*, and she was embarrassingly close, her panties drenched with desire. *"Blaine...?"*

He slowed his efforts, placing feathery kisses along her heated flesh, his hand sliding down her stomach to the button on her shorts. She knew he wasn't the type of man who asked permission for anything, but those all-seeing eyes searched hers for approval. Her heart was thundering so hard, she was sure he could feel it. Once this line was crossed, there was no turning back. But turning back was the last thing she wanted to do. *"Kiss me,"* she whispered.

As their mouths fused, she rocked her hips, giving him the green light he sought. He opened her shorts, his big hand pushing into her underwear. *"So fucking wet for me,"* he rasped against her lips.

Swallowed by embarrassment, she turned her head.

"Don't you dare hide from me."

His rough tone brought her eyes to his. The lust looking back at her was underscored with something dark, visceral, and surprisingly caring. "That's it, baby. Be with me. That damn blush gets me every time." His fingers slid from her clit to her center, pushing inside her and crooking, hitting the spot that caused her toes to curl under. He stroked her so perfectly, she clenched her teeth to keep from making a sound.

"Don't hold back. *Own* your pleasure." He dipped his head to her breast, eyes trained on her as he sucked and used his teeth and moved his fingers to her clit, quickening his efforts. She ground her teeth together, pressure mounting inside her. Her eyes fluttered closed, and she forced them open, her vision blurring as he took her to the edge and held her there. "*More*," she begged. "*Please.*"

His eyes glimmered devilishly. He knew *exactly* what he was doing to her, keeping her on the verge of madness. Just when she was sure she'd combust, he added pressure, stroking faster, sucking harder, until pain and pleasure raced down from her chest and up her core, colliding in an explosion of fire and ice inside her. His name flew from her lungs like a battle cry as wave after wave of the most intense climax she'd ever felt ravaged her. She held on to him, nails puncturing his skin, anchoring her in their dizzying world.

When she finally started to come down from the peak, he quickened his ministrations, sending her right back up to the clouds, a string of lustful sounds spilling from her lungs. Without missing a beat, his fingers still stealing her ability to think, he took her in a penetrating kiss, intensifying every sensation. She couldn't get enough of him, kissed him as hungrily as he devoured her, as ripples of aftershocks rolled through her.

She felt him smiling against her lips and opened her eyes, slayed by the emotions in his.

BLAINE FUCKED UP. He thought he could tamp down his carnal urges with Reese, but now that he'd whet his appetite, he wanted more, and he wanted it *his* way. But the sweet girl gazing up at him in a post-orgasmic haze wasn't ready for the likes of that.

"Welcome back, beautiful."

Reese sighed. "I'm pretty sure I just died and went to heaven."

He pressed his lips to hers. "There is nothing sexier than seeing you come for me. Except maybe that satisfied look in your eyes."

She buried her pink cheeks in his neck.

He nipped at her earlobe. "Just wait until I get my mouth on that sweet pussy of yours."

"Are you *trying* to embarrass me to death?" She tried to glare at him, but her stifled grin was fucking adorable. "Give a girl a minute to get used to your filthy mouth."

"Don't kid yourself, little bunny. I know how much my dirty talk turns you on, and before you deny it, remember, I *felt* it."

"*Fine*, I won't deny it, but for the record, I much prefer death by orgasm."

A deep laugh tumbled out. "So do I, but your pink cheeks are a force to be reckoned with." He shifted lower, admiring her bare breasts, making her blush even harder. He kissed the marks he'd left on them, filling with a warped sense of pride, like an animal marking his territory. "I'm going to come on these gorgeous tits one day."

"Blaine."

He smirked, knowing he should back off but wanting to push her boundaries. "Just giving you a warning so you can get used to the idea."

"What makes you think I'd let you?"

He had no fucking idea if she'd let him or not, but he sure hoped she would. He didn't bother answering as he clasped her bra and kissed a path down her soft curves. Every touch of his lips earned a sharp inhalation. He was dying to sink his cock into her and feel those luscious thighs wrapped around him, but her expressive baby blues and innate sweetness were doing strange things to his emotions.

He needed to rein it in, but he could no sooner do that than he could walk away.

As he buttoned and zipped her shorts, he said, "If I wasn't afraid you'd run for the hills, I'd strip these off and make you come with my mouth." He perched over her, rubbing his erection against her center, loving the way her eyes darkened, and reclaimed her mouth in a brutal kiss. He was a bastard for pushing her boundaries even further, but he wanted her to know what she was getting into. He brushed his lips over hers. "And then I'd flip you over on all fours and fuck you from behind."

"No, you would *not*," she said sharply, but her smile remained.

"Oh, yes, I definitely would."

"That's not very intimate."

"I don't do intimate, buttercup. I fuck for pleasure. Mine and yours."

Her eyes narrowed. "I don't get you. You have such a big heart that you go to great lengths to do really nice things. Why are you such a Neanderthal about relationships?"

"If I were a Neanderthal, I'd have done both of those things I mentioned, wouldn't I?"

"So you're just messing with me?" Her brow furrowed. "Trying to make me blush?"

He brushed his nose along her cheek, breathing her in. "Like I said, just giving you a glimpse of what's to come."

"You don't *know* that," she challenged. "Maybe I was using you for the benefits you've already given me, and I'm ready to move on."

"Well, that'd be a shame, wouldn't it?" He lay on his back and pulled her against him. "I like you, Wilder, but you fuck with my head."

"I like you, too, Wicked, and don't talk to *me* about messing with your head. You're the king of it. The master head effer."

He laughed and kissed her forehead. "So you'll come with me next weekend to the Hog?"

"Maybe."

"Two orgasms and all I get is a maybe? Damn, woman, way to cut a guy off at the knees."

She laughed. "I'll talk to Colette, but we'd better get the tools put away. I have to get going. I told her I'd be back by seven."

"I'll take care of the tools." He helped her to her feet. She looked like an angel with the sun shimmering along the horizon behind her. *Since when do I notice those things? Shit.* She really was fucking with his head.

She fidgeted with the edge of her shorts as he walked her to her car. "I guess I'll see you tomorrow."

"I make you nervous, don't I?"

"No."

He cocked a brow.

She sighed. *"Okay.* Sometimes. Maybe a little."

"Why?"

"I don't *know.* Maybe because your kisses make me weak, and we just did things I haven't done in a long time, and you say dirty things to me that no one ever has, and I *like* it, and we're only friends. How's that for a laundry list?"

God, he liked her.

He took her face between his hands, and the way she looked at him, full of tentative hope and sheer embarrassment, made his heart stutter. "Weak knees are a good thing, and I'm honored that you allowed me to touch you." He kissed her softly. "I can't change who I am, Reese, and you should know that I'm a dirty bastard in the bedroom."

She swallowed hard, eyes wide.

"Don't overthink it, beautiful. I'll never make you do anything you don't want to, and that's a promise I can keep."

"I trust that you wouldn't hurt me. If that was your goal, you've had plenty of opportunities."

"Good, and as far as the rest goes, all you need to know is that I will never disrespect you by touching anyone else as long as we're involved with each other. We don't need labels for that. Now take a deep breath and give me that sexy mouth for one last kiss."

She smiled and went up on her toes, meeting him halfway. Her mouth was so sweet and she was kissing him so eagerly, he needed to be closer. He lifted her and set her on the hood of her car, guiding her legs around him. "That's better," he said against her lips, and took the kiss deeper. He tangled his hands in her hair, blood thundering in his ears at the sinful sounds she made and the feel of her wrapped around him. He ached to carry her inside and spend the next several hours exploring every inch of her beautiful body. Finding every erogenous zone, until he knew the sounds she made, the way she moved, and the way she felt and tasted, by heart.

He tore his mouth away. "*Fuck.* I'm like a horny teenager around you. You've got to get out of here before I bend you over this hood."

She giggled.

"You're killing me, Wilder."

"You mean you're not like this with every woman you're attracted to?"

"Hell no. You've got some kind of superpowers hidden behind those gorgeous eyes of yours. And I'm going to suck those powers dry if you don't leave." He helped her off the car and opened her car door. "Get in before I change my mind."

She climbed in, grinning from ear to ear. *Man, what a sight.* He put a hand on the roof and leaned in, cupping her cheek with the other, and brushed his thumb over her lips. "I'm going to dream about doing very dirty things to this mouth."

"I will not blush. I will not blush."

They both laughed.

"Don't ever stop blushing. It's a good reminder for me."

"What do you mean?"

He wasn't about to tell her it was a good reminder for him to take things slow, which he sucked at with her. "Just that you're new to my kind of debauchery." He gave her a quick kiss, knowing she'd overthink his answer all night long. "Text me when you get home so I know you're okay."

"I'll be fine. It's a fifteen-minute drive."

"Jesus, woman, stop arguing and do it."

"Ever hear the saying 'you'll get more bees with honey'?"

"I believe it's flies, but I'm not interested in insects. I've got my sights set on a buttercup." That earned another slightly bashful smile. "Text me when you get there." He closed her door, stepping back.

She started her car and rolled down the window with a mischievous grin. "Better be careful, Wicked. I hear the first step to wanting a girlfriend is thinking about her too much."

"Don't get your hopes up." He gritted his teeth against the acrid taste of that comment, but her smile didn't fade. Her gaze swept down his body with renewed confidence, and *damn* he liked that.

"See you tomorrow, *Blaine.*" She said his name seductively and a little breathily.

As she drove off, he wondered if he'd misread her innocence.

A little while later, tools put away and freshly showered, he was still thinking about Reese when he realized she hadn't texted to say she'd gotten home. He bit out a curse, headed out to his truck, and peeled out of his driveway.

His phone rang, and Cuffs's name flashed on the screen. He answered, but Cuffs spoke before he could. "Hey, Blaine. Got a minute?"

"I'll call you back in a few. I've got to take care of something."

"Tell me it's not the dealer."

"I gave you my word I wouldn't move on that until we talked."

"We both know when you get a hair up your ass about something, nothing stops you, and you can't go after this guy alone."

"I'm *not*." He ended the call, trying to keep that fury compartmentalized, and focused on Reese.

When he pulled up to her house, the state of the yard grated on him. He'd take care of it tomorrow. Right now he had to set his woman straight. As he strode up to the house, that thought ate away at him, but he wasn't going to pick that shit apart. For now she *was* his woman. He rapped on the door.

Reese peered out from between the curtains in the living room, her eyes widening.

The door opened, and she stepped outside, quickly closing it behind her. "Hi. What are you doing here?"

"You didn't text."

"I'm a big girl. I told you I'd be fine."

He closed the small gap between them, their bodies brushing. "Did I have my hands on you an hour ago?"

"Yes. Why? Did you forget already?" she asked sassily. "Maybe I need to rethink this age-gap thing."

He narrowed his eyes as her voice whispered through his mind. *I hear the first step to wanting a girlfriend is thinking about her too much.* Holy shit. Was she fucking with him? Was this a ploy to get his attention, or was Little Miss Autonomous just standing her ground?

"Don't fuck with me, Reese."

She smirked. "Why would I do that?"

"You know damn well why." He couldn't be near her without wanting to be closer. He took her face between his hands, as had already become a habit, and crushed his mouth to hers. When she went soft against him, he grinned against her lips and continued kissing the ever-loving daylights out of her. "Don't defy me again, Wilder." He spun on his heel and strode toward his truck, leaving her hazy-eyed and breathless.

"Hey, Wicked."

He turned to look at her.

She folded her arms, lifting her chin, defiance shimmering in her eyes. "Just because you make my knees weak doesn't mean you own me."

If his little bunny knew what her challenges did to him, she wouldn't be shaking her tail quite so hard. All that gumption wrapped up in an adorably sweet, sexy package made him want to wrap her wrists in silk and show her what it really meant to be *his*.

"Lock your doors, buttercup. See you tomorrow."

Chapter Ten

"WHAT'D YOU FIND out?" Blaine asked Cuffs as he drove away from Reese's house.

"The guy is bad news. His real name is Nelson Taneks. He goes by the nickname Ice. He's only been around the Cape for a few years and usually sticks to the Upper Cape. I don't know how your girl's mother got involved with him. The club has a handle on dealers in our area, and he's not on our list."

"I know. I checked. What about his crew?"

"He's got about a dozen guys working for him, about half on Cape, half off. But again, they're known around the Upper Cape, not up our way, and as far as I can tell, Ice collects from certain customers himself. Usually the women he's fucking. If they miss a payment, things get ugly."

Blaine gripped the steering wheel tighter. "He's not fucking Reese."

"No shit, but he might've been fucking her mother, and a guy like that doesn't give a damn who fills that need."

"He's not getting anywhere near Reese or Colette," he seethed. "Where can I find him?"

"I've been trailing him for the past few hours. I've got eyes on him at the Watering Hole, but Ice has half his crew with him." The Watering Hole was a dingy bar in a skeevy area about forty minutes away. "They're not packing visible heat, but that doesn't mean they're not armed."

"Cowards usually are." Guns didn't scare Blaine. It was the unpredictable assholes wielding them that were the issue. But he was a hell of a fighter and as fast as lightning when he needed to be. If they caught up to them in public, he didn't think it would come to blows. "Can you get a tracker on his vehicle?"

"Already done. I'll send you the link."

Blaine heard the text come through a few seconds later. "Got it. I'll get ahold of the guys and meet you there." He ended the call and put one through to Tank.

His cousin's gruff voice rumbled through the phone. "What's up, B?"

"I've got a situation and need backup." He explained what was going down.

"Where are we meeting?"

"My place as soon as you can get there."

"I'll round up the boys."

The line went dead, and Blaine called Maverick. It rang so many times, he was about to hang up when his brother answered with an abrupt "This better be urgent. I'm rubbing my wife's feet."

"It is." He filled him in. "Can you get ahold of Zeke? I'll call Zan."

"On it."

Blaine ended the call and rang Zander.

"What's up, bro? You coming to the Hog tonight? There's a group of hot chicks passing through from Norfolk, and there's a brunette with your name on her."

The only hot chick Blaine wanted was the blonde he was

protecting. "No." He told Zander what was going down. "I need you to have eyes on Reese and Colette tonight." He didn't like the idea of anyone but himself watching over them, but Zander didn't fuck around when it came to this kind of safety. He'd keep eagle eyes on them, and Blaine would be there soon enough.

"*Damn.* No problem. Shoot me the address, and I'll head right over."

"Thanks, but I'm driving. Grab a pen." He gave him Reese's address. "Zan, don't sit in front of their house. I don't want to frighten them."

"Don't worry, bro. I've got it covered. If they go out, I'll follow, but she knows what you're doing tonight, right?"

"Hell no."

There was a long silence before Zander said, "After what happened with Madigan, don't you think you should talk to her first?"

"She's not Mads, and she thinks the asshole is her mother's boyfriend, so no. I'm not talking to her first and scaring the shit out of her until I know it's handled and she's safe. Do me a favor. Call Justice and ask him to be your backup in case Reese goes out without Colette, and keep your distance if you follow her. I don't want to spook her or make her think I don't trust her."

"You must really be into this girl if you're worried about that."

No shit. "Just do it, Zan."

"I'm on it. Don't worry. Good luck."

"Thanks, man. Sorry about your night."

"No worries. Plenty of other fish in the sea. Let's keep yours safe."

Blaine chewed on the idea of Reese being *his* for the rest of the way home.

He headed inside to get his cut and sent a group text to his parents, as had become his habit after they'd lost Ashley. Life was too short not to say the important things.

Blaine: *The boys and I are taking care of some business tonight. Love you both.*

Preacher: *Need me and Con?*

Blaine: *No. We're good.*

Mom: *You boys be safe. I love you.*

Blaine: *Always.*

He thought about Madigan and the strain he'd put on their relationship. She was an adult at twenty-five, but he'd been eight when Madigan was born, and in his heart, she'd always be the little sister he couldn't protect when Ashley died and she'd lost her best friend, and when she'd had her heart broken by some asshole overseas. He thumbed out a text to her.

Blaine: *Something's going down tonight. I'm not worried, but know I love you and I stand behind you and Tobias.*

Madigan: *How could you not?* A laughing emoji popped up. *Seriously though, be careful. I need your pushy, annoying self around so I have someone to tease. And I LOVE Reese and would really like another sister-in-law, so...* A smiling emoji with hearts around it appeared.

Blaine shook his head.

Madigan: *Don't shake your head at me. You look at her like she's a shiny new Harley you can't wait to ride!* A heart-eyed emoji appeared.

He laughed and thumbed out, *This isn't a fairy tale, princess.* As the daughter of the president of the club, Madigan was considered a biker princess, and she hated that title.

Madigan: An eye-roll emoji popped up. *Please don't get hurt. I love you!* Three hearts appeared.

The sound of motorcycles approaching drew his attention. He grabbed his cut and put it on as he went outside. After giving the guys a quick rundown on the plan, they headed out. Blaine led the charge, followed by Maverick, Zeke, Baz, and Gunner, with Tank bringing up the rear.

An hour later they rolled up to the Watering Hole, an old brick building with a BAR sign over the door. As Blaine climbed off his bike, he spotted Cuffs crossing the street toward them.

"Hey, brother." Cuffs clapped him on the shoulder.

"Thanks for tailing this guy," Blaine said.

"It's all good. One of his posse left about fifteen minutes ago with a chick. You've still got five of his guys in there, and they've had quite a few drinks."

"A bunch of drunk assholes." Gunner rubbed his hands together. "This ought to be fun."

"We're not here to cause trouble," Blaine reminded him. "We're here to make sure there isn't any."

Gunner held his hands up. "I know. But if it goes south, I'm here for it."

"There are about twelve or fifteen other customers inside," Cuffs said. "If this goes south, keeping them safe is our top priority."

"Remember, let me do the talking. The plan is to take it nice and easy. Let him know Reese and Colette are protected by the Dark Knights and are off-limits." Blaine eyed the others, thinking about Ashley and the other women and children in their lives, grief fueling his anger. "Fuck it. We're not leaving anything to chance. They need to know our *towns* are off-limits."

"Damn right," Baz said.

"Fuck yeah," Tank gritted, and the others agreed.

"Let's do this." Blaine strode into the bar, flanked by Tank and Cuffs. Maverick and Gunner took up residence by the door.

Blaine scanned the room, zeroing in on Ice's shaved head. He was sitting at the bar chatting up a blonde. It took about three seconds to spot his posse. One guy was sitting to his left, flirting with a redhead, two idiots were playing pool and doing a shitty job of showing off for a couple of chicks, and a rather large guy was sitting at a table eyeing Blaine and the others. He must be their muscle. As Blaine made his way toward Ice, Baz and Zeke headed for the open pool table, and Tank planted himself between Blaine and their muscle.

Blaine and Cuffs sidled up to the bar on either side of Ice and his other guy. The blonde who was talking with Ice eyed Blaine from head to toe, but he kept his eyes trained on Ice and said, "We need to talk."

"Check it out. Goldilocks's sugar daddy is a Dark Knight." Ice looked at the blonde. "Beat it."

The blonde scoffed, grabbed her bag from the bar, and strutted off. Ice's cohort sent his girl packing, too. Blaine took the blonde's seat, noticing the guy from the table was on his feet, but Tank was a formidable barrier.

"Since you're familiar with the club, I'll cut to the chase. You and your crew aren't welcome in our area, and if you show up again, there's going to be trouble."

"I don't deal in Dark Knight territory, but until your pretty lady pays up, I'll be there every week."

Fuck. Reese lied? Anger roared inside him, at Reese, at her mother for putting her in this situation, and at the smug fucker in front of him who facilitated it. "How much does she owe?"

"*Five* grand. She's damn lucky her mother did my boys some favors before her stupid ass got her into rehab, or your precious Goldilocks would be bear meat by now." He cocked a grin. "I'd happily forgive half of it for a week with her. If she's as good at sucking dick as her mo—"

Blaine's fist connected with Ice's jaw, spewing blood from his mouth. Chaos erupted around them as Blaine grabbed Ice by the collar, dragging him to his feet. The bartender hollered, and customers ran for the door as Ice's crew battled Blaine's. But Blaine was lost in fury, holding Ice by the neck. "Disrespect her again, and it'll be the last thing you *ever* do."

"If she doesn't pay up, you'll never see her again."

Blaine saw red. His fist flew, sending Ice stumbling back. Ice quickly recovered and came at Blaine full force. Blinded by rage, Blaine landed one punch after another, sending Ice reeling into a table. As he hauled Ice back up to his feet, he caught sight of Maverick and Gunner pulling Tank off a guy who was lying on the floor, Baz dragging someone out the door, and Zeke holding a guy against the wall with his forearm at his neck. He heard Cuffs arguing with the bartender. *Fuck.* They had to end this before it got any further out of hand and they all landed in jail.

Blaine slammed Ice's back against the wall. One of Ice's eyes was swollen shut, his mouth and nose bleeding. "Take a good look around you. This is what happens when you fuck with Dark Knights. You're on our radar now, and there are dozens more of us who'd love to get their hands on a piece of trash like you. You want your money? Meet me back here at midnight, and if I *ever* catch wind of you within ten miles of Reese or her sister, or crossing into Mid Cape for so much as a fucking U-turn, I'll bury you under two tons of crushed stone. Are we *clear?*"

Ice spit blood on the ground, giving Blaine a menacing look. "Clear."

Blaine released him with a shove, and Ice caught himself on a chair.

"She must have a sweet pussy for you to go this far—"

A *crack* rang out as Blaine's fist slammed into Ice's face, but the thud of him dropping to the floor, out cold, could be heard for miles.

Chapter Eleven

"SURE YOU'RE COOL with this?" Blaine asked Maverick as he opened the safe at Cape Stone. The other guys were waiting for them outside the office so they could come up with a plan to keep Reese and Colette safe. "I'll replace it tomorrow when I can get to the bank."

"You know I don't give a shit about the money." Maverick crossed his arms, leaning against Blaine's desk. "But level with me. What's up with you and Reese?"

"I don't know. She's got my head all fucked up." He took five grand out of the safe, locked it, closed the compartment, and pushed the bookcase that hid it back into place.

"Yeah, I noticed. Want to talk about it? Remember how messed up I was over Chloe?"

"I remember you wouldn't touch another woman and were a bitch to deal with until you two got together."

Maverick laughed. "I'm surprised y'all didn't kick my ass for it, but she was worth it. What about Reese?"

"Like I said, I can't think straight around her, and when I'm not with her, she's all I think about. But she lied to me, man. She told me she and that douchebag were square, so I don't even know if she really believes he's her mother's boyfriend or if that was a lie, too. It's all fucked up."

"It seems far-fetched to think she doesn't know."

"No shit. I'm giving her the benefit of the doubt."

"That's something coming from you. I know you'll help anyone who needs it, but I was beginning to think that when it came to connecting with women, your heart had turned to stone."

He gritted his teeth, feeling a tinge of pain. He'd taken a few solid hits and was sporting some ugly bruises. "You sound like Preach."

"He taught me well. You told me you'd never met a woman who was worth getting emotionally involved with. *So...?*"

"Look, I'm not some lovesick fool like you. I like her, but I don't know where we'll go or how long we'll last." He didn't like lies, but that wasn't the only obstacle they had to overcome. He might want to get his sweet little bunny into his bed, but once she got more of a taste of his wicked ways, it could very well be the end for them.

"Stop avoiding the question. You're different with her. I saw it when we went riding and you blew us off afterward to head over to her place." He paused, as if he was letting that sink in. "I'm asking you, here and now, *is she worth it?*"

"*Yes*, you pain in the ass," Blaine barked. "She drives me fucking insane, challenging everything I do and say, but she's worth it." He angrily counted the money again and put it in an envelope. "And so is her sister. They deserve better, and *right now* I'm here for them."

"Cool." Maverick clapped him on the shoulder. "Was that so hard?"

Blaine glowered and strode out of the office. He saw Cuffs and Tank on their cell phones by the stone fountain displays and headed to the other guys by the reception desk.

"We started without you," Baz said.

"You hear that often, Baz?" Gunner chuckled.

"It's better than finishing without him," Zeke said.

"Baz would never let a lady finish alone," Blaine said, giving Baz an *I've got you* nod as Cuffs and Tank joined them. "Everything okay?"

"Yeah, I was just checking in with Leah," Tank said.

Blaine felt bad for taking some of the guys away from their significant others, but the girls knew what they were getting into with the club. "I really appreciate you all helping me with this. I heard from Zander. All is well for now. Hopefully this asshole learned his lesson and will take the money and disappear, but until we know for sure, we've got to be vigilant."

"Absolutely," Tank said.

"That's this guy's MO. He's all about the money. But I set up extra drive-bys for Reese's house, her office, and Colette's route to and from school," Cuffs said. "A little police presence is a good deterrent."

"Great. I'll take over for Zan after the drop, but I'll have to leave before Reese goes to work. I don't want her or Colette to know they're being watched. I don't want to frighten them."

They worked out a schedule to make sure the girls were covered in the mornings. When Gunner offered to make sure Reese got home from work safely in the afternoons, Blaine said, "She'll be coming to my house after work." He had no idea if she'd still need the money, or if she only needed it to pay off that asshole. But he intended to find out.

Maverick arched a brow. "Every day?"

"*Yes.* She needed to earn extra money fast, and all the jobs she was considering weren't safe. She likes gardening, so I told her our company picked up a new job and was short-staffed. We're putting in gardens and another patio at my place, but she doesn't know you and I own the company. She thinks I'm just a hardscaper."

Gunner scoffed. "That's one way to make sure a girl's not after your money."

"She doesn't want a damn thing from me." Which pissed him off all over again. "She wouldn't have taken the job if she knew I owned the company."

"Oh, man." Baz shook his head.

Tank's brows slanted disapprovingly. "Dude, you're lying to your girl?"

"She lied to him, too, about owing money to that dickbag," Cuffs pointed out.

"That's not the best way to start a relationship," Maverick added.

"We weren't starting a relationship," Blaine snapped. "*Jesus.* Can we just focus? We have to leave here in five minutes to meet that asshole. The bottom line is, she'll come to my place after work, and I'll watch her after that. But Colette will be home alone after school until Reese gets there. I'm going to talk to her tomorrow afternoon, but if she really thinks this guy is or was her mother's boyfriend, the fact that he's a dealer might be too much for her to handle. I'll get her home as quickly as I can, but it might take some time, and I need to know Colette is safe."

"I'm off duty tomorrow afternoon. I've got her," Cuffs said. "What about when we're at church?" Church was what the club called their Wednesday-night meetings.

"I'm going to ask Tobias to keep an eye on them. If Mads doesn't have a gig tomorrow night, I'll ask her to hang out with

Reese and Colette, too."

"If Mads can't do it, I'm sure Chloe would be happy to have the company," Maverick said.

"Leah, too," Tank said. "The more hands with the kids, the better."

"If they have a hen party, count Sid in," Gunner added.

"We'll see what Mads says." The thought of Reese having all those women as her friends had Blaine feeling pretty damn good, but it lasted only a second before reality hit him. "We've got to go."

FOUR BLOCKS OUT from the bar, Blaine glanced in his mirror as Cuffs, Tank, and Gunner turned off the main road. In case Ice decided to do something stupid like bring weapons, Cuffs and Gunner were armed. Cuffs was going to take up residence behind the bushes on the hill next to the bar with Ice in his crosshairs. Tank and Gunner were going to come in from the other end of the street, hopefully giving them the advantage of having Ice, and any other assholes he brought with him, surrounded.

Ice was leaning against the building smoking a cigarette when they arrived. The guy who had been sitting with him at the bar was on his right, the guy Tank had knocked out, on his left. The other nitwits were talking a few feet away. They were all in shit shape. Blaine climbed off his bike, sizing up the situation as Maverick and Zeke stepped beside him. Baz moved closer to the guy standing near Ice.

Ice pushed off the wall and tossed his cigarette on the sidewalk, the streetlight illuminating his swollen eye and bruised face. "Lost some of your guys, huh?"

"That'll never happen," Tank said as he and Gunner came up behind the other guys who had been talking and were now whipping their heads from side to side, unsure who to watch.

"You bring my money?" Ice asked.

Blaine closed the distance between them, and Ice took a step back. "Once I give you this cash, Reese's family no longer exists to you or any of your crew. Is that *clear*?"

"Yeah, man. It's clear. Now give me my fucking money."

"Remember what I said about crossing into our territory."

Ice's jaw clenched. "I follow the cash, and it never leads upstream."

"Good. Now we're going to frisk you and your buddies to make sure you don't decide to shoot us in the back."

In the next breath, Blaine had Ice against the wall, forearm at his throat, and the other guys restrained his men, as he felt for a gun. He found one tucked into the back of his jeans. He pressed the barrel to Ice's chin. "Bad idea, sweetheart. Turn the fuck around, hands on the wall."

"That's not for you, man," Ice said as he turned around. "If I wanted you dead, I'd've already shot you."

Blaine ignored him and searched for more weapons, confiscating a knife that was strapped to his ankle. "I'll hold on to this, too, in case you don't heed my warning." He spun Ice around, hooking his arm around Ice's neck from behind, and pointed the gun at his head. Ice's crew struggled to get free, but they were no match for the Wickeds. "Now, my men are going to search your boys, and if any of them try anything, you die."

They confiscated the other men's weapons and had them line up against the brick wall with Ice.

"You can't take our guns," Ice fumed.

"We just did," Blaine said. "It's always better to be safe than sorry. Didn't you learn that in kindergarten?"

"First grade," Baz said.

Blaine furrowed his brow. *"Really?"*

"Nah, he's wrong. It was definitely kindergarten," Zeke said.

"I thought so," Blaine said, his eyes never leaving Ice. "Another thing we learned in kindergarten was how to show respect and listen to those in charge. Hopefully you learned that much." He held out the envelope. Ice snagged it and counted the money. "We done here?"

Ice pocketed the cash. "Yeah. We're done."

Blaine pinned him with a dark stare. "Be smart and stay the fuck away from Reese's family, or when I put you in the ground, it'll be with bullets from your own gun."

Chapter Twelve

REESE CHANGED HER clothes before leaving work, excited about seeing Blaine. She'd been hoping he might text after all they'd done yesterday, but she hadn't heard from him since he'd appeared on her doorstep last night. She didn't know what to make of him with his Neanderthal possessiveness and swoon-worthy gestures. How could a guy with such a big heart carry on without developing warm and fuzzy emotions? He was a walking dichotomy of hard and…definitely *not* soft. *Less hard.* Yes, that worked. Although there was nothing physically less hard about the man. She giggled, giving herself a quick once-over in the mirror. She'd worn her glasses because she loved the way Blaine looked like he was restraining himself from kissing the heck out of her when she wore them. She'd also taken a few extra minutes this morning to find shorts that actually fit and had chosen her SCIENCE. IT'S LIKE MAGIC BUT REAL T-shirt, which had a picture of a half-full chemistry flask with three hearts coming out the top. Colette thought it screamed *science nerd*, but Reese loved it.

She pushed open the bathroom door and headed to the lobby.

"You look cute," Terry said. "Are you gardening with Blaine

again?"

She'd asked Reese why she'd changed her clothes yesterday, and without thinking, Reese had told her she'd taken a part-time gardening job with the company Blaine worked for. Now she wished she hadn't mentioned Blaine. "Yes. I've got to pay off my loans somehow."

Terry tucked her shoulder-length dark hair behind her ear and leaned forward like she was sharing a secret. "I think you should garden with him even if you didn't need the money. He's such a nice young man."

An incredible kisser, too.

Now she was blushing *and* nervous about seeing him. She'd definitely done the right thing when she'd turned down Madigan's offer to hang out tonight. If she and Blaine got together again, she'd never be able to keep a straight face in front of his sister.

"I'd better go so I'm not late." Reese headed out to her car, hoping she could calm herself down before she saw him. She didn't remember dating being this nerve-racking. Then again, she and Blaine weren't dating, a fact that nagged at her like an itch she couldn't scratch. She was trying not to drive herself crazy over it, but how should a person act around someone they weren't dating but were exclusively making out with?

In a stranger's yard.

Not just a stranger. A client of the company she was now working for.

She cringed. *How could I be so reckless?*

When she arrived at the client's house, she parked next to Blaine's truck and spotted the answer to her question pacing the yard, talking on his phone. Mr. Deliciously Wicked raked a hand through his hair, back muscles flexing. She remembered just how good that hard body had felt against her and shuddered with memories of his strong hand and talented mouth making fireworks go off inside her. Her hormones must be on overdrive, because she suddenly wanted to throw caution to the wind and let the insanely handsome dirty talker who had turned her into a puddle of desire wreak havoc with her good senses.

She rested her head against the headrest and gave herself a reprimand. *You are here to work, not to end up on the grass making sounds right out of a porn movie.* Not that she'd watched porn, but she had a pretty good imagination. She could resist him. She'd done much harder things than resisting temptation. *I've got this.*

Determination firmly in place, she headed into the backyard. The flowers and plants had been delivered and were lined up in the grass by the areas she'd cleared. Blaine was still on the phone. He sounded angry. She couldn't make out what he was saying, but his body language was enough to know he wasn't relaxed. Did he even know how to relax? She had a feeling they had *that* inability in common. Her gaze slid lower to the faded jeans hugging his ridiculously perfect butt. She reluctantly turned away from that nice sight, found the gloves she'd left yesterday by the tools, and started to turn the soil in the first bed.

"*Fuck,*" Blaine said loudly.

She turned around at the same time Blaine did and gasped at the sight of bruises on his cheek. "What happened?" She hurried over to him, reaching up to touch his face, but he caught her wrist.

"How's it going, buttercup?" His voice was gruff, the muscles in his jaw flexing.

"I'm fine, but you're obviously not." Her gaze dropped to

his fingers around her wrist and his bruised knuckles. "How did you get all those bruises? Are you okay?"

"I'm fine. I ran into your mother's boyfriend last night."

His voice was dead calm, sending an icy chill down her spine. "You *ran into* him? Where?"

"Why'd you lie to me, Reese?" he said sternly.

She stepped back, her walls stacking up like a fortress. She didn't know which lie he was referencing. "What do you mean? Lie to you about what?"

"Did you really think he was your mother's boyfriend?"

She crossed her arms, holding his stare. "Why does it matter?"

His eyes narrowed. "Answer the question."

"You answer *my* question. Where did you run into him?"

"At a bar," he gritted out.

"So you just happened to see him at a bar, and what?" Her voice escalated. "You started a fight with him because you were jealous or something?" This was exactly what she'd wanted to avoid. Those bruises were *her* fault.

"I don't get jealous," he seethed.

His words stung, fueling her anger at his intrusion into her life.

"And I didn't *happen* to run into him." Blaine's angry eyes drilled into her. "I tracked his ass down and went to warn him away from you and Colette. He said some shit, and I set him straight. Why did you lie to me about owing him more money? Did you know he's a drug dealer?"

Shaking, furious, and embarrassed, she lost it. "How *dare* you question me. You're not my father or my boyfriend. What I *know* is none of your business. You have *no right* to come into my life and try to take over. I had that situation handled."

"You owed him thousands of dollars," he shouted. "How is that even remotely handled?"

"I was handling it *my* way! You had no right to go behind my back."

"I paid the fucker off and made sure he'd never come near you or Colette again."

"I never asked you to do that!" It was an ungrateful thing to say when he'd only been trying to help, but she couldn't stop herself.

"A simple thank-you and an explanation will suffice," he barked.

"I can't believe your arrogance. I don't owe you anything. This is *my* life and *my* shit to handle *my* way, *not* yours."

His nostrils flared. "Do you have any idea of the things that asshole does to women?"

"I don't effing care what he does to anyone else! I was *fine*. I was taking care of it, and I don't need *you* or anyone else saving me." She couldn't stop hollering, the words spewing as fast and as poisonous as venom. "I never should have let you bulldoze your way into my life. I'll find a way to pay you back, but you can take your white-knight complex, and this job, and shove it." She stalked toward her car.

"*Don't* walk away from me, Reese."

On the verge of tears, and furious about the whole situation, she did something she'd never done to anyone before. She lifted her hand and flipped him off.

Chapter Thirteen

BLAINE WAS STILL breathing fire hours later at the Dark Knights' clubhouse. Meetings were mandatory, and he'd never wanted to miss a single one, but tonight it had taken a lot to get his ass there instead of hitting the open road again to try to outrun the shit in his head. But he'd done that after making sure Reese had gotten home okay and arranging for Gunner to keep an eye on her house. Going for a ride had been the only way to keep himself from banging on the door and demanding she talk to him. It hadn't helped.

He'd purposely shown up late for the meeting to avoid having to speak to anyone and had started to take a seat in the back until fucking Baz waved him over. He'd saved him a seat with his brothers and cousins. They'd spent the last half hour giving him questioning looks. Who knew support could be smothering? These were the men he respected most, whose presence usually eased him out of a shitty mood. But while Preacher and Conroy sat at the head table discussing club finances, prospects, and other business, Blaine was chewing on nails, and Reese's voice was slicing through his mind. *You're not my father or my boyfriend...I never should have let you bulldoze your way into my life.*

Baz nudged him. "You're up." He nodded to the front of the room. Preacher's ice-blue eyes were locked on Blaine.

Shit. He needed to get his head in the game. He'd filled his father in about what had gone down last night, and his father had given him hell for taking on such a dangerous mission without discussing it with him first.

"You going to join us tonight, son?" Preacher asked. "We're waiting for an update about last night's situation."

Blaine cleared his throat and pushed to his feet. He explained what had gone down to the group, concluding with, "We've got eyes on Ice, and Reese and Colette are covered for the time being. We'll keep tabs to be sure Ice and his crew stay off our turf, and if there's a need to continue watching the girls, we'll coordinate with volunteers at next week's meeting. Cuffs, do you have more to add?"

Cuffs stood. "We're working with the other jurisdictions and tracking Ice and all members of his crew. We busted one guy today. Caught him in the act of selling to a minor. We'll get these guys, but make sure your contacts are aware, and report any leads back to me."

They answered questions, and after they sat down, Conroy said, "Zeke, you're up next with an update on the Young Knights mentoring program."

Zeke stood. "I'm happy to report that the program is going well. We've got three kids in it right now. Saint's son, TJ, started a few months ago. Gunner is mentoring him, and he's volunteering at the rescue on the weekends. The other two boys have no prior affiliation with the Dark Knights. Colonel and I are mentoring them." Brian "Colonel" Carver was Sid's father. He was retired military and a Dark Knight. "I want to remind everyone that this program is about brotherhood and helping kids grow up on a good path. Some kids just need someone to listen and help them navigate problems. Others might need to learn a trade or get help with schoolwork. This is our chance to help kids understand how to make smarter decisions and give them reasons to do so. I encourage you to get involved if you can."

Gunner stood, waking Milo, one of Preacher's dogs, who had been asleep at his feet. Milo gave him the side-eye. "I second that. It feels good to make a difference, and the kids will be volunteering at our adoption event the weekend after Mother's Day. I hope you'll come out and meet them, and maybe take a dog or a cat home with you..."

As they talked about the program and the event, Milo wandered over and brushed against Blaine's leg. Blaine reached down to pet him, his thoughts returning to Reese. He'd bet she'd never had the luxury of owning a pet. It would have been just another mouth to feed, something to take care of. That pissed him off almost as much as her giving him shit and walking away had. He couldn't stop thinking about his call with Madigan this morning. When he'd asked her to hang out with Reese while he was at church, she said she'd already reached out to Reese because she'd wanted to see her and had figured since he'd be at church, it would be the perfect time for her to get to know Colette. She'd had no idea why Reese hadn't taken her up on the offer, and he had no idea why Reese turning her down had bugged him so much. It wasn't like she was alone, and Tobias was keeping an eye on things.

"Remember to bring your families to Preacher's sixtieth birthday party at the Salty Hog next weekend," Conroy said, drawing Blaine from his thoughts.

"You're getting old, Preach!" someone hollered.

"Like motorcycles, bikers don't get old," Preacher retorted with a smirk. "We level up to *classic*."

A rumble of laughter rang out.

Blaine bit back the uncomfortable feelings piling up inside him as they wrapped up the meeting. He'd been looking forward to introducing Reese and Colette to everyone and widening their circle of friends.

When everyone started milling about, racking billiard balls and talking about next weekend's ride, Blaine was ready to cut and run.

Baz eyed him. "You look like you're ready to kill someone."

"I'm guessing it didn't go well with Reese?" Zeke asked.

Blaine shook his head. "She's pissed."

"Because we're watching her place?" Gunner asked.

"No," Blaine bit out. "She doesn't know about that."

"The idiot didn't tell her what we were doing last night before we did it," Zander said.

Blaine glowered at him.

"What did she have to say about lying to you?" Tank asked.

That she's not mine. He was choking on that jagged pill. "Not much. She was too busy giving me hell for going behind her back, and walked off."

"Why do women always walk away?" Zander shook his head.

"Because they're smarter than us," Maverick said. "They take time to cool down instead of saying shit they don't mean."

"Fuck that. I'm going over there, and she damn well better talk to me," Blaine said.

"That is *not* a good plan, brother," Gunner said. "Trust me, when Sid is pissed, I stay as far away as I can."

"Women need time to process arguments," Baz added. "I'll

take your shift watching her house tonight."

"I've *got* it," Blaine insisted.

"No, man, really," Baz said. "You need to take it down a notch. If you grit your teeth any harder, they'll crack. Have a drink with the guys, cool off, and talk to her tomorrow."

"Fuck that." Blaine felt a heavy hand grip his shoulder and knew it was his father before he even heard his voice.

"Why don't you boys clear out and give us a minute," Preacher said with the air of authority they'd all learned to respect when they were knee high. With slicked-back salt-and-pepper hair, pitch-black brows and mustache, and a short silver beard, his old man could look menacing and didn't have to speak to demand respect. But he'd never used that to his advantage with his kids. He didn't have to. He taught through words, not anger, which was probably why his lessons stuck.

Blaine wondered what lesson he was in for now.

"I'm heading to Reese's." Baz pointed at Blaine. "And don't give me any shit about it."

"We'll meet you at the Hog," Zeke said as they headed for the door.

Not one to beat around the bush, Blaine turned to his father. "What's up, old man?"

"I was about to ask you the same. You got here late. Everything okay?"

Shit. Showing up late showed a lack of respect. Blaine hadn't thought about that before he'd chosen to do it. "Sorry. I've had a hell of a day and didn't want to get roped into talking about it."

"You know that doesn't fly here."

Blaine drew his shoulders back. "Like I said, *sorry*. I meant no disrespect. I've just got a lot on my mind."

"That's understandable after what went down last night, but that's what these men are here for. To support you when things get tough."

"It's not that. That's been handled." Blaine crossed his arms. "It's Reese. The woman I'm helping."

"What's the issue? Maybe I can help."

"Nobody can help. She's got my head all screwed up."

One dark brow arched. "That's the first time I've ever heard those words come out of your mouth. She must be something special, which would explain you going off the way you did."

"She's something all right. She's got way too much shit on her plate, and all I want to do is clear it. But every time I do anything, she pushes back. I took care of that asshole, and she's pissed at me for not talking to her about it first. She lied to me, and *she's* pissed? What the hell is that?"

Preacher chuckled.

"I'm glad you find this funny."

"I can't help it. You're so damn thickheaded, she's got you all befuddled."

"I'm not fucking befuddled."

"Then you know why she's pissed. Your heart was in the right place, and I'm sure you had your reasons for taking action before talking to her, but don't act like you don't get it."

"Damn right I had good reasons. She said the guy was her mother's *boyfriend*. I didn't want to scare her before knowing he was handled."

"That sounds reasonable, but even so, there are consequences for our actions. Whether those actions are right or wrong makes no difference. You stepped onto her turf and took over without her approval, just like you did with Madigan."

"This is totally different. Madigan was right. I probably

should have gone to her first. But Reese isn't Mads. She was in over her head. She's taking care of a teenage sister, trying to make ends meet, and cleaning up the shit her mother left behind. It's too much for her."

"And yet she's pissed that you took care of it, which tells me that maybe *she* didn't think it was too much for her. Did you talk about it, or did you blow in there and tell her how things were going to be, the way you do?"

Blaine ground his back teeth.

"You did the latter, didn't you?"

"I was pissed. She lied to me, and I wanted to know why."

Preacher shook his head. "Sit down, son. We need to talk."

"I'm good."

He lowered his chin. "Sit your ass down."

Blaine reluctantly complied.

"You're a smart man, Blaine, but you're so used to making sure everyone falls in line, sometimes you forget to slow down and take other people's feelings into consideration. That's my fault to a large degree, because you've had a big flock to watch over since you were a boy. You took it on naturally. You've always excelled at taking charge, and most of the time that serves you well. You've managed to build one of the most successful stone businesses in New England, and you're well respected by the community and every man in this club. But, son, women are a different breed. They're not followers. They're leaders in their own right. Sure, some will follow, like the women you tend to hook up with, but if you think about it, they're taking what *they* want, too."

"How do you know who I hook up with?" He was discreet, and he didn't talk about his trysts.

"The same way I knew when you'd taken Susie Beedrum to

the old quarry." Susie was a girl Blaine had gone out with when he was sixteen. They'd gone to the old quarry to have sex, but Preacher had shown up before he'd even gotten past second base.

"I never did find out who tipped you off."

"And you never will. She was *fifteen*. Right or wrong in your eyes, I wasn't going to let that happen. The point is, I did some checking on this girl of yours. She's been running the show for a long time."

"No shit. I'm trying to make it easier for her."

"By accusing her of lying to you?"

"She *did* lie."

Preacher shrugged. "People lie, Blaine. We're all guilty of it. If you bully them, they're going to either lie more often or stay the hell away from you."

"If you're telling me to sit her down and talk nicely when I'm pissed, it's not going to happen. I'm not Zeke. I don't have that in me."

"I know you don't, and I'm not telling you what to do. I'm simply imparting some knowledge to try to save you more grief. There's an easy equation to being happy with a partner. You've got to build trust, and that takes more than good intentions. If you want her to respect you, treat her with respect."

"I respect the hell out of her."

Preacher's brows slanted again. "In that case, I strongly suggest you take a moment to look at what transpired between you and the young woman who's got you all tangled up and ask yourself this. If some other guy spoke to her the way you did about that lie, would you have stepped in?"

Blaine's chest constricted.

Preacher pushed to his feet. "Do yourself a favor, son. Give

Reese a day or two to figure out what she wants. What we do is a lot for any woman to handle, and you've always been an enforcer. It might all be too much for her. It's often the toughest women who need a soft place to land. Carrying around all that armor takes a toll. If that's the case with Reese, only you can decide if that's something you can give her." He patted Blaine's shoulder. "You're a good man, son. Take Baz's advice. Go to the Hog tonight and blow off some steam."

Blaine didn't move. The visual he'd conjured of his argument with Reese was stuck on repeat in his mind.

CROUCHED IN THE moonlight, Reese uttered, "So stupid," for the hundredth time as she yanked handfuls of weeds and grass and whatever else was in reach and threw them aside. "Stubborn ass." She stabbed at the dirt with a hand shovel and yanked another weed. She'd spent the last few hours fuming at herself, at Blaine, and at her freaking mother as she'd made dinner for Colette and scrubbed the dishes like they were to blame. She'd finally retreated to her room so she wouldn't snap at Colette. But the silence had made her feel like the walls were closing in on her.

The walls she'd spent years trying to escape.

But there was no escaping the hell her mother had left her with. She'd finally come outside to work through her frustrations, but her argument with Blaine clung to her like humidity.

"Reese? Reese, are you out here?" Colette called out the back door.

"Back here!" She yanked another weed, then grabbed another fistful. "Stupid." *Yank.* "Pushy." *Yank.* "Butthead." The weed broke free, and she threw it aside.

"Are you okay?" Colette was staring down at her in the moonlight, looking younger than her fifteen years in a hoodie and shorts.

"I'm effing *great.*"

Colette crossed her arms. "What's wrong?"

"Nothing." She stabbed at the dirt.

"Obviously something is wrong. You're not all over me to do my essay."

Shoot. How did I forget your essay? "Did you start it yet?"

"*No,*" she said with attitude. "Why are you so mad?"

"You wouldn't understand." How could she when Reese didn't even understand the hurt, anger, and guilt battering her from the inside out? This was one of the many times she wished she had a best friend, someone she could spill all her awful truths to, who wouldn't judge her or make her feel bad for sharing her dirty laundry. She'd stupidly thought Blaine might end up being that person. She'd also thought he might come back and apologize, but she hadn't heard from him, and that hurt as much as his going behind her back had. The tears she'd been refusing to let fall since she'd gotten home burned her eyes, but she willed them away.

"How do you know?"

"Because you're fifteen." *And I'm supposed to protect you.* She stabbed at a root.

"So?" Colette fumed. "I'm not a baby. I know things."

"Lettie, *stop,*" she snapped. "Just let it go and get your essay done."

"You're such a jerk." Colette stormed into the house and slammed the door.

"Damn it." She threw the shovel and looked up at the stars, physically hurting from missing her grandmother so much. "I'm trying my best to do all the things right, but I'm not sure I know what right is anymore. I need help, Gram. I *like* Blaine. I mean, *really* like him in a way I wasn't sure I could ever like anyone, and I don't know what to do. I wish you were here. Can't you send me a sign or something? Tell me if I'm doing the right thing by shutting him out?"

With a heavy sigh, she plunked down to her butt, feeling more alone than she ever had. She pulled her knees up to her chest as the tears she'd been holding back broke free.

Chapter Fourteen

"WHAT DO YOU mean it's delayed another three weeks? I needed that product last Friday," Blaine barked into the phone Thursday afternoon. He paced his office, listening to his contact in Italy drone on with another fucking excuse he had no patience for, when Maverick walked into his office, brows slanted, and closed the door. "If I don't have the product in two weeks, it'll be the last time I use you." He ended the call and continued pacing, feeling like a caged animal. "The fucking travertine is delayed again."

"Okay, so we'll tell the client. You need to get out of here."

"Why?" Blaine snapped.

"You've been yelling at everyone today. I just came from accounting, and they're afraid to leave because they have to walk by your office."

"That's ridiculous."

"Is it? They've never seen you like this. You never lose your cool at work."

He gritted his teeth, as he'd been doing all damn day. "Excuse me for being fucking human."

"Want to talk about it?"

"There's nothing to talk about."

"You can't bullshit me, bro. You have to be exhausted. I know you took over for Baz last night, watching Reese's, and made arrangements for Colonel to take over keeping her safe in the afternoons since she's not coming to work at your place. It's got to be killing you to give Reese space, but we don't need to scare employees over it."

Damn right it was killing him. He'd been fighting the urge to text her all day.

"Go work on that project at your house. It'll do you good to get your hands dirty."

"I'm *fine.*"

Maverick opened the door. "Don't make me drag your ass out of here."

Blaine narrowed his eyes. "You want to dance, bro?"

He smirked. "I only dance with my wife."

"That's what I thought," Blaine said as he strode out the door.

BLAINE STOOD IN his backyard, staring at the flowers he and Reese had picked out and the extra ones he'd ordered for her garden at her mother's house. He'd wanted to surprise her with them, and now everything was fucked up. Their argument came back to him in full-blown color and surround sound. The sadness and anger that had welled in her eyes slayed him anew, and his reaction to her anger drove that pain deeper. His father's voice traipsed through his mind. *What we do is a lot for any woman to handle...It might all be too much for her. It's often the toughest women who need a soft place to land...If that's the case*

with Reese, only you can decide if that's something you can give her.

His hands curled into fists.

If anyone needed the Dark Knights, it was Reese and Colette, and he was *exactly* the man Reese needed. How much time did she need to figure that out? If he bided his time any longer, he was going to lose his mind. He loaded up his truck with the extra flowers he'd bought for her and headed over to her house.

When he turned onto her street, he spotted Colonel on his motorcycle and pulled up beside him. "Hey, man. Thanks for taking over."

"No problem. Colette is home, but Reese hasn't shown up. Fish said she hasn't left work yet." Fish was another Dark Knight. He was watching over Reese's office.

Shit. "He's sure she's okay?"

"Yeah. Nobody concerning has come or gone."

Blaine looked down the street at the jungle around their house. "A'right. Can you give me ten minutes to run a quick errand before you take off?"

"Of course."

Blaine drove to the gas station, filled a gas can for the mower, grabbed a bag of potato chips, and headed back. He waved to Colonel on his way to Reese's and saw him drive away as he parked in front of her house. He was grabbing the gas can from the back of the truck when Colette walked outside, wearing jeans and a green belly-baring shirt.

She crossed her arms, lifting her chin with the same defiance Reese did so well. "Reese isn't here."

"Oh?"

"She's working late."

"Okay. I'm just going to cut the grass before this jungle swallows your house. You hungry?"

She shrugged.

He grabbed the chips from the passenger seat and headed up the walk. "I had these left over from lunch. You want them?"

"I guess." She took the bag and opened it. "Did you piss off my sister yesterday?"

He didn't know what Reese had said to her, so he went with a safe answer. "Probably. I piss off a lot of people."

She ate a chip, eyes narrowing. "What did you do?"

"You want a list?" He smiled. She didn't.

"That's not an answer."

Reese had obviously taught her the art of interrogation. "I did something that I thought would help her without asking permission first."

"That was stupid." She ate a chip. "You've hung out with her enough to know she has to control *everything*."

"She's got a lot on her plate." He wasn't going to get in a pissing match, but he would like to get to know her better. Maybe even find a way to get her to ease up on Reese. "Do you know where Reese keeps the key to the shed?"

"Uh-huh." She tossed another chip into her mouth.

"Would you mind getting it so I can use the mower?"

With an annoyed exhalation, she went inside, then returned a minute later, holding the key out for him.

"Walk with me. I could use your help."

She exhaled loudly again but came off the deck and walked with him through the long grass.

"What are you doing today?"

"Apparently I'm helping you." She ate another chip.

"Did you learn that snark from your sister?"

She rolled her eyes.

"What were you doing before I got here?" He set the gas can

on the grass as she unlocked the shed.

"Working on a stupid essay."

"Tell me about it." He surveyed the mess of gardening tools, electrical cords, empty flowerpots, boxes of who-knew-what, paint, pieces of wood, baby toys, and a dozen other miscellaneous items.

"There's nothing to tell. I haven't written anything yet."

He grabbed a box and set it to the side. "Help me clear a path, will ya?"

"You can change locks, but you can't clear stuff out of a shed?"

"There's nothing I *can't* do."

"Then why do you need my help?" she challenged.

"Because it'll go faster with two of us. I'll tell you what. Give me a hand, and I'll help you with your essay. I aced English."

"Like you've even read *The Outsiders*," she said sarcastically.

"Are you kidding? It's a classic. I've read it, seen the movie, and lived many parts of it."

"I forgot you were in a gang."

"Give me those." He took the bag of chips and handed her a box. "Put this in the corner." He put the bag of chips on an old chair and started moving other items. "The Dark Knights isn't a gang. It's a club of guys who enjoy riding motorcycles and biker culture. We work together to keep our communities safe. We don't go out and stir shit up for fun, and unlike the Greasers, who were poor, and the Soces, who weren't, everyone is welcome in our club. We've got members who are well off and guys who live paycheck to paycheck." He handed her another box. "What'd you think about the book?"

She shrugged and set the box aside.

"Did you read it?"

"Mm-hm." She didn't look at him and began moving things out of the way without any prodding.

Blaine knew avoidance when he saw it. "What did you think of the way Dally killed Bob?"

She shrugged.

"Were you sad when Johnny moved away?"

"Kind of," she mumbled.

He stopped working and looked at her. "A'right, Colette, level with me. You didn't read the book, did you?"

"I just said I read it."

"Then you read a different book than I did. Fess up."

"I hate reading. It's boring."

"Not this book. It's exciting."

She rolled her eyes.

"When is your essay due?"

"Tomorrow."

"Then we have some work to do. Let me tell you about *The Outsiders*." As they cleared a path for the mower, he said, "The thing I love most about that story is how real it is. Every kid feels like an outsider in some way. It doesn't matter if you're rich, poor, top of the class, or just getting by. We all have insecurities, and teenagers have it the worst because kids can be real assholes."

"You swear a lot."

"Do I?" He'd never thought about how much he swore. "I'll try to watch that." He moved an ancient bag of potting soil out of the way.

"Which would you have been when you were a kid? A Greaser or a Soc?"

"I was the son of the president of the Dark Knights, so I was expected to behave. I had a lot of responsibility, like Reese does, but I also liked to push limits. I was too rough around the edges to be a Soc, but we weren't poor. I guess I'd've been like Ponyboy and Johnny and tried to do good. Strived to cross social barriers and change things for the better."

"I thought the book was all about two gangs fighting."

"There is a lot of fighting, but there's much more to it." He stacked boxes along the wall. "It's about family and friendship, navigating the inequities of life, and figuring out what's important. Ponyboy's parents died, and his older brother, Darry, is raising him and their other brother. Darry works hard to keep the family going, and he gives them hell when they screw up, but only because he loves them and wants something better for them. Like Reese does with you. But Johnny, and their buddy Dallas, weren't so lucky."

She moved the last tool from in front of the mower. "Why?"

"Their parents are abusive shitbags." As soon as the words left his lips, he regretted saying it. But if it bothered Colette, she didn't let it show.

"That sucks," she said cavalierly.

"It does suck, and it affects them both differently. Dally is a real ass ki—*sorry*—butt kicker because of it. Even though he loves the other guys, he acts like a prick to everyone else most of the time. He's just so angry, he doesn't know what to do with the anger. My brother Maverick used to be like that." *Hell, I'm like that.*

She eyed him cautiously. "Were your parents abusive?"

"No. He's adopted. He lost his mom when he was a kid, and his dad was a real piece of work. But with time, some therapy, and lots of love, Maverick dealt with his past and learned to trust our family. He's a great guy."

"What about Johnny? You said he was like Ponyboy." She grabbed her chips, following him as he pushed the mower out of the shed.

"Even though Johnny's parents were just as bad as Dally's, he's a really good kid. All heart. Although he does kill a guy during a rumble to save his friends from getting hurt."

"Ohmygod. He *kills* him? Does he go to jail?"

"No," he said more thoughtfully. "He and Ponyboy hid out in an old church and save a bunch of kids from a fire. But Johnny gets hurt real bad. He doesn't make it."

Sadness rose in her eyes. "He *dies*?"

"Yes, but he saved those kids." He began filling the mower with gas. "I told you it was real. That's the thing about life. Good people can do bad things, and you never know how much time you have. It's up to each of us to decide how we want to live our lives and how we want to treat others." His mind veered straight to Reese, and his chest constricted. "Anyway, it's a great book. You should get started reading it while I cut the grass."

She tilted her head. "What are you now? A Soc or a Greaser?"

"Neither. I'm a Dark Knight."

"So, like, you're a badass, but you try to do good things?"

"That pretty much sums me up, and sometimes I do bad things but for good reasons. What about you?"

She was quiet for a minute. "I'm just an outsider."

"Not anymore you're not. Nobody's an outsider when they're in my circle."

Her lips curved up, but then her brows knitted. "Even if Reese hates you?"

"Reese doesn't hate me. How could she hate this face?" He flashed a cheesy grin, earning another eye roll. "Even if she did,

I'd still have your backs, and I always will."

"Because you're a stalker?" she challenged.

"Yes, smart-ass. Because I'm a stalker. Now get inside and start reading so you don't fail your class."

"I CANNOT *WAIT* to get home," Joy said as she and Reese walked out of work Thursday evening. "I'm starving, my feet hurt, and Willa doesn't know it yet, but she's going to give me a foot rub and migrate north if I'm lucky."

I'm exhausted, my heart hurts, and I have a teenage attitude waiting for me at home. She hadn't slept a wink last night, and everything that could go wrong at work, did. Her head felt like a dumpster fire. Colette was barely speaking to her, and she felt crappy about yelling at Blaine, but at the same time, she was still furious over what he'd done. All she wanted was to go home to her quiet apartment above Mr. Wilson's garage and be alone in her misery...or to crawl into Blaine's arms. But *that* was out of the question. It irritated her that she could be this angry and still feel like she could find a protective, comforting place to catch her breath in his arms.

"Earth to Reese." Joy nudged her.

"Sorry, what?"

Joy stopped walking and put her hand on her hip. "Are you sure you don't want to talk about whatever's bothering you?"

"I'm fine."

"Nobody is fine every day, and you've been walking around like a zombie looking for a human to eat."

"I'm just a little tired. I didn't sleep well last night, and working thirteen hours was a lot."

"We share an office, remember? I know you had your panties in a twist when you got to work this morning. You don't have to tell me what's wrong, but I'm here if you ever want to talk. God knows I bend your ear enough about my troubles."

Our troubles are from different planets. "Thanks. I appreciate it, but I'd better get going. I'll see you tomorrow."

She hurried to her car. The feeling in the pit of her stomach was worse than usual, and she knew it had to do with Blaine. He was the one good thing in her life, and the minute she'd let herself believe in him, he'd disappointed her like everyone else. Well, not exactly like everyone else. He had good intentions, and she probably owed him an apology, but didn't *he* owe *her* one, too?

This was why she didn't bother with relationships.

We aren't even in a relationship.

She cranked the music to drown out her thoughts and steeled herself for another night of being ignored or scowled at by Colette.

Chapter Fifteen

REESE'S STUPID HEART skipped at the sight of Blaine's truck in front of her house, but annoyance quickly shut that down. What was he doing there? She was *not* in the mood to be bossed around.

She got out of her car and slammed the door. As she stalked toward the door, she realized the lawn had been mowed, ratcheting up her irritation. Why did he have to do nice things and take care of them *all* the time? Couldn't he just be an all-around jerk like other guys? That would make this so much easier.

Ready to give him hell despite the lawn, or maybe because of it, she climbed the steps to the deck and heard Colette laughing. It was such a foreign sound, it stopped her in her tracks. She peered through the screen door and saw them sitting on the couch. Blaine was typing on Colette's laptop, and she was watching something on her phone. A half-eaten plate of spaghetti sat on the coffee table in front of Colette.

"Did you watch the whole scene?" Blaine asked.

"*Yes.* Stop asking me that every time." Colette shoved him, but it was a playful gesture, so different from the way she treated Reese.

Furious, Reese threw open the door and stormed inside. "What's going on?" she demanded, glowering at Blaine as he stood up. "Why are you in my house?"

Blaine set the laptop on the coffee table. "I came by to talk to you."

"And made yourself right at home, alone with my little sister?"

"He's helping me with my essay," Colette argued.

"Stay out of this, Colette," Reese warned.

"You're such a *jerk*. He cut the grass *and* fixed the leaky sink *and* made dinner, and all you can do is bitch at him." She grabbed her laptop and stormed into her room, slamming the door behind her.

"Reese, this is on me, not Colette."

"I'm not doing this with you here. She doesn't need to hear it." She turned on her heel and stalked outside and across the yard.

Blaine followed. "I didn't come over to piss you off."

"Well, you screwed that up, didn't you?" She turned on him, all of the anger and hurt from the past twenty-four hours pouring out. "You can't just show up and insert yourself in my life whenever you want to, like everything is okay. *Nothing* is okay."

"I didn't try to insert myself into your life," he seethed, his voice escalating. "I came over to apologize for yelling at you."

"You're yelling at me right now."

"Because you're yelling at me and pissing me off! *Jesus.*" He paced. "I can't win with you."

She crossed her arms, hating herself for being a bitch but too upset to stop. "I'm not a game to be won."

"I didn't mean it like that," he gritted out.

"If you think whatever that was in there is going to win me over, you're wrong. She's just using you to get to me."

"I didn't help Colette as some kind of manipulation. I helped her because I was here, and it's what I do."

"We don't need your help. We're *fine*."

"Are you fine, Reese?" he asked in a lower, serious voice. "Because I'm fucking not. I hate arguing with you. All I want to do is help you, and you've got a hair up your ass about letting me do that."

She scoffed. "Is that supposed to win me over?"

His jaw clenched. "This *isn't* a game to me. Don't you get it?" He stepped closer. "You got under my skin, buttercup. I care about you."

Had she heard him right? He'd said he never got feelings for women. Her focus waned, and her walls started to crack, but she pulled it together. "You say you care, but I trusted you. I opened up to you emotionally and physically, and you went behind my back to do what *you* wanted without even consulting me, when it was my life you were messing with. That's not how you treat someone you care about."

"In my world, you do whatever it takes to keep the people you care about safe." His voice was low and serious, not as angry, and that took the edge off her anger. "I'm sorry that I upset you, but you said that asshole was your mother's boyfriend, and I believed you really thought he was. I didn't want to scare you by telling you he was a drug dealer until I knew he was taken care of."

He'd tried to protect her, like she'd tried to protect him? "I guess I see your point, but *still*. This is my life, and it's *my* job to keep Colette safe. I like you a lot, Blaine, but I don't want to be with someone who doesn't respect my boundaries."

His jaw tightened, and his face pinched, like he was trying to solve a complicated equation. When he spoke, his tone was softer, more caring. "I get why you're mad, but hear me out. I'm sorry I went around you, and I can't promise I'll never do it again. But I can promise to think twice about it, and hopefully, the decision I come to is the right one for both of us. I can also promise that I'm going to try my damnedest not to yell at you again. You don't deserve that, and it pisses me off that I lost my cool. But you're not innocent in this, Wilder. You said you trusted me, but you lied to me about that guy."

"Because I didn't want you getting involved. Look at your face. Those bruises are *my* fault. And for what? You're not going to stick around anyway. Nobody ever does." Emotions clogged her throat. "You act chivalrous, but you'll be like the other guys who claimed to be interested in me, wanting more than I can give, because, like it or not, I'm the only person my sister has, and I'll never be a carefree girl who can stay out all night and party it up."

His eyes drilled into her. "I'm not some nitwit kid who's led around by his dick. I'm a grown man who not only understands responsibility but respects it, and I'm right here, Reese. For you *and* Colette, and I'm sorry I screwed up, but I'm not going anywhere."

"Yeah, but for how long? Until we have sex enough that you get bored? You've already admitted to being a commitment-phobe."

"Have I?" He sounded irritated again. "I've been with the club for sixteen years, and I've never wanted to walk away. I'm not afraid of commitment. I'm just a different breed than the guys you're used to. I don't take commitments lightly. When I give my word, it's with everything I have. Mind, body, and soul.

I know other guys go from one person to the next, catching feelings and professing them, but that's not who I am. Relationships are *not* disposable to me."

"You don't *do* relationships with women, remember? You said you can't make any promises, and I'm not asking you to. I'm just saying that opening up and trusting isn't easy for me, and doing those things with a guy who says he won't commit is a scary proposition."

The muscles in his jaw were jumping again. "I don't do relationships *because* they're not disposable. I said we were exclusive. Isn't that a commitment?"

"Yes, but you know what I mean."

"I do, and I'm sorry, Reese, but this is who I am. I'm not an easy guy to be with, and I wouldn't blame you for telling me to fuck off. I hope you won't, and I'm not saying I would even if you asked me to. But until we know we're compatible in every sense and you're sure you can handle me and my world and want me in yours, faults and all, I won't put a label on us. I know that's not what you're used to, but it's the best I can do."

Exclusivity was a label in and of itself, even if not a public label. That was something, but it was his honesty that softened her resolve. "I think you forgot to say until you're sure you want to handle my world, too."

"No, I didn't. I already know where I stand on that. I just need to slow down and think twice so I don't fuck it up again."

Her heart stuttered.

"Shit, Reese. I don't even know how to do this."

"What's *this*?"

"Caring enough to argue with a woman. Asking for another chance. Hell, thinking about you so damn much."

Her heart took another hit.

"I can defend myself from four guys at the same time, but you wreck me without even trying." He framed her face with his warm hands, gazing deeply into her eyes. "I'm flawed, Wilder. I say shit I probably shouldn't, and I go off when someone I care about is in danger, and I don't know if that will ever change or how much I want it to. But the last thing I want to do is hurt you. I can only promise to try to do better, and if you want to be with me, then I need the same promise from you. No more lies. And if you don't want to be with me, that won't change the fact that I'll still be here for you and Colette day and night, whenever you need me, and even when you don't."

Her eyes teared up. "Why is this so hard?"

"Because we're both stubborn." He caressed her cheek, giving her the tender touch she craved. "We've lived a certain way for so long, we don't know how to open the doors that have been nailed shut. I break them down, and you peer out the peephole, and both of us do it armed for battle."

They were so similar and so different. How did he already know her so well?

"You've been trying to hold a big, complicated world together all alone since you were thirteen, and you've done a great job at being both mother and father to Colette. But you don't have to carry the weight of the world alone anymore. It's okay to need someone to lean on. I'm here if you want it to be an ornery biker who makes a mean spaghetti."

She laughed softly. "Why is it impossible to stay mad at you?"

"Because you know I'm not a bad guy, and maybe you like me a little, too."

She did. *God.* So much more than a little.

"I need to kiss you now, so if you're going to give me any

more grief, can you do it quickly?"

"Just kiss me."

He pressed his lips to hers, wrapping his strong arms around her, unraveling the anger and knots of discontent and fear. She soaked him in like they were longtime lovers reunited, which made no sense, but the feeling was too real to deny.

"God, I've missed you," he said against her lips. "How is that even possible?"

"I was just wondering the same thing."

His lips curved up, but there was confusion in his eyes. "What are you doing to me, Wilder?"

"Kissing you." She pulled his mouth back toward hers, but he stopped short of kissing her.

He brushed his thumb down her cheek again, speaking softly but firmly. "Don't walk away from me again."

She blinked innocently up at him. "I can't promise I'll never do it again. But I can promise to think twice about it, and hopefully, I'll make the right decision for both of us."

He shook his head, flashing that devastating smile, and drew her into another kiss. She felt him smiling against her lips, but that lasted only a few seconds before he took the kiss deeper, his fingers tangling in her hair, sending scintillating shocks down to her core. She rose onto her toes, returning his efforts with fervor, wanting to get lost in them, as she had the other day.

He growled and tugged her head back by her hair, eyes blazing with desire. "If we don't stop, I'm going to haul your gorgeous ass into my truck."

She was too turned on to stop herself. "Then what?"

A rapacious grin curved his lips, and he brushed his nose along her cheek. "I'll make up for all my wrongs by having you ride me until you come so hard, you can't feel your legs."

She couldn't speak for the desire that sparked.

"Don't look so shocked, baby girl. You know how that turns me on, and your sister is right inside." He lowered his face beside hers, his breath warming her ear. "Have you ever been fucked in a truck?"

Prickles of heat seared between her legs, her sex clenching needily. "Uh-uh."

"Have you ever gone down on a guy in one?"

Holy cow. Why did that make her want to? "No," she whispered.

"*Good.* I look forward to popping both of those cherries. Don't worry. I have tinted windows." He dragged his tongue around the shell of her ear and nipped at her earlobe. She inhaled sharply, and he pressed a quick kiss to her lips. "Those pink cheeks are going to be the death of me."

"Then I'll meet you in heaven, because your dirty mouth will be the death of me."

"Now, *that* sounds like a great way to die." He hoped she never lost that innocence, although he hungered to steal it. "I know you're probably starved and you need to talk to Colette, but I want to talk to you about her first. Help me bring these flowers into your backyard?"

She blinked several times, trying to switch gears from the X-rated images he'd sparked. How did he do it so fast? "Flowers?"

"Yeah. I ordered the ones you mentioned wanting to plant here when we went to the nursery, plus a few others I thought you'd like. I was going to surprise you yesterday, but I didn't get the chance."

She couldn't believe he'd paid that much attention to what she'd said that day, much less that he'd gone to so much trouble for her. "That's incredibly thoughtful, but you don't have to keep—"

"Don't give me shit, Wilder. Your whole face lit up in that nursery. If flowers bring you that much joy, you should be surrounded by them all the time."

Some girls wanted gold and diamonds, but all she'd ever wanted was someone to see her, and appreciate her, for who she was, caretaker for Colette and all. Blaine had his faults, just as she did, but he was honest and he never missed a thing. She glanced at his truck, shocked to see so many gorgeous flowers in the back of it. How had she missed them? Her gaze caught on beautiful black-eyed Susans, her grandmother's favorites. She got chills. Smiling, she threw a silent thank-you up to her grandmother for giving her a sign that maybe she wasn't screwing things up after all.

She looked at the complicated man who had pissed her off to protect her and was nurturing her damaged heart, one selfless act at a time, and wondered if her grandmother had had her hand in their meeting all along. "Thank you. They're beautiful, and that was really thoughtful of you."

"*Finally.* Can you say that again? That sounds so much better than you yelling at me."

She laughed. "Not a chance. Let me take a better look at these flowers."

"Does that mean I get to look at your flower?"

"Ohmygod. You never stop."

"There's the blush I love."

She filled with happiness as they started bringing the plants to the backyard. "You wanted to talk to me about Colette?"

"Yeah. Does she have issues with reading?"

"She hates it."

"I think it might be more complicated than that. She hadn't read the book for her essay, and we got to talking about it.

When I was fixing the leak in the bathroom sink, I asked her to read me the opening of the story. She was struggling through it."

"Really?"

"Yeah. We worked around it. We watched the movie, and she was going to type her paper, but that was hard for her, too, so she dictated what she wanted to say, and I typed it for her."

"She's never been great at reading and her spelling is atrocious, but she doesn't even try. When she does homework, she can't focus for more than a few minutes at a time, and she doesn't like school at all, so you played right into her hands."

"I don't think so." He set down the plants, his face serious. "I think she might need help. Zander has dyslexia, and he masked it for years by being the class clown. The teachers didn't pick up on it. If it weren't for Zeke realizing something was wrong when he stepped in to make sure he got his homework done and understood the assignments, who knows how long he would've gone undiagnosed."

"You think Lettie has dyslexia?"

"I can't say for sure, but when we watched the movie, she was engaged and excited about the story, and when it came to reading and writing the essay, all I saw was pain."

"Oh my gosh. How could I have missed something so big?"

"I could be wrong, but if I'm not, it's not your fault. These things go undiagnosed and misdiagnosed all the time. Have her teachers ever mentioned the possibility of a learning disorder?"

"Not that I know of. They've always talked about her behavior and needing to stay on top of her assignments, but not anything like a learning disability. I would've gotten her help."

"I figured you would have."

"I've tried to help her with homework, but she shuts down

with me."

"I think that's to be expected. Some kids are embarrassed that they have difficulties. There's no reason to be, but Zander was, too. He hated that he had trouble, and my parents tried to get him tutors, but the only person he'd let help him was Zeke. So Zeke met with the tutors and learned how to help him. Then he walked him through every assignment in every grade. After Zeke graduated from high school, instead of going away to study like he wanted to, he went to community college his first year, just to make sure Zan graduated from high school."

"That's amazing. He sounds really special."

"He is. They both are. There are lots of ways to make things easier for Colette. Do you think you can get her to talk to someone?"

"I'll try, but she fights me on everything. I'm a little worried if I mention it, she'll feel like I'm putting her down. She thinks I look down on her because I was a good student. Little does she know, doing well in school was the only thing I could control. But I will talk to her about it."

"You should probably share that with her."

"I don't want her to know how hard things were back then. She might think it was her fault."

"I get that, but I think she could benefit from knowing your life wasn't perfect either. There's a lot to be said about common ground, you know? Maybe you can find a way to tell her it was hard without saying too much about the things you don't want her to know." They headed back to the truck for more flowers. "Actually, I might have a better idea about how to approach her reading issues. I'll talk to Zeke about this, but if you'll come with me next Saturday to my old man's party, Colette can meet him. He's really good at helping kids and getting to the root of problems. He might be able to figure out what's going on without putting her on the spot or making her feel singled out. If he's concerned, he'll probably have suggestions, and you can decide what to do from there."

She'd been too wrapped up in their falling-out to see straight, and she knew he was just as upset. But it hadn't overshadowed *his* concern for Colette. Other than their grandmother, there hadn't been anyone in their lives who had taken the time to care, much less try to help. Guilt tightened like a noose. "I'm sorry I jumped all over you about her earlier."

"You had a right to, but I hope you know I'd never do anything to hurt her."

"I know you wouldn't. I shouldn't have gone off like that."

"We already said our *sorry*s. No need to hash it out anymore."

"Okay, but I want to finish that gardening job if you think it's still open to me. I like working with you, and I need the money to pay you back."

He shook his head. "You don't need to pay me back."

"I do, and I will. Forty-five hundred dollars is a lot of money."

His brows slanted. "Reese—"

"Don't even try to change my mind, or I'll sell pictures of my feet and do OnlyFans."

He laughed and pulled her against his side. "You're a stubborn girl." He kissed her temple. "What do you think about the party?"

"I'd like to go, but I don't know if I can get her to, and I don't want her to find out about everything that's happened with Ice."

"You don't have to worry about her finding out. We don't

talk about club business with anyone other than members. Why don't you go see if you can clear the air with her? I'll finish bringing the flowers out back, and if you want me to talk with her about the party, I'm happy to. I'd like you guys to meet everyone, not just Zeke."

Reese took a deep breath, telling herself not to get too caught up in the way he was drawing her into his circle. It felt big, and after all he'd said, maybe he meant it that way, but she was about to face another difficult situation. She needed a clear head, not one muddled with confusing emotions.

Throwing a silent prayer up to the apology gods, she hoped for the best as she headed inside.

Chapter Sixteen

COLETTE WAS COMING down the hall when Reese walked in. "If you came to yell at me about my dishes, I'm on my way to get them."

"I didn't. I wanted to apologize. I shouldn't have gone off when I came home."

"Whatever." She stalked into the living room, and Reese followed.

"Colette, I'm really sorry. I didn't sleep at all last night, and I had a crappy day. I shouldn't have blown up when I got home."

"It's no different from any other day." Colette picked up her plate of spaghetti and carried it into the kitchen.

"Lettie—"

She spun around, her angry glare cutting like a knife. "What? You're sorry. Okay. I get it. What do you want me to say? It's not like you won't do it again tomorrow." She dumped the spaghetti into the trash and went to wash her plate.

Unexpected tears welled in Reese's eyes, but she refused to let them fall. This wasn't the way their relationship was supposed to turn out. Colette was supposed to be protected from the stress and ugliness, and instead, she was bearing the brunt of it. "You're right. I've been stressed since Mom went back to rehab, and I've taken it out on you. It was wrong, and I'm sorry. All I've ever wanted was to make your life better."

Colette put the plate in the dish drainer and turned to face Reese, crossing her arms. "You treat me like I'm a little kid, and sometimes I wish I was. At least then you *liked* me."

Reese was taken aback. "Colette, I *love* you."

"But you don't *like* me. You look at me like I'm the enemy, and I get it. You're always stuck taking care of me. I know you moved out because you didn't want to do it anymore, and you still have to come back all the time because Mom is such a shithead. And I'm not as smart as you, or—"

"Stop!" Reese hollered, her heart breaking, tears reemerging. "Just *stop* for a second. Mom *is* awful, but I didn't move out to get away from you or because I didn't want to be around you. I moved out to get away from *her*. I wanted to take you with me, but she wouldn't let me. I asked you to come with me. Don't you remember?" She was too upset to wait for a response. "And I came back all the time because I love you, and I care about you, and I wanted your life to be better than it was. That's why I get on you about school and staying out of trouble. I don't think you're stupid, Lettie, and I'm *not* smarter than you. Schoolwork was the only thing I could control when I was growing up. I worked my butt off because I got positive feedback from my teachers, and I needed that."

Her heart was racing, tears burning. "I'm sorry our mother is a mess, but from the second you were born, I have loved you with all my heart. So did Grandma, and after she died, I hated going to school and leaving you behind. It was *always* you and me. We were a team for so long, and then it all fell apart. But there has *never* been a time in my life when I didn't want to be your sister, and it kills me to think I've made you feel like the enemy or like you're not smart enough." Tears streamed down her cheeks. "No wonder you hate me."

"I don't *hate* you." Colette looked down at the floor. "I just wish we could go back to the way we were."

"I want that, too." Reese held her breath, waiting for Colette to look at her or say something.

It seemed like a lifetime before she looked up. "Did you *really* want to take me with you?"

"Yes, more than anything. I begged Mom to let me."

"I thought you didn't really want to," Colette said sadly.

Reese shook her head. "I would've sold my soul to get you away from her. I thought if I moved out, she'd stop comparing you to me and treat you better. I hate how she is with you. I always have. The reason I tried so hard to get her to clean up her act was for you. You deserve better than her, and I don't *ever* want to make you feel bad." She swiped at her tears. "But you snap at me all the time, too."

"Because you never just talk to me. You only tell me what to do or say I'm doing something wrong."

Reese sighed and leaned against the counter beside her. "Then that makes me a crappy sister, and I'm sorry. I promise to try harder."

"Then I'll try not to snap at you, too." She met Reese's gaze, her eyes sad and glassy but still wary. "Are you and Blaine still fighting?"

"No. We're working through things."

"Good. I know you don't like anyone in our business, but I like him, and he obviously likes you. He helped me a lot today, and he fixed that leak in the bathroom sink."

"I'm glad he helped you and that you like him, but how did

he even know the sink was leaking?"

"I told him. He said he was going to stick around until you came home anyway, and it's been broken forever."

"But you were alone. What if he was a bad guy?"

"Then you wouldn't have let him in the house in the first place."

"That's true. But from now on, you should let me know if anyone is here with you."

"Fine."

Reese felt like they'd stepped onto a broken bridge, and she trod carefully. "Blaine invited us to his father's birthday party next weekend. Will you go with me?"

"You don't have to drag me along on your date."

"It's not a date," Reese said.

"Uh-huh. I can stay home alone. I promise I won't throw another party. Blaine said if I did, he'd camp out in the yard and scare everyone off."

"I bet he'd do it, too." Reese grinned. "He invited both of us, Lettie. He wants you there."

"He probably thinks you won't go without me."

"That's *not* why he invited you. He wants you to meet everyone."

"Who am I going to meet at some old guy's birthday party?"

"I don't know. His family and friends? Ask him yourself. He's outside."

"Fine. I will." She strutted toward the door.

Reese exhaled with relief, glad they were talking instead of arguing.

BLAINE WAS SITTING on the steps to the deck when the screen door opened, and Colette walked out. He pushed to his feet, trying to read her expression. She didn't look angry, which was a plus, but she looked tense. "Hey, Colette."

She crossed her arms. "Do you want me to go to your father's party with you guys, or are you just afraid Reese won't go unless I do?"

Reese walked out behind her and mouthed, *Sorry*.

"I want you both there. It'll be fun. It's going to be at the Salty Hog, and there'll be lots of good food, music, and cake. You've got to come for the cake."

"We like cake," Reese said.

"Will there be anyone my age there?" Colette asked.

"Yes. All the Dark Knights and their families are coming. My buddy Saint has a daughter your age and a son who's a little older. I'm sure there'll be other teenagers, too."

Colette's eyes narrowed. "Why do you want us there?"

He climbed the steps, joining them on the deck. "I thought we were buds, and that's what friends do. They invite each other to hang out. I want you to meet my family and all the guys who will have your back."

"I thought *you* had our backs," Colette said.

Reese gave him a curious look.

Answering the question in Reese's eyes, he said, "I told Colette I wasn't going anywhere even if you decided to hate me, and I meant it." He turned to Colette. "I have your backs, and the guys have mine, which means they have yours, too. I'll even sweeten the deal. If you come to the party, I'll give you a ride on my motorcycle."

Colette's face brightened. "Really?"

"Is that safe?" Reese asked. "She could fall off."

"I'm not going to fall off," Colette said.

"I'll be careful," he promised. "And you're getting a ride, too, so get used to the idea."

Reese's eyes widened. "I don't know about that."

"Don't be such a fraidy-cat," Colette teased.

"I'm not," Reese insisted.

Blaine leaned closer, meowing like a cat.

They all laughed.

"You're a pain," Reese said.

"That's old news, Wilder." He looked at Colette. "So, we're on for the party?"

"I guess, but you better give me that ride," Colette said.

"You don't have to twist my arm to get me on my bike," Blaine said. "How much more do you have to do on that essay?"

"Just the conclusion," Colette answered.

"I could help you with it," Reese offered. "I loved *The Outsiders*."

The hope in her voice tugged at something deep inside Blaine. As much as he'd hoped to spend more time with her tonight, he'd much rather she and Colette connected and pushed in that direction. "A'right. Why don't you guys get to work on that."

They turned to go inside, and he headed for his truck.

"Aren't you coming?" Colette asked.

"Yeah, you don't have to leave," Reese said. "We could watch a movie or something afterward."

He felt himself grinning like a fool. "Sounds good to me. I'll heat up some spaghetti for you while you two are working."

"I want more spaghetti," Colette said.

"Spaghetti party it is," he said, and followed them inside.

THEY SAT AT the kitchen table, talking about Colette's essay while they ate. There was some eye rolling, but there wasn't any yelling. Blaine offered to do the dishes while they worked on the essay in the living room. He didn't know what had gone down between them when Reese had gone inside to talk with Colette, but whatever it was, it took the chill off the air between them. He even heard a few laughs while they were finishing the essay.

"That's a great paper, Lettie." Reese closed the laptop. She'd typed for Colette, just as Blaine had. "What movie do you want to watch?"

"I'm not in the mood for a movie. I'll be in my room." Colette grabbed her laptop and book off the coffee table and looked at both of them. "Thanks for helping me."

"Anytime," Blaine said.

"It was fun," Reese said.

"You have an odd sense of fun." She headed down the hall to her bedroom.

After her door closed, Blaine did what he'd been dying to do all night. He pulled Reese into his arms and kissed her. It was just a quick press of his lips, but it was enough to loosen the knots in his chest. "That seemed to go okay."

She grinned. "Yeah. I'm really happy. This is the first time we've eaten dinner together in forever, and I really did enjoy helping her."

"I guess your talk did some good."

"What you said helped. Opening up to her was the right thing to do. But it wasn't easy. She said some hurtful things, but they were true, and I needed to hear them to open my eyes to the way I've treated her. I've been so wrapped up in holding our lives together that I didn't see what my reactions were doing to her. But I feel good. At least for tonight. I have to be much more aware of how I speak to her."

"Funny enough, I'm working on that, too."

She laughed softly. "Will you stay and watch a movie with me?"

"There's no place I'd rather be."

"I haven't watched a movie in ages. The last thing I watched was *Big Bang*."

He cocked a grin. "They have porn on Netflix? I must have missed that."

"I meant *The Big Bang Theory*."

"You don't have to pretend. It's cool if you're into porn. We can watch it together but probably not when Colette's home."

"I'm *not* watching porn with you."

"You're right. It'll be better if we make our own."

She swatted him, and he laughed as she picked up the remote. "I have a Netflix account, but you're not supposed to use it at more than one household, so we can watch something on one of the free stations."

He lowered his voice. "Why do I find your rule following so sexy?"

"Because you think about sex all the time."

"That's not true. Sometimes I think about foreplay." He kissed her temple, damn glad to be there with her. "I bet you were a hall monitor, adorable in your little schoolgirl outfit."

"Your mind never stops."

Her wide smile told him she liked his mind. "You're lucky I wasn't around back then. I'd've had fun turning you into a very good *bad* girl."

"I wouldn't admit to that if I were you. When I was thirteen, you were…what? In your twenties?"

"I meant if we were the same age, but now that I know you're into older guys…"

She laughed. "Would you stop?"

"Probably not." He took the controller from her and signed into his own Netflix account. "Now you can watch anything you want."

"If they find out, they'll charge you extra."

"I think I can handle it. What do you like to watch besides porn?"

She narrowed her eyes. "How about we watch one of your movies? Let's see." She typed *James Marsden* into the search bar.

He tugged her closer and tickled her ribs. She squealed with laughter. "I'm a hell of a lot better looking than James Marsden."

"If you say so." She giggled, and he tickled her again.

Her laughter was music to his ears. He stole the remote and kissed her temple, keeping her close as he clicked on romantic comedies. "Here's one that's right up your alley. *How to Lose a Guy in Ten Days.*"

"I got that beat. I lost you in less than a week."

"Nice try, Wilder, but in case you haven't noticed. I'm still here."

She tipped her face up, smiling. "You must be a glutton for punishment or something."

Since you blew into my life, I have no idea what I am. "Let's go with *or something.*" He lowered his lips to hers in a tender kiss.

They decided to watch *How to Lose a Guy in Ten Days.* An hour into the movie, Blaine was completely enamored. With

Reese, that is. He didn't know what the hell was going on in the crazy-ass movie. Kate Hudson would've been gone from his life in the first ten minutes. But Reese? He could look at her beautiful face every minute of the day and never tire of it, even if they argued about everything under the sun. She was probably the only woman on earth who could get him to sit through a romcom.

She was tucked beneath his arm, her eyes at half-mast. He pulled the blanket off the back of the couch and put it over her.

She smiled sleepily up at him.

"I should go so you can get some sleep."

"No. Please stay."

"Then why don't you lie down? You had a long, emotional day."

"Can I lie on you?" she asked sweetly.

"I wouldn't have it any other way."

She lay on her side with her head in his lap, cute as could be with her legs curled up on the couch. He wanted to lie behind her and wrap her in his arms as she watched the movie. The urge was so unlike him, he was struck by two thoughts at once. *What the fuck?* and *That's a first.*

He tried to shake off the unfamiliar feelings taking root inside him and ran his hand down her arm and up her hip, squeezing the swell of it. He expected to feel a jolt of arousal, but knowing she was resting and safe by his side brought a sense of contentment. He hadn't felt content a day in his life. He brushed her hair away from her face and caressed her cheek, testing himself, waiting for thoughts of a blow job to creep in. But her sweet smile brought the urge to see her face on a pillow beside him in the morning. He was shocked, since he didn't do overnights with women, and much to his surprise, the thoughts that should send him running made him want to hunker down right there with her.

That made him a little edgy.

He'd never imagined himself enjoying spending time with a woman like this. He was the kind of guy who was always doing something. Blaine didn't *do* quiet nights with anyone, much less a woman who gave him grief about damn near everything he did.

He felt like a nitwit, bowled over by the depth of his emotions for a woman he hadn't even had sex with yet. But when the credits finally rolled, with Reese fast asleep on his lap, he wanted to carry her into the bedroom and sleep with her in his arms. He quickly nixed that idea for two reasons. The first was because that wasn't who he was, and the second? He was so damn glad she'd allowed him back in her life, he didn't want to risk her pushing him away again.

Then there was Colette—a third, and unexpected, reason.

He'd connected with her this afternoon, and he'd seen a sweet, vulnerable side, which she hid so well under all that rebellion. He wanted to help her, too. To give them both the stability they deserved. But now that she and Reese were making an effort with each other, he didn't want to screw that up.

He turned off the television and eased off the couch, putting a throw pillow beneath Reese's head. He brushed a kiss to her forehead and turned to leave, locking the door before pulling it shut. Hell if walking out of there wasn't the hardest thing he'd ever done.

Chapter Seventeen

KISSING BLAINE WAS euphoric. Reese wanted to live in that moment, with his fingers taking her to new heights as they ate at each other's mouths. They were lying in the grass, his thick erection pressing against her leg, and he was making those growling noises that made her feel animalistic. She gathered all her courage and pushed him onto his back, kissing his neck and working her way south. He was shirtless, his skin salty and hot. She ran her fingers down the dusting of chest hair, following the treasure trail to the button on his jeans, and nimbly set him free. His cock was heavy in her hand, thick and hot and bigger than she'd imagined, but she wanted him so bad, she lowered her mouth over it. "That's it, baby girl, take my cock—"

His deep voice startled her awake.

She was panting, wet between her legs, and *alone* on the couch. Disappointment gripped her, leaving her bereft. She closed her eyes and put her hand over her racing heart, trying to calm herself down. But the thrum of desire was still there. The feel of him and the sound of his deep voice had felt so real, her brain didn't want to make sense of it or write it off as a dream. She wanted to go back to sleep and pick up where she'd left off, which was a little nutty since the few times she'd taken part in that activity, she hadn't enjoyed it.

But I want it with him.

She stared up at the ceiling. There were a lot of things she hadn't enjoyed previously that she wanted to try with Blaine. His dirty talk and confidence, coupled with the way he looked at her and made her feel as safe as she did needy every time they kissed, made her crave more. She desperately wanted to see and feel that powerful man lose control at *her* touch, too. Maybe she shouldn't want those things so fast, given the fact that they'd only just made up, but Madigan was right. Beneath that rough exterior was a heart of gold as real and true as her desires, and she knew how rare that was.

She got up from the couch and peeked in on Colette on her way to the bathroom. She looked so peaceful when she slept, reminding Reese of when they'd shared a room and she used to read to her until she fell asleep. She missed their closeness and vowed to work hard to rebuild their relationship. She closed the door softly behind her and headed into the bathroom. After brushing her teeth and washing her face, she changed into sleeping shorts and a long-sleeved shirt, thinking about Blaine. *You got under my skin, buttercup. I care about you.*

The in-control man who said he didn't ever catch feelings was catching them for her.

Did he realize he'd revealed so much of his heart tonight?

She went to close the curtains and saw Blaine's truck parked out front. Her pulse quickened, and she glanced at the clock. It was *3:27.* Had he just left her house? She waited to see if he started his truck, but minutes ticked by and he was still there. She hurried to the front door and quietly stepped outside. The freshly mowed lawn tickled her bare feet as she went out to the street. His head was tipped back, eyes closed. She lifted her hand to tap on his window, and his eyes opened as if he'd sensed her presence.

He opened the door. "You okay, buttercup?"

She warmed with the endearment. "Yeah. Why are you out here?"

"Until we know that asshole dealer isn't going to come back, we're keeping an eye on you and Colette. Please don't give me shit about it. This is nonnegotiable. I'm sorry I didn't mention it earlier, but I didn't want to scare you."

Her heart filled up. "I'm not going to give you a hard time, but should I be scared?"

"No. We've got eyes on him. He hasn't made any moves in this direction. We're just being extra cautious."

"Okay. Then let's not tell Colette."

"That's the plan."

"Thank you for making sure we're safe. Were you out here last night?"

"Yes. Down the street, which is where I should've gone tonight, but I didn't want to be that far away. I left before you went to work so you wouldn't see me. My brothers and cousins and some other guys have been helping during the day, making sure you and Colette didn't run into issues when you went to and from work and school."

"You arranged all of that even though I basically told you to eff off?"

"Of course. I told you I had your backs. That's not dependent on how you feel toward me."

His heart truly knew no limits. "Can I come in there?"

"Hell yeah." He pushed the seat farther away from the steering wheel and reached for her. She intended to climb over him, but he grabbed her hips, settling her on his lap so she was straddling him. "Look at you." He cupped her cheek, brushing his thumb over her lips. "So fucking pretty."

His hand moved up her thigh, his gaze shifting lower, lingering on her breasts as his hand pushed into her shorts and he grabbed her ass. He growled, eyes flaming. "I want you bare-assed like this when you come to work tomorrow."

She was as shocked as she was turned on. Her dream came rushing back, making her ache for his touch. Before she could chicken out, she crushed her mouth to his, kissing him with everything she had. He tightened his grip on her ass, his other hand diving into her hair, taking her in a savage kiss that sent a thrilling mix of pain and pleasure between her legs. She ground against his hard length, earning the greedy growl that emboldened her to reach between them and fumble with the button on his jeans, determined to finish the dream she'd started.

He grabbed her wrist. "You want my cock, baby girl?"

"Yes," she said desperately.

"Tell me you want it."

She shuddered at the demand. Was he serious? His eyes bored into her. *Yup.* Dead serious. *I can do this.* "I want it."

"Tell me you want my *cock.*"

"*Blaine...?*" She lowered her eyes, too embarrassed to say more.

He took her chin between his finger and thumb, lifting her face so she had no choice but to meet his gaze. "It's just you and me in here, baby. If you want it, you have to say it."

Her heart raced, heat crawling up her chest as she said words she never in her life imagined saying. "I want your cock."

"How do you want it? In your pussy or in your mouth?"

Lust coiled hot and tight inside her as *both* sounded in her mind. "*Really?* You want me to say it?"

"Yes." His authoritative tone left no room for negotiation.

Ohgod. She was breathing so hard, her words tumbled out too fast. "Inmymouth."

"Good girl. I fucking love it when you tell me what you want." He stroked her cheek and moved his thumb to her lower lip. "You have no idea how badly I want to come in that pretty mouth of yours."

Wait. What? Maybe she hadn't thought this through.

His hand moved from her ass to between her legs, his thick fingers pushing into her wetness. She gasped at the intrusion, zings of pleasure shooting through her as he pumped them in and out of her.

"You like when I fuck you like this?"

"*Yes—*"

He quickened his efforts, making it hard for her to breathe. He withdrew his fingers so abruptly, she whimpered at the loss.

"Show me how much you want me." He painted her arousal on her lips and dragged his tongue along the same path. She tried to kiss him, but he drew back, eyes narrowing in warning, and pushed his damp fingers into her mouth. "Suck them like they're my cock."

She was so far out of her league, she couldn't even see the playing field, but she didn't want to stop. She grabbed his wrist with both hands, feverishly sucking and licking his fingers. He rocked his hips, his erection hard and insistent beneath her as he tangled his other hand in her hair, sending prickles of heat skating over her flesh. She moaned, her eyes fluttering closed.

"Eyes on me," he gritted out.

Her eyes flew open.

"That's it, baby." His praise spurred her on, and she continued licking and sucking harder, more dramatically, grinding against his shaft. "*Fuck.* You're going to worship my cock so good, aren't you?"

He pulled his fingers from her mouth, and in one swift move, he lifted her off his lap and laid her on the bench seat. His mouth came roughly down over hers, tongue thrusting deep, hips rocking to the same fierce rhythm, sending her into a moaning, clawing, lustful frenzy. His mouth left hers and "*No*—" sailed from her lips.

He was halfway down her body, his mouth on her stomach, fingers hooked in the waistband of her shorts. His head shot up, eyes filled with concern. "You want me to stop?"

"*No*" came out as a plea. "I…nothing…sorry."

His brows slanted. "Baby girl, if you need me to stop, it's okay. I respect that."

He started to unhook his fingers from her shorts, but she grabbed his hands, keeping them in place. "Don't stop. I just liked kissing you."

"Would you rather we just kiss?"

She was floored that he was giving her complete control. "*Nonononono.* Carry on…" She bit her lower lip.

"You're killing me." He nipped at her stomach, eyes still locked on hers as he stripped her bare from the waist down. Those hungry eyes moved between her legs. "*Mm-mm.* There's my sexy little pussy. Nice and wet for me." Her cheeks burned. He slicked his tongue along her center, drawing a needy moan from someplace deep inside her. "So fucking sweet."

He did it again, and she moaned louder. "That's it. I want to hear every sound you make, and when you come, it better be my name flying from your lips." He guided her legs over his shoulders, teasing her clit ever so lightly with his tongue. She felt her sex swell, her inner muscles reaching for him. He applied more pressure, causing a gust of toe-curling sensations. She dug her fingers into the leather seat, rocking against his mouth, her thoughts reeling as he took her to the edge of madness. He pushed his fingers inside her, stroking her until her entire body felt like a bundle of nerves. He withdrew and buried his mouth between her legs, using his other hand on her clit to perfection. Without warning, his wet fingers moved to her ass, teasing that forbidden spot, shattering her ability to think or speak. She couldn't do anything more than moan and plead and rock, chasing the pleasure mounting inside her.

"Ohgod, *Blaine...Don't stop.*"

He quickened his efforts, and then the tip of that wet finger pushed past the tight rim of muscles, catapulting her into ecstasy. She went off like a bomb, rocking and thrusting, crying out, grabbing his hair, trying to still her careening world. Then she was soaring, enveloped in pleasure, unable to see or hear or—

He intensified his efforts, sending her right back up to the peak. She exploded in a crescendo of lights and sounds and overwhelming sensations. Her climax felt like it lasted a lifetime, and when she finally sailed down from her high, he was licking her, soft and sweet between her legs. Every slick of his tongue on her oversensitive nerves earned a gasp or a whimper. His mouth came down over her clit, his teeth and tongue wreaking havoc with her senses. Violent waves of pleasure crashed over her as "*Blaine. Ohgod, Blaine*—" tore from her lungs like a curse.

She was shaking, her teeth chattering as she sank back to the seat. He kissed his way up her body, slowing to tease her nipples, causing whimpers and sharp inhalations.

He didn't relent. "Come for me again."

"I can't," she panted out.

"The hell you can't." He moved down again, using his mouth and fingers to make her come again and *again*, draining her of everything she had to give, until she lay spent and trembling.

He moved up again, kissing her deeply and sensually, filling her lungs with his breath. Her mind slowly started functioning again, bringing the feel of his strong arms around her, the weight of his body pressing down on her, the rugged taste of his mouth mixing with the taste of her.

He brushed his scruff along her cheek. "Your body is *mine*," he said against her lips. "Say it."

"Not unless *your* body is *mine*," she said groggily.

He laughed. "You and your fucking mouth."

"You like my mouth."

"You're right, Wilder. I do. Now say it."

"My body is yours as long as your body is mine."

He bit her neck *hard*, and she squealed with shock. "What did I tell you about defying me?"

"I don't make one-way deals with my body or anything else."

"*Why* do you need labels?"

"Excuse me? I'm not the one demanding ownership."

He gritted out a curse, and then all conversation was lost in long, luxurious kisses.

Chapter Eighteen

REESE KNELT IN the dirt, squinting against the sun as she planted the last of the flowers on the job with Blaine. It felt good to be working with Blaine again. Her phone vibrated in her pocket. She took off her gloves to check the message and saw Colette's name on the screen. Reese didn't want to count her chickens or anything, but Colette had actually thanked her again that morning for helping her with her essay.

Colette: *We have Netflix?!*

Reese: *It's Blaine's account. He said we can use it.*

Colette: *Cool. Tell him I said thanks.*

Reese: *Will do. Did you turn in your essay?*

Colette: *No, I did all that work for nothing.* An eye-roll emoji popped up.

Reese: *Sorry.* She added a face-palm emoji. *I'll probably always bug you about homework.*

Three dots appeared, indicating Colette was typing. Reese hoped she wasn't going to get mad, but the dots disappeared.

No text was better than fighting. She was pocketing her phone when it vibrated with another text.

Colette: *I'll probably always get annoyed at you.* A smirking emoji popped up.

Reese smiled as she thumbed out, *That's okay. I wouldn't recognize you if you didn't.* She added a laughing emoji for good measure and pocketed her phone.

She glanced at Blaine, hard at work finishing the patio, muscles flexing against his T-shirt. *You want my cock, baby girl?* Her cheeks burned, just as they had about a million other times today as she'd mentally replayed every sinful word, touch, and sound he'd made last night. She'd told Joy she'd added too much spice to her lunch and was having hot flashes.

She wasn't sure she'd bought the excuse.

Reese had no idea who that brave girl was in Blaine's truck last night. He was bringing out a side of her she hadn't realized existed, and she wasn't sure that was a good thing. What did it say about her that she enjoyed giving up control and obeying his dirty demands? She didn't want to be his sex toy, being told what to do at his whim. Good girls didn't act like that, and she'd always been good.

She couldn't afford not to be. Colette needed her to keep her head on straight.

She watched Blaine setting the last stone in place, brow furrowed in concentration. He wasn't all demands. He'd given her control of how far they went, and he was romantic in lots of little ways, with the things he did and said. He'd walked her to the door last night and had told her how glad he was that they were done fighting and how much he'd enjoyed being close to her. Of course, he didn't say it in those words. *I loved feasting on you, feeling you come on my mouth. Next time it's going to be my dick in your mouth.* She shivered with arousal. He definitely had a unique sense of romance. This morning he'd surprised her and Colette with muffins and had whispered in Reese's ear, *Leave the panties behind this afternoon, buttercup.*

She'd been revved up all day just thinking about showing up pantiless. She'd taken them off when she'd changed after work, and now she was wet just thinking about last night and what was yet to come. She bit her lower lip at the double entendre.

Blaine looked up, a slow grin climbing across his handsome face.

Her nerves flared. She was sure he could tell what she was thinking. She turned away, looking at the garden. "How does it look?"

"Hot as fuck."

She turned back and found him striding toward her with a predatory look in his eyes. "The *garden*, not my butt."

"That's nice, too." He pulled her into his arms, taking her in a ruthless kiss, and grabbed her butt with both hands, his long fingers sliding up the legs of her shorts. "I've been thinking about your bare ass all day."

"Is that all you think about?" she teased, secretly thrilled by his confession.

"No." He nipped at her neck. "I also thought about how sweet you taste and how good you're going to feel wrapped around my cock, and don't get me started on your mouth."

"Blaine..." Now she was really wet.

He rubbed his scruff down her cheek, heightening her desire. "And the feel of you grinding on my lap."

"That's *all* sexual," she pointed out.

He brushed his lips over hers. "Are you telling me you haven't been thinking about how good it felt to come until you could barely breathe? Because those innocent eyes of yours are begging me to strip you naked and bend you over the patio table."

"Blaine? *Honey!*"

Reese practically jumped out of his arms at the female voice. A pretty middle-aged woman was hurrying across the lawn toward them. She wore jeans and a red blouse, and she was carrying a large dish covered with tinfoil. Blaine gritted out a curse as she approached.

"Hi, honey." The woman kissed his cheek and smiled at Reese. "Hi. I'm Reba, Blaine's mom."

His mom? "Hi. I'm Reese. It's nice to meet you." She saw the familial similarities now: a hint of Blaine's smile, and her hair was the same pretty shade of mahogany as Madigan's. The muscles in Blaine's jaw were bunching, which she didn't understand, since he'd said they had a good relationship.

"You didn't tell me you were putting in more gardens, and look at that patio," Reba said. "Wow, you've been busy. I would have come out to help if I'd known."

"Do you work for Cape Stone, too?" Reese asked.

Blaine uttered a curse and scrubbed a hand down his face.

"Goodness no," Reba said. "I could never work for my boys. We'd probably kill each other. I run the office for our family business and leave Cape Stone to Blaine and Maverick. I was a little worried when they said they were putting all their money into starting a business, but I'm so proud of the way they've handled their company. They're great businessmen. But I love helping them pretty up their yards. My daughter and I helped Blaine plant the gardens around his patio and in the side yard. They've filled out so much since then."

Reese felt like she'd had the ground kicked out from under her. She folded her arms, glowering at Blaine. "You *own* the company?"

"I can explain," he said sharply.

"This is *your* house, and that must be *your* boat, and you lied to me about all of it?"

"Uh-oh. I'm so sorry," Reba said.

"It's okay, Mom," Blaine bit out.

"I think I'd better go. I made you lasagna." Reba handed Blaine the dish. "It was nice meeting you, Reese."

"It was nice meeting you, too." She forced a smile.

As his mother hurried back toward her car, Blaine said, "Reese, I can explain."

"Don't bother. You don't mind if I wash up in *your* house, do you?" She stalked toward the back door without waiting for an answer.

"Reese," he said angrily, coming after her. "You said you wouldn't walk away again."

"I'm not walking away. I'm giving myself space to think twice." She pulled open the patio door and walked into a massive recreation room with leather sofas, hardwood floors, a big-screen television, and a pool table and realized she had no idea where to go. "Bathroom?"

"This way."

He led her through a spacious bedroom with dark wood-and-iron furniture, into a luxurious bathroom with marble floors, granite countertops, an enormous Jacuzzi tub, and a shower big enough for several people with glass doors and multiple showerheads. She went to the sink and started washing her hands.

"Reese, I'm sorry I lied about my house and the job—"

"And owning the company," she pointed out.

"Technically, that wasn't a lie. We never talked about it specifically."

She glared at him.

"I'm sorry about all of it. I only did it because I knew you wouldn't take my money, and after everything you'd already been through, the idea of you driving strangers around or doing any of the other jobs you mentioned made me crazy. I hated lying to you, but I just wanted to help you and keep you safe."

"It's *my* life, Blaine." She scrubbed her hands furiously. "I have a right to know who I'm working for."

"You're absolutely right. I fucked up, and I shouldn't have done it, but those lies happened before last night. I would *never* lie to you again."

She looked at him in the mirror, seeing the anguish in his eyes, and she knew he was telling her the truth. "Why didn't you tell me last night?"

"I honestly didn't think about it until my mother showed up." He wrapped his arms around her from behind as she turned off the water. "I get why you're mad, but we have a good thing, buttercup. Let's not get lost in a stupid spur-of-the-moment decision I made to try to help you pay your bills when we first met."

She didn't want to get lost in that stupid decision, either. She just wanted a clean slate. No more surprises. "Are there any other lies I need to know about?"

"No. I swear it. I know we got off on the wrong foot, but I will *never* lie to you again, and that's a promise. I won't be another guy who lets you down. I give you my word." He held her gaze in the mirror. "I don't even need to think twice about it."

She couldn't suppress her smile. "I'm going to find a way to pay you back for everything."

"I don't want your money, babe. But if you're dead set on it, fine." He cocked a devastatingly sexy grin. "I need gardens all over my property."

She shook her head, smiling. "Don't be a jerk."

He turned her around. "I can't help it. I'm part jerk, but I fucking love being with you, and we both know you want me to be your jerk." He brushed his lips over hers.

"That's debatable," she challenged.

"No, it's not." He cradled her face in his hands. "You *want* this to be *my* face. You want these to be *my* lips." He brushed his thumb over her lips. "*My* neck." He kissed her there. "Tell me I'm wrong."

Her heart was racing, but she remained silent, because it would be a lie.

"That's what I thought." He ran his hands up her ribs and palmed her breasts. "These are *my* tits." Desire burned through her as he grabbed her ass, eyes blazing. "This is *my* ass." He cupped her sex through her shorts. "This is *my* sweet little pussy." He crushed his mouth to hers in a brutal kiss that sent her thoughts skittering away. "Do you want to be mine?"

"*Yes—*"

"Then you need to know what I'm really like." He turned her around roughly, so she was facing the mirror, and held her gaze in the reflection, jaw tight, eyes boring into her so powerfully she felt them reaching into her soul. "I'm not a guy who will spread rose petals on the bed for you and rub your back as a means to get laid." He put her hands on the counter, rubbing his erection against her ass, his eyes never leaving hers. "I get off on your innocence, but I also want to steal it. I fucking love your sweetness, and I don't *ever* want to ruin it. But you're a smart girl. Once you've been with me enough times, you'll figure out how to use it to your advantage, and I like that, too, buttercup. Challenge is good, but make no mistake about who's in charge. I like sex *my* way. Raw and rough and animalistic."

Her eyes widened. She was having flashes of *Fifty Shades of Grey*. She'd thought the heroine was crazy to go along with Christian's rules, but now she understood the thrill of it. The white-hot desire it sparked. But this wasn't a movie, and she needed clarification. "That could mean a lot of things. Will you...*hurt* me?"

His brows slanted like he was appalled by the question. "Never cruelly. Some of the things we do might be slightly painful, but the pleasure will outweigh the pain threefold, and I won't ever force you to do anything you don't want to do. If you tell me to stop for any reason other than the pleasure being too immense, I always will." He palmed her breasts again, teasing her nipples to hard peaks through her shirt, speaking huskily into her ear. "But you won't tell me to, because everything I do will bring you pleasure."

She swallowed hard, thinking about his finger in her ass and the shock of pleasure it had brought. She was so turned on, she was afraid her arousal would show through her shorts.

Eyes still trained on hers in the mirror, he brushed his scruff along her cheek. "Still on board, little bunny?"

"*Yes*" came out shaky.

"Good girl." He brushed his thumb over her lips. "Tell me you still want to be mine."

"I want to be yours," she said breathily.

His eyes flamed, and he wrapped his fingers around her neck. His hand was hot, his grip firm but not too tight. A chill ran down her spine, but she wasn't scared. She was *intrigued* and desperately wanted to experience whatever it was that he was warning her about. She tried not to let that frighten her about herself as he rubbed his thumb over the spot he'd bitten last night. "Wash that shit off your neck and let me see the mark I left there."

"I had to cover it for work, and I didn't want Colette to see it." She quickly washed off the concealer.

"You do what you need to in public, but when you're with me, I want to see all of you. Every mark, and you can be damn sure I'll wear the ones you give me proudly." He took a step back. "Take off your clothes, and don't turn around."

She was so turned on, she was trembling. It took a minute for her to process his demand. He pushed his hand into her shorts, his thick fingers sliding through her wetness, sending heat rippling through her as he spoke gruffly into her ear, eyes on hers in the mirror. "It's okay to want this, baby girl. It's okay to enjoy it." He massaged her clit, and she whimpered. "That's it. Let go of your need for control."

"It's not easy."

His eyes narrowed, and his lips curved up wickedly. "If it were easy, it wouldn't make your heart race, would it? It sure as hell wouldn't make you this wet. Now take your clothes off, or walk out that door. I won't ask again." He withdrew his hand and sucked his fingers clean. "So fucking sweet."

With shaky hands, she stripped naked. His eyes never left hers as he took off his boots and socks and stood behind her. Her skin was fair and splotched with pink from embarrassment; her stomach was far from flat. She had love handles and dimpled thighs, and they were all on display for him.

"There's the sweet girl who climbed onto my lap last night wanting my cock." He caressed her ass and grabbed it hard enough to make her gasp. "Remember how good my finger felt in your ass last night? How hard you came on my mouth?"

A shock of desire heated her inner thighs. "Yes," she panted out.

"One day I'm going to fuck you there."

She could barely breathe for the lust consuming her as he reached behind his back and tugged off his shirt, tossing it aside. He was still behind her, but her eyes locked on the ink beneath a dusting of chest hair on his pecs, along his shoulders and the tops of his arms, stopping just short of his T-shirt tan lines. Holy smokes. She had thought she wasn't attracted to tattoos, but she was wrong. She just hadn't been attracted to other men with tattoos. He pressed his chest to her back, fondling her breasts as he sealed his mouth over her neck, his eyes never leaving hers in the mirror, obliterating her ability to concentrate on anything else but the feel of his rough hands and hard body and the hunger in his eyes.

"Look at these perfect tits. I'm going to make them feel so good." His hand slid lower, and she instinctively sucked in her stomach. His eyes narrowed. "*Don't.* You're gorgeous, Reese. I get off on your curves. When you're with me, don't waste one second wondering if I'm attracted to you. Know I am, or you wouldn't be here."

Why did that make her even more nervous?

BLAINE KNEW HE should go easier on her, but he couldn't take it anymore. He needed to know she could handle him, or he needed to get her the hell out of his head for good, and the only way to do that was to push her boundaries. He excelled at pushing boundaries, but he was struggling to keep from easing the worries shining in her innocent eyes with a softer touch.

But softer wouldn't give him the answers he needed. He was already being far more patient than he normally would. He never coaxed or gave step-by-step instructions. If she were anyone else, he'd have torn off her clothes and bent her over that counter already or sent her home.

"Tell me you want to worship my cock."

She hesitated.

He gritted his teeth. "You went for it last night, Reese. If you can't handle this, you can't handle me. Either own it, or walk out that door."

She lifted her chin. "I want to worship your cock."

"Good girl." He stepped back. "Turn around and get on your knees."

She hesitated for only a second before doing as he'd asked. What a beautiful fucking sight she was, big blue eyes gazing up at him as he opened his jeans, perky nipples aching to be squeezed, drenched pussy begging to be fucked. He withdrew his cock, and her eyes widened. He was blessed in the dick department and was used to that reaction. He fisted his cock, giving it a few tight strokes. Her breasts rose with her heavier breathing, and she licked those luscious lips. His chest constricted.

Still stroking himself, he put his other hand beneath her chin, lifting her face. "This isn't going to be like a high school blow job, buttercup. I'm going to *fuck* your mouth, and you're going to learn to relax your throat so I can fuck it hard and deep. Now be a good girl and wrap that pretty little hand around my cock." As she did, he threaded his fingers into her hair and fisted it. "That's it. Let me feel you stroke it." She did as he asked. "Tighter." She tightened her grip. "Good, now give me your other hand." He guided it to his balls, showing her just how to hold them. "When I tell you to, you're going to hold my balls just like this. Now guide my cock into your mouth."

He watched half his dick disappear between her lips. Her mouth was hot, but her jaw was tense. Desire and worry battled in her eyes, tugging at his emotions. He struggled to push them away. "Grab my hips and hold tight, baby."

She grabbed him, innocent eyes wide as saucers as he withdrew, then drove in deeper. Her throat closed against the head of his cock. He tugged her head back a little. "Relax your throat, baby." He withdrew again, pumping deeper. She gagged. *Fuck.* He withdrew from her mouth, tugged her head back, and crushed his mouth to hers, kissing her hard and rough, thrusting his tongue deep, forcing her mouth open wider, eating up her moans and whimpers. With another tug on her hair, he broke the kiss. "You like kissing me?"

"*So much,*" she panted out.

"Then learn to suck me off, and my mouth will be yours."

She nodded with hunger in her eyes and guided him into her mouth. This time he pushed, thrusting harder, ignoring her gags, pulling her hair as he pumped deeper, until she opened for him. "Fuck yeah, sexy girl. That's it. Let me go down that throat." He pumped and thrust, as she clung to his hips, her throat opening for him, victory shining in her eyes. "Good girl, taking my cock so well." He gritted his teeth against the need to come. Her mouth was heaven, her throat tight around the head. Fucking perfect.

"Touch your pussy. Feel how wet you are from sucking my cock." She put her hand between her legs. "Now rub that clit until you come, and *don't* stop sucking while I fuck your mouth." Her skin flushed as he pumped his hips, her fingers quickening between her legs. She whimpered as he neared release, her body trembling. "Grab my balls with your other hand." She cupped his balls. "*Fuuck*, that's good." Her eyes and throat slammed shut as her orgasm hit. He pulled out of her mouth, grabbed his cock with one hand, still fisting her hair with the other, and pumped come all over her tits as she cried out with her orgasm, her body quivering and quaking. *"Fuck, baby. Fuuck."*

When the last of the aftershocks rolled through him, Reese's face came back into focus. She was watching him, breathing hard, her skin flushed, lips swollen and pink, breasts streaked with his come. His fucking heart brought him to his knees in front of her. He grabbed her face with both hands, caressing her jaw. "You did good, baby girl. Next time I'm going to come down your throat, and you're going to swallow every drop." He took her in a hard, sensual kiss, running his fingers through his come and smearing it down her stomach. "Are you on birth control?"

"Yes," she said, breathy and soft.

"Good." He pushed his fingers inside her. "I never fuck without a condom, but I'm going to fuck you bare. I want to feel your tight, hot pussy wrapped around me and brand you from the inside out." He took her hand and pushed to his feet, bringing her up on shaky legs. "But first I need to eat, and you need to come again." He lifted her onto the counter and stripped off his jeans and boxer briefs. He splayed his hands over her thighs, spreading her legs wide, and holding them there as he lowered his mouth and took his fill. She writhed and moaned as he feasted, fucking her with his tongue and devouring her clit, until she came so loud, it echoed off the walls.

As she came down from the high, he lifted her off the counter, setting her down on her shaky legs, and spun her around, widening her stance with his knees. He pushed his fingers inside her, and then he spread her ass cheeks, rubbing her tightest hole with her arousal. "I can't wait to see you on your hands and knees, ass in the air as I fuck you here." He let that sink in. "Does that turn you on, knowing I'm going to claim you here?" He pressed against that hole.

She swallowed hard, nodding, big blue eyes still on his in the mirror.

"Say it, baby."

"Yes," she panted out.

"Feel how wet you are from thinking about my cock in your ass."

She touched herself, her eyes brimming with lust.

"Good girl. Now hold on to the counter and watch me fuck your pussy, buttercup." Holding her gaze in the mirror, he grabbed her hips and buried himself to the hilt in one hard thrust. She cried out, clinging to the counter, eyes wide. Gritting his teeth against the need to pound into her, he stilled. "Need me to stop?"

"*No.* Don't stop," she pleaded.

"That's my girl." Holding one hip, he gathered her hair in his other hand and tugged her head back as he thrust and pumped, grinding and growling with the exquisite pleasure of her hot, drenched pussy surrounding him. "So fucking tight." He held nothing back, taking her roughly and demanding. Her pleas for more were music to his lecherous ears. He released her hair and reached around her, stroking her clit.

"Oh God. So good...*Blaine*—"

Hearing his name sail from her lips like a plea nearly did him in. "That's it, baby girl. Let me hear every fucking sound. Tell me to fuck you harder."

"*Yes.* Fuck me harder. Make me yours."

Those words unleashed a beast of desires. He jackhammered his hips and quickened his fingers, until his name shouted from her lips, her pussy squeezing his cock like a vise, drawing come from the depths of his soul. *"Fuuck—"*

He came so hard, he saw stars. He could do little more than curse as his body jerked and thrust through the last of his release. When he finally pulled out, he turned her roughly, claiming her mouth with such force, she bent backward. He wrapped her in his arms, holding her upright as he ravaged her, unable to get enough. He'd never wanted so viscerally, never craved or kissed like this, and he wasn't nearly done. He wanted to take her to his bedroom, tie her down, and use and pleasure every inch of her until she had nothing left to give.

But he wasn't a complete asshole.

At least not with Reese.

He broke the kiss, needing to see her face. She felt unsteady in his arms, her sated smile bringing an abundance of satisfaction. But it was those innocent eyes, glassy and brimming with lust, that made him want to take care of her. He allowed himself one embrace, soaking in the feel of her gorgeous, supple body. The urge to get lost in her instead of fucking her crept in, and he pulled back. He should help her dress and send her on her way. His body simmered at the thought of her walking around marked by him, but she had a younger sister waiting at home who didn't need her innocence shattered.

"Shower time, buttercup."

"You want to shower with me?"

Even after all he'd done, she was still so damn sweet. He gritted his teeth against the emotions that stirred. He'd never showered with a woman, but he was damn near salivating at the thought of showering with Reese. "I can't very well send you home to Colette smelling like me, can I?"

She absently touched her hair. "I can't get my hair wet."

"Then we won't use the ceiling-mounted showerheads." He turned on two wall-mounted showerheads, three body jets on either side, and the handheld unit.

As they stepped into the expansive marble shower, she said, "This is so extravagant. Do you have *parties* in here?"

"No. It helps my muscles when I'm sore. But if that's your way of asking if I'm into multiple partners, the answer is from time to time. Women only, that is, and never in my house."

"*Oh*," she said softly. "I wasn't asking, but I guess I was curious. I've never…done that."

Her innocence cut him deep, bringing a dose of guilt for getting off on stealing it, but it also had that green-eyed monster perching on his shoulder, digging its talons into his flesh. "Don't worry, little bunny." He wound his arms around her, the feel of her slick body instantly arousing him. "I have no interest in sharing you."

He kissed her neck the way he knew drove her wild, but she put her palm on his chest, pushing him back. "I thought we were in here to get clean."

"I never promised not to dirty you up first."

"You've had your fun. Now I want your sweeter side."

Was she joking? "I don't do *sweet*."

"That's too bad, because I enjoyed what we did." She stepped from his arms. "But if you don't do sweet, then you don't do *me*."

What the fuck? "Reese, I warned you that I wasn't a rose-petal guy."

"I don't need rose petals. You can be the boss in the bedroom. I don't mind being your plaything, or sex toy, or whatever you think of me as, but I need you to give me this."

He didn't think of her as a plaything or a sex toy, but he kept that from coming out. "You said you enjoyed it, and you came like you fucking loved it."

"I *did* love it. I honestly wasn't sure I could handle it at first, but you were right. It turned me on to give you control. But I've never done anything like that before. I just gave you *all* of myself, and now I need to get centered and know that I made the right choice with the right person, so if you want what we did to continue, then in here, I want you to touch me like you care, and I don't want it to lead to sex."

His heart hammered against his ribs, unease prickling the back of his neck. "*Reese,*" he warned.

"I don't think I'm asking for too much. You needed to see if I could handle you, and I just want the same respect. I *know* you care about me. You told me you do, and I'm sure on some level that's as terrifying to you as standing here naked is to me."

He swallowed hard against the truth in that statement and the hope in her eyes.

"I need this, Blaine." She'd never looked so innocent or so vulnerable. "If you can't give it to me, then I guess I do need to walk out that door after all."

There was a reason he kept walls around himself, but he couldn't look at the only woman he'd ever wanted to give more to and not give her this. "Get over here, baby." He gathered her in his arms, their hearts pounding rapidly. "I'll always try to give you what you need."

"Thank you," she said softly, the tension in her body easing a tad.

Ignoring the knots tightening in his chest, he stepped way

the hell out of his comfort zone and reached for the bodywash. He gently bathed her neck and shoulders and washed away the evidence of their passion from the swell of her breasts. His muscles corded, the devil in him aching to do a hundred dirty things to her, but after all she'd given him, the magnitude of trust she'd put in him hit hard, and his fucking heart spoke louder than the darkness within him, forcing him to give her what she needed.

He took extra care bathing the marks he'd left last night. She sighed gratefully. He felt the tension easing from her body as he trailed kisses in the wake of the suds down her chest, stomach, and that sweet haven between her legs. A new type of pleasure seeped beneath his skin. He found himself appreciating her in a different way, wanting to earn more of those surrendering sighs, to feel the way she relaxed when he touched her like this. The pleasure in her eyes was vastly different from the sexual gratification that had shone in them earlier, but it was every bit as intense, and he knew he'd crave that now, too.

He washed her back, kissing his way down her spine, feeling her breathing hitch when he kissed the soft globes of her ass. It was hell not taking it further, but this wasn't about him.

When he finally finished, the tangle of emotions consuming him had him turning away to wash himself.

She took his hand, shaking her head. "Let me."

"Reese..."

She ignored the warning, pouring bodywash into her palms. She ran those delicate hands over his shoulders. Her touch was sensual, a small smile playing on her lips, as if his giving her this comforted her in a way nothing else could. "You're so tight," she said softly.

He cocked a grin. "So are you."

She shook her head as she bathed his arms. "Don't you ever fully relax?"

"Yes. Like you, after I come I'm pretty relaxed."

Her smile widened. "We're quite a pair that way, aren't we? Two people who have to be lost in the throes of passion in order to relax?"

He wound his arms around her, his erection pressing into her belly. "A little relaxation sounds great right now."

"This is not supposed to be sexual," she reminded him, stepping back again.

"Talk to the boss." He looked down at his dick.

"No." She laughed, her cheeks pinking up. "That bad boy will rope me into doing more dirty things, and I have to leave soon to get home to Colette."

He knew she was right, but the emotions inside him were too big. He needed to get them out before they consumed him and pulled her into a kiss.

"*Hey*, now." She waggled her finger playfully. "What did I say?"

"There are worse things than me being unable to keep my hands or mouth off you."

"Very true, but I *need* you to behave."

She fucking killed him with that sweetness. "You're adorable, Wilder."

"You're not bad yourself, Wicked." She began washing the left side of his chest, tracing the boulder with the word FAMILY tattooed on it and the shading and grass around the bottom of the boulder that made it look like it was embedded in his flesh.

He'd never been studied so closely. The urge to stop her was strong, but it was no comparison to the weight he'd felt rising off her shoulders when he'd agreed to this, and he wasn't about to shut that down.

"I like that family is so important to you," she said.

"You're the same way, babe."

She shook her head, eyes trained on that tattoo. "Only with Colette. It's awful to say, but while I love my mother, it's more obligation than heartfelt."

He put his fingers beneath her chin, lifting her face, wishing he could obliterate the regret looking back at him. "That's not awful. It's *life*. There's no comparison between your feelings for a woman who has put you and Colette through hell and anyone else's love. You love hard, Reese, and it shows in everything you do for your sister." He pressed his lips to hers. "You're a good person. Don't ever question that."

"Thanks. Sometimes it helps to hear it."

He wondered if anyone had ever told her how special she was since she'd lost her grandmother and silently vowed to let her know more often.

She washed the right side of his chest, running her fingers over the tattoo there. "This looks like the skull on your club sweatshirt and the vest you wore the other night but with flowers around it."

"It is. The flowers are my mom's favorites."

"That's so sweet. I like this one, too." She touched the large infinity tattoo on his upper arm and shoulder. It was drawn to look like a road with a compass in the top part and a motorcycle wheel at the bottom. The upper-right side of the road shattered into birds that flew across his shoulder. "What does this one signify?"

"My love for the open road. Freedom."

"You said you're always watching over your siblings and cousins. Do you ever feel really free? Because I don't think I ever have until today. In here."

Christ. That made him want to embrace her and never let her go as badly as it made him want to give her every ounce of freedom she deserved. He'd enjoy every sinful second of freeing her from the confines that society had drilled into her head.

"That's when I feel the freest, too." He'd never admitted that to a soul.

"I like knowing that." She stepped behind him, dragging her fingers along the wings tattooed across his upper back. "You were hiding a lot beneath your shirts. Why don't you have tattoos where people can see them?"

"I got them for me, not to impress others."

As she washed his back, her small hands moved across the wings and over the names tattooed there. "Who is Hilda?"

"My grandmother. She passed away several years ago."

"Oh. I'm sorry." She was quiet for a minute. "Were you close?"

"Yeah. We talked a lot."

"Did she know all your secrets?"

"Not the dirty ones," he teased to take the weight off the truth. "My grandfather left home at sixteen to escape an abusive father, and he met my grandmother when they were seventeen. They were married a year later, and madly in love right up until the day we lost her."

"It must have been so hard for him."

Blaine swallowed against the emotions thickening his throat. "It wasn't easy for any of us. But you lost your grandmother. You know how it is."

"Yeah," she said softly. "Who are the other people? Ashley and Axel? Are they gone, too?"

"Yes. My cousin Ashley was a year older than Madigan. We

lost her to an accidental overdose when she was nineteen, and my uncle Axel was my mom's brother. He died from cancer about fifteen years ago." He missed the hell out of both of them, but he kept that to himself.

"I'm sorry." She pressed a kiss to the center of his back.

He soaked in her touch, wishing he could push her against the wall and bury himself to the hilt to chase away those painful memories. But he cared too much about Reese to use her in that way, and that realization fucked with his head anew. He drew her into his arms, taking one *last* kiss. But the urge to fuck away his hurt morphed into the desire to talk to her about it, sounding alarm bells in his head.

He was definitely on the verge of losing his mind. "You'd better keep your hands off me and let me finish washing up."

"Why? Did I overstep?"

"No. It's just getting late, and Colette's waiting."

Her brow furrowed, but he turned away, finishing quickly. He shut off the water and stepped out of the shower, grabbing a towel from the rack and holding it up for her. As he wrapped it around her, she gazed up at him with a dreamy, trusting look in her eyes, driving those confusing feelings deeper.

"Thank you."

He didn't know if she was thanking him for being sweet with her or for the towel, but it didn't matter. The fact that he even wondered *why* told him he needed to get his head on straight.

BLAINE CLIMBED OFF his motorcycle as Reese parked in

her mother's driveway. They'd passed Zeke on the way in. He was keeping an eye on Colette this afternoon and agreed to stick around a while longer so Blaine could take a ride to clear his head.

Reese looked like an angel getting out of her car in her shorts and T-shirt, smiling a little bashfully and holding the lasagna his mother had made. "Do you want to come in and have dinner with us?"

"Yes, but I'm not going to." He needed space to sort out his feelings. "You and Colette can probably use a little alone time, and I need to take care of a few things."

"Oh, of course you do. Okay."

He set the dish on the hood of her car and pulled her into his arms. "Listen, I have your money for making the gardens, but I don't want you to think it's payment for what we did this afternoon."

"I wouldn't think that, but keep it. I owe it to you anyway."

"I'm not keeping it." He handed her the envelope. "Use it for your school loans or the other bills that are piling up, or buy yourself and Colette something special. You worked hard for that money."

"*Blaine*, I can't take your pity money."

"I didn't offer you that job out of pity, and I'm not giving you the money out of pity. You didn't ask for the debt your mother left you with, but you took it on to keep Colette safe. I'm giving the money to you out of respect for all you're doing. It would mean a lot to me if you'd keep it." He kissed her forehead. "And if you don't, I'll go into your house right now and get the bills that are piling up and pay them myself."

"No, you will not," she said with a laugh.

"You know I will. The only reason I didn't do it yesterday

was because you were already pissed at me. I didn't want to give you a reason to be any angrier."

"That was a wise move, but I can't take your money," she said.

"Reese, please don't argue with me for the sake of arguing. If you're determined to pay me back, then when your mom is home and things are under control, we can figure it out. Until then, take the damn money."

She sighed heavily. "*Fine.* I don't want to argue."

"Thank God. Do you still need to earn extra each week?"

"This will help me catch up, and without having to pay her dealer, I can get by without it."

"Okay, if you need more—"

"Don't say you'll give it to me. I'm going to work for every penny I receive."

"I get it, my prideful vixen. I was going to say that we've got clients who would love it if we'd do landscaping with the stonework. I can hook you up anytime."

She narrowed her eyes. "*Real* clients or your family members? Or maybe your friends?"

"Smart-ass." He nipped at her lower lip, wrapping his arms around her again. "Yes, real clients. I know better than to lie to you anymore."

"You better." She wound her arms around his neck, smiling sweetly.

That smile got him every time, and sweetness rolled off his tongue without thought. "Thank you for trusting me today." She blushed, heat rising in her eyes, drawing him in for another kiss. "That blush…Have fun with Colette tonight. I'll be back later with my truck to keep an eye on things." He cocked a grin. "Come out and see me if you get lonely after Colette's asleep."

He kissed her again, hating to let her go.

She picked up the lasagna dish. "I don't know if I can take all that alpha bossiness twice in one day."

"If I had it my way, it would go on all day, every day."

Her eyes widened as she headed up to the door. *"Blaine."*

"You might want to get used to that idea." He sauntered over to his bike. "See you later, buttercup. Lock your doors."

"I always do."

When she closed the door behind her, he headed for the highway, hoping like a kid on Christmas Eve that she'd come out after Colette was asleep.

Chapter Nineteen

THE NEXT WEEK flew by in a whirlwind of busy days and sexed-up nights. They spent the weekend finishing the garden at her mother's house. Reese tried to get Colette to join them, to no avail. She and Blaine had a blast spraying each other with the hose and stealing kisses. At one point, an innocent water fight had turned into Blaine wanting to drag Reese into her bedroom, but with Colette home, he'd doused himself with cold water instead. Reese had made it up to him in the truck later that night, driving him out of his mind with her mouth. She could still see the look of pure euphoria on his face as she'd swallowed him down.

Blaine had joined them for breakfast a few times early in the week, and Colette had loved it as much as Reese did. Colette challenged or teased Blaine about everything from the treats he brought them to the way he looked at Reese. Blaine took it all in stride and had even driven her to school a few times. Seeing their friendship grow made Reese all kinds of happy. She loved that he never excluded Colette from their plans, and that had the added benefit of strengthening her relationship with her sister. They were getting along better, which made everything easier. Blaine spent evenings with them, too, and had fixed a dozen little things around their mother's house as he and Reese helped Colette with her homework. One night they'd all gone out for burgers and eaten at the beach. Reese had never seen Blaine as relaxed as he'd been that night, barefoot in the sand, stoking the bonfire, ever-watchful eyes keeping them safe. She didn't know if it was the sea air or something else, but *wow*. A relaxed Blaine caused a whole new swarm of butterflies.

The best news was that the Dark Knights had called off their stakeout since Ice and his two henchmen who hadn't yet been arrested had steered clear of their territory. Reese hadn't realized how much she'd worried about that whole situation until relief had swept over her like a storm.

It was a great week, although saying good night to Blaine was becoming increasingly difficult. Their endless kisses were as blissful as they were torturous, since she was always left wanting more. But he never left her hanging for long. When she'd told him as much Tuesday night, he'd shown up at midnight in his truck. A simple I-miss-you text had brought him over late Wednesday night, and since then, their good-night kisses had become see-you-later previews to sinful hours in his truck. He was just as demanding—*Ride my cock. Eyes on me. Suck harder. Straddle my face.* That one was tricky in the truck, but they'd managed it. She was becoming the type of sexual creature she never envisioned herself being, and she was loving it. But she knew she'd never cross those lines with anyone else. Blaine was a demanding lover, but his unwavering confidence and desire for *her*, combined with the way he claimed her body as *his* own, brought a level of trust and security she'd never known. For the first time in her life, she felt beautiful and wanted and cared for. Sneaking around was thrilling, and she couldn't be more grateful that he respected that Colette's welfare came first, but she couldn't wait to get a night alone with him in a real bed.

It was Saturday, and Reese was getting ready for Preacher's birthday party. She was slipping on her sandals after changing her clothes for the umpteenth time, when Colette walked by her bedroom. "Hey, can you zip this for me?"

"I thought you were wearing jeans." Colette zipped the back of her dress.

"I was going to, but I want to make a good impression." She looked down at her cute red sundress with tiny white flowers all over it. "Why? You don't like this? I've gained some weight since I bought it. Does it show too much back fat? Or is it my stomach pooch? Should I change back into jeans?"

"No. *God.* Back fat? Really, Reese? You look pretty, but it's just a birthday party and you've changed a hundred times. Why are you so nervous? It's not like you don't see Blaine every day."

"We're meeting his family, and all the Dark Knights will be there. It's a big deal that he's bringing us around the people who are important to him."

"You must really like him." She sat on the bed, looking cute in jeans and a black midriff tank top.

"I do, but it's complicated."

"Why?"

Reese had never talked with Colette about the other guys she'd gone out with, but she needed to stop thinking of her as a little girl. "We haven't been seeing each other that long, and I'm not sure how he'll treat me around everyone, or how I should act toward him. It's not like he's my boyfriend."

"He acts like he is."

She tried to figure out how to explain their relationship without revealing too much. "I know, but he doesn't like labels, and as you get older, not all relationships lead to being a couple, and he's much older than me."

Colette's brows knitted. "How do you know so little about boys?"

"What's *that* supposed to mean?"

"They don't ever know what they want until they can't have it, and even then, they're too thickheaded to realize it sometimes."

"How do *you* know that?"

"Because I'm not stupid. I've liked boys before. You got pissed at him, and he came back, didn't he? He may not say he's your boyfriend, but anyone can tell he wants to be. He looks at you like he can't *stop* looking at you, even when you're yelling at him."

"No, he doesn't." Reese laughed softly, but she was secretly overjoyed to know her sister saw it, too.

"Yes, he does. He's also here every night, and you two kiss like you'll never get another chance."

Reese sank down to the bed beside her. "You've seen us kiss?"

Colette gave her a deadpan look. "You kiss a lot, and even when he just kisses your cheek, it feels bigger."

"I guess we haven't been very discreet. Sorry about that."

"Why are you sorry? I'm not a little kid. Even if I hadn't seen you kiss him, I'd know you've slept with him."

"Colette!" She hoped Colette hadn't seen her sneak out last night.

"What? You act different. You're happier, and when he comes over for breakfast, you look like you want to eat *him* for breakfast. I've never seen you look at anyone that way."

"Ohmygosh. I'm the *worst* big sister ever. You shouldn't have to see that or know that about me."

"You're so weird. I'm happy that you're finally happy."

"You are?" Reese warmed all over.

Colette nodded. "Just don't let him hurt you, and be yourself at the party. You're great, and whoever doesn't think so sucks anyway."

Reese got choked up. "Why do I feel like we've swapped roles, and you're the older sister in this conversation?"

"Because you're a weirdo."

The roar of a motorcycle had Reese jumping to her feet. "He's here."

"I'll alert the press," Colette said sarcastically, heading for the door.

"Wait." Colette didn't stop, so Reese caught up to her and settled for walking beside her instead of the hug she'd wanted. "Thank you for talking me off the ledge."

"Whatever, weirdo."

Colette headed into the bathroom, and Reese answered the door with a happy heart and a nervous flutter in her belly. Blaine stood on the porch in a black T-shirt, his leather vest, worn jeans, and black leather boots. She knew what was beneath all that fabric, and as glorious as his body and all those tattoos were, it was the part of him she couldn't see that made her the happiest. The part he didn't realize he wore on his sleeve a little more every time they were together.

"Damn, buttercup." His eyes glowed with appreciation as he tugged her into a kiss. "You look hot."

"You get me hot."

"I'd like to get you naked." He kissed her again, deep and delicious, though quick. "Is it still cool if I give Colette a ride before we go?"

"Yes." She lowered her voice. "She said she's seen us kiss,

and she knows we've...*you know.*"

"Shit. How does she know *that?*"

"She said I act different. Happier."

His lips curved into a sexy grin. "I'm not going to apologize for that."

She heard the bathroom door open seconds before Colette walked into the living room and said, "Are you going to give me a ride on that bike?"

"Will it get rid of that attitude?" Blaine asked.

Colette smiled but quickly schooled her expression and crossed her arms. "I guess it'll depend on how fun the ride is."

Reese got a kick out of the challenging banter that had become their thing.

"Nobody but me gets on my bike with an attitude."

Disappointment rose in Colette's eyes. "Is that your way of saying you were never going to give me a ride anyway?"

Reese's heart squeezed at Colette's expectation of being let down. She didn't blame her. She still had moments of looking for the other shoe to drop, but Blaine noticed every little thing about her, and he was quick to reassure her. She knew he would find a way to do it for Colette, too.

"Nope. Wickeds don't break promises. But the attitude thing still holds true."

Her eyes lit up with her smile. "You're really going to take me?"

"With that smile? How can I say no?"

"*Yes!* Let's go!" Colette ran out the door.

"I don't think I've ever seen her so happy, but promise me you'll be extra careful," Reese said. "Please don't drive too fast or let her fall—"

He silenced her with a hard press of his lips. "Have a little faith. It won't be long before I get your pretty little...sorry. Your fine womanly ass on the back of my bike."

She laughed. "I don't know about that."

"I do."

COLETTE RATTLED ON about how much she loved the motorcycle ride the whole way to the party, and her excitement was contagious. "You need to try it, Reese."

"Maybe someday." Reese was nervous just thinking about it. The idea of holding on to Blaine was tempting, but what if something happened to her? Where would that leave Colette?

"*Soon,*" Blaine said authoritatively, underscoring it with a curt nod.

Her oversexed brain took that tone to more enticing places. As they turned into the Salty Hog parking lot, she tried to shut off that naughty part of her brain. She'd thought the party would be inside, but about two hundred people were milling around the grounds of the restaurant. They climbed out of the truck, and she saw a band playing eighties music on a makeshift stage.

She was glad Blaine had warned them about how many people would be there and had filled in Colette on his family members so she wouldn't feel so overwhelmed. Although the sight *was* overwhelming. Dozens of men wore black leather vests. Some of them looked rough, some were tattooed and bearded, and others were clean-cut, like Blaine. A group of teens was hanging out by the band, and children were darting across the lawn, gathered around a clown making animal balloons and climbing in and out of an enormous bounce house. Several long tables were draped in silver and blue and littered with food and drinks. Balloons danced from long strings tied to the legs of tables and the backs of chairs, and a massive HAPPY 60TH BIRTHDAY banner hung across the front of the rustic two-story restaurant and bar.

"This is how your family throws birthday parties?" Colette asked with surprise.

"When the president of our chapter turns sixty? Damn right. My aunts and uncles and their families are here from the East and West Coasts, and a bunch of Dark Knights came from other chapters to celebrate, too."

As they headed onto the lawn, Blaine kept his hand on Reese's back, pointing out his friends and family and sharing a little bit about each of them.

"Do your relatives feed their boys growth hormones?" Reese asked. "Your cousin Kingston is even bigger than Tank and Bullet."

Blaine chuckled. "My cousins from Upstate New York are the biggest of all of us. Kingston's father, my uncle Jacob, is six seven." He looked around and pointed to the tallest man Reese had ever seen. "That's him over there, talking with Denver Whiskey. He's also from Upstate New York."

"Some of your cousins are scary-looking," Colette said.

"They might look intimidating, but they're some of the best men I know," he said. "I'll introduce you, and then you can tell me if you still think they're scary."

Reese loved the way he encouraged her to make her own decision.

"Deal, but I doubt I'll remember who's who," Colette said.

"That's okay. We all answer to *Hey, you.*"

"Blaine, wait up."

Reese turned at the deep voice and saw a broad-shouldered, rough-looking guy with dark hair, wearing a black leather vest, holding the hand of the most gorgeous pregnant woman she'd ever seen, hurrying toward them from the parking lot.

Blaine lifted his chin in greeting. "Reese, Colette, this is my brother Maverick and his wife, Chloe." Chloe was tall and chic with straight blond hair. She was wearing a clingy mauve dress and looked like she had a basketball strapped to her otherwise-slim body.

"Hi. It's nice to meet you," Reese said.

"You, as well," Maverick said, nodding at Colette. "Blaine's told me great things about both of you."

"He has?" Colette asked skeptically.

Blaine's brows slanted. "Why do you say it like that? Of course I have."

"Because I'm a pain," Colette said.

"You're a teenager. You're supposed to be a pain," Maverick said. "And if anyone knows that, it's Blaine. He was a big ol' pain in the butt at your age."

Colette grinned.

"When is your baby due?" Reese asked.

"Not soon enough." Chloe rubbed her baby bump. "Next month. Madigan told me you guys had dinner together. It's too bad you couldn't join us last week while the guys were at church."

That was the night she and Blaine had fought. It seemed like it was a month ago. "Maybe another time?"

"I'd like that," Chloe said. "I'm looking forward to getting to know you and Colette, but if I don't get to a bathroom in the next five minutes, we're going to have an issue. This baby is sitting on my bladder."

"Go," Reese urged. "We'll catch up later."

"Nice to meet you both," Maverick said, and off they went.

"I'm *never* having babies," Colette said.

"You might change your mind one day," Reese said as they headed into the crowd.

She spotted Blaine's mother wearing a gorgeous red dress, standing by one of the tables with a tall woman with strawberry-blond hair and wearing tortoiseshell glasses and two incredibly handsome men wearing leather vests. One of them looked like a movie star with longish wavy silver hair, deep dimples, and friendly bright blue eyes. The other man had tattoo sleeves on both arms, slicked-back salt-and-pepper hair, a trim mustache and beard, and the same piercing ice-blue eyes as Blaine's. Those serious eyes were locked on them.

Reba waved.

"There's your mom." Reese waved awkwardly, remembering the circumstances under which they'd met last week. "Is that your father watching us?"

"Yeah. That's Preacher, and the other two are my aunt Ginger and my uncle Conroy. They own the Hog. I'll introduce you." He put a hand on Reese's back, leading them toward his parents.

"You call your dad Preacher?" Colette asked. "Is he religious?"

"No. That's his road name," Blaine said.

She looked questioningly at Reese.

"That means his biker name," Reese explained.

"Cool," Colette said. "What's yours, Blaine?"

His lips quirked. "According to your sister, it's Bulldozer."

"That's fitting." Colette laughed.

"Hi, honey," Reba said as they approached. "Reese, it's good to see you again." She hugged her. "I'm so glad my son didn't scare you away."

"He tried his best," Reese said.

"He's good at that," Preacher said.

"Thanks, old man." Blaine shook his head. "You guys, this is Reese Wilder and her sister, Colette. Reese and Colette, this is my mother, Reba, my father, Preacher, and my aunt and uncle, Ginger and Conroy."

"Hi," Reese and Colette said in unison.

"It's a pleasure to meet you both," Ginger said, giving Blaine an approving glance.

"It sure is," Preacher said. "I'm glad you could make it."

"Wilder, huh?" Conroy eyed Blaine. "That sounds like a challenge."

"You have *no* idea," Blaine said with a loud exhalation, and they all laughed.

"You sure know how to throw a party," Reese said.

"I told them not to make a big deal out of it," Preacher said.

"Oh, please." Reba slid her arm around Preacher. "You love being the center of attention."

"The center of *your* attention." Preacher leaned in and kissed her.

Reese warmed at their open affection.

"Here comes trouble." Conroy lifted his chin in the direction of two tall, broad, dark-haired guys heading their way. One had hair a shade lighter than the other, more tattoos on his arms, and wore a smirk, while the other guy looked relaxed with an affable expression.

"The big man made it to the party," the smirker said, eyeing Blaine. "And I see you brought me a friend, bro." He held out his hand to Reese. "Zander Wicked at your service. I'm great with my hands and even better with my mouth."

"*Zander,*" Reba chided.

"What? You taught us to be honest." Zander snickered, earning a laugh from Colette.

Blaine glowered at him.

"Sorry. I forgot his muzzle," the other guy said. "You must be Reese and Colette. I'm Zeke. Sorry about our brother."

"He's talking about Blaine," Zander said.

Colette giggled.

Reese smiled, loving their energy and Zeke's ability to roll with Zander's mischief. Hopefully, he'd be able to help them figure out what was going on with Colette. "It's nice to meet both of you." She looked at Blaine's parents. "I can only imagine what it was like raising these guys."

"Some days it was heaven; others, not so much," Reba said. "But I wouldn't trade a day of it for anything."

"Zekey! Zekey!" A little dark-skinned girl with puffy pigtails and the biggest grin and deepest dimples ran over and grabbed Zeke's hand. She looked about four years old, and she was wearing a fairy outfit and wings. She had a heart painted on her cheek and fake tattoos on her arms. "We *need* you to be our fwog pwince!"

"It looks like Papa Tank is your frog prince." Zeke nodded toward one of Blaine's cousins he'd pointed out earlier. Tank wore a sparkly pink crown, and he was sitting with two little girls on his lap, while a little fair-skinned girl with red curly hair drew on his arm and another little girl with long brown pigtails hung on his back with her arms around his neck.

"He's our fairy king!" the little girl told Zeke.

"That's the story of Zeke's life. Always the prince, never the king," Zander teased.

Zeke shot him a dark stare, then turned a kinder one on the little girl. "Why can't I be a king?"

"She's obsessed with *The Princess and the Frog* movie," Ginger said. "Just go with it."

"Yeah! Go with it!" The adorable girl smiled at Reese. "Hi! I'm Wosie. You're pwetty!"

"Thank you. I'm Reese, and this is my sister, Colette."

Rosie's dark eyes found Colette, and she gasped. "Our fairy queen! Junie! Lila! I found our fairy queen!" She grabbed Colette's hand.

Colette shot a panicked look at Reese. "*What?* I'm not a fairy queen."

"How do you know?" Zeke asked with a mischievous grin.

"She *is*! You are!" Rosie insisted. "We *need* you. *Pleeease* come with me." Big brown eyes implored Colette.

"How can I say no to *that*?" Colette relented.

"You can't," Zeke said.

"None of us can, and she knows it." Blaine winked at Rosie.

As Rosie dragged Zeke and Colette away, Preacher called out, "Just so you know, they sacrificed the last queen."

Colette looked over her shoulder and said, "Let them try. Our Dark Knight has my back. Right, Blaine?"

"Always," he hollered.

Everyone looked at him curiously except Reese, who fell a little harder for the man who'd had a more positive impact on her sister in a week than her own mother had in fifteen years.

"I can't believe she went with them. This is so good for her." As Reese said it, she realized she didn't mean just playing like a kid. She meant the whole event. These welcoming people, seeing what a loving, functional family looked like, hearing them joke around without any ire. It was good for Reese, too. She turned her attention to Preacher and Conroy. "Blaine told me about the Dark Knights watching over us. Thank you. No one has ever done anything like that for us. I never meant to be a burden to anyone, much less so many people. If there's anything I can do to repay you or the club, please let me know."

"You and Colette are not a burden," Preacher reassured her. "This is what we do, sweetheart, and we're proud to be there for both of you."

"And as far as repaying the club goes," Conroy said. "We don't work that way. Our payment, if you want to see it like that, is knowing you and Colette are happy and safe."

Blaine's hand slid around her waist. "What'd I tell you? You two are in our circle now. You'll never be alone again."

"Coming from you, that might not be so appealing." Zander chuckled at his own joke.

Blaine's hand tightened on her hip, like he was keeping himself from going off on Zander.

"I'm only kidding, bro," Zander said. "I talk shit a lot, Reese, but Blaine is the glue that holds us together. I got nothing but respect for the old guy."

"Old guy, my ass. He's the old guy." Blaine motioned to his father. "Happy birthday, Dad. I'm going to introduce Reese around."

Preacher nodded. "Enjoy yourselves."

"It was really nice to meet you, Reese," Ginger said.

"You, too."

"We'll catch up later," Reba said sweetly.

"I'd like that." As they walked away from his family, Reese said, "I really like your family, and Zander is too funny."

"He's a good guy with no filter."

"Well, I really like his oldest brother who also lacks a filter, so that's not such a bad thing."

"I don't lack it, buttercup. I get off on those pink cheeks of yours." He pulled her closer and whispered, "Keep that dress on tonight. I want to see it hiked up around your waist while you ride my cock later."

"*Blaine*," she whispered, cheeks burning, body not far behind. "Don't say stuff like that here. You'll get me hot and bothered."

"I like knowing you're wet for me while I introduce you around."

He took her hand, ignoring her whispered threats, and proceeded to introduce her to more family and friends, while whispering dirty things in her ear every time they walked away. Thrills ricocheted through her with every filthy promise.

When they neared the stage, she saw Madigan. She looked cute in a miniskirt and boots, dancing with an exotic-looking brunette wearing a dress almost identical to Reese's, but hers was white with red flowers. Madigan was a good dancer, but the brunette had killer moves. Reese watched with envy, remembering what Blaine had said about her dancing the night they'd met. *You might want to practice dancing in those heels... You were pretty awkward.*

"*Shit*," Blaine gritted out, snapping her back to the moment.

"What's wrong?"

Those muscles in his jaw bunched repeatedly as he guided her away from the crowd, tension rolling off him. "I need to tell you something. When I said I didn't bring women I'd hooked up with to these events, it wasn't a lie."

"*Okay.*" She didn't like where this was heading.

"We have a family friend who I hooked up with for a while, and we hang in the same circles. She's here."

Her chest constricted. "Are you still seeing her?"

"*No*, and I haven't for a long time. She's seeing the guitarist in the band that's playing tonight."

She looked at the handsome shaggy-haired guitarist and saw a few women watching him. "Which one is she?"

"She's dancing with Madigan."

Her stomach seized. "The gorgeous brunette?"

"Yeah," he said tightly. "Her name is Marly."

Reese felt sucker punched and didn't think before her insecurities rolled out. "Look at how she dances. I can't compete with that kind of confidence, and I'm sure it carried over into the bedroom. If a woman like that couldn't get you to commit, it's no wonder you don't want to commit to me."

"Reese, baby, don't say that. It was *just* sex. Neither of us was looking for more, and no one even knows we hooked up."

"How could they not? I'm sure you whispered dirty things to her at events like this, too. It was probably obvious to everyone that you were more than friends." *Why can't I stop talking?*

"No, it wasn't, because I never did those things with her." His muscles tensed, and he looked almost angry, like he was struggling. "Don't you get it? There is no competition. I've never taken her or anyone else to events, but I'm here with *you*."

Her heart raced as he took her face roughly between his hands, brows slanting, eyes brimming with emotions so real, she felt them wrapping around her.

"Hear me when I say this, Reese. I would take your awkward dancing and your sweet heart over her or anyone else, every minute of every day."

"You would?" came out as an incredulous whisper. The gravity of his words sank in the way rain fell from the sky, with purpose, weightless and soul-drenching at once.

"*Yes.* There could be a hundred women of all shapes and sizes lined up, and I'd *only* see you, with your innocent eyes and gorgeous figure. But it's not just your looks, buttercup. It's all of you. It's the things you say, how you think, and the way you take care of Colette. It's how you look at me, the way we connect, and, believe it or not, it's even the way you give me hell. I can't explain it, but whatever this is between us, it grows deeper every time I think of you."

Choked up for the second time that day, she took a deep breath. "I'm sorry. I shouldn't have said—"

He pressed his lips to hers, keeping her close as their lips parted. "Don't apologize for telling me how you feel, and please don't compare yourself to anyone else. You obviously have a skewed idea of how gorgeous and special you are."

"Okay," she said softly, floored by his outpouring of emotion.

"In case you're still doubting how attracted to you I am—maybe *obsessed* is a more accurate word—if Colette hadn't been with us, I'd've already fucked you in the truck."

Why did that Neanderthal proclamation turn her on so much? Unable to string words together for the lust pooling inside her, she merely blinked.

His eyes narrowed. "Get that look off your face, or we might have to take a ride."

A nervous laugh tumbled out. "Is that supposed to be a threat?"

"I don't threaten. It's a *fact.*"

She had no doubt it was. She caught movement in her peripheral vision and saw Madigan and Marly heading their way. Her nerves flared, and it must have shown on her face, because Blaine followed her gaze, and tension billowed off him again.

"Shit. Are you cool with this?" he asked. "If not, we can leave."

"After everything you said, how could I not be okay with it?"

"That's my girl." He took her hand, and happiness bubbled up inside her.

"Hi, Reese! I was hoping you'd be here," Madigan said excitedly and hugged Reese at the same time Marly said, "Hey, stranger," and hugged Blaine.

Reese's insecurities came rushing back. Marly was even prettier up close, with almond-shaped eyes, tanned skin, and a body like a Victoria's Secret model.

"I've missed your sorry ass," Marly said to Blaine. "You never hang out with us anymore."

"I've been a little busy," he said tightly. "Reese, this is Marly. Marly, Reese."

"I don't blame him for hiding you," Marly said appreciatively. "*Girl*, you are gorgeous. I bet he didn't want one of the other guys stealing you away."

Insecurities be damned, Reese liked her. "I don't think anyone could steal me away from him."

"You know we're talking about this guy, right?" Marly hiked a thumb at Blaine.

"She knows." Madigan took Reese's arm. "Come on. We want to introduce you to our friends."

Reese was excited to see Madigan again, and although she still had some unease about Marly, it wasn't enough to stop her from wanting to go with them.

"Hey," Blaine barked, looking at Reese like he was trying to figure out if he should save her.

"You've had her all week," Madigan said sassily. "Go hang with the other broody boys. She'll find you later."

"She's *fine*. We'll take good care of her," Marly promised as they led her away from him.

"Did we just clamjam you?" Madigan asked.

"Did you *what* me?" Reese asked.

"It's like cockblocking for girls," Marly explained. "And for the record, I've been telling her not to use that word for months."

"Oh. *Oh*. No, you didn't do that. We were just talking."

"More like sucking face," Madigan said as they neared Chloe and a group of girls standing by the water, watching them approach.

"You two are hot together," Marly said.

"*Thanks*," she said a little uncomfortably as they joined the others.

"Hey, you guys, this is Reese, Blaine's girlfriend," Madigan said.

Reese was about to correct her when she realized she didn't know what to say. He'd never used that word, but after everything he'd just told her, it seemed like he was saying it without saying it.

"Those are words I never thought I'd hear," a vivacious brunette said. "Hi, I'm Evie, Baz's bestie, and his assistant at work."

"Baz is the veterinarian, right?" Reese asked.

"The one and only," Evie said. "Is it weird that I feel like I'm meeting a celebrity? No one can believe Blaine brought a woman to an event. Everyone's talking about you two."

"They are?" *Gulp.* "That's embarrassing. We're not really boyfriend and girlfriend. We're—"

"Yeah, yeah. We don't care how you label yourselves. We see the sparks flying, and we think it's fantastic," Madigan said.

"Besides, we get the no-label thing. Wicked men aren't like other guys who go through a dozen girlfriends before settling down. They don't *claim* women until they're sure they're the one. I'm Sid, by the way, Gunner's fiancée, and if anyone knows about that, it's me." Sid was slim, with side-parted, shoulder-length hair a dozen shades of brown. In jeans and a Wicked Rescue T-shirt, she could pass for nineteen, though Reese could tell by her demeanor she was closer to her age. "Gunner and I were in the military together. I pined for him for *years*, but he was so hardheaded, he treated me like one of the guys."

"Until Sid played the player and got her man," a curvy brunette with red streaks in her hair standing beside Sid said. "I'm Steph, Gunner's other bestie. I've known the Wickeds and the Dark Knights forever. They're all a little stupid when it comes to women, and when they fall, everyone talks about it."

"I can vouch for that. I'm Leah, Tank's wife." Leah was soft-spoken with a Southern drawl and a mass of reddish-brown corkscrew curls framing her freckled face. She was holding an adorable baby boy. "They had a similar reaction when we got together. I know it can be overwhelming to have so many people trying to dissect your relationship, but they're good people, not the kind that talk bad behind your back."

"Well, that's a relief," Reese said nervously.

"We love Blaine," Evie said. "Even if he is a bossy bastard who needs his head handed to him sometimes."

"You can say that again," Madigan agreed. "But we're hoping he doesn't scare you away."

"Well, I guess it's good to be cheered on," Reese said. "I just don't want Blaine to feel pushed or my sister to hear anything that would make her uncomfortable."

"You can't push that man. He's unbudgeable," Marly said. "He's easily the most stubborn person on earth."

Reese had thought that was true, too, until he'd given in to her request to be gentle in the shower.

"Zeke introduced us to your sister when she was with the kids earlier," Leah said. "My girls *love* her. I think she's Rosie's newest obsession."

"Her treasured fairy queen," Chloe added.

"Rosie has been looking for their queen for weeks," Leah said. "Colette *really* connected with Junie, which is always a little harder than with Rosie because Junie's more reserved. She's like a little mother to both Rosie and our baby, Leo." She kissed the baby's forehead.

"Leo's adorable, and so is Rosie. I met her earlier, but I didn't meet Junie. Which one is she?" Reese asked.

"She has bright red curly hair, and she's wearing green fairy wings." Leah looked into the crowd, pointing across the grass to the fair-skinned redheaded little girl. She was holding Conroy's hand. "There she is."

"She is *so* cute," Reese said. "You look so young to have three kids."

"I adopted my brother's girls when they were born." Leah told her about how she'd raised her younger brother, River, after their father had died.

Reese never imagined she'd have so much in common with other girls. She was tempted to tell Leah that she was raising Colette, but she didn't want to get mired down with talk of her mother.

Leah went on to tell her how she'd lost River, and Tank and his family and the Dark Knights had been there to help them every step of the way. "So when I say I understand how overwhelming it can be to come into this group, I mean it," Leah said. "The Wickeds and the Dark Knights don't just help people. They take them under their collective wings, and before you know it, you're part of this incredible family made up of people from all different walks of life. After I lost my father, I never had anyone to help me." She looked at the gaggle of girls chatting around them. "Now I have more family than I could have ever imagined."

Reese was starting to understand exactly how special the Wickeds and the Dark Knights were. "I can't imagine going through what you have. I'm so sorry about your father and brother. I'm glad you have Tank, and all these friends."

"We *love* her," Madigan said, embracing Leah.

"And I love all of you," Leah said.

"Okay, huggers, stop hogging Reese. Hi, I'm Starr. I work at the Hog, and I have a little girl named Gracie. I'm wondering if Colette babysits." Starr had long, kinky blond hair and colorful tattoos on her arms.

Leah's eyes lit up. "I was going to ask, too. Ginger and Conroy do so much for us, it would be great to have another babysitter."

"I don't know. She's never babysat." Reese couldn't imagine Colette wanting to babysit, but she'd seen her playing with the girls, and she seemed happy. "I'll have to talk to her about it, but she'd probably need me to go with her the first time or two, to make sure it's not overwhelming."

"I can show her the ropes," Evie said. "I love babysitting

Gracie and the girls and Leo. Then you and Blaine could have a little private time."

That piqued Reese's interest, but she didn't want to seem needy. "You don't have to do that."

"It's no problem. I've got tons of experience with kids," Evie said.

"That's really nice of you. I'll talk with Colette about it."

"Great. Now give us the scoop on you and Blaine," Evie said. "Mads said you met at a party. How did you guys get together?"

Reese wasn't used to sharing her private life, but she liked these girls, and she didn't want to shut them out. "He's like a boomerang. No matter how many times I tried to send him away, he kept coming back."

"Really?" Steph said. "He doesn't strike me as a repeat performer."

Evie nodded. "Yeah. I think he's the king of once and done."

Reese knew better and glanced uncomfortably at Marly, who was looking at her. Her knowing expression sent a shiver down Reese's back.

"Okay, you guys, I think that's enough of that. Not everyone wants to talk about their sex life," Sid said.

"You're right. I'm sorry," Evie said. "Has Mads told you about the book club?"

"Of course I did," Madigan said. "We have a meeting in a few weeks. You should join us."

"It sounds fun, but I don't like to leave Colette alone at night."

"Blaine can hang with her," Madigan offered.

"I wouldn't ask that of him," Reese said.

"It's *Blaine*," Marly said. "He'll want to stand guard over her anyway."

"If Reese isn't comfortable asking him, don't push her," Leah said.

"Leah's right. We can have an afternoon meeting instead of evening," Chloe suggested. "When there's a will, there's a way."

"Careful, Reese. You're stepping from the frying pan into the fire." Sid shook her head. "First they try to get you to spill all the deets about your sex life, then they rope you into the book club, and the next thing you know, you're wearing leather pants and eating penis-shaped food."

"What?" Reese laughed.

"Didn't I tell you it was an erotic book club?" Madigan said. "We had a BDSM-themed meeting. Everyone had to wear leather, and Chloe brought erotic snacks, and I brought some toys to share."

When Madigan had first mentioned the book club, if she'd said it was erotic, Reese probably would have said she wasn't interested. But since coming together with Blaine, her views on a lot of things had changed.

"You didn't mention that, but the book club sounds fun." *Did I really just say that?*

"Did I hear book club?" A tall tough-looking and beautiful redhead asked as she joined them. She had tattoos on both her arms and ink sneaking out of the top of her tank top. "Hi, new girl. I'm Dixie Whiskey."

"I'm Reese."

"She's Blaine's girlfriend," Madigan announced cheerily.

"Then you definitely need to join our book club so he can reap the benefits," Dixie said. "But fair warning. One of our book club reads is responsible for Baby Stone." She patted her stomach.

The girls gasped. "Are you *pregnant*?" Madigan asked.

"Nine weeks!" Dixie announced.

The girls squealed and hugged her, all of them talking at once.

Reese took a step back.

Marly sidled up to her. "Hey," she said carefully. "From the look you gave me, is it safe to assume that Blaine told you that we—"

"Yes, he did." Her heart raced.

"Good. This is awkward, but you should know that there wasn't anything real between me and Blaine. We were both sick of the games people play, and one night we got drunk and ended up together. It was fun and easy, so we did it a few more times, but never with the hopes of it ever turning into more, and we ended it when I met Dante. The girls don't even know we hooked up, and I just didn't want you to think there was anything more between us."

Reese appreciated her honesty, but her heart was beating so fast, she was afraid to try to say too much. "Thank you for telling me."

"Well, you seem nice, and I have a feeling we'll be seeing a lot more of each other, so I'm hoping we can become friends."

Reese looked at the girls she'd only just met but could see herself becoming closer friends with and caught sight of Blaine talking with his cousins from Maryland. *There could be a hundred women of all shapes and sizes lined up, and I'd only see you.* He wasn't a man who said things just to appease anyone. He didn't have to tell her about their trysts, and he sure as heck didn't have to share his feelings the way he did. Being with Blaine tested her on many levels, but she was already stepping outside her comfort zone in other ways, and she and Colette were happier because of it. Blaine did so many things for them. Marly was his family's friend, and obviously close to Madigan. She could do this for him, couldn't she?

Gathering her courage like a cloak, she managed a smile and said, "To be honest, it's a little weird knowing you two were together, but I think with time we can get past it."

Chapter Twenty

"MAN, WE USED to rock these parties, and now look at you guys," Blaine said to his cousins Bones, Bullet, and Bear, who were holding their adorable toddlers. "You traded your beer bottles for baby bottles."

"Best thing I ever did was marry Finlay and have Tallulah." Bullet nuzzled his little girl's cheek. Her blue eyes lit up with her giggles. It was quite a sight to see a man who rivaled Tank in size and had suffered from PTSD so badly he spent years rarely doing more than grunting at people, happily in love and snuggling his precious baby girl.

"We're still badass bikers, right, Axel?" Bear tickled his dark-haired little boy's belly, earning sweet giggles. "Now we're just badass bikers with their badass toddlers."

"Badass Daddy." Axel patted Bear's cheek, and they all chuckled.

Bear cracked a grin. "That's right, little man. Just don't let your mama hear you say that."

"This is where it's at, man." Bones shifted Maggie Rose to his other arm, her fine dirty-blond hair curling at the ends. When Bones met his wife, Sarah, she'd had two young kids and was pregnant with Maggie Rose. The way Bones loved those babies, you'd never guess they weren't his biological children. "Ask Maverick in about six months. He'll tell you."

"Nah. Ask him in a year," Bullet said. "Nobody gets any sleep the first few months. You vacillate between being madly in love and out of your mind with fatigue."

The clown walked by waving balloon animals, and the kids started shouting for balloons, trying to wriggle out of their daddies' arms.

"Duty calls," Bear said. "We'll see you later, man."

Blaine felt a tinge of something akin to jealousy as he watched his cousins set down their toddlers and take their hands as they chased after the clown. He wondered how they did it. He looked around at the men he'd known since he was a kid. Some were old and gray now, others raising families or flying solo, and unfortunately, a few were long gone, their lives taken too early. They all dealt with demons. Their own and those of others. They suffered grief and other heavy shit, and he had no idea how they separated from the weight of any of it and were able to make promises of forever and bring babies into the world when there were already so many people who needed protecting.

He took a swig of his beer, watching Colette eating cake with Saint's kids, Kendra and TJ, and a few other teenagers beneath the umbrella of a tree. He wanted to stand by her side every minute to make sure she was okay and making good decisions. He'd had the same protective urges when he'd seen her reading to Tank's kids earlier. Zeke had been with her, and he knew he wouldn't let her flounder, but he'd still worried she might be uncomfortable. His mother had convinced him to let her be—*This is how kids learn to navigate tough situations*—but *Jesus.* Hadn't Colette been through enough tough situations for one kid? The instinct to build a fucking moat around her and Reese was as intense as the need to keep his siblings safe.

He looked across the lawn at his blond beauty talking with the girls and noticed a handful of guys checking her out. He didn't fucking like it, but he couldn't blame them. She was a vibrant buttercup in a sea of grass. He knew he'd done the right thing being honest with her about Marly, but her worries had slayed him. None of this was easy for her, and he wanted to *make* it easy.

His grandfather stepped into his line of sight, holding two plates of cake. "You look like you could use this." His craggy voice was comforting. It had been raspy and rough for as long as Blaine could remember, but his grandfather's wispy gray hair and the wrinkles mapping his sunken cheeks and square jaw were ever-present reminders that he wouldn't be around forever. Worst of all, his blue-gray eyes had never lost the emptiness that had appeared when his grandmother had passed away.

"I'm good, thanks, Gramps."

"I was counting on that. Hold this for me, will ya?" He handed Blaine the plate. "If your mama sees me with extra cake, she'll hand me my ass." Not only did they have to watch his grandfather around card tables, as he was a cardsharp, but they also had to monitor his sugar intake. His doctors didn't want him eating too much of it, and he was always bribing someone to get him a treat.

"You're going to get me in trouble."

"Not if you keep your trap shut." He stabbed the cake with a fork and ate a mouthful. "I hear you got yourself a girl. What the hell are you doing over here by yourself?"

"Just trying to get my head on straight." He stole another glance in Reese's direction, but the crowd had shifted, blocking his view, adding to his frustration.

"What's going on? All the talk about you two getting your goat?" he asked between bites.

"You know I don't give a shit what people say."

"'It's not the fork in the road that causes the quandary. It's the decision of which to take and all the possibilities of what could happen along the way.'"

Blaine smiled at the wisdom his grandmother had shared with him. "God, I miss her."

"You and me both, son. Every damn minute of the day. I know she was your confidant, and I can't claim to be as wise or as patient as my Hilda was. But she's still right here." He patted his hand over his heart. "So if you want to give me a try, maybe she can impart something other than shit for me to share with you."

"I don't even know where to start."

"Just spit it out. I'm getting older by the minute." He finished his cake and swapped Blaine's plate with the slice of cake on it for his empty one.

"It's just…Shit, I don't know. I brought Reese and Colette today without thinking about how big of a deal it was, but at the same time, I knew *exactly* what I was doing. I wanted them to meet everyone and be part of our world. I wanted them here with me. But now that we're here and I'm watching Reese get to know the girls and Mom and Dad and everyone else, and Colette is making friends and actually smiling like she's so fucking happy, the significance of it is…"

"Overwhelming?"

"*Bigger.* It's all-consuming. I take care of people in one way or another every day, but from the moment I met Reese, there was something else there. Something more powerful than me, which I didn't think was possible. I tried to ignore what I felt for her, but from day one she was never just a girl I was helping. She and Colette are *always* on my mind. Are they safe? Do they need anything? Are they happy or sad or frustrated?"

"Women have a way of getting to us." He ate another forkful of cake.

"No one ever has with me. But these feelings are so big and they hit so fast, I don't know how to handle it."

"It's scary, caring so much for someone."

"It's fucking terrifying. I don't ever want to go through what you did when we lost Gram. I don't know how you go on breathing every day without her, or how Ginger and Con survived losing Ashley. I've had these walls around me for as long as I can remember, protecting me from getting too close to anyone, and I never once wanted to bring someone into them. But when I look at Reese, I want to fucking demolish those walls. I want to give her and Colette the best life and fuck up anyone who tries to hurt them or get in my way. But there's still this part of me that *needs* those walls, because if something happened to them, I'd lose my fucking mind, and we've only known each other a couple of weeks. What the hell is that? What'll it be like a month or a year from now? It's like they've become a bigger part of me than my own identity, and I know that doesn't make any sense." He scrubbed a hand down his face, shocked he'd said so much. "It's messed up."

His grandfather finished the second slice of cake. "Walk with me. Let's get rid of the evidence." They headed for a trash can. "Women are put on this earth for many reasons, and one is definitely to mess us up."

"You say that like it's a good thing."

"Because it is. You know how fast I fell for your grandmother."

"Day one, and married her a year later."

"That's right. Your father and Conroy fell for their sweethearts the same way. Hard and fast. Look at Maverick and Tank. Wickeds are no-bullshit men. We know who we are and what we want, and when the right woman comes along, ain't nothing gonna stand in our way except our own damn selves."

Blaine threw the plate in the trash. "What are you saying?"

"I'm saying you're looking at this all wrong, and it's causing you to be your own roadblock. Let me ask you something. When you get on your bike and go for a solo ride, do you map out your route?"

"Hell no. Half the fun is seeing where I end up."

"Then why are you dead set on missing out on the adventure of a lifetime with the only woman who has ever brought your heart into play?"

"I'm *not*," he insisted.

"If you want to know what your grandmother would have said, that's easy. She would've looked you in the eye and said, 'That's a load of malarkey, honey.' She was all about the here and now, and she always led with her heart. She'd tell you to get out of your own damn way. Stop spinning your wheels and holding back feelings because you're afraid there might be an end to the road, and put that energy into making Reese and Colette's world everything you want, and they need, it to be. Otherwise, the pain of not doing it will haunt you until the end of the road comes. And trust me, regrets hurt more than any crash ever could."

"Do you have regrets about Grandma?"

"Some that are private, but not about loving her or how I treated her. You want to know how and why I'm still breathing?"

"If you don't mind sharing."

"Don't go blabbing it, or they'll think I've lost my mind. Every morning I get up and reach for my wife on the other side of the bed, and for a few blessed seconds, I feel her hand in mine and hear her saying, *Morning, handsome. Come over here and kiss me,* just like she did every day since the first time I woke up next to her. I breathe because she's giving me a reason to. I go on because I know I gave her the best life I could, and she wanted me to live the life she couldn't. At some point she'll tell me it's time to join her, and when that happens, I'll happily go. Until then, I'll eat cake and spend time with the grandchildren and great-grandchildren she missed out on so I can tell her about y'all when I see her again."

Blaine's throat thickened with emotion. He futilely tried clearing it. "Is that true? You hear her?"

"Absolutely. You'd hear her, too, if you ever let yourself."

Blaine steeled himself against the hope that brought.

"You're a damn fine man, and I could not be prouder to call you my grandson. But you'll never fully live until you allow yourself to face your losses and feel the pain you've been hiding from behind those walls you started building when you were nine years old, when you suffered your first real loss."

Blaine's chest tightened, and he narrowed his eyes. "What're you talking about?"

His grandfather eyed the people milling around them and lowered his voice. "When you suffered your first loss in your old man's shed. That's when you learned that turning off certain feelings was easier than dealing with them."

"How do you know about that?" Blaine had never told a soul about the old stray dog that had wandered into their parents' yard when he was nine. It was a tiny thing. A terrier of some sort. He'd had to share everything with his siblings and the kids they'd fostered, and he'd wanted that dog all for himself. He'd loved it so damn much, he'd named it Clover, because clovers were lucky. He'd secretly fed it, made it a bed out of old blankets, and had snuck out every night to sleep with it in the shed for almost three weeks. Until one awful morning when he'd woken up before dawn and realized Clover wasn't breathing. He'd been devastated, and he'd done the only thing he could. He'd wrapped him in blankets and buried him behind the shed.

"Your grandmother figured it out one night when we were all having dinner together. While the other kids were eating dessert in the dining room, you said you were going outside to play, but you went into the kitchen. You didn't realize your grandmother was in the pantry looking for something. She saw you going through the trash, filling your pockets with steak scraps from dinner. That's how she knew something was up. When we left that night, we went out back to investigate and found that scrappy little dog in the shed wearing the belt you cut up and made into a collar. You did a good job of carving *Clover* into the leather."

Even after all these years, Blaine couldn't think of that dog without feeling gutted. "I used the pocketknife you gave me for my ninth birthday. Did my parents know?"

"I went to clue in your father, and he said he'd been sleeping outside the shed every night to make sure you were safe."

Blaine looked across the yard at his father, emotions swallowing him whole again. "Fucking Preacher."

"That's love, boy. It can definitely mess you up, but it's worth it. If you want a shot at experiencing it with your little lady, I suggest you let her know before Bayside's most charming bachelor makes his move."

He followed his grandfather's gaze across the lawn to Reese and Baz. She was laughing at something he was saying, his cousin's panty-melting dimples in full force. *Fucking Baz.* Baz was a couple of years younger than Blaine, charming as a Southern gentleman, with puppy-dog eyes that made women go wild. He'd also inherited Conroy's ability to remain calm and rational in any situation. If Blaine was a bulldozer, Baz was a sailboat. But Baz wasn't a pushover. He was every bit as lethal as the rest of them, and he was the kind of guy Reese should probably be with.

That realization hit like a punch to the gut.

Blaine knew that while women called Baz *husband material,* Baz was in no hurry to settle down. But he hadn't been looking to settle down, either, and now he couldn't imagine a day without Reese in it. He knew better than to assume Baz wouldn't fall prey to those innocent blue eyes, her sweet demeanor, sexy-as-sin body, and sassy challenges. His hands curled into fists. He'd be damned if he'd let Reese get roped into Baz's net.

"Thanks, old man. The next time you talk to Gram, tell her I miss her."

"Tell her yourself."

And people say I'm pushy? Blaine set his sights on Reese and didn't slow down until she was within reach. "Hey, buttercup." He slid his arm around her waist, pulling her closer. "Hope you're not falling for this guy's charms."

"Just keeping her company, man." Baz shook his head.

Reese batted her beautiful eyes. "In case you haven't no-ticed, I'm a little busy falling for yours."

Baz arched a brow. "You'd better lock this one down before

she figures out what you're really like."

"I don't need to lock her down." He pulled Reese closer, lowering his voice for her ears only. "But tying you to my bed is definitely going to happen."

Her cheeks flamed, eyes riveted to his.

Baz said something about it being his cue to leave and took off. Blaine ran his fingers along her cheek and pushed his hand into her hair, kissing her in a way that left no doubt for anyone watching, and hopefully for her, too, that she was *his*.

REESE WAS LOST in the most incredible kiss of her life. It was primally possessive, consuming and *claiming*, turning her entire body to liquid heat, and leaving her head spinning and her heart thundering. She clung to him as their surroundings came back into focus. "Was that the equivalent of a dog marking its territory?"

"Isn't that what you wanted?" His voice was thick with desire, his eyes a little victorious.

"Yes, but it was one thing pulling me aside to tell me how you felt privately, but that was... *Whew.* I thought you didn't want to label us."

"I didn't. Now I do."

She felt a little giddy and was unable to resist teasing him. "You mean, you want to be my *boyfriend?*"

"We're a little old for that, sweetheart. I'm your *man*, and I don't want there to be any doubt in your mind or anyone else's who you belong to."

"You don't *own* me," she said cheekily.

"You're mine, and I'm yours. End of story." He sealed those words with another deliciously passionate kiss, leaving her a little weak in the knees.

"I can live with that."

He slung his arm over her shoulder. "Let's go check on Colette."

"She seems happy with those kids."

"I need to put a little fear into those boys."

"Why?"

"Because she's ours, and I'm not letting anyone disrespect her."

He rolled his shoulders back, strutting like the biggest cock in the henhouse, and Reese felt herself walking a little taller, too.

Chapter Twenty-One

BLAINE BARELY LEFT Reese's side as they mingled with his friends and extended family. People came and went, and as evening crept in, tiki lights were lit and dinner tables were brought out, battery-operated candles dancing in the center of them. Lights twinkled to life along the railings of the restaurant and illuminated the edges of the makeshift stage, giving the party a romantic feel. The din of conversation and laughter hung in the air as Reese refilled her iced tea, soaking in the sight of Colette sitting at a table, surrounded by new friends her age, looking happier than ever. She'd seemed to like it when Blaine made his presence known to the boys she was with. Reese could tell she'd felt special. She glanced at Blaine, chatting with Preacher at a table with a handful of their relatives, his arm casually draped along the back of the empty chair beside him where Reese had been sitting. *The Neanderthal in you is doing good things for both of us.*

Reba sidled up to her, smiling warmly. "I'm so glad I finally caught you alone. My son has kept you glued to his side."

"I think he's introduced me to everyone. I'm glad we have a moment, too. I wanted to apologize for the way I acted when we first met at Blaine's house. It wasn't my finest moment."

Reba waved her hand dismissively. "Don't give it a second thought. Young men don't always use their heads. It's up to us to straighten them out. Especially my boys. The only one who doesn't act before he thinks things through is Zeke. Maverick is better than he used to be. Chloe slowed him down a bit. I don't know if there's any hope for Zander in that department, but I'm a little surprised that Blaine lied to you. He's always been honest to a fault, even about things we might not want to hear, which means either you have bamboozled him or he had a very good reason to lie."

"I think it was a little of both, and to be fair, I had told a few fibs of my own. But I'm happy to report that we've gotten past all that."

"That's good. It's nice to see him letting his guard down. That's not easy for him."

Reese nodded. "It's not easy for me, either, with anyone. I spent some time with Madigan and her friends, and they're all so upbeat and friendly. I hope I didn't turn them off by not sharing much."

"I'm sure you didn't, honey. Not everyone needs to be an open book, and I have it on good authority that Mads is thrilled about you and Blaine."

She exhaled with relief. "I'm glad to hear that. I really like Mads and Leah and the others. They talked me into joining their book club."

"That's wonderful. They're such a nice group of girls. I take it you're having a good time?"

"*Yes.* I've never been to anything like this. I'm in awe of how well orchestrated it is. I have to admit, when Blaine told me how the families in the club are like one big, extended family, I didn't really believe that it could feel that way. But everyone has been so welcoming, they made me feel like I was part of the group instead of an outsider, and I've never seen Colette smile so much. Thank you for allowing us to celebrate with you."

"We're so happy you and Colette are here with us. Does that mean you don't come from a big family?"

"No, we don't. I guess Blaine didn't tell you about our family? It's just me and Colette and our mom, but I've pretty much raised Colette. Our mother is nothing like you and the other ladies I've met here." She looked out at the families and friends sitting around large tables, talking and laughing, support and camaraderie thickening the air. "This is good for Colette, to see what families and friends should be like."

"It sounds like it's good for you, too," Reba said thoughtfully. "Not everyone comes from a perfect family. Lord knows I didn't. I want you to know that Blaine didn't tell me anything about your family. I know the club was watching out for you and Colette, but even as the president's wife, I'm not privy to club business, so I don't know why they were, and I'm not asking for details." She took Reese's hand, giving it a gentle squeeze. "Some secrets are okay to keep, but if you ever want to talk, know I'm here for you, anytime, day or night, whether you're with Blaine or not."

Reese's throat thickened. "Thank you. I appreciate that."

"I hope we'll be seeing a lot more of you."

"Me too."

Reba motioned to Blaine, getting up from his seat, eyes locked on Reese. "Looks like my son is missing you. That makes my mama heart feel good. I'm going to grab a drink. I'll see you at the table."

As she walked away, Reese went to Blaine. He put his arm

around her, drawing her close. "Did my mom give you the third degree?"

"Not at all. I really like her."

He pressed a kiss to her temple. "I'm glad, and I'm really happy you and Colette are here."

"Me too, even if it was a little overwhelming at first."

"I'm sorry about dropping the Marly bomb on you and for Mads stealing you away so fast."

"I didn't mind Madigan stealing me away. I got to meet her friends, and I liked them too. The Marly thing was awkward, but we talked, and I'll get over the jealousy I feel."

He cocked a grin. "Why does that turn me on so much?"

"Because you're a caveman." She rolled her eyes.

He stopped walking, his gaze serious. "Don't be jealous, baby girl. You've already gotten more of me than she, or anyone else, ever has."

Her breath caught. She knew how much of himself he was giving by bringing them with him today, but hearing him say it magnified the significance. "I know, and that means the world to me, but it's not like I can just turn off the jealousy. If you met someone I had been with, would you be jealous thinking about them touching me? Wondering if I said the same things to them as I do to you?"

His jaw ticked, his eyes narrowing. "As far as I'm concerned, I'm the only man you've ever been with."

"Okay, then." She laughed softly. "I hope that little fantasy works for you."

"I've got to think that way, or I'll hunt the poor bastards down and tear their heads off."

She shook her head. "Has anyone ever told you that you're a little *extra*?"

"Only you, baby." He kissed her as they went back to their seats.

Zeke sat beside Reese. "Hey, Reese. Do you have a minute?"

"Sure."

"I don't know if you saw Colette reading to the girls earlier, but Rosie begged her to, and you know…nobody can say no to Rosie."

Worry tiptoed in. "I didn't see that. How did it go?"

"She struggled, but she handled it well. I was going to step in, but before I could, she closed the book and told them a story instead."

"I'm glad she didn't get upset. I didn't even know she knew any stories."

"A lot of kids who have learning disabilities find clever ways to hide them. She made up a story about a chipmunk in a magical forest, and the girls ate it up."

She remembers. Reese's heart thudded harder.

"I had a chance to see what was going on with her reading, and after the girls moved on to play something else, I talked with Colette a little bit. She's a smart girl, so I took a chance and broached the subject of dyslexia with her. I normally wouldn't do that without clearing it with you first, but we were talking about school and friends, and I told her how Zander had been a troublemaker when we were kids and how he used it as a way to distract people from realizing he had a reading disorder."

"Did she clam up?"

"No. She was relieved that she wasn't the only one who had to read things multiple times to understand them or who gets distracted when she's trying to concentrate. I asked her about issues that are common for people with dyslexia, and she seemed to answer me honestly."

"I can't believe she opened up with you about all of that."

"Zeke has a way of getting people to drop their guards," Blaine said.

"He must. Zeke, don't worry about stepping on my toes. You're experienced with this, so you have my permission to talk with her anytime. I wouldn't even have known she had this issue if not for Blaine, so thank you both. But what can I do to help her?"

"Technology has made it a lot easier to navigate than when Zan was in school. There are reading and writing programs that'll make life easier for her, and I showed her a virtual planner she can use on her phone so she doesn't forget assignments." He went on to explain the types of accommodations the school can make for Colette, and since it was almost summer break, he suggested scheduling a meeting with the school to get the ball rolling for next year. "I'd be happy to walk you through how to advocate for Colette, but it's best to teach Colette to advocate for herself. It'll empower her, and she strikes me as someone who would take pride in handling things herself, or at least leading the charge."

"She definitely likes to be in control of her life, like the rest of us, and I'd appreciate any help you're willing to give." Reese probably shouldn't be floored that a guy who had been a complete stranger before today was willing to go to such lengths to help them, especially since he was Blaine's brother, but she was. "I can't thank you enough. Can I get your number so we can figure out a plan?"

After they exchanged numbers, Zeke said, "Fifteen is a hard age, and feeling a step behind can make it even harder. I'm glad Blaine caught it." Starr walked by looking annoyed. Zander was close behind, trying to talk her into something. Zeke pushed to his feet. "I'd better go save Starr from Zan."

"Thanks, man. We really appreciate your help." Blaine motioned in the other direction. "You might want to check on Aria, too. Looks like the drummer's got her cornered."

Zeke's eyes narrowed, and he made a beeline for her.

Reese put her hand on Blaine's leg, leaning closer as Zeke walked away. "Your family really believes it takes a village, don't they?"

"Look around you, babe."

She glanced across the table at Preacher, holding Tobias's sister Carrie's little girl, Lynnie Loo, while Reba told her a story. A few seats down, Rosie was sitting on Ginger's lap, chatting animatedly with her and Conroy. Chloe was holding baby Leo, and Junie sat on Gunner's lap, making sure Chloe was holding her baby brother's head up.

"It's not just a belief." Blaine covered her hand with his. "It's a way of life."

Colette ran over, interrupting them. "Hey. Kendra and TJ volunteer at Gunner's rescue on the weekends. They invited me to help tomorrow from ten to two. Can I go?"

Reese had liked Colette's new friends when she'd met them earlier, and Blaine had introduced her to their parents, who seemed nice and low-key. Kendra was a willowy, energetic blonde, and TJ was tall and lean with a mop of light brown hair that hung over his eyes and a rascally grin. But the thing that had really struck Reese was the clarity and openness in their eyes. All kids had secrets, but theirs didn't seem like storm clouds looming overhead. "We should probably ask Gunner."

"He won't mind. Hey, Gun," Blaine called out, and Gunner looked over. "Would it be okay if Colette volunteers with Kendra and TJ tomorrow?"

Gunner flashed a grin. "Does she mind cleaning out animal cages?"

"I've never done it, but I don't mind," Colette said.

"How do you feel about playing with animals and feeding an ornery goat?" Sid asked.

"Have you met Blaine?" Colette eyed him playfully. "If I can handle him, I think I can handle an ornery goat."

The guys roared with laughter.

"Watch it, or I'll lock you in a pen, *Halfpint*," Blaine said with a grin, and more laughter rang out.

Colette crossed her arms, eyes narrowing, but her stifled smile warmed Reese's heart.

Gunner gave her a thumbs-up. "You're in, Halfpint."

"Yes!" Colette did a fist pump and beamed at Reese. "Can you drop me off and pick me up?"

"Of course."

"Awesome!"

She ran back to her friends, whose excited voices nearly brought tears to Reese's eyes. "I'm not dreaming, am I? Did that really just happen?"

"It sure did." Blaine put his arm around her. "How would you like to go for a ride with me tomorrow while she's with her friends?"

Feeling ridiculously happy, and closer than ever to Blaine, she whispered, "What kind of *ride* are you talking about?"

His eyes darkened, his grin turning wicked. "I was suggesting a motorcycle ride." He tugged her closer, speaking gruffly in her ear. "But now you're going to follow that up by riding my face while you suck my cock."

The breath rushed from her lungs, igniting the embers he'd sparked with his dirty whispers all afternoon. He'd been torturing her all day, so she decided to do it right back. "Now, that's just cruel. You have no idea how much I want to *taste you* right now."

His eyes flamed, and he gritted out, "Sure, I'll walk you to the ladies' room."

Before she had a chance to catch her breath, he tugged her to her feet and hurried toward the restaurant. "Blaine, we can't—" He crushed his mouth to hers, devouring her with a fierceness that left her wet, wanting, and practically salivating for more.

"The hell we can't." He led her into a staff bathroom and locked the door. "On your knees."

She dropped to her knees as he withdrew his cock and wrapped her hand around his heavy length. "Keep your hands out of my hair, or everyone will know."

"Fuck."

"It'll be worth it," she promised, and took him in deep, earning a low, lustful moan that seared through her like liquid fire.

"God, your mouth was made for my cock, baby."

Chasing his praise and his pleasure, she stroked and sucked, bringing him to a jaw-clenching, growling frenzy of greed. His hands fisted by his sides. "That's it. Squeeze tighter." She did. "Head back. I want your *throat*." She was quick to comply with his gruff demand, taking him deeper, his every muscle cording tight. "*Fuck it. Sorry, baby.*" Voice thick with need, he grabbed her hair with both hands and thrust *hard*, driving his cock down her throat. He let out a guttural hiss as he pounded into her, gritting out, "So damn sexy taking me deep." She grabbed his hips, pulling him in deeper with his every thrust. "*Fuuck yeah.* You want my come, baby?" Refusing to slow down, she heightened her efforts in answer. She felt him swell impossibly bigger and cupped his balls the way he loved, tugging just hard enough to sever his control. His hips jerked as hot jets slid down her throat. His fists tightened in her hair. *"Christ, Reese. Fuuck."*

She swallowed every last drop, soaking in the pleasure in his voice and reveling in the lust it stirred. When he pulled out, she licked her lips clean, desperate for more of him. He lowered his chin, eyes drilling into her with his every hard breath. He brushed his thumb down her cheek. "You're killing me, baby girl. I'm so obsessed with you, when you say shit like you did out there, I lose my mind." He lifted her to her feet, running his fingers through her hair. "My sweet girl. I shouldn't have dragged you in here. I'm sorry. I hope I didn't embarrass you."

She was touched by the unexpected sweetness. "You didn't. You said you were walking me to the bathroom, and you did, like a perfect dirty gentleman."

"I'm not sure anyone else would agree with the gentleman part." He kissed her. "I can't get enough of you, baby. Does taking my cock make you wet?"

Her desperation came out in a breathy plea. *"Yes."*

"Let me take the edge off for you." He hiked up her dress and tugged down her panties, his thick fingers finding just the right spot. "I want to fuck you against this wall." She whimpered needily, and he quickened his efforts. "But I don't have a condom, and you don't need to walk around with my come dripping down your legs." He crushed his mouth to hers, taking the edge off with one mind-numbing orgasm after another, until her legs felt like Jell-O and her body hummed with pleasure. She clung to him as he eased their kisses, breathing air into her lungs. He drew back, eyes lustful. Without saying a word, he gathered paper towels and cleaned her up. Maybe she should be embarrassed, standing there like a boneless doll as he washed her most intimate parts, but he was so tender and loving, she couldn't think past her swelling heart.

Blaine held her possessively and protectively close as they made their way outside. His mother was making her way to the stage. Blaine stopped in the grass a short distance from the tables and brushed a kiss to her cheek. "I just want to be with you for a minute before we join everyone else."

She snuggled into his side, feeling good all over. Colette was still with her friends, and if anyone thought twice about her and Blaine's abrupt departure, she couldn't tell. No one was paying particular attention to them, which was a relief.

His mother took the microphone from Dante, smiling as she waited patiently for the din to quiet. "Hi, everyone. It warms my heart to see all our friends and family joining us to celebrate Preacher's birthday."

"Preacher's the man!" someone hollered, eliciting applause and whistles.

"Yes, he is." Her loving gaze moved to her husband. "Most of you know that my granddaddy was the original founder of the Dark Knights. I was brought up around rough and tough guys, and not much surprises me. But nothing could have prepared me for the day Preacher rolled into Peaceful Harbor, Maryland. Imagine that fine man over there at twenty-one years old with tar-black shoulder-length hair and an arrogance that led the way when he swaggered into a room."

"Still does," Conroy called out, causing a rumble of laughter.

"Preacher walked into Whiskey Bro's, my daddy's bar, where I happened to be giving my brother, Biggs, crap about something."

"That's *still* an everyday occurrence," Biggs called out.

Reese had met the six-foot-five president of the Peaceful Harbor chapter and his wife, Red, earlier. He walked with a cane and spoke with a slow drawl due to a stroke, but that took nothing away from his powerful presence.

"Someone's got to keep you in line," Reba said. "On that fateful day, Biggs raised his voice to me, as siblings do on occasion, and Preacher, who didn't know me from Eve, cut through the crowd and planted himself between me and Biggs. He stared down my brother and said, 'How about you back off, big man, and learn some manners? That's not how you talk to a lady.'"

"That's my daddy!" Madigan hollered, and chuckles rang out.

"Yes, baby girl, and what a magnificent daddy he is. Preacher has always been fearless," Reba said. "It didn't matter that Biggs had a couple of inches and probably twenty-five pounds on him or that he didn't know anyone in town. He didn't seem to care that there were about a dozen Dark Knights surrounding him that night, with expressions that could make a dead man get up and run. Fearless Preacher stood his ground. At least until I asked him who the hell he thought he was." More laughter rang out.

Blaine squeezed Reese against his side. "Sounds like someone else I know."

"Needless to say, we had an interesting start," Reba said. "He and Biggs butted heads for quite some time, but nothing would dissuade my bossy man from getting his girl."

"Sounds like you come by your bossiness honestly," Reese said.

"I learned from the best." He leaned in for a kiss.

Reba walked across the stage as she spoke. "Preacher put a ring on my finger, and he didn't waste any time prospecting the club. Once he was a member, he learned how things were run, and a couple of years later we were settled here and gearing up to open the Bayside chapter with Con and Ginger." Reba set her eyes on Preacher again. "I have had thirty-nine years with the love of my life. A man who showed me the meaning of unconditional love, respect, and admiration. As many of you know, Preacher is not an easy man, but I'd venture a guess that he'd tell you I'm not an easy woman, either."

"You can say that again," Preacher called out. Laughter rose around them.

Reba held his gaze. "Honey, everyone here knows you wouldn't last a day with an easy woman." She looked directly at Blaine, and Reese felt him tense up beside her. "Like someone else I know."

"She's not wrong," Blaine said in Reese's ear, and rested his cheek on her head.

"We raised a gaggle of rambunctious children and shared the joys of success." Reba stopped walking, her gaze moving from Ginger and Conroy to Preacher. "We've faced unimaginable tragedies and devastating losses, and I can honestly say, I don't know how we got through much of it. But I know two things for sure. I couldn't have done it without Preacher by my side, and we couldn't have done it without all of you by our sides. I hope we are all blessed with many more years together. Robert Wicked, my heart, my soul, my love, this is for you."

The band began playing "Happy Birthday," and Reba proceeded to sing *Happy Birthday, Mr. President* slowly and seductively à la Marilyn Monroe, earning hoots, howls, and roars of laughter. Reese listened with awe, aching for that kind of soul-deep love that would not only stand the test of time but also make each partner stronger and better. She looked at the light in Blaine's eyes, the contented smile on his lips, and wondered if they could have that one day.

When Reba finished singing, everyone shot to their feet, giving her a standing ovation as Preacher made his way to the stage, where he kissed the heck out of his wife. Whistles, shouts, and applause rang out, and Blaine hollered, "That's what I'm talking about!"

"I see the apple didn't fall far from the tree there, either," Reese said as she clapped.

Blaine pulled her into a kiss that put his parents' scorching-hot kiss to shame.

As Preacher and Reba stepped from the stage, Dante said, "How about we bring the music back to this decade?"

The band started playing "Flowers" by Miley Cyrus. Madigan and some of the girls pushed to their feet. Madigan and Evie ran to Reese, and Madigan said, "Come dance with us!"

Reese waved them away. "I'm not a very good dancer."

"So what?" Evie said.

"We don't care." Madigan took her hand, dragging her toward the other girls, who were dancing like they were born to do it.

Reese looked over her shoulder at Blaine, hoping he would save her. He was *right* behind them, brows knitted, jaw rigid, giving her an *I've got you* look. She sent him a silent *thank you* as he said, "*Mads*," but one of his cousins from Colorado stepped into his path. The last thing Reese saw was Blaine trying to get around them as three more cousins joined him.

Shoot.

She stood with the girls, awkwardly trying to keep up and

follow their moves, but she was sure she looked like a flapping chicken. Colette was dancing with her friends, and even *she* had great moves. Evie said something about Reese being a fine dancer, but Reese knew she was just being nice. Evie put her hands in the air, and Starr and Steph moved in, dancing with her.

"You're doing great!" Madigan shouted.

I feel foolish. "I think I'm just going to go sit down." She turned to leave and smacked into Blaine's hard chest.

His arms circled her. "Hey, gorgeous. Where do you think you're going?"

"To sit down before I embarrass myself anymore."

"Not a chance. I want to dance with my girl." He guided her arms around his neck as "Trustfall" by Pink started playing.

"Blaine, you know I can't dance."

"What I *know* is that you're the only woman I want to dance with, and you have nothing to be embarrassed about." He held her tighter. "Close your eyes for me, baby."

She closed them.

"That's my good girl," he rasped in her ear. "Now just breathe, and give yourself over to me."

One of his hands pressed firmly on her lower back. The other threaded into her hair, holding just tight enough to prickle her scalp. Her body tingled with anticipation, budding desire, and that overwhelming sense of safety she felt each time she surrendered control to him, easing her tension.

"That's it, beautiful. It's just you and me. Picture us in your grandmother's garden, surrounded by all your favorite flowers. Feel my arms around you." He pressed a kiss beside her ear. "My breath on your cheek." He tightened his grip, one hand sliding down to her butt. "Feel me, baby. Let yourself go. Move with me."

She was utterly mesmerized by his voice, the words he said, the feel of his strong arms, the heat of his hand, and the sway of his hips. She couldn't think, but she didn't have to. Her body was already following his lead.

"That's it, baby." He brushed his scruff along her cheek. "You're the sexiest woman out here, and I'm the lucky bastard who gets to call you *mine*."

Her heart was full to near bursting.

He gently tugged her hair, bringing her eyes to his. "Still embarrassed?"

The depth of emotions brimming in his eyes was almost too much to take. "No, but I thought you liked it when I blushed, and I'm sure I was blushing a red streak when you came out here."

"Your pink cheeks are two of my favorite things, but not when they're caused by something that makes you feel bad about yourself."

Oh, her *heart*. "You're pretty good at this being-my-man thing."

He brushed his lips over hers. "I told you. You wreck me."

"If this is wrecking you, then maybe I need to go for full-on demolishing."

His eyes narrowed. "Don't push it, buttercup."

Chapter Twenty-Two

COLETTE WAS READY early Sunday morning without any prompting from Reese, and she looked cute with her hair pinned up in a high ponytail, wearing a light blue T-shirt and cutoffs. But it was the new light in her eyes that made Reese's heart sing. She must have thanked Blaine about a dozen times last night for taking her to the party, and she'd been talking about her new friends nonstop. She'd even asked Reese if she thought she'd be good at babysitting because Kendra had been babysitting for the past year and loved it. There was no way to know if her excitement would fade after a few hours of working at the rescue or not, but Reese was eating up every happy second while it lasted.

"I can't wait to see the animals," Colette said as they waited for the gate to open at the entrance to Wicked Animal Rescue.

"I'm sure you're going to have fun with them, but you know you have to work, right?" While Reese was excited Colette was interested in doing something other than hanging out in her room, she was also a little nervous about leaving her sister where she was expected to follow rules and actually work.

Colette rolled her eyes.

"I'm sorry. It's just that you've never had a job or volunteered before, and there's a lot of responsibility that goes along with it." The gates opened and she drove in.

"I *know*. I like animals, and I want to hang out with Kendra and TJ. I don't care if I have to clean out cages."

"Okay, *good*. I hope you really enjoy today." As always, Reese did her best to prepare her in ways their mother never had. "Remember, it's okay to ask questions if you get stuck and you're not sure what to do, and be sure to listen to Gunner and Sid. This is their facility, and it's really nice of them to let you help today, so please try not to lose your temper, and be careful not to go near animals that aren't friendly—"

"*Reese*, I can handle it."

"I know you can, but I can't help worrying about you. You're my sister."

"Well, *try*." She sat up, eyes brightening. "Look how big the shelters are. That must be Gunner and Sid's house." She pointed to a farmhouse in the distance. Gunner had given them the lowdown on the property, which was composed of several fenced-in acres, two large shelters, Baz's veterinary clinic, which he lived above, and Gunner and Sid's farmhouse. "There's Baz's clinic, and that must be Chewy!" Chewbacca, aka Chewy, was a beloved rescued goat. She pointed to the goat pen.

Reese laughed, excited for Colette to have something new and fun in her life. "I never thought I'd see you this happy over a goat."

"They're cute."

"If you say so." As she pulled up in front of the main shelter, she saw Blaine talking with Zeke. A few feet away, Gunner and Sid were chatting with Kendra and TJ. Blaine looked over as she parked, his sexy smile stirring those ever-present butterflies. He looked as different as Colette did this morning, and

Reese had to admit, as different as *she* looked, too. His eyes looked clearer, his sharp edges less severe. Could coming out as a couple have done that for him, the way it had for her?

Reminding herself this morning wasn't about her, she focused on Colette. "I didn't know Zeke was going to be here. Did you?" Colette hadn't mentioned the talk she'd had with Zeke last night, and she'd been in such a good mood, Reese hadn't brought it up.

"He reads to the animals that are having trouble acclimating. I might try to do that with him."

"Really?"

"Yeah. He thinks I might have dyslexia, like Zander. He told me about programs I can use and offered to show me some tricks that might help. See you later!" Colette threw open the door and ran to her friends, leaving Reese in awe of how easily she'd relayed that news.

"I'm so glad you're here!" Kendra's excitement floated through the open car windows as she hugged Colette, her blond ponytail swaying.

Blaine opened Reese's door. "Hey, buttercup."

He kissed her as she got out of the car, and she heard TJ say, "Hey, Lettie. I'm glad you came." She glanced over as his and Colette's gazes met and held, as her sister said, "Me too."

"Colette looks excited to be here. I'll tell the guys to keep an eye on her and TJ." Blaine took out his phone and thumbed out a text to Gunner and Zeke.

That protectiveness no longer rubbed Reese the wrong way, and she was thankful he didn't single them out in front of Kendra. "She is excited, and she just told me very matter-of-factly that Zeke thinks she has dyslexia. She said she might read to the animals with him so he can help her. Does he always read to the animals?"

"No. He was just telling me he thought it might be a good way to work with Colette."

"That's so nice of him to give up a Sunday morning. Even though he said he'd be happy to help us come up with a plan, I thought helping her one-on-one would fall solely on my shoulders and started researching dyslexia in teens last night." She glanced at Colette, smiling and nodding as she talked with the others. How had their worlds changed so fast? One glance at her bulldozer and she had her answer.

"Remember when I said you didn't have to bear the burden alone anymore?"

"Yes, but experiencing it is totally different from hearing it. Thank you for not staying away when I pushed you to."

"Trust me, buttercup. I tried like hell to stay away. I didn't want my darkness to dim your light, but it's like the universe wouldn't let me." He tucked her hair behind her ear. The intimate touch was as unexpected as the clarity in his eyes.

Her heart squeezed. She'd never thought of herself as having *light*, but he was helping her see everything differently. "You didn't dim my light. You blazed a path that uncovered it and helped *me* finally see it."

He pressed his lips to hers. "Are you ready to ride today?"

"I'm nervous, but Lettie still raves about how much fun she had when you took her for a ride, so let's say I'm cautiously excited."

"That's my girl. Come on." He took her hand, and they headed over to the others.

"Hi, Reese." Kendra smiled brightly. "Thanks for letting Colette come today."

TJ pushed his hands into the front pockets of his jeans,

moving his hair out of his eyes with a flick of his chin. "Yeah, thanks."

"Thanks for inviting her. I hope you guys have fun." She turned to Zeke, Gunner, and Sid. "Thanks for letting Colette help." She held Zeke's gaze, sending extra gratitude his way without calling attention to Colette. "And for taking the extra time to show her the ropes."

"We need all the help we can get," Gunner said.

"And we're looking forward to getting to know Colette better," Sid added, earning a proud grin from Colette.

Now, *that* was a sight to behold.

Blaine set a serious stare on Colette. "Remember to listen to the adults. Don't leave the property, don't cause trouble, and—"

"And there he is, folks," Gunner said. "Buzzkill Blaine, crushing teenage girls' social lives for decades."

Everyone laughed, except Blaine, who shot him a narrow-eyed look.

"We were around when Ashley and Mads were teenagers," Gunner reminded him. "We can handle this."

"Hey. Buzzkill." Colette crossed her arms and lifted her chin. "Don't crash with Reese on the bike, and don't upset her, or you'll have *me* to deal with."

"Someone's got your number," Sid teased in a singsong voice.

Blaine pointed two fingers at his eyes and then at Colette, indicating he was watching her.

"Get outta here, and go have some fun before you kill ours." Gunner gave Blaine a shove toward the parking lot. "Let's go inside and get this party started."

Reese looked over her shoulder as they headed to Blaine's motorcycle and saw Colette heading inside with the others.

Blaine gave her the same lecture he'd given Colette on motorcycle safety, and then he took her hand, his expression turning thoughtful. "This is *your* ride, baby. Lettie is safe. She's with friends, and she's happy. This is your chance to let go of your responsibilities and just be a twenty-six-year-old woman who's out with her man, enjoying the open road."

"That sounds amazing, but it's not like I can just stop worrying about her. What if she doesn't like it or gets bored in an hour?"

"If anyone knows how hard it is to let go, it's me, but as Zeke reminded me, kids don't always like what they sign up for. That's part of life. She needs to learn to handle it without losing her shit, and she will. She tries your patience, but she's not a child, and she's in good hands. They'd never let anything happen to her, and we have to trust that."

"I can't promise, but I'll try." She got anxious just thinking about trying to let her worries go, but she was also touched that he'd had the same thoughts and had spoken to Zeke about it.

"Attagirl." He helped her onto the bike and handed her a helmet. "Don't put that on yet." He stepped back and admired her.

"What are you doing?"

"Burning the image of you on my bike into my brain." He came closer, taking her chin between his fingers and thumb. "And thinking about fucking you on it." He lowered his mouth to hers in a toe-curling kiss. "Oh yeah, baby. We're definitely going to do that."

Her body heated at the thought, but she was feeling spunky. "You'll do that *if* and *when* I let you."

A wolfish grin appeared. "You know how I love your challenges."

"Yes, I do." She put on her helmet as he climbed onto the bike.

She wrapped her arms around him, anticipation mounting inside her. He tucked his fingers under her thighs and hauled her forward. Then he took her hand and lowered it over his crotch, squeezing tight.

"Blaine!"

"That's how I'd *like* to ride." He pressed her hands to his ribs. "But this is how we're going to ride."

"Someone could have seen you put my hand there, you know."

He glanced over her shoulder. "Does that idea turn you on?"

"Ohmygosh. *Stop it.*" She laughed, but there was no denying the thrill his question brought. "One day I'm going to learn how to stop blushing so you can't make me do it."

"No, you won't. You like hearing all my dirty thoughts."

She didn't even try to deny it.

The bike roared to life, the vibrations heightening her already titillated body. She held on tight as he cruised down the long driveway, his back muscles flexing against her chest, abs rigid beneath her palms. Her pulse raced, her temperature rising despite the brisk air kissing her skin. The gate opened, and he drove through it but stopped at the main road.

He took off his helmet, turning to look at her. "You okay?"

To her surprise, she wasn't scared. She was exhilarated and nodded excitedly.

He faced front and lifted her hand, pressing a kiss to her palm before flattening it on his stomach and putting on his helmet again. She soaked up that unexpectedly sweet gesture. Then they were off, cruising down the main road, the roar of the engine competing with the blood rushing through her ears.

When he turned onto the highway, they picked up speed. The scintillating vibrations and the feel of Blaine's powerful body brought a thrum of desire. But she'd spent so many years stressing about every little thing and watching out for Colette without anyone to lean on or hand the reins to for even a minute. Her mind was now tiptoeing in the garden he'd seeded with the idea of letting go. As the world sped by, she reminded herself that Colette really *was* safe, and she truly was happier than ever. Little by little she pushed those worries aside, making way for a burgeoning sense of freedom she barely recognized.

And craved.

Holding Blaine tighter, she forced herself to let go a little more with every passing mile. By the time they crossed the bridge leading them off the Cape, that sense of freedom pounded inside her like a second heart. The air felt crisper, the sky looked bluer, and she allowed herself to revel in it.

Miles later, they turned off the highway, weaving through back roads. Reese had no idea where they were, and she was too busy enjoying her newfound freedom to care, just as she reveled in pleasure every time she surrendered control to Blaine. Her analytical brain picked that apart, and she realized the act of surrendering was incredibly powerful. In the next breath, an even bigger revelation hit her. By surrendering, she had actually taken control of her sexuality and her worries. As that sank in, she felt braver, more empowered.

Like there was nothing she *couldn't* do.

They turned onto a winding dirt road buffered by trees, her emotions deepening for the man who was helping her learn to let go and discover who she was as a woman, separate from her role as Colette's caretaker or her mother's babysitter.

A breathtaking view of the ocean appeared in the distance, and she innately knew it looked a hundred times more beautiful now than it would if she'd stumbled upon it by herself, because she was with Blaine. Sharing in one of *his* greatest pleasures: the open road.

She wondered if he was thinking about her, too, feeling anything like the overpowering emotions billowing inside her. Or if he was too focused on keeping them safe to think about anything else.

BLAINE TRIED TO sort out the emotions pummeling him as he drove to the end of the dirt road. Seeing his beautiful bunny on the back of his bike had gotten him all twisted up inside. But having her wrapped around him? Knowing she trusted him with not just her body but her life? *That* did him in. He'd thought they'd go for a long ride and stay on the road until it was time to pick up Colette. But his damn heart, the organ that had lain dormant for so many years, had other ideas, leading him to the place that had been so sacred, he'd never shared it with anyone.

He cut the engine and planted his boots on the ground, trying to center himself before climbing off the bike.

It didn't work.

He climbed off the bike and took off his and Reese's helmets, setting them on the seat.

"That was amazing," she gushed as he helped her off the bike. "And look at this view. Where are we?"

She was even more radiant than usual, driving those feelings deeper. He tried to distract himself from them. "If I told you,

I'd have to kill you."

Failing to ground himself yet again, her sweet laugh had him pulling her in for a kiss. He took her hand, leading her along the dirt trail he knew by heart to an outcropping at the edge of a rocky bluff overlooking the ocean as far as the eye could see.

"Wow," she said as they sat on the patchy grass. "This is serene. Do you come here a lot?"

He put his arm around her, needing her close. "Not that often, but enough."

"Okay, Mr. Mysterious," she teased. "You got me to spill all my secrets, but you're still holding yours."

"Opening up isn't easy for me."

"You're preaching to the choir. But I highly recommend it, so if you ever want to, I'm here, and I'd really like to be the person you trust enough to share your secrets with."

His chest tightened at her willingness to be what he wanted—*who* he needed—and not demand the same in return. It was that gentleness that had nearly made him spill his feelings in the shower. Those feelings had magnified tenfold since then, and the urge to let her in had grown, too. He *wanted* to open up to her. She deserved that, but he was still struggling. The need to give her something, to show her that the old cliché—*it's not you, it's me*—was real and, in his case was strong, but all he could come up with was "Sorry I'm not easier to be with."

"I'm not easy, either, and I honestly don't think we'd be together if you were."

"What do you mean?"

"I was afraid to let you in because nobody had ever stuck around, and you refused to let me believe you wouldn't stick around. If you were a different person, you'd have walked away, and I would have gone back to shutting out the world and being terrified about Ice and arguing with Colette. I might never have realized that she needed help or that I was treating her like she couldn't grow up. I'm a better person with you in my life."

He tightened his hold on her, gazing out at the water, silent minutes ticking by as sharp as razors as he tried to convince himself that she could ever be a better person because of him. "I'm too intense."

"You? Intense? Who's been lying to you?"

"I'm serious. It's not fair to you. I don't know how to open up, and I *still* dragged you into a bathroom because the need to be closer and connect on a visceral level was as strong as my need to breathe. I've never felt that way with anyone else, and I don't know how to turn that off."

Her brows knitted. "Do you think I want you to turn it off?"

"You should. You deserve a guy who won't cross those lines."

"Do I act like I don't enjoy being with you?"

"*No.* But I'm a lot. You said it yourself. I'm *extra*."

"I admit, your intensity took some getting used to, but I have never felt safer than when I'm in your arms. I might submit to your dirty demands, but I *am* perfectly capable of telling you no. I wouldn't be with you if I didn't enjoy it or if I felt disrespected or like I didn't matter to you."

"I know you wouldn't, but it's more than that. I learned a long time ago that it's easier to shut down my feelings than to deal with them, and that doesn't make me a great partner."

"You may not wear your heart on your sleeve, but you show me how much you care with everything you do, and you have since day one."

"And you think that's fair?"

"There is no relationship scoreboard. It's about what makes us happy, and I'd rather be with someone who shows me they care than someone who says they do but whose actions prove otherwise."

"But I do hold back with everyone," he said sharply, unable to hold back his frustrations with himself. "That makes me a tough person to be around. I see it in your eyes when I clam up."

She was quiet for a minute, brows knitted.

He knew she agreed with him. He could feel it hanging between them like a villain he needed to slay. "It sucks, I know, but it started when I was a kid, and you know what they say about old habits."

"I knew you had your reasons, but I didn't realize they went back so far. What happened?"

"Nothing. It's stupid."

"How can you say that when it's caused you to feel this way? It must have been traumatic to impact you this much." She put her hand over his, interlocking their fingers. "I felt freer when I told you the truth about my life. I'm right here, and I'm not going anywhere. Won't you let me do that for you?"

He didn't know how to do this or where to start, but he fucking wanted to. His grandfather's voice traipsed through his mind. *I'm saying you're looking at this all wrong, and it's causing you to be your own roadblock...If you want to know what your grandmother would have said, that's easy. She would've looked you in the eye and said, "That's a load of malarkey, honey." She was all about the here and now, and she always led with her heart.*

He grabbed ahold of that advice, hoping like hell he didn't sound like an idiot, and opened the throttle. "I found this stray dog who I just fucking loved…" He forced himself to tell her everything, from how he'd found it to the very moment he'd put the last shovelful of dirt on his grave.

Her eyes were damp with tears. "Oh, Blaine. That's sweet and so sad."

"That little dog filled me with a different kind of happiness."

"*Clover*," she said softly.

"*Right.* I felt protective of it, but at the same time, I was anxious that someone would find the dog and take it away."

She squeezed his hand. "Blaine, it's no wonder you shut off your feelings. You kept Clover a secret, and you had nobody to share those worries or your grief with, but I think you're still shutting down your feelings."

"What the hell are you talking about? I'm telling you about them."

"But you're treating Clover like an object by calling him *it* and *the dog*, which lets you keep your feeling for him at arm's length instead of seeing Clover as the only dog who found a special place in your heart that only he could fill. I've read a lot of information about trauma because of my mother, and I know it's not the same, but she *rarely* says Colette's name, and that's one way to disassociate from her. I just wonder if it could be the same with you and Clover."

Holy shit. He did do that. Even in his own head.

"You pushed me to own my feelings and let me know it was okay to like what we did. I know it's different, but maybe if you allowed yourself to use Clover's name and allow that pain in, it might help with other emotional stuff in the future."

His jaw clenched, and his gut followed. *It's not the fork in the road that causes the quandary. It's the decision of which to take and all the possibilities of what could happen along the way.* This time the voice he heard in his head wasn't his grandfather's. It was his grandmother's, rattling him to his core. He hadn't realized he was standing at a fork in the road, but he sure as fuck was. One way led to burying more feelings. The other led to the truth...and to Reese's heart.

His words clawed painfully up his throat. "I never told anyone about Clover, because I worried that I'd done something to kill him."

"But you loved him, and you said you took care of him."

"I did. I tried so fucking hard. But maybe I fed him the wrong food or hurt him by keeping him in the shed. Who the fuck knows, but that was only the beginning. My parents had dogs when we were growing up, and when they died, Madigan and Zander were a mess for weeks. Watching them grieve was like death itself. And it wasn't just the dogs that caused that kind of pain or just the kids who suffered. When my uncle Biggs had that stroke, it hit my mom really hard, and my brothers and Mads were terrified that our old man would have one, too, so I was constantly trying to reassure them and distract them from those worries. Our family took another blow when we lost my uncle Axel. He was my mom's brother, and a few years later we suffered again when my grandmother died."

"That's a lot of loss."

"It sucked. My grandmother was the only person I could share my shit with and not feel guilty about it."

"What about your parents? They seem to really care about all of you."

"They do, but they had all of us and foster kids and the club. They didn't need one more burden to carry. They needed me to be strong to watch over the other kids, and my grandfather was such a force of nature back then."

"The sugar thief? He still is," she said warmly. "But why couldn't you talk to him about things that worried you?"

"Because I didn't want him to think I was weak. But my grandmother understood what it was like for me to constantly make sure everyone else was okay and how hard it was to navigate foster kids and siblings and cousins. Everyone lost it after my grandmother died, and my grandfather was completely shattered. He suffered the worst pain I'd ever seen."

"You must have been devastated, too."

"I was, but by then I'd honed the ability to shut it down so I could take care of everyone else. But just when I thought we'd faced the worst of it, we lost Ashley." Tears burned, and he turned away, trying to regain control. "That was even worse than losing my grandmother, because she was just a kid, and she had this zest for life that you could feel a mile away. Then she was just...*gone*. It was unfathomable. I don't know how Ginger and Con survived, and I can't even begin to explain how messed up Tank was, because he's the one who found her. Everyone was a mess. Maverick was pissed all the time, Zeke shut down, Zander got into a shitload of trouble, and Mads had lost her best friend. She cried for weeks. I tried everything to help them through it, but I couldn't save them from the pain, and that fucked me up pretty bad."

Reese threaded her arm through his with tears in her eyes. "Nobody could have saved them from it. That's the thing about grief. We can't escape it. We *need* to process it and experience it so we can find a new normal, like after my grandma died. It hurts and it sucked, but it's necessary."

He shook his head. "Fuck that. Eventually my brothers and cousins got through it, but Mads escaped *us*. She went to study overseas and got her fucking heart broken by some married asshole. I knew something was wrong when she came back, but she wouldn't tell me what had happened. Suddenly my sister, the girl who was like the brightest star in the sky and believed the world was her oyster, locked herself in her bedroom for months, writing songs that ripped my fucking heart out. I had always protected her. *Always.* And right or wrong, the fact that she shut me out fucked me up even more. And all these years later, Tobias came along, and you heard about how I nearly ruined our relationship over him."

"But they both said it was because you were *protecting* her."

"Exactly," he gritted out. "Don't you get it, Reese? I don't know how to love like other people do. I've spent my life protecting people I love no matter what the consequences. I'd fucking take a bullet for anyone who was at that party last night."

"And for strangers," she said softly. "You didn't hesitate to step in to protect me the night we met."

"I'd do it for anyone."

"That's not a bad thing, Blaine."

"It is when you don't know how to put it aside or temper it, and it overshadows everything else," he barked. "I see my brother and cousins getting married and bringing children into the world, and I have no idea how they can let themselves love that deeply when anything can happen and they could lose them tomorrow, much less how they can protect them without smothering them."

Her brows knitted, but then a small smile curved her lips. "To a girl who has never felt fully loved, being smothered by it doesn't sound so bad."

"You're not being honest with yourself, buttercup. Think

about how mad you were when I showed up to fix your locks or when I helped Colette or told you what went down with Ice."

"And yet I'm still here. We're not so different, you know. I was afraid to let anyone in because I thought everyone would let me down, and you're afraid to smother someone with love because you might suffer another loss." She climbed into his lap, putting her arms around him. "You don't scare me, Blaine Wicked. But all that heartache trapped inside you does. You helped everyone else through their grief, but it sounds like your grief is stacked up inside you like cars on a highway with no exit. Maybe we should build some exit ramps and see what happens."

He wrapped his arms around her, swallowing against the lump in his throat that was threatening to suffocate him. "God, baby. What did I ever do to deserve you?"

"You went to an asshat's bachelor party."

He laughed softly and kissed her. "My grandmother would say it was fate."

"Mine would say we're like wildflowers thrown into the wind who came together in the most unlikely of places. Different but nourished by the same sun."

"I wish I had met her. I think our grandmothers would have been good friends."

"Me too. Now start smothering before we run out of time and have to go back."

As their mouths came together, his heart cracked open, and Reese slithered in, healing the crack behind her, one sweet kiss at a time.

Chapter Twenty-Three

REESE GRABBED THE groceries she'd bought on her way home from work Thursday afternoon and headed inside. She smiled at Colette, sitting on the couch with her earbuds in, listening to something on the iPad Blaine had given her earlier in the week. He'd been there every night after he got off work, with the exception of last night, because he had church. Goodbyes hadn't gotten any easier, and Blaine continued to come back after Colette was asleep.

He'd gone extra wild the night she'd come out wearing only his Dark Knights sweatshirt. They were always ravenous for each other, but one night he'd brought blankets, and they just lay in each other's arms in the back of his truck, enjoying their time alone under the stars. He showed up every morning to have breakfast with them, claiming the few hours they spent apart were grueling. Reese was glad she wasn't alone in that feeling. It was funny, ever since their talk last week, everything felt better, brighter, and happier. Even Colette was opening up more.

"Have you thought any more about Woody?" Colette asked as Reese put the grocery bags on the kitchen table. She'd loved volunteering at the shelter and had been begging to adopt

Woody, an ornery dachshund she'd fallen in love with last weekend. She'd been so helpful, Gunner and Sid had said she could volunteer every weekend with Kendra and TJ. Colette was not only excited to continue volunteering, but she also beamed with pride at a job well done.

"Lettie, I told you we can't get a dog. They're too expensive, and you know Mom won't let you have it when she comes home." She didn't want to think about her mother coming home or not living under the same roof as Colette anymore.

"What if I babysit like Kendra does and I pay for it, and you keep it at your place?"

"How about we get through the school year and make sure Mom's not a mess, and then deal with it."

"Fine." She came into the kitchen and peered into a grocery bag. "Did you remember chocolate chips?" She wanted to make Reese and Blaine chocolate-chip pancakes tomorrow morning.

"Yes. Were you working on your homework?"

Zeke had gone with them to meet with the school about setting up a plan to help Colette next year, starting with having her evaluated by a reading specialist. Zeke worked with several kids in the area, and based on his assessment, they agreed to give Colette extra time for testing for the remainder of the year. It was a start. Meanwhile, Zeke offered to help Colette prepare for finals, and Reese was filling out the necessary paperwork to start the evaluation process for a formal individual educational program for Colette. She had worried that Colette might feel different from the other kids and fight getting help from the school, but Zeke was right. It seemed to have the opposite effect, bolstering her confidence.

"I only had one reading assignment, and I already listened to it." Colette started to help unload the groceries. "I was listening to a book Kendra told me about."

In true bulldozer fashion, Blaine hadn't wanted to wait to get approval from the school for financial assistance before setting Colette up with the programs that could help her. He'd loaded her iPad with the reading and writing programs Zeke had suggested, and since Colette had enjoyed *The Outsiders* so much, he'd downloaded an audiobook app and purchased her a subscription, which she was free to use with one caveat. She had to actually listen to the books she downloaded. Reese had fought him on spending so much money, but when it came to Colette, she didn't have the heart to put her foot down. Colette was beyond grateful, and they'd had three stress-free homework days.

Reese was determined to do something special for Blaine in return for everything he was doing for them. She just didn't know what yet.

"Good job on the homework." She put the milk and eggs in the fridge. "What book are you listening to?"

"*The Summer I Turned Pretty.*"

"Do you like it? I think they made it into a show on Netflix."

"They did. It's gritty like *The Outsiders*, but the main character is cool. Kendra invited me over Saturday night to watch it at her house with a couple of her friends. Is that okay?"

"Will her parents be home?"

"*Yes*," she said with attitude.

"Okay. What time does she want you to come over?"

"Six."

"That's fine. I can come get you at eleven. Does that sound good?"

She put the chocolate chips and pancake mix in the pantry.

"Midnight sounds better."

"That's too late. It's not fair to her parents. How about eleven thirty?"

"Fine."

They finished unloading the groceries, and Reese changed out of her work clothes. She was heading into the living room when a knock sounded at the door.

"I thought Blaine wasn't coming over until later," Colette said.

"He's not." Reese headed for the door with Colette on her heels and saw Blaine's truck out front. She opened the door, and her stomach flip-flopped at the sight of him wearing a gray T-shirt that hugged his muscles, low-slung jeans, and a panty-melting smile.

"Hello, ladies."

"Hi. What are you doing here?" Reese asked. "I thought you had a late meeting with a client."

"I rescheduled it so I could take my girls out."

"Out *where?*" Colette crossed her arms. "And why are you wearing sneakers?"

Blaine's brow furrowed. "What's wrong with sneakers? You wear them."

"Your boots are cooler," Colette said.

"Yeah? Well, they're not good for going on my boat." He winked at Reese.

Excitement bubbled up inside her.

"You have a *boat?*" Colette asked.

"I do, and I figured you two might like to take a sunset ride with me, do a little fishing, and eat dinner on the water."

"Really?" Reese and Colette asked in unison.

"Yes, really. Why don't you grab sweatshirts, and—"

"Okay!" Colette ran for her bedroom, and Reese laughed. "I guess she's excited."

Blaine drew her into his arms. "How about you?"

"I'm elated, but you shouldn't put off work for us."

"My boss doesn't mind." He kissed her smiling lips.

AS THEY CLIMBED out of the truck at Blaine's house, Colette said, "This is *your* house?"

"Yeah," Blaine said.

"Are you rich or something?"

"*Lettie*," Reese chided.

"What? Look at this place, and he has a boat, a motorcycle, *and* a truck."

"I do okay for myself." He slung an arm over Reese's shoulder. "Do you want to see the inside?"

"*Yes.*" Colette said it like he'd asked an inane question and headed for the front door.

"Sorry," Reese said.

"Don't be. It's a cool house." He kissed her temple as they followed Colette. "You know what those glasses do to me. Think she'll notice if we disappear for an hour?"

She laughed.

He opened the door and waved them into a vast two-story foyer with steps leading upstairs to their right and downstairs to the left. The stone mosaic floor was a beautiful mix of grays and browns, and the walls were a soft gray with white trim. Blaine's black leather boots and brown work boots were neatly placed beside a rough-hewn table by the door.

"Whoa," Colette said.

"Did you make this floor?" Reese asked.

"Yeah. I did all the stonework in the house."

"Can I go upstairs?" Colette asked.

He waved to the stairs, and she bolted up them, exclaiming, "Whoa!"

They made their way upstairs to a gorgeous open living area. The wood floors were a pale, almost gray, wood. The walls were the same pale gray with white trim as the foyer. The kitchen was white with sparkling stainless-steel appliances. There was an enormous island with three shiny silver lights hanging down over it and four expensive-looking stools on one side. The island had a stone base unlike anything Reese had ever seen. Every stone was round or oblong, not flat like she'd seen in magazines. The dining room table seated eight and was made out of the same rough-hewn wood as the table in the foyer. The living room had a two-story stone fireplace with the same type of stones as the island, a comfortable-looking brown leather corner couch, and a round table with stones under a glass top. Several framed photographs of Blaine's family and friends decorated the walls and mantel.

"Reese! Look at the view." Colette went to the nearly floor-to-ceiling windows overlooking the backyard.

"This is incredible," Reese said with awe. "I've never seen floors like this or stones like the ones you used on the island and fireplace."

"The floors are bamboo, and the stones came from the Mad River."

"That sounds fake," Colette said.

"It's not. It's in Vermont," Blaine explained. "My grand-mother lived in Mad River Valley until she was about your age.

Her family owned a small tract of land that had gotten passed down through three generations. She used to tell me stories about helping her grandfather in the fields and how he made piles of the prettiest round river stones."

"Why would they find river stones on land?" Colette asked.

"They farmed the bottom fields, which is the low area by the water. It has the richest soil, and farmers are always turning up rocks. When I bought this house, I went out there with my grandfather and bought a couple of truckloads of the stones from the farmer who now owns the property where my grandmother grew up. I still have about half a truckload left."

Reese was continually amazed by the love he carried in that broad chest of his. She reached for his hand. "I love knowing that. You always have a piece of your grandmother with you."

He nodded.

"Like you and Grandma, Reese," Colette said. "You always make sure you have flowers around." She picked up a framed photograph of a much younger Blaine from the mantel. He was probably around twenty, with his arms around a pretty blonde and Madigan, who looked to be around twelve or thirteen. "Who's the blonde?"

"That's my cousin Ashley."

Reese held his hand a little tighter, hearing a hint of deeper emotion in his voice that she would have missed had she not been looking for it.

Colette studied the picture. "I don't think I met her at the party."

"No," he said in a low voice. "She passed away several years ago."

Colette's brow furrowed. "She *died*?"

"Yeah. She tried drugs for the first time, and they were laced with something. It was an accidental overdose." He took the picture and set it on the mantel.

"I'm sorry. I didn't mean to upset you," Colette said sincerely.

"You didn't," he reassured her. "Just promise me you won't do drugs."

"I saw what drugs and alcohol did to our mom. I don't want to have anything to do with that stuff." Colette glanced at Reese. "Just so you know, the night I had that party, I didn't do any drugs or anything."

Relief flooded Reese. "I'm so glad to hear that."

"Me too," Blaine said. "We should get a move on."

"Wait, what's down there?" Colette pointed down the hall.

"Nothing exciting. A few bedrooms and bathrooms," Blaine said. "The master bedroom and rec room are downstairs."

"Can we go down?" Colette asked excitedly. "I promise to be quick. I've never been in a house this nice."

Reese had butterflies as Blaine gave them a tour of the rest of the house, remembering the first time they'd gotten together in his bathroom. She took in his masculine wood-and-iron furniture, which looked as strong and stable as the man himself, and noticed the feet of the leather couches were made from the same stone as the fireplace and island. Colette raved about everything from the pool table and big-screen television to his massive bathroom and enormous bed. Reese wondered what it would be like to share that bed with him and to wake up in his arms instead of sneaking around and missing him all night.

"Your house is huge. You should get a dog," Colette said.

Blaine looked at her like she was out of her mind. "What would I do with a dog?"

"Let me come play with it."

"You're going to see dogs every weekend at the rescue. I think you're good," Blaine said as they headed outside.

"But there's a dachshund I really want to adopt at the shelter, and Reese won't let me get it."

"I wish we could, but we can't handle a dog right now," Reese said apologetically.

"But Blaine can," Colette said hopefully. "Woody is *so* cute. You'd love him."

Blaine cocked a brow. "A wiener dog named Woody? Did Gunner name it?"

"Yeah, you know, like Woody from *Toy Story*? Sid said he loves that movie," Colette answered.

He shook his head. "Sure he does. Sorry, Halfpint, but I'm *not* getting a dog. Let's go outside."

"Whatever." Colette followed him out and gaped at the patios and gardens.

"Your sister planted the gardens by the wall down there." Blaine motioned farther down the lawn.

"And Blaine did the stonework," Reese said.

"It's all awesome," Colette said. "I can't believe you live here, and you spend all your time at our crappy little house."

"Your house isn't crappy," Blaine said. "And the roof over my head doesn't matter if I'm with people I care about."

"Still. Can we hang out here sometime?"

"Lettie, you can't just invite yourself over." Reese gave Blaine an apologetic look.

"I think it's a great idea," Blaine said. "How about we have dinner and watch a movie here this weekend?"

"I'm going to Kendra's house Saturday night," Colette said.

His lips tipped up. "Then how about tomorrow night? I'll throw some steaks on the grill, and we can watch whatever you want or play pool."

"Can we have a bonfire?" Colette asked.

"Absolutely. I'll buy some marshmallows."

"And graham crackers and chocolate bars for s'mores?" Colette asked hopefully.

He laughed. "You've got it."

"Are you sure you don't mind?" Reese asked.

"I can think of worse things than having two of my favorite people in my house." His eyes remained trained on hers. "How would you like to go out with a hot biker Saturday night while Lettie is with Kendra?"

A thrill tickled her skin. "I'd love that. I have to drop her off at six, but we can go after."

"Why don't I pick you both up, and we'll drop her off together, then go out on our date?"

Reese felt giddy. A real *date* with the guy she was crazy about? "Sounds great."

"Does that mean I can stay out until midnight?" Colette asked.

"No," Reese said. "I'm picking you up at eleven thirty."

"Blaine, don't you want more time with her?" Colette urged.

"*Lettie*," Reese warned.

Blaine hooked his arm around Colette's shoulder, pulling her closer as they headed down to the dock. "Don't try to play me against your sister. It won't end well."

"Whatever," Colette said like she was bored. "Oh my God. Look at that boat! You *are* rich."

"Possessions don't make you rich. Friends do. I'd give away everything I own to keep the people in my life safe with a roof over their heads."

"Okay, so you're a rich weirdo," Colette teased. "But you're still rich."

She ran toward the dock, and Blaine reached for Reese's hand. "I think she likes it here."

"Who wouldn't? But I hope you know by now that I don't like you for your money."

"I wish you did. It would negate all the arguments about me spending too much on you and Colette."

"Dream on, *weirdo*." She went up on her toes and kissed him.

"Hurry up!" Colette hollered.

"You heard the boss. Get going." He smacked Reese's butt. She squealed, and he chased her all the way to the boat, the three of them cracking up.

THE LATE-AFTERNOON sun shimmered off the water as they trolled for fish. Colette was fishing off the stern, and Blaine stood at the helm, admiring Reese sitting on the bow reading on her phone. A gentle breeze blew a lock of hair into her face, despite her continual efforts to keep it tucked behind her ear. She was wearing his Dark Knights sweatshirt he'd given her the night they'd met. That seemed like forever ago. It was hard to believe how much had changed.

"Am I just supposed to stand here holding this thing?" Colette's voice tugged him from his thoughts.

"I'm pretty sure the fish won't jump into the boat on their own."

"But nothing's happening. Maybe they're all sleeping."

"You'll get one. Just give it time."

She sighed, her shoulders slumping. "It's boring."

"Some people think it's relaxing." He glanced at Reese, who was watching them with a sweet smile. "What're you reading, babe?"

"Nothing." She pressed her phone to her chest.

"It's a dirty book for the book club," Colette called out.

He held Reese's gaze. "You can tell me all about it later."

Her cheeks pinked up, tweaking his heart. She'd told him at Preacher's party that she was joining their book club, and he was glad she was doing it. Not just because he liked the idea of her reading steamy scenes they could later act out and improve upon but also for the camaraderie. He wanted her life to be filled with family, friends, and *him*.

"*Blaine!* Something's happening!" Colette's line was arching toward the water.

"You've got a fish on the line! Start reeling it in." He cut the engine and went to help her.

"It's too hard. The line's gonna break," she complained as Reese ran over.

"No, it's not. Keep reeling," he said firmly. "You've got this, Lettie. You're stronger than the fish. Use your body for leverage." He shifted the rod so it was resting against her body near her hip.

"That's a *lot* better." She continued reeling.

"Attagirl. Keep going."

"This is so exciting!" Reese exclaimed, taking pictures.

The fish came into view just below the surface, and Colette shouted, "There it is! Look! Reese, look!"

"I see it! I'm getting lots of pictures!" Reese said.

Colette reeled it in, and as Blaine grabbed the line, bringing the fish onto the boat, she exclaimed, "I did it! Look at it! It's *huge*," and hugged Reese.

"She's a beauty. About thirty-two inches. Reese, come hold the line up and I'll take a picture of the two of you." Colette held the rod, and Reese held the fish up by the line as he took the picture.

He knelt to take the hook out, and Reese winced. "Doesn't that hurt it?"

"I try not to think about it."

"Is it okay?" Colette hovered over him. "Don't kill it."

"It's fine. It's just a hook." He set the hook aside.

"Put it back in the water so it doesn't die," Colette urged.

He cocked a brow. "Are you sure you don't want to eat it for dinner tomorrow?"

"Ew," Colette said.

Reese nudged him. "Put it back."

"A'right." As he leaned over the side to release the fish, Colette said, "Can I catch another? Reese, you have to try it. It's *so* fun."

Reese had opted not to fish earlier, but Blaine had a feeling she was giving Colette the spotlight. "Are you ready to try it, babe?"

Her grin widened, and she nodded. "I think so."

"Yes!" Colette exclaimed. "Okay, here's what you have to do..."

She rattled off the same lesson Blaine had given her. He loved how their relationship was working itself out.

They fished for a while. Reese was so excited when she caught one, she squealed as loud as Colette had and hugged both of them. Blaine knew it was a moment he'd never forget.

The sun was setting as they sat down to eat the subs and

chips he'd brought. He told them fishing stories from when he was younger. They had lots of laughs making bad fishing jokes at his expense.

Reese eyed his sub. "What's in your sandwich besides roast beef?"

"Horseradish, cheese, lettuce, tomato, and pickles." He'd bought turkey, ham, and roast beef subs, and had offered them their choice, taking whatever was left for himself.

"That sounds good."

"Here, see if you like it." He held it up for her.

"No. It's okay." She sat back. "I've got my own."

"Reese, take a bite," he encouraged.

She took a small bite. "*Mm.* That's really good. I've never had a roast beef sandwich."

He swapped the other half of their subs on their plates.

"You don't have to do that," she complained.

"What's mine is yours." He kissed her cheek and held the sub out toward Colette. "Want to try it?"

"No thanks."

As he took a bite, he noticed Colette watching him more closely. "Is something wrong?"

"No." She ate a chip. "It's just...you're so nice to us. I mean, I get why you're nice to Reese. She's your girlfriend, but I'm not."

He didn't know much about Reese's past boyfriends, except that once they realized she was Colette's primary caretaker, they'd split. "That doesn't make you any less important to me, and when you start dating, if boys don't treat you at least as well as I do, and treat Reese with the same respect, they don't deserve you." He took a drink, letting that sink in. "But you're not dating until you're thirty, so we don't have to worry about that yet."

"Thirty?" she snapped.

"Yup." He took a bite of his sandwich.

Colette glared at him. "You're not my father. You don't make the rules. Reese, tell him he's nuts."

"I think he's kidding, right? I'm only twenty-six."

"But you're with me," he said arrogantly.

"I'm not waiting until I'm as old as Reese," Colette insisted.

"Is there a basement in your house? I feel the need to lock you up for a few years." He laughed with the tease.

Colette narrowed her eyes. "Why is she dating you again?"

"Because I'm awesome." He winked, and she rolled her eyes.

Reese was looking at something on her phone. "I just got a text from Leah. Tank is taking her to Boston overnight next Saturday and Evie's babysitting. She wants to know if Colette wants to help. She said she'll pay you."

"That's the night before Mother's Day," Blaine said. "I was going to ask if you guys wanted to help me and Mads and my brothers that night. We're repairing and repainting the gazebo in my parents' backyard, putting in a pond, and adding a big garden as a Mother's Day surprise for my mom."

"That sounds fun," Reese said.

Colette wrinkled her nose. "Painting and planting or getting paid to play with kids? I'll take the babysitting job."

"Are you sure? Kids can be demanding," Reese pointed out.

"I had fun with them at the party, and Evie's cool. It'll be fun to spend the night there." Colette ate another chip, eyeing Blaine. "Is that okay with you? I don't want you to think I don't like your mom."

"Don't worry. I get it." He wasn't about to complain about having a whole night alone with Reese. "Do you guys have plans to see your mom on Mother's Day?"

"Why would we do that?" Colette said with disgust.

"She doesn't want us to visit, remember?" Reese said.

"Right." He shoved his irritation at their mother down deep. "I was just making sure, because I'd really like it if you'd join us for brunch with my family. I know my mom would love to see you."

"I'd like that. What do you think, Lettie?" Reese asked hopefully.

"If I'm done babysitting by then, sure."

"Tank's family has brunch with us, so I'm sure he'll be back by then."

"Do you celebrate every holiday together?" Reese asked.

"Pretty much. Will that be too overwhelming for you?"

"No," Colette and Reese said at the same time.

"Good."

"But I want to get your mom a gift," Reese said. "I felt bad for not bringing something for your dad on his birthday."

"Nobody got him gifts. We donated to a suicide prevention fund, and I put your names on the donation with mine. As far as my mother goes, you're going to help get her surprise ready. That's enough."

"But that's from you and the rest of your family."

"You guys are a big part of my world, so now that includes you and Colette." As he said it, he realized how much he wanted to make it real.

Chapter Twenty-Four

REESE FELT LIKE she was living a dream as she and Blaine waited for their dessert to be brought to the table Saturday evening. Blaine had brought her a beautiful bouquet of flowers when he picked her and Colette up. After dropping Colette off at Kendra's house, they'd gone to Provincetown, an artsy community at the tip of the Cape. Reese had never been before, and it was like a different world, full of artists, street performers, and outlandish shops. They'd walked hand in hand, listened to a guy play guitar, watched a mime perform, and meandered through a dozen stores.

They'd walked to the beachfront restaurant, where they enjoyed a delicious lobster and steak dinner and talked without the distraction of entertaining Colette or worrying about what they said or how they touched each other. Reese had gotten so used to eating dinners with Blaine and Colette, she'd wondered if it would be awkward with just the two of them. But they talked and held hands and laughed almost as much as they kissed. It was fun and romantic, and with Blaine, there was never a lack of sexual tension to keep her on her toes. It was already, without a doubt, the best night of her life.

She looked out at the water from the deck of the elegant

restaurant, the sandy shore and gentle waves a romantic backdrop to the din of conversation. Blaine was sitting next to her in a curved chair for two with their backs to the other diners. He looked strikingly handsome in a steel-gray button-down and jeans. He was so attentive, he hadn't taken his eyes off her all night and must have told her she looked gorgeous in her black strapless dress a million times. If he wasn't holding her hand, his hand was resting on her leg, like he couldn't go a minute without touching her. She'd caught him looking at her a few times like she was a complexity he desperately wanted to figure out. She didn't even try to figure him out anymore. She loved being surprised by the private bits of himself he shared.

He covered her hand with his. "Penny for your thoughts."

"I was just thinking about how much I've loved everything about tonight. I feel like we're on vacation. This place is beautiful, and it's so nice just being alone with you." She finished the last of her wine.

"I'm glad you're enjoying it. Would you like another glass of wine?"

"Oh gosh, no. I've already had two."

"Reese, I'm driving. You can have as many as you want."

She leaned closer, lowering her voice. "Did you see how expensive it was per glass? And we had lobster *and* steak, and you ordered that big dessert."

He pressed his lips to hers in a tender kiss. "Turn off that beautiful, brilliant mind of yours, and just enjoy yourself. I can handle a lot more than a few glasses of wine and dinner. I want to do nice things for you." He slid his hand up her thigh, eyes darkening. "And dirty things *to* you."

A shiver of heat rippled through her. They had all night together, and she was aching to be alone with him. They'd had a wonderful time on his boat Thursday night, and hanging out at his place with Colette last night had been wonderful. The bonfire was fun, and the s'mores were delicious. They'd watched a movie snuggled up on the couch together while Colette lounged on the other sofa. It had been easy to let her mind, and her heart, wander down a tempting path filled with drama-free evenings and steamy, sensual nights. But she knew it was a dream that would be upended once her mother finished rehab. She couldn't even pretend it was going to be any easier once she came home. Nothing was easy with her mother. Reese knew she'd worry endlessly about how she was treating Colette and whether she'd fall off the wagon.

But she had eleven more weeks to be happy, and she wasn't going to let her mother steal a second of that time. She was a little tipsy and feeling too good to be shy. She leaned closer to Blaine and whispered, "Yes, please."

A wicked grin curved his lips as the waitress arrived with their dessert, a mouthwatering concoction of flakey pastry filled with custard, topped with a flower drawn with chocolate and whipped cream around the edges. Reese's mind tiptoed down a dirty path, imagining licking that chocolate sauce off a particular body part of his. Her body ignited at the thought of being on her knees for him.

As the waitress walked away, Blaine handed Reese a spoon and said, "Do you know how badly I want to eat this off your body?"

"I was thinking about doing the same thing to you." She wanted him wild for her tonight, unable to hold back, the way he was so often. Holding his gaze, she scooped a spoonful of ice cream and licked the sweet treat as seductively as she could, hoping she didn't look ridiculous.

His eyes narrowed, his hand sliding up her thigh, fingertips brushing between her legs as she sucked the spoon clean.

"It's not quite as good as you," she said with an extra dose of innocence.

"Listen to my naughty girl." He stroked her through her panties, speaking gruffly into her ear. "I want to lay you on this table and dribble chocolate down your body."

Her sex clenched needily.

"You like that, huh, baby? I want to suck it off your nipples, drip ice cream on your pussy and lick you clean."

His words were like candy to a sugar addict. "Then what?" she panted out.

"Then I'd do this." His fingers slipped beneath her panties and pushed inside her. She gasped, gripping his leg as he said, "With my *cock*."

She suppressed a whimper. His eyes darkened as he stroked that magical spot with deathly precision. Her breaths came faster, desire burning up her limbs, blazing in her core, charging toward the finish line.

"You can tell me to stop," he gritted out, fingers taking her higher.

She gripped his leg tighter, knowing she should tell him to stop. It was crazy to let him get so dirty in public, but her heart was racing, and after such a sweet, romantic evening, she felt like a princess and had a bone-deep desire to test her own boundaries and be *his* naughty vixen. "I don't want you to stop."

His eyes flamed, and he growled low and primal, heightening her arousal.

"Then come for me," he demanded, fingers quickening.

Her body caught fire, inner muscles swelling, skin tingling.

He angled himself in the seat, blocking her even more from the possibility of being seen. It was harder than she thought to let go of the fear of being caught, but it was also beyond thrilling doing something so high risk and naughty. Blaine's gaze was reassuring and hungry at once. She felt how much he wanted this, and he must have sensed her hesitation, because he said, "Close your eyes."

She obeyed, knowing he'd find a way to get her there.

"It's just you and me, baby. Let yourself be free."

She wanted that so badly. Her breathing hitched, and she concentrated on the feel of his thick fingers quickening as they moved in and out of her body.

"This sweet pussy is mine, and I can't wait to fuck it later."

"I'm yours," she panted out, feeling delirious.

"Prove it. Give yourself to me. I want *all* of you, right here, right now." His thumb pressed on her clit, and she detonated, clenching her teeth to keep from crying out as her inner muscles pulsed. Her fingernails dug into his leg, and she buried her face in his neck, riding out her pleasure to the sound of his voice. *"That's my girl. You're fucking beautiful…I'm so lucky you're mine…"*

When she went boneless and breathless against him, she couldn't believe she'd done it. And she wanted to do so much more.

He put his arms around her, his breath hot and taunting on her cheek. "I need to be inside you."

THEY STUMBLED INTO his house in a tangle of greedy

gropes and devouring kisses. Her back hit the wall, and he pinned her hands above her head, grinding against her, the two of them feasting ferociously on each other's mouths. Blaine felt like he'd waited a lifetime to have her in his bed. He had no idea how something like that could make him physically ache, but if he didn't get her there soon, he was going to lose his mind. He lifted her into his arms, earning a sweet laugh and more urgent kisses as he carried her downstairs to his bedroom.

He set her down beside the bed, his chest tightening with the impact of the moment. She was the first woman he'd ever wanted in *his* bed, *his* room, *his* house. Desire pounded like a drum through his veins as he took off her glasses and placed them on the nightstand. Her innocent, hopeful eyes brought a different type of ache.

She held up her phone, which he hadn't realized she was holding. "In case Colette needs me."

He tried to wrap his head around the emotions engulfing him as he placed her phone on the nightstand and pulled back the blanket. He felt her watching him with an eagerness that tugged at him to be gentle and wanted to give her more of what she craved. *Fuck.* He took her beautiful face between his hands, brushing his thumb over the dimple in her chin, wanting to give her everything and knowing she needed his control as much as he did. "Seeing you come in that restaurant was so damn sexy. Did you enjoy it?"

"Yes."

He ran his thumb over her lower lip, soaking in her sweet smile and the trust she put in him. "Did you get off knowing someone might see us?"

"I got off on your touch and your voice," she said breathily. "No one else even existed."

Jesus. That was exactly how he'd felt, and he wanted to tell her, but he struggled against the roaring emotions, afraid he'd say too much, and gritted out, "That's my girl," and began unzipping her dress, moving into safer territory. "I want to be inside you, but first you're going to straddle my face while you suck my cock." Her dress slid down to her feet, leaving her bare, save for her panties and heels. He stroked her cheek, speaking softer. "You're going to take me deep, and you're not going to stop when I make you come." He dipped his head, licking her nipple, earning a sharp inhalation. "Do you want that?"

"Yes," she said lustfully.

"Yes, what?" He met her gaze, palming her breast.

She lifted her chin, showing him that confidence he adored. "I want to suck your cock while I come."

"That's my good girl." She breathed harder every time he praised her, and it made him want to do it more. "Take off those sexy panties." When she did, he dragged his fingers along her slickness. "You listen so well, and you're already drenched for me. I'm going to give you extra orgasms tonight. Now get on the bed and let me see *my* pretty pussy."

She lay on her back, her golden hair fanning out around her face like an angel as she spread her legs, high heels digging into the sheets. Her nipples were rosy and tight, her pussy practically dripping.

"Look at you, beautiful, so wet and ready." He took off his boots and socks and began unbuttoning his shirt. "Touch yourself." Her fingers slid through her wetness, eyes on him as he stripped off his shirt. "That's it." He unbuttoned his jeans. "Stroke your clit." Her cheeks flamed as she did it. "That's my girl. Faster." He stripped off his jeans and boxer briefs, and her eyes locked on his dick as he fisted it. "Like that, baby girl?"

"*Yes.* I like watching you touch yourself."

He fucking loved when she took the initiative to say more. "Sit up against the headboard." She hurried to the new position. He climbed between her legs and sealed his mouth over her pussy. She smelled like heaven and tasted even sweeter.

"Oh God...*Blaine*..."

He reveled in every moan, every sinful sound she made as he used his teeth, tongue, and fingers, taking her right up to the edge. Wanting her needy, he went up on his knees, leaving her trembling and whimpering. "I need to fuck your mouth." She reached for him like a starving woman reaching for a meal, taking him deep. "Your mouth fucking owns me," he roared out.

He fisted his hands in her hair, thrusting and pulling as she sucked him off. She moaned, and the vibration nearly made him come. He pulled out and crushed his mouth to hers, kissing her ravenously, but nothing was enough. He tore his mouth away. "I'm going to lie down and you're going to sit on my face, and I mean smother me with that fine pussy of *ours*."

He lay down on his back, and she crawled over him, wrapping her hand around his cock.

"I want to feel my cock go down your throat." He wetted his fingers with her arousal and pulled her down to his mouth. She moaned as she lowered her mouth over his cock, the vibration searing through him. She sucked and stroked, taking him balls deep as he feasted on her. He intensified his efforts, earning more moans and quicker strokes. He teased her clit with one hand and brought the other to her ass, teasing her tightest hole. She sank deeper onto his mouth, moaning and grinding her hips, urging him on. He pushed one finger past the tight rim of muscles, and she moaned around his dick. His hips bucked. She sucked harder as he fucked her ass with his finger and quickened his efforts on her clit. She came hard against his mouth, sending his climax crashing into him. His girl stayed with him, taking everything he had to give, until they both went slack.

He repositioned, gathering her body in his arms, stroking her back, feeling like she'd sucked a piece of his heart right out of him. "*Jesus, baby.* Still with me?"

She snuggled into him, warm and soft and so damn sweet, whispering, "Always."

How could one little word make him feel like his chest was going to burst? He nuzzled against her neck, breathing her in. The shrill ring of her cell phone startled them both.

"Colette." Reese scrambled onto her hands and knees, reaching for it. "Lettie?"

She paused to listen, too tempting on her hands and knees to resist. He moved behind her, caressing her ass and teasing her with his hands and mouth. She glowered over her shoulder as she spoke into the phone. "Her parents don't mind if you sleep over?" She went quiet again, and he spread her cheeks, running his tongue from one hole to the other. Her muscles tensed. He rubbed the length of his cock along her wetness and brought his fingers into play again, teasing her tightest hole. "Okay," she said fast and breathy. "See you tomorrow." She ended the call and went down on her elbows, panting out, "Colette's spending the night with Kendra, and good *God*, you're killing me."

"Does that mean you want me to stop?"

"No. *Don't stop*," she pleaded.

"That's my greedy girl." He continued teasing her ass and pushed only the head of his cock into her pussy. She moaned and rocked back, trying to take him deeper, but he didn't let her. "You want more, baby?"

"*Yes.* I want your cock. All of it."

"Do you have any idea how sexy you are with your ass up in the air, begging me to fuck you?" He pushed his finger into her ass, and she fisted her hands in the sheets. "Like that, baby girl?"

"*Yes.* I like everything you do."

His fucking heart stumbled. He pumped his finger. "I'm going to fuck your beautiful ass soon." He withdrew his finger, dripped spit between her cheeks, and pushed two fingers into her ass. She gasped and stilled. "Too much?"

She shook her head.

"Good girl. Get used to the feel of it."

He thrust his hips, slowly burying himself to the hilt, two fingers pumping into her ass. "How does that feel?"

"So full. So good."

"You feel incredible, baby. So tight and hot." He fucked her faster with his fingers and cock and used his other hand on her clit.

"*Ohgod, Blaine...Harder...Don't stop...*"

"Stop? I want to fucking live inside you."

Her fists tightened in the sheets, her moans growing louder. His name shot from her lungs, and she rocked in time with his efforts, her pussy and ass squeezing him like a vise. His entire body flexed, fighting the urge to come as she cried out his name again and pushed up on her hands and knees, thrusting back feverishly, taking his fingers and dick like she needed them to breathe. The sight of her fully letting go, head thrashing, hair swinging, the sounds of pleasure streaming from her lips— giving him everything he asked for—made him want to take more.

But once again his heart took over, making him want to

give her everything she wanted and didn't ask for.

When she came down from the peak, he shifted her onto her back, gazing into her lustful, luminescent eyes, overwhelmed with love for this amazing woman who'd come out of nowhere and seeped into every aspect of his life, bringing him light and warmth and a reason to want to be a better man.

She smiled, reaching for him as he came down over her. She opened her mouth to speak, but it was all too much. He covered her mouth with his as their bodies came together and poured all of his emotions into their connection. As they found their rhythm, he guided her legs around his waist, taking her deeper, soaking in every pleasure-filled sound, every sinful plea. But it still wasn't enough. He wanted to give her more of what *she* wanted. The trouble was, he'd fucked and he'd taken, but he'd never made love to a woman. He didn't know if he was capable of letting go of his need to demand and control.

But for Reese, he wanted to try.

He shifted their positions, lying on his back, letting her ride him, and held back the curses and demands vying for release, giving her the reins. She pressed her hands to his chest, her beautiful breasts bouncing with her efforts, her gaze soft and sweet and still painfully innocent.

"I don't know if I'm doing this right," she said just above a whisper. "Does it feel good?"

"Everything feels good with you. Use me, baby. Make yourself feel good."

"Will you help me? Touch me?"

"Always," he parroted, hoping it did as much for her as it had for him when she'd said it.

He teased her clit and groped her breast, squeezing her nipple. "*Yes*," she panted out, beyond beautiful angling her hips, finding her stride, taking him at an excruciatingly perfect pace.

"I could watch you fuck me all night," he gritted out, earning a smile, but her eyes were fluttering open and closed, and he knew she was lost in them, close to letting go, her fingernails digging into his chest.

"Ohgodohgodohgod."

"That's it, baby. Fuck me. Take what you want."

She rode him faster, harder. "Pinch my nipples."

"Fuck yeah." He pinched them, and she cried out as her orgasm ravaged her, taking her from a sweet bunny to a wild jackrabbit. He gritted his teeth, staving off his own release, needing to give her even *more*. When she collapsed over him, he rolled her onto her back, cradling her in his arms, kissing her sensually, and then he loved her slowly, deeply, *passionately*, until she was chasing the high just as he was, and they spiraled into ecstasy, lost in a tangle of moans and thrusts and heartfelt pleas.

They lay spent and sated in each other's arms as their breathing calmed, their bodies slick with a sheen of sweat. He kissed her lips, her cheeks, and that sexy dimple in her chin, biting back the three terrifying words vying for release.

"That was...*wow*," she said breathily.

She was so damn adorable, she made him feel like a lovestruck fool. "Do I really get to spend all night with you tonight *and* next Saturday night?"

"If you want to."

"If?" He nipped at her lower lip.

"I don't want to assume."

It pained him that she'd never been able to take anyone for granted. It was time for that to change. "I can't leave your house at night without coming back two hours later to hold you in my arms. I'm there every morning for breakfast with you and Lettie. It's safe to assume I can't get enough of you, baby girl."

"Are you sure?"

"I wouldn't say it if I wasn't." He might not be good with verbally sharing his emotions, but from now on he'd make damn sure he left no room for questions. "And I don't want to waste a second of tonight."

Her brow furrowed. "I don't know if I have enough energy to do more."

He laughed and kissed her lips. "You don't have to. I'll be right back." He went into the bathroom and started filling the Jacuzzi.

She peered in a minute later. "Can I use the bathroom before you take a bath?"

"That bath is for *us*, and sure." He kissed her as he walked out.

When she was done, he went into the bathroom and dimmed the lights. He climbed into the tub and reached for her hand. She started to straddle him. "No, baby. Sit with your back against my chest." He helped her get comfortable and put his arms around her. "Just relax." He turned on the jets and began gently bathing her.

"This feels nice." She melted against him. "What did I do to deserve this?"

You put up with me. You're the sweetest, strongest woman I know. You're always there for your sister. You make me want to be a better man. You deserve the world, and I want to give it to you. "You exist" was all he could manage, and kissed her cheek.

After a long, lazy bath, he gave her one of his long-sleeve shirts and a pair of his sweats to sleep in.

"You're getting me dressed? This is new."

He laughed. "Just put them on."

"You really want me to sleep in these?" She was sitting on the edge of the bed with a towel wrapped around her. "I thought you'd want to sleep naked. If I wear these, you'll never see me as sexy again."

"First of all, you would look sexy wearing a tarp. You're sexy, baby. The way you talk, the way you move, the way you look at me. It's you, not the clothes." He pulled her to her feet, kissing her again. "Secondly, if we were sleeping inside, we'd definitely be naked. But tonight we're sleeping under the stars, and you'll be lulled to sleep by the sounds of the water kissing the shore."

Her face lit up. "Really?"

"Yes, and when you look at me like that it makes me want to toss you back in bed and do dirty things to you. So get dressed while I get us set up outside, and if you want to wear something different, just go through my drawers and grab whatever you like."

A LITTLE WHILE later, they were cuddled beneath blankets on a lounge chair beside a roaring bonfire. Reese lifted her head from Blaine's chest. "I can't believe we both fit on this."

"Still think I don't want you with me?" He kissed her forehead.

She smiled up at him. "This is the best night ever."

"If I had known we'd have all night, I would've been prepared and blown up an air mattress and done it right."

"This is perfect." She snuggled in tighter against him. "This is Lettie's first sleepover since she was little. I'm happy for her."

"I am, too. I called Saint to make sure TJ doesn't wander down the hall tonight, but he was already all over it."

"I hope that's not why she's staying over."

"I asked him about that. He didn't think it was. He said there's definitely an attraction between them, but she and Kendra have really connected."

"I can't believe you're not going ballistic about the attraction between them."

"Who said I'm not?"

She laughed softly.

"Saint's on it, and that's about all I can do without stepping on your toes."

She feigned a gasp. "Blaine Wicked, are you learning to respect boundaries?"

"I plead the Fifth. But I will admit that this is my first sleepover, too."

"Seriously? I mean, it's mine, but…"

"It's mine, baby. No woman has ever woken up in my arms."

Her smile sparkled in her eyes. "You'd better be careful sharing those kinds of secrets and doling out all this goodness. I could fall for a sweet guy like you."

His chest constricted at the thought of her falling for him, but was she fooling herself? He'd never been called sweet in his life and for good reason. He tightened his hold on her. "Don't kid yourself, Wilder. You know I'm not sweet. Do I have to remind you of just how much of a savage boundary breaker I am?"

"You do excel at breaking boundaries, but you're also sweet in your own way. At least to me. So maybe I just like a little of everything."

"There is no *maybe* about it." He squeezed her butt. "You get off on the dark side as much as I do."

"*Shh*. Don't tell anyone."

A comfortable silence fell around them. Blaine lay listening to the sounds of the fire crackling and the water kissing the shore, thinking about how much his life had changed in three short weeks. He'd gone from working late and hanging with the guys at the Hog most nights to wanting nothing more than to be with Reese and Colette. He looked up at the stars, thinking about his conversation with his grandfather, and sent a silent message up to his grandmother. *I'm trying to get out of my own damn way, Gram. I don't think I'll ever be the kind of guy who pours his heart out, but I'll never stop trying to be the best man I can be for Reese and Colette.*

His grandmother didn't give him a sign, and he didn't hear any words of wisdom to help him figure things out. But under the cover of night, with Reese asleep wrapped tightly in his arms, his heart whispered, "You're everything to me, too, baby girl."

Chapter Twenty-Five

"WATCH IT, YOU'RE dripping," Zeke chided Zander as they painted the gazebo in their parents' backyard with Tobias the day before Mother's Day.

"That's what she said." Zander laughed.

"Just do it right," Zeke snapped.

"What're you talking about? My side looks better than yours," Zander said arrogantly. "Doesn't it, Tobias?"

Tobias shook his head. "Keep me out of this."

"Don't want to get on Zeke's bad side?" Zander challenged. "Pussy."

"Careful, dude," Tobias warned.

Zeke glowered at Zander. "He knows you're wrong, dip-shit."

Zander flicked his paintbrush at Zeke, splattering him with white paint, and Zeke went after him.

Reese couldn't help but laugh at how much the Wicked brothers bickered as they chased each other around the yard. Preacher had taken Reba out for the evening so they could get her surprise ready in the backyard. Blaine and Maverick were building the pond, and Reese and Madigan were making a beautiful garden, while Chloe sat in a lounge chair with her feet up, eating popcorn and talking with them.

It had been a week since she and Blaine had spent the night in his yard, and what a magical week it had been, even with Colette bucking Reese about doing homework some nights while simultaneously begging to adopt a dog. Blaine had backed Reese up without taking over, which was nice. They'd spent most evenings hanging out at his place, thanks to Colette's begging to spend time there, and Reese was glad. It was hard to relax in her mother's house. They'd gone for another boat ride, and Blaine was teaching them how to play pool, which Colette loved. She was good at everything she tried, while Reese was not very good at pool. But she loved having Blaine's arms around her as he taught her how to make certain shots.

Zander darted past, and Reese laughed. "Are they always like this?"

"For as long as I can remember," Madigan said.

"At least they're not wrestling," Chloe added just as Zeke tackled Zander. "Never mind."

"Okay, you guys. I think I've got a great idea for a card," Madigan said as she passed Reese another pot of flowers. She'd been gabbing since they got there, sharing details of her and Tobias's sexy night on the beach and trying to come up with new cards for her Booty Call line. "The front of the card will say *You're a pain in my ass*, and the inside will say *It's a good thing I like anal.*"

Reese's eyes widened with surprise, and Chloe snort-laughed.

"You okay, babe? Need me?" Justin hollered.

"No. I'm *fine*." Chloe lowered her voice. "I love him to no end, but every time I hiccup, he thinks I'm going into labor."

"I love how much he adores you." Reese glanced at Blaine

and had the strange thought that if she were pregnant with their baby, he'd jump at a hiccup, too.

"What do you think about the card idea?" Madigan asked.

"You might be going a little too far with that one," Chloe said.

"Don't try to tell me you don't like doing it. You were all about acting out the scenes from the BDSM book we read for the club, and anal was definitely in there," Madigan said. "What do you think, Reese?"

"I...*um*...I don't know anything about greeting cards." Her cheeks burned. She'd been thinking about that particular position with Blaine ever since he'd first mentioned it a few weeks ago, and she'd nearly told him she wanted to last weekend when they spent the night together, but she couldn't tell them that. She also couldn't tell them that they'd taken a chance and had snuck Blaine into her bedroom after Colette had fallen asleep twice this week and had quietly acted out some of the steamy scenes in the book she was reading for the book club.

"I guess you're not into butt play?" Madigan's smile faded fast, and she held up her palm. "Wait, I don't want to know that about you and my brother."

"Here we go again." Chloe rolled her eyes and tossed a piece of popcorn into her mouth.

"What?" Madigan's brow furrowed.

"Sometimes you can be one-sided with girl talk," Chloe said.

"Oh my God. You're right," Madigan said with a frown. "I'm so selfish. I've been living my best sexy life, enjoying everything my man has to offer and sharing all the good stuff, and here I am telling you not to do the same. What a jerk."

"Ya think?" Chloe teased.

Reese was envious of how open Madigan and some of the other girls had been about their personal lives at Preacher's party. She couldn't imagine sharing something so private, but hearing them talk about it made her feel less like she was different or depraved for enjoying the things she and Blaine did. "It's okay, Mads. I don't mind."

"No, it's not," Madigan insisted. "We're friends. I want to be here for you guys, and I can't expect you to hold back all the girl talk. What fun is that for you?"

"It's a bit stifling," Chloe said. "But I get it."

"Well, you shouldn't have to," Madigan insisted. "How about this? If you want to talk about dirty stuff with my brothers, either start the conversation with *I have this friend* or just change their names to Fred and Barney so I don't have to think about my brothers like that."

They laughed.

"It's really okay with me." Reese focused on the flowers she was planting. "I'm not used to sharing those things, anyway."

"And you don't have to," Chloe reassured her.

"But if you ever want to, I'm here for you," Madigan said. "And I promise not to cringe if I think of my brother."

Reese glanced at Blaine, arguing with Maverick about where to place the stones around the pond, and her heart beat a little faster. Blaine looked across the yard at her, with that secret smile that said she was too far away. Thinking about Madigan's comment, she said, "There is nothing cringeworthy about that man."

"You must be head over heels to overlook all *his* flaws," Madigan said.

"I think I'm head over heels partly because of his flaws and the way he owns them."

"Aw, I love that," Chloe said. "We all have flaws."

"Not me. Tobias says I'm perfect." Madigan flashed a cheesy grin.

Chloe said, "That's man-speak for *give me sex*," and they laughed.

"Since we're allowed to talk about Fred and Barney, can I get your opinion on something?" Reese asked.

"Yes! I'm all ears," Madigan said.

"Blaine has done a lot for me and Colette, and I want to do something special for him, but I'm not sure what. I don't have a lot of money, so I can't do anything too big. Do you have any ideas?"

"We could make him a memory board," Chloe suggested, and proceeded to tell her about memory boards she'd made using images and keepsakes.

"Your memory boards are awesome, but *Fred* wouldn't know what to do with a memory board." Madigan waggled her brows. "He'll want hot lingerie he can tear off your body."

"Yeah, you're probably right," Chloe said. "You can't go wrong with sexy lingerie."

She was thinking of something even more special that was *just* for him, but she could use a recommendation on where to buy lingerie. "Do you know of any lingerie shops that aren't too expensive?" She couldn't spend much, but she'd caught up on her mother's bills, and she knew Blaine would appreciate seeing her in pretty lingerie.

"Only about a dozen," Madigan said.

They worked on the garden as they discussed lingerie shops, which led to talking about other clothing shops they loved and how fun it would be to shop for baby clothes. The more they chatted, the more excited Reese became, and they made plans to go shopping together the next weekend while Colette was volunteering at the rescue.

Blaine and Maverick walked by on their way to get something out of Maverick's truck, and Blaine pulled Reese into a kiss. "The garden looks great. Are you doing okay?"

"She's *fine*," Madigan reassured him.

He scowled at her.

Madigan rolled her eyes and shooed him away.

The pond and the gazebo were almost done. "I can't believe your mom doesn't know about any of this."

"My dad has always been good at helping us pull off secret gifts for her," Madigan said. "He won't let her near the windows or the backyard until we get here tomorrow."

"He'll probably keep her in bed until then," Chloe said.

"Ew, you're right. Sexy talk about my parents is definitely off-limits," Madigan said as Blaine and Maverick returned, carrying a gorgeous stone fountain with intricately sculpted tiered bowls to the pond.

"Did Maverick make that?" Reese said as she and Madigan grabbed the last of the flowers to plant.

Blaine had taken her and Colette to see Cape Stone the other night. Their operation was impressive, and the fountains Maverick had made were stunning. But what Reese had loved most was the passion and pride in Blaine's voice as he showed them pictures of the many jobs they'd done, the equally stunning hardscapes he'd designed and crafted himself, and the praise he had for his staff. Colette had asked a million questions, and he'd been patient, answering each one in detail. Every time they'd been with him, he acted like he was just a regular guy, but he was so much more. He was a successful businessman, a proud Dark Knight, a phenomenal lover, and he was also becoming the best friend she'd ever had.

"Yeah, Justin has been working on it for weeks. There are five bowls, one for each of their kids," Chloe said.

"That's so thoughtful. I hope Reba loves the garden as much as she loves the pond and gazebo. Chloe, will you and Maverick be here for brunch tomorrow, or are you visiting your mom?"

"We're definitely *not* seeing my mom. It's my first Mother's Day, and I want it to be a good one. Right, baby?" Chloe rubbed her belly. "We'll be here for brunch, and then we're having dinner with my sister, Serena, her husband, Drake, their new baby, Jayden, and the rest of our Bayside friends."

"You don't like seeing your mom?" Reese asked.

"My mother is a hot mess who cares more about men and what they can do for her than she does about her own children," Chloe said. "I basically raised my younger sister, Serena."

"I guess we have that in common," Reese said. "My mom is a hot mess, too, and I've pretty much been raising my sister since she was born."

"I'm so sorry. I know how hard that is." Chloe's voice dripped with empathy. "Do you still see your mom?"

"I have to if I want to take care of Colette. She wouldn't let me take her when I moved out, but she's in court-ordered rehab for the next several weeks, so we get a reprieve."

"How did I not know this?" Madigan asked.

"I don't really tell people about it."

"I didn't either," Chloe said. "It's hard when your family is dysfunctional and you see other families with mothers who would bend over backward for their kids, like Reba and Ginger and Leah and Starr and Carrie. If it's that bad for Colette, why doesn't she get emancipated?"

"The stress took a toll on our relationship for a long time, and we weren't in a place where I could suggest it. We're doing better now, but I'm hoping rehab works this time. Do you mind if I ask when you decided you'd had enough and cut ties?"

"Not at all. It wasn't until Justin and I got together. I went with Serena and Drake to see her, and she was beyond awful. Something inside me snapped, and I just knew I couldn't do it anymore. It was the hardest, and the best, thing I've ever done. She was like a noose around my neck my whole life, and now instead of worrying about shielding our baby from her, I can focus on being happy and becoming the kind of mother I always wished I'd had."

Focusing on being happy was exactly what Reese was doing. "You're going to be an amazing mother. Your baby is lucky."

"Thanks. If you ever want to talk about your mom, I'm here," Chloe said.

"We both are," Madigan said.

"Thanks. I appreciate that."

They finished planting and stepped back to see how it looked. They'd made the garden along the stone wall Blaine had helped his father build as a boy. She imagined him carrying those stones, bearing the burden without complaint, because that was who he was, and accepting his mistake of not realizing the hardships Justin had faced as a boy, because that was who he was, too.

"Watch it!" Blaine hollered at the same time Madigan said, *"Oh shit."* There was a *splash*, followed by cursing and shouting. Reese turned around just in time to see Maverick catch the fountain and Zander scramble out of the pond, chased by Zeke and Blaine.

"Oh no. What happened?" Reese couldn't help but laugh as

they sprinted around the yard, hollering threats and cursing, while the others cracked up.

"Zander was walking backward, giving Zeke crap about something, and tripped into the pond, knocking over the fountain," Madigan explained.

Blaine tackled Zander, and Zeke jumped in. Maverick and Tobias tried to pull them apart. Madigan shouted, "Tobias, don't get invol—" Zander grabbed Tobias's ankles, toppling him to the ground as Zeke and Blaine jumped on Maverick.

"Don't hurt Justin!" Chloe hollered. "My baby needs its daddy!"

"You've got *me*, Uptown Girl!" Zander hollered.

"Like hell she does!" Maverick shouted, going after him.

"Someone's going to get hurt!" Reese worried aloud.

Blaine went up on his knees. "It won't be me, babe!" Maverick jumped on his back, and Blaine flipped him over his shoulder as Zeke and Zander tried to take on Tobias.

"Shouldn't we stop them?" Reese asked. She and Madigan looked at the hose, still filling the pond, at the same time. "Should we?"

"Hell yes!" Madigan exclaimed, and they ran over to it. Madigan started spraying the guys as they rolled around in the grass, wrestling, laughing, and cursing. They stopped cold, exchanging troublemaking glances.

"Uh-oh," Reese said as they pushed to their feet.

"Run!" Madigan hollered.

She and Reese took off, but the guys were too fast. Blaine and Tobias caught them around their waists, and Zander turned the hose on *them*. The girls shrieked as Chloe and the guys cracked up. Reese tried to bury her face in Blaine's chest, but she was laughing too hard, and so was he as Zander turned the hose on Chloe, and Maverick tackled him again.

Reese looked up into Blaine's smiling eyes. "I hate to tell you this, but I'm falling pretty hard for your wacky family."

"That's a'right, buttercup, because I'm falling pretty damn hard for you."

He crushed his lips to hers in the passionate kiss she'd been dying for all night. *Whoops* and cheers and "Get a room!" rang out, and someone turned the hose on them. Reese shrieked and tried to hide behind Blaine as everyone howled with laughter.

Blaine's strong arms circled her, his eyes dark and sexy as he said, "I like you wet," and lowered his lips to hers, his brothers' catcalls turning to white noise to her thundering heart.

Chapter Twenty-Six

IT WAS LATE when they finished cleaning up his parents' yard and finally made it back to Blaine's house. They stripped off their wet clothes and stepped into a warm shower, reaching for each other. Everything they did lately was in sync, and that was an incredible feeling. They had so few nights alone, their kisses were deep and lustful, their hands roaming greedily over each other's bodies. Blaine backed her up against the wet tiles, teasing her with his fingers as they ate at each other's mouths. Without breaking the kiss or losing his rhythm between her legs, he wrapped her hand around his cock, helping her stroke him tight and fast.

God, what that did to her.

He focused on her clit, and her head fell back with a moaning whimper, but she didn't close her eyes. She craved his virility, drinking in his corded muscles and the restraint in his jaw, his eyes blazing into hers as he squeezed her hand tighter, stroking faster. "You want to see me come on you, don't you, dirty girl?"

"*Yes*" came out as desperate as she felt.

He squeezed her hand tight around the base of his cock and sank his teeth into her neck, sending pleasure radiating through her. She cried out, and his mouth came down over hers in a deliciously deep kiss, continuing his magnificent manipulations between her legs until she lost it again.

As she came down from the high, he eased their kisses, and their grip on his cock, guiding her to stroke him again. He growled into her mouth, kissing her harder. His cock was rock hard, his strong hand rough over hers. He was usually so verbally demanding, his silence brought another level of excitement. Need pulsed in the air between them hot and sharp. His other hand pushed into her hair. She longed for the sting of pleasure and pain she knew would follow. But he took his time, kissing her deeper, stroking faster, their moans competing with the sound of the shower raining down around them, heightening her anticipation.

He was so different tonight, as if he were lost in his own head, intent on *only* her pleasure. All at once, he tugged her hair, sending scintillating sensations streaking down her body, and broke their kiss, angling her face so she could watch as warm streaks of come painted her sex and inner thighs. There was something so real and vulnerable about seeing him that way, it drew a whispered confession. "*I love that.*"

He gritted out, "*Fuuck, baby,*" and tugged her head back, searching her eyes as if he were weighing the truth of her words. He brushed his lips over hers, whispering, "We're not nearly done," and then he kissed her slow and deep, his fingers sliding through the come and pushing inside her. He released her hair and grabbed both of her wrists, pinning them above her head. "Don't move when I let go." She kept her arms above her head as he poured bodywash into his hands and proceeded to bathe, caress, and titillate every inch of her until she was squirming and begging for more. He lowered her hands, and she reached for him, but he shook his head, stepping out of reach as he washed himself. Leaving her *wanting* with a vengeance, jealous of *his* hands.

He turned off the shower and dried her off before tending to himself. He led her into the bedroom and pulled down the blanket. "Sit on the edge of the bed, baby girl. I have something special for you."

She sat down, her pulse quickening as he opened his nightstand drawer and removed a box wrapped in black paper and tied with a pretty red ribbon. With shaky hands, she took the box. "What have you done, Mr. Wicked?"

"Probably not what you think." He tucked her hair behind her ear and kissed her. "Open it and see."

She untied the ribbon and lifted the top. Her body ignited, and so did her nerves, as she withdrew a black lace blindfold, two long black silk ties, and a bottle of intimate massage oil. "Who knew just the sight of these things could make me so nervous?"

He gazed deeply into her eyes. "Do you trust me, baby?"

"Yes. Explicitly."

"Do you want to play tonight?"

She nodded. "Yes. With you, I always want to."

"That's my girl." He kissed her. "This is the start of our sexy collection." He placed the gifts on the mattress and set the empty box on the nightstand beside their glasses of ice water. "I hope we'll add more to it as you feel comfortable. Tonight is all about you, baby. Do you want a drink before we get started?"

She nodded and took a sip of ice water. He downed the rest, the ice cubes clinking as he set down the glass.

"Close your eyes, buttercup." She closed them, and he put the blindfold on her. "I'm going to tie it on the side so you can put your head on the pillow. How does that feel? Is it too tight?"

"No. It's good." Her heart was thundering, and she was already wet between her legs. "It's kind of thrilling."

"I was hoping you'd like it. Now I want you to lie down." He helped her to the middle of the bed and began wrapping a silk tie around her wrist.

"Are you going to bind my wrists together?"

"No." He stretched her arm out to the side, and she felt a tug on the tie. "I'm tying them to the metal rungs on the headboard."

She swallowed hard as he tied one, then tethered the other. She'd never felt so exposed and vulnerable. She was breathing hard, sweating a little. She was nervous but not scared. She knew he'd never hurt her.

"If either is too tight or if they become too tight, I want you to tell me. The only pain you should feel tonight will be from overwhelming pleasure."

Her sex clenched at his lust-drenched voice. "They're not too tight." She heard him walking, and then he was spreading her legs wide.

"Look at my beautiful buttercup. Willing and trusting and so gorgeous and open for me."

She swallowed hard and felt the bed dip on one side. Now that she was enveloped in darkness, her other senses were heightened. She felt him move between her legs and felt the drip of liquid on her stomach and breasts, a gentle scent mixing with the rugged scent of him. Then his hands were sliding in the oil, moving over her stomach and up her ribs, caressing and groping her breasts. The sensation of his strong, rough hands and the slick, soft liquid was intoxicating. His mouth came down over one nipple, and he sucked hard as he pinched her other nipple. She cried out, bowing off the mattress, pain and pleasure burning through her like lightning. His body heat blazed over her skin. She sensed him leaning or reaching over her and heard the ice in the glass. An ice cube touched her nipple. She gasped at the fiery sensation as he held it there. "Feel that burn, baby."

She bit her lower lip, her nipple burning and prickling. "I can't take it."

"You *can*. Stay with it just another minute." He lowered his mouth to her other nipple, sucking and using his teeth. She writhed and moaned, dizzy with desire, unable to think as scintillating sensations rained down over her. She bucked, and thrashed, the pleasure excruciatingly intense. Just when she was sure she'd pass out from it, he moved the ice and slicked his tongue over her nipple.

"Suck it. *Please*, suck it."

"I fucking love hearing you beg for my mouth." He sucked her frozen nipple, sending heat and ice whipping through her. He dragged the ice over her other nipple and down her body, leaving a cold trail of wetness on her hot skin, and followed it with his mouth. She wanted his mouth everywhere at once. "Like that, baby?"

"*Yes.*"

He touched her clit with the ice. She cried out, her hips shooting off the mattress with the burn. He pushed them down with one hand, keeping the ice in place. "Next time I'll bind your ankles, too."

That enticing thought sent her into a greedy frenzy. She writhed and pleaded for more as he trailed the ice along her swollen lips and the center of her sex, sending shocks of scintillating pain and pleasure ricocheting through her. He was relentless, taking her right up to the edge of madness, then drawing back. "You like that, baby?"

"So much."

"Good girl, playing all my games." She felt the mattress dip and his body heat over her again. He rubbed the ice over her lips, and she opened her mouth, trying to capture what was left of it. "Hold the ice between your teeth until it melts, and don't drop it." She opened her mouth, and he put it in place. She felt him come down over her. His chest hair tickled her skin, and she realized he was putting his nipple on the quickly melting ice. "*Fuuck*, that feels good." As soon as it melted, he growled, "Suck my nipple *hard*." She opened wide and sucked. "That's it, use your teeth...*Fuck*. I like the pain. Bite me, baby. Mark me as yours."

His demand was exactly what she wanted, what she *needed* to let go. She bit and sucked and held nothing back, wanting to give him the same pleasures he gave her. He gritted out, "*God*. You're so fucking good. I need your mouth." He tore his nipple away so fast, she tasted blood and crushed his mouth to hers, tongue plunging deep. She was ravenous for him, but his mouth left hers as quickly as he'd given it to her.

The mattress shifted with his weight as he moved lower on the bed and gripped her ankles with oil-slicked hands. He lifted one of her legs, dragging his tongue along the underside of her knee, sending heat slithering through her core. He lingered there, licking and sucking, so focused on that one spot, she felt every slick of his tongue as if it were between her legs. She moaned and rocked as he nipped, bit, and grazed his teeth along her inner thigh. Every touch sent shocks of pleasure through her core. She writhed as his mouth traveled up her leg. Lust pooled tight and hot inside her as he sucked the space between her thigh and her sex. She felt her arousal dripping down her ass. She should probably be embarrassed to be so exposed, but she was so turned on, she felt fully electrified, fully alive. Like she'd been barely breathing before Blaine came into her life, and all she wanted was more. More of this *and* more of him.

"Your sweet pussy is begging for my cock." His fingers followed the slick trail.

"Give it to me," she begged. She felt more oil being poured over her sex, dropping thick and warm between her ass cheeks.

"Soon, baby girl." He moved his slick fingers to her ass, teasing her there, and pushed one finger into her ass. It was so slick, and she was so ready, pure loud, lustful sounds of pleasure burst from her lungs. "Feels good, doesn't it, baby?"

"So good."

"I'm going to fuck this beautiful, tight ass tonight."

She couldn't stop another moan from escaping as he pumped his finger.

"Does my little bunny like the thought of me claiming her there?"

"*Yes*," she panted out, spreading her legs wider. "*More.* I want more."

"That's my dirty girl. I need to taste you." He shifted again, lifting her legs over his shoulders as his mouth claimed her center, and that thick finger pushed into her bottom again. Her body caught fire. She couldn't control the bucking of her hips or the pleas spilling from her lips. *"More...Don't stop...There. Ohgod, there!"* He pushed a second finger into her ass, praising her for taking him so well, for being so beautiful, so *giving*. His praise helped her let go even more, allowed her to be louder, to thrash and beg the way she knew he loved. *"I need you. I want your cock inside me."* He took her clit between his teeth, and waves of pleasure engulfed her as he pumped his fingers, taking her up, up, *up*, until she shattered like glass.

Just as she started coming down from the peak, he moved up her body, driving his cock into her, as his mouth claimed hers in a ravenous kiss. The unique taste of him mixed with the taste of her. The weight of his powerful body and the feel of his thick thighs pressing down on her were like a drug. He remained buried deep and gyrated his hips, grinding against that secret spot inside her, until she went off like a bomb, thrusting and crying out into his mouth. Her shoulders ached from the tethers, but the pain only heightened the pleasure ravaging her, seeping into every nook and crevice.

She was lost in a world of ecstasy, floating in a post-climactic haze, vaguely aware that he was still hard, as he untied her blindfold and unbound her wrists, his loving eyes coming into focus.

"Welcome back, beautiful." He kissed her softly.

"Hi," she whispered, her body still vibrating with pleasure. "That was incredible."

"You're incredible, baby." He rubbed her shoulders. "How do you feel? Do you still want to play?"

She shivered with anticipation. "Yes. Do I get to tie you up?"

"SORRY, BABY, IT doesn't work that way." It physically pained him to see disappointment in her baby blues. He would never give up that kind of control, but if there were ever a woman who made him wish he could, if only to show her how much he cared, it was Reese. His heart thudded to a different beat, harder and somehow also softer, making him want to give her more to make up for the things he couldn't change.

Shoving those feelings down deep, he kissed her sweet lips. "Turn over for me, sweetheart. Let me make you feel good." He helped her onto her stomach, and she started to go up on her hands and knees. He ran his hand down her back. "Stay on your stomach."

As she settled onto the pillow, he dripped oil across her shoulders and massaged them, working his way down her arms, giving extra attention to her wrists. He worked his way back up to her shoulders, easing the discomfort with his capable hands.

"That feels so good."

"I need to take care of my girl."

"You're definitely sweet, Mr. Wicked."

"Let's see if you still think so when I'm buried nine inches deep in your ass, Miss Wilder."

"Blaine." She laughed and buried her face in the pillow.

"Aw, come on, don't hide the blush." He kissed her shoulder, and she rested her cheek on the pillow again. "Just keeping my rep intact." He dribbled oil down her spine, over the curve of her ass, and down the crack, earning a sharp inhalation.

"You really are wicked."

"You get off on my wickedness." He massaged his way down her back, kissing down her spine, and nipped at the dip in her waist. "Look how gorgeous you are."

"You always make me feel that way."

"Because you are, baby. You're the sexiest, most beautiful woman I've ever seen. I want you to hear my voice telling you that every time you look in the mirror. Got it?"

"Okay."

"That's my girl." He skimmed his hands down her hips and caressed her supple cheeks, gritting out, "*Mine.*" He couldn't resist taking a bite out of one soft globe. She yelped with surprise. "I ought to have my name tattooed right here." He rubbed his hand over one cheek and gave her a smack, just hard enough to sting. She flinched and moaned and buried her face in the pillow again.

"Why are you hiding?"

She lifted her face. "Because I *liked* it."

"Fuck yeah, you do. Don't ever hide what you like from me. *Own* it." He ran his fingers between her cheeks. She was slick from the oil. His fingers brushed over her tightest hole, but he didn't focus on it. He wanted her to *crave* it. "I can't get enough of you." He poured oil along her thighs, letting it drip between her legs. She squirmed and moaned, lifting her ass. "Feel good, baby?"

"Yes," she said breathily.

He massaged from the backs of her knees and thighs, teasing her pussy with his thumbs. She moaned and lifted her ass, giving him better access. "Good girl, letting me in." He pushed his fingers into her slick heat, finding the spot that made her entire body shudder. "That's it, baby girl. Let me feel you come." He put his other hand on the top of her ass, teasing her hole with his thumb.

"Oh *God.*" She gyrated her hips.

"You want more, baby?"

"*Yes.*"

He continued teasing as he fucked her with his fingers, making her mewl and *want,* until she was trembling and gasping, on the verge of coming.

"Blaine...*please.*"

"Own your pleasure, baby. Tell me what you want."

"Your thumb," she panted out. "In my ass."

He pushed it in, and "*Yes*" sailed from her lips, her hands fisting in the sheets as her climax ravaged her. He gritted his teeth against the urge to drive his cock into her, to feel every pulse of her desire along his dick. "You're so damn sexy."

When the last of the aftershocks rolled through her, she sank into the mattress, breathing harder. "*More.* I want *you*."

His chest tightened. "There's nothing I want more than to claim the rest of you. Up on your hands and knees, baby girl." She rose up, her body glistening. "So fucking beautiful, giving in to your desires and fulfilling mine." He poured more oil between her cheeks, working her open with his fingers while teasing her between her legs. "Feel good?"

"Mm-hm."

When he was sure she was ripe for his taking, he pressed a kiss to her spine. "Are you ready for me, baby girl?"

"*Yes*," she said with as much confidence as desire.

He lubed his cock, and rubbed the head of it on her hole. She tightened up. "Relax, buttercup. I'm going to take good care of you." He stroked her bottom. "It might hurt a little at first, but then you'll feel so good you'll forget the pain." He eased into her, breaching the tight rim of muscles. Her hands fisted in the sheet. "Breathe, baby. Open up for me." His entire body was tight with restraint, fighting the need to pound into her. He forced himself to go slow, her slightly pained sounds slowing him down even more. "Is it too much?"

"No. I want this."

"That's my girl. Let me know what you need. You feel so good, baby." He pushed in farther, and she exhaled loudly, her head dipping between her shoulders. He stilled. "Want me to stop?"

She shook her head. "It's better now. Keep going."

He clutched her hips, pumping slowly. "Christ. Your ass is so fucking tight." Exquisite pleasure coiled around him like a snake at the grip her body had on him, every thrust heightening the intensity. It took everything he had to keep from chasing that high. The desire to take care of her, to bring *her* pleasure, drove his efforts. She rocked in time with his thrusts, her sounds morphing to sensual moans, taking him deeper, faster, *harder*.

"Fuck, baby. Our bodies are made for each other." He quickened his thrusts and moved one hand between her legs.

"Feels so good," she said breathlessly. *"Don't stop."*

Her plea cut him loose, and he pounded into her, teasing her clit, gritting his teeth to keep from coming. *"Fuck.* So tight...So fucking good."

"Blaine...I'm gonna—"

Her body clamped tighter, and he spiraled into oblivion, thrusting and cursing as violent gusts of pleasure tore through him. He jackhammered into her, clinging to her hips, unable to think or speak as exquisite sensations and fierce emotions battered him, the erotic sounds of their passion and his bunny's sweet sounds of surrender drawing him into a sexual vortex.

As the storm passed, he was enveloped in a state of bliss unlike any other, his heart rising to the surface. He pressed kisses to Reese's back and wrapped his arms around her. "Jesus, baby. I got so lost in us. Did I hurt you?"

"No. I was a goner, too," she said just above a whisper.

Every little thing she said and did made him want to be closer, to have more of her. More of her time, her heart. Hell, he wanted to be the very air she breathed. He rested his cheek on her back, her racing heart thrumming against it. There were so many emotions stacking up inside him, so many things he wanted to say to let her know how special she was to him and how unbelievably hard he was falling for her, but all he could manage was "You're in for it now, baby girl. I'm never letting you go."

Chapter Twenty-Seven

REESE AWOKE IN the same position in which she'd fallen asleep, lying on her side, her head resting on Blaine's arm, their bodies flush. One of his legs was tucked between hers, the other rested on her outer thigh, and his other arm was still wrapped tightly around her, as if he couldn't stand the thought of any space between them. She felt herself smiling as his voice tiptoed through her mind. *You're in for it now, baby girl. I'm never letting you go.*

Did he know how big those words were? How much they meant to her?

She didn't have to look far for the answer. Blaine wasn't an off-the-cuff type of man.

She thought about all the things they'd done last night, the loving way he'd worshipped every inch of her, and the sweet things he'd said, taking care of her head and heart as much as her body. He always seemed to know exactly what she needed. She'd never felt so loved or so connected to anyone. She hoped he really wouldn't ever let her go.

"Morning, buttercup." He kissed her forehead. "What's got your heart racing?"

"You," she said softly, meeting his gaze. "Us."

"Mm. That was pretty intense last night." His hand slid down her back, and he cupped her bottom. "How do you feel?"

"A little sore and aware of muscles I haven't used before."

"I'll run you a hot bath when we get up."

She kissed his chest. "You sure know how to romance a girl."

"I don't know about that, but I like taking care of you, and I like waking up with you in my bed."

"I'm sorry my life is the way it is, and we don't have more time alone."

"There's nothing to be sorry for. I'd never wish Colette away. Just know that if it were up to me, we'd wake up like this every day."

"Me too."

"How are you feeling about Mother's Day?"

"I was so lost in being happy, I forgot it was Mother's Day. It's strange, I guess."

He went up on his elbow, giving her his full attention. "Just this year because she's in rehab? Or every year?"

"It's always been a weird holiday for me. Remember when you were in elementary school, and everyone would make Mother's and Father's Day gifts?"

"Vaguely."

"Those times were so anxiety inducing for me, I couldn't forget them if I tried."

He held her tighter. "Why, baby?"

"Because while other kids were drawing pictures of things their parents enjoyed, like golf, or baking, or a hundred other things, I had no idea what my parents liked besides partying. It wasn't like I could draw a picture of beer cans or bottles of wine or liquor or the high heels my mother wore when she went out."

"I can only imagine how tough that was." He brushed a kiss to her lips. "Did you resent the other kids?"

"No. I resented my parents, but mostly I longed for what I'd never have. I thank God I had my grandmother, and I hope and pray I'm doing right by Lettie."

"You are. She loves you, and now that she's letting go of some of that anger, she's really coming into her own. That's all because of you, baby."

"I had a little help from a pushy biker lately." She touched his scruff.

He grinned, then kissed her. "I'm sorry today is hard for you, and if you'd rather not hang out with my family, we don't have to."

"I'm looking forward to it. I like your family, and it's good for Lettie to see what normal looks like."

"Your life with her is normal right now. She's thriving. But either way, I'm glad, because I want you there. I got you a little something." He leaned over and opened the nightstand.

"More play toys?"

"No, but we'll do that soon."

A thrill chased over her skin.

He dangled a small black velvet pouch from his fingers. "This is for Mother's Day. For all the love and support you give Lettie."

"But I'm not her mother."

"You don't have to give birth to a child for her to be yours. You're the reason Colette is a smart, strong young woman. Not a day goes by when you're not thinking of her welfare, making sure she's healthy and safe and doing all the things she should be doing in order to secure a future she can be proud of. You've given her someone she can count on. You are, in every sense of the word, Lettie's mother, and you deserve to be honored on this special day."

Tears welled in her eyes.

"Oh shit. Did I fuck up?"

She shook her head, tears spilling down her cheeks as she choked out, "No one other than my grandmother has ever acknowledged the things I do for her, except you, and you noticed from the start."

"How could I not? You don't just live and breathe for her. You chose a career that would give you access to another way to possibly help her. I can't do anything about your longing for a better mother, but from now on this is *your* day, baby."

He poured the contents of the pouch into his hand, revealing a beautiful gold necklace with an infinity symbol on one end and a diamond teardrop that must have cost a fortune on the other. Her breath hitched. She'd never seen anything so beautiful.

"The infinity symbol represents us."

"Like your tattoo."

He winked. "The diamond is Colette's birthstone. It threads through one end of the infinity symbol, showing your connection, and hangs down real pretty."

More tears fell as he put it on her. She touched it with a shaky hand. Too choked up to speak, she reached for him. He pressed his lips to hers, salty tears slipping between them. "I've never owned anything so beautiful. How can I say thank you for something this nice?"

"You don't have to say anything." He wiped her tears. "I have one more gift for you."

"*Another?* This is already too much."

"You opened the door to smothering. You can't close it

now." He reached into the nightstand again and handed her an envelope. "It's actually for you and Colette."

"Blaine, you didn't have to—"

"Open it." He left no room for negotiation.

She opened the envelope and withdrew two gift certificates for a day of pampering at the Spa at Ocean Edge. Ocean Edge was the most glamorous resort on the Cape. "Blaine, we can't accept this. It must have cost a fortune."

"You can, and you *will*. You two deserve it, and you can use it whenever you want. It's good for a year. Happy Mother's Day, buttercup."

Fresh tears slid down her cheeks. "When I okayed smothering, I meant with hugs and kisses and opening your heart, not luxurious gifts."

"Then I'd better get busy." His wolfish grin made her laugh.

As he lowered his lips to hers, she said, "I couldn't love the gifts"—*or you*—"more."

LIKE MOST HOLIDAYS with Blaine's family, Mother's Day brunch was a loud, festive affair with endless food, too many desserts, and hours of heckling. His mother had raved about all the work they'd surprised her with. She showered Reese and Colette with affection and was thrilled they were sharing the special day with their family.

It was midafternoon, and his family was scattered around the yard chatting and cheering on Junie as she lined up for her turn at Wiffle Ball. Red ringlets framed her face, which was pinched in concentration. Junie, Rosie, and Lynnie had dragged

Blaine and Reese and a handful of others into the game.

"Let's go, Junie!" Colette called out from the other side of the yard, where she was talking with Zeke and Conroy.

"You've got this, Junie," Blaine said. His gaze slid back to Reese, as it had been doing all day. She was playing second base and looked adorably sexy in olive-green shorts and a white V-neck shirt that accentuated her curves.

"Go, Junie!" Rosie hollered as she twirled in the grass.

"Hey, you're cheering for the wrong team," Gunner teased.

Rosie giggled.

"Take your time, Twitch," Tank encouraged, using the nickname that always made Junie smile.

Cheers rang out as Junie hit the ball off the tee and ran toward Sid, who was playing first base and ushering Lynnie toward second. Reese cheered for Lynnie as she ran over the base, launching herself into Reese's arms. Reese spun her around, and Blaine was filled with an unfamiliar, happy sensation.

Gunner stood on the pitcher's mound. He pointed at them, giving Blaine a thumbs-up, earning laughter from the guys. Blaine might struggle with the idea of ever having kids of his own, but there was no denying the tug in his chest at the sight of Reese hugging the towheaded little girl. Just as there was no ignoring the selfish part of him that didn't want to share her with anyone other than Colette for a long damn time. Despite all that, he knew he would give Reese whatever she wanted, including children.

"Give you any ideas, son?" Preacher asked with a chuckle.

"She looks awfully good with a little one in her arms," Madigan said.

Yeah, she fucking does. He shut them down with "She looks

good all the time."

Baz handed him the bat. "You're up, Daddy Blaine."

Blaine gritted out a curse and went to hit the damn ball.

"Huwwy!" Rosie hollered.

"Hit those girls home, Blaine," Tank said.

As everyone cheered him on, the word *home* rang different-ly. He set his gaze on Reese again. He'd been wrestling with the idea of moving her and Colette into his place since they'd started spending more time there. Once their mother was out of rehab, they could figure out the next step for Colette, but that woman had a lot to prove before he'd let Colette go back to living under her thumb.

"Go, Blaine!" Rosie shouted.

Blaine swung and missed the ball altogether, causing an uproar of laughter. *What the...?*

"Forget hitting them home," Maverick teased. "He can't even get on first base."

"Just like with women," Zander shouted.

Blaine gritted out, "I was sidetracked." He looked at Reese, laughing behind her hand, and couldn't help laughing, too.

"Sidetracked by lack of skill," Tobias shouted.

"I'll show you lack of skill." He eyed Reese as he lined up his shot. *This one's for you, buttercup.*

A crack rang out as he beaned the ball in a low line drive straight to Reese. Whoops and cheers erupted as he ran to first base and scooped up Junie on his way to second. Reese was holding the ball, moving from side to side, blocking second base and waiting to tag him out. He set Junie down and said, "Run all the way home, Junie." As she ran around Reese and touched the base, sprinting toward third, Blaine lowered his shoulder and barreled into his girl, tossing her over his shoulder. She shrieked with laughter, dropping the ball.

Everyone was laughing and cheering as he sprinted to third base with Reese over his shoulder, scooped Junie up under one arm, Lynnie under the other, and ran all three of them home. He'd never heard so much cheering as he set down the giggling girls, and Reese slid down his body to her feet.

"You're crazy!" she shouted over the commotion, beaming brighter than the sun.

"Crazy about you, baby." He pulled her into a kiss.

"Show-off!" Gunner hollered.

Blaine kept an arm around Reese. "We all know which Wicked is toughest *and* better with the women."

"All right, you two, that's enough," Madigan said. "We've got a game to finish."

"Yeah! Let's play!" Rosie shouted.

"I'm out. Uncle Blaine needs a drink." He looked at Reese. "Want a drink, baby?"

"No, thank you. I have a base to cover."

As Reese sauntered away, he asked Maverick to take his place and went to get a drink out of the cooler. His mother was pouring herself a glass of iced tea at the beverage table.

"Hi, honey. That was quite a show."

"Sometimes you gotta put the boys in their places." He chuckled and opened a beer.

"I can't remember the last time I saw you smile this much."

"It's been a good day." He took a drink.

"It has, but I think we both know it's more than that. I'm really glad Reese and Colette are here. They're having such a good time, and it could have been a really difficult day for them."

"Did Reese tell you about her mom?"

"Yes. We talked at Preacher's party and more today about her parents and how hard it's been for her and Colette. You know how difficult my father was and how his view on women was not the kindest."

"Yeah. That sucks. I'm glad we weren't raised that way." He hated that his mother had experienced that.

"That was by design," she said sweetly. "I understand what it's like growing up with a mother who doesn't stand up for you, but Reese and Colette have had it much harder. I knew my mom loved me, but I didn't know what a mother's love should really feel like until I met your grandmother. I know Reese had her grandmother, but she died when Reese was so young. I don't think Reese knew what love felt like from anyone else until you came into her life."

His chest constricted. He took another drink to ease his thickening throat.

"She showed me the necklace you gave her and told me about the spa package you got for her and Colette. You did good, sweetheart."

"They deserve a lot more than that."

"Yes, but you know it's not about the gifts. It's about how you make each other feel, and I know from talking with Reese and Colette that you make them feel special and valued and loved. Am I right in thinking they make you feel the same?"

"I'm not with Reese to feel better about myself."

"I know, sweetheart, but it's okay to admit that she makes you feel that way. I know you're used to being the top gorilla, who makes sure everyone else has what they need. But you deserve to feel special and valued and loved, too."

"I feel good, Mom. No worries there."

"Good. That makes my mama heart happy. I have to admit,

I never thought I'd see you fall in love."

"Now you're living in Madigan's fantasy?"

She smiled and ran her fingers along the side of his hair. "My sweet boy, you don't have to say it. I've seen enough Wicked men fall to know what love looks like. Your girls have brought out your heart, and Reese told me how much their lives have changed since you two got together. Just look at how happy they are."

He glanced at Reese, crouched in the grass looking at something with Rosie, and had that weird sensation in his chest again. He looked for Colette and found her sitting at a table playing cards with his grandfather and Conroy. "*Shit.* You don't think they're teaching her to cheat at poker, do you?"

"You *know* they are."

"Not anymore." He downed the rest of his beer, tossed the can into the trash, and went to set them straight.

His grandfather looked up as he approached. "What's got your britches in a knot?"

Blaine put his hand on Colette's shoulder. "Are these guys teaching you unsavory habits?"

"No," Conroy said. "We're teaching her to win."

"By cheating, *Con*?" His uncle's nickname didn't come from shortening his given name.

Conroy squinted against the sun. "Where did you get such a low opinion of us?"

"I've played cards with you." He took Colette by the arm, lifting her to her feet. "Come on, Lettie. Let's find something else to do."

"You're always ruining my good times," his grandfather complained. "I was about to win a spa package."

Blaine glowered at Colette. "You bet the gift I gave you?"

"It's all I have, and it's not like I was going to lose. They taught me tricks."

"Tricks, huh?" He set a dark stare on his grandfather. "What did *you* bet?"

"A trip to the ice cream store," his grandfather said.

"You have no shame." His grandfather was no longer allowed to drive. "She's not old enough to drive, Gramps. Stop trying to swindle sweets out of the kids." He dragged Colette away from the table.

"Bring me back some cake, Lettie!" his grandfather shouted.

"You got it, Gramps," she called over her shoulder. "Why can't I keep playing?"

"You don't need to be learning bad habits." He loved and trusted his grandfather and Conroy, but Colette was on a good path, and there was no need to add temptations. She'd volunteered at the rescue again yesterday and had loved it, and she'd had so much fun babysitting, she'd offered to do it again.

"Gramps said he taught *you* to play, and you didn't turn out so bad."

"There are plenty of people who'd disagree with that."

"I've got your back. Where are they?" she said sharply. "I'll take them down."

He laughed.

She stopped walking, her expression thoughtful. "Seriously, though, I wouldn't have given away the spa package. This is the best Mother's Day ever. Thank you for thinking of us."

He hooked his arm around her shoulder, walking toward the others. "Are you going soft on me, Lettie?"

"*Never.* Can we spend the night at your house tonight?"

Yes, absolutely, was on the tip of his tongue. "You'll have to ask Reese."

"*Fine.* I want to get Gramps some cake. Stand behind me so Reba and Ginger can't see me."

"What makes you think I'll do that?"

She gave him a deadpan look. "As if you wouldn't?"

She had him there. "You'd better be quick, or we'll both get in trouble."

Colette went to the dessert table. As Blaine positioned himself between her and everyone else, Reese walked over, eyeing him curiously. "Why do you look like you're up to no good?"

He pulled her into his arms. "Maybe because every time I see you, I want to be very"—he kissed her—"*very*"—he kissed her deeper—"*bad.*"

"Good cover. Nobody wants to see that," Colette said as she walked by with a plate of cake.

Chapter Twenty-Eight

REESE SUBMITTED THE last report for the day and began gathering her things, excited for the weekend. She, Blaine, and Colette were meeting Blaine's brothers, Madigan and Tobias, and some of their cousins and friends at the Salty Hog for dinner, as they'd done half a dozen times since Mother's Day. Kendra and TJ usually came with their parents, and Marly and Dante were usually there, too. Thankfully, the jealousy Reese had initially felt had diminished, making that situation less awkward. It was hard to be jealous of anyone when Blaine showed her how special she and Colette were to him every single day.

She touched her necklace, unable to believe it had only been almost three weeks since Blaine had given it to her. She was still thinking about the special spa day she and Colette had shared. Things were going so well, it felt more like three months since that romantic morning. Colette was still volunteering at the rescue and falling in love with every dog she met. She and Kendra were as thick as thieves, and she was better prepared for finals thanks to Zeke's tutoring and her hard work. Blaine continued to surprise them at every turn, spending too much money and ignoring Reese's complaints about it. Reese came home every week to find her mother's lawn had been freshly mowed. Two weeks ago he'd had a batch of beautiful flowers delivered, because Reese had mentioned that she hoped to convince her mother to get into gardening when she got out of rehab, to keep her mind off drugs and alcohol. He'd also taken Colette and Kendra out to dinner and a movie the night Reese had attended the book club meeting, and he'd gotten them both cool iPad cases while they were out.

Reese was still trying to figure out the right gift to get Blaine to show her appreciation for all he did for them, but the man had everything, and all he seemed to want was her and Colette in his life.

"I can't get used to seeing you all dreamy eyed," Joy said as she pocketed her phone. "What does Mr. Romance have planned for you and Colette this weekend?"

She smiled at the nickname Joy had coined for Blaine when he'd surprised Reese at work a couple of weeks ago to take her on a lunch date and had brought her flowers. Reese was learning to let go of the embarrassment of being her mother's daughter and had been trying to open up more to Joy and, to a lesser degree, to Terry. She wasn't spilling all her dirty laundry or raving about her sex life, but she wasn't hiding from the world anymore, either. She'd told Joy the truth about where her mother was and had learned that Joy's wife's younger brother was in recovery from a substance use disorder. As awful as that was, it made it easier for Reese to open up and had shown her once again that nobody's life was perfect. Although with Blaine, hers and Colette's sure felt that way.

"We're meeting everyone at the Salty Hog tonight, and tomorrow we're taking his boat out with his sister and her boyfriend and Colette's friends." They headed for the door to leave for the day. "I really wish you and Willa would meet us at the Hog one evening so you could get to know everyone. Or maybe you guys can come fishing with us sometime."

"Willa's not into crowded bars, but fishing is right up her alley. I'll ask her about it, but I'm not getting near any fish guts."

"You and me, both."

"Those look like *thank goodness it's Friday* faces to me," Terry said when they walked into the lobby. "Have a great weekend, and tell Willa, Blaine, and Colette I said hello."

"Will do," Joy said.

"See you bright and early Monday morning." Reese followed Joy out the door and headed home.

COLETTE WAS SITTING on the couch listening to music on an app on the television and eating a bowl of cereal when Reese walked in. She smiled around a mouthful, and Reese swore it lit up the warm, clean living room, which no longer felt like a neglected penitentiary.

She set her things on the table by the door. "Hi. How was your day?"

"Boring. Are we still going tonight?" She ate another spoonful of cereal.

"Yes, and Madigan said she'd be happy to bring her guitar and show you and Kendra a few chords." They'd taken Colette and Kendra to hear one of Madigan's musical storytelling gigs last weekend, and the girls had been enamored with the idea of learning to play. Reese was worried about Colette reading music, but Madigan said plenty of people played by ear.

"Awesome. Will Gunner and Sid be there?"

"I think so. Why?"

"I want to see how Woody's doing."

"I'm sure he's okay. Did you text them?" Woody had gotten a rather large sliver in his paw last weekend.

"No. I've texted every day, and I don't want to be a pain."

"I doubt it would bother them." As wrong as it was, when they'd attended the rescue's adoption event, Reese had prayed Woody wouldn't get adopted, because she knew it would break Colette's heart. She didn't know why that adorable old dog hadn't been scooped up yet, but she was relieved. "I'm going to pack a few things for the weekend and take a quick shower. Have you packed yet?"

They'd been spending a lot of time at Blaine's house and were spending more nights there, too, which deepened all of their relationships. Colette liked sleeping upstairs and having that floor to herself, except when Kendra spent the night. On those nights they usually sacked out on the couches in front of the big-screen television. She also seemed to appreciate that Reese didn't try to hide the fact that she slept in Blaine's room. Sometimes she even texted Blaine early in the morning with something like *Get up, lazy, I'm hungry*, and they'd meet in the kitchen and make breakfast together before Reese was even awake. Knowing Colette had a good male role model in her life who loved and protected her like she was his own sister brought a special kind of happiness.

"No, but Blaine isn't coming until six, so I have time."

Biting her tongue against the urge to micromanage, Reese headed into her bedroom to pack. She'd mentioned that struggle to Reba when she'd seen her at the adoption event, and

Reba had said, *Micromanaging a teenager is like holding a toddler's hand when everything they want is right in front of them. Better to let them stumble and fall and be there to help them back up than to have them break free and never look back.*

Reese was getting there.

She packed the pretty pink lace lingerie she'd bought with Madigan and Chloe and the other things she'd need for the weekend. Even on sale, the lingerie was still a splurge, but Blaine was worth it. The last time she'd worn it, Blaine hadn't been able to keep his hands off her.

She chose a cute outfit to wear to dinner, pinned her hair up so it wouldn't get wet, and went to take a shower.

Tipping her face up to the warm water, she felt the stress of the day washing away and wished Blaine were there to wash her back...*among other places.* Bathing together had become one of her favorite things. She loved their sweet showers as much as she enjoyed their sexy showers, and maybe most of all, she adored their tender baths, when she could lie against his chest, and his love came through in sweet and sexy whispers and gentle caresses. She was soaping up, reveling in thoughts of him, when she heard what sounded like shouting.

What is Colette listening to? They liked a lot of the same music, but Colette liked rap more than Reese did.

She rinsed off and was washing her face when she heard a door slam. When she turned off the water, the squeal of tires had her pulse spiking.

"Lettie?" she yelled through the door as she wrapped the towel around herself. She opened the door and heard the same type of pop music Colette had been listening to when she'd come home. She ran into the living room, stopping cold at the sight of her mother digging through *her* purse, her light brown hair a tangled mess curtaining her face.

Bile rose in Reese's throat. "What are you doing here? Where's Colette?" She looked in the kitchen, but it was empty. "Lettie?" she hollered. Answered with silence, the hair on the back of her neck stood on end. "*Where* is Colette?" She yanked her purse from her mother's hands, bringing her mother's frenetic, glassy eyes to hers, fueling her rage.

"Where's the money?" Her mother started pulling open drawers on the cabinet by the television, her hair flying wildly with her actions. "I know you have it. Look at this place. It's a fucking castle now."

Reese's mind reeled. She was shaking all over, fury raging inside her as she ran to the door and tugged it open, hurrying out to the deck, screaming, "*Lettie! Colette!*" Her shouts went unanswered. She stormed into the bathroom, pulled out her hair clip, and threw on her clothes, frantically searching for her phone before remembering it was by the front door. She bolted into the living room.

Her mother was tearing open the kitchen drawers and rummaging through them, sending silverware and other utensils to the floor. She looked at Reese with hatred in her eyes. "If you won't help me, then *get out* of my house!" She stormed down the hall to Reese's bedroom shouting about money.

Reese grabbed her phone and saw several messages from Blaine but none from Colette. She called Colette's phone and heard it ringing. Her heart sank as she followed the sound to the floor between the couch and the coffee table. Tears sprang to her eyes as she sprinted down the hall. Her dresser drawers were open, her belongings strewn across the floor, and her mother was digging through her overnight bag, raging about money. Reese lost it. She grabbed her mother and shook her. "Where is my sister? What did you do?" She heard the front door open. "Colette!"

She ran out of the bedroom just as Blaine's deep voice called out her name. She burst into tears at the sight of him, saying, "Colette's gone—" At the same time, he said, "Your mother is missing."

His nostrils flared, every muscled corded tight. "What do you mean *gone*? Who's shouting?"

"My mother—" She told him the rest as he tore down the hall.

Blaine grabbed her mother by the arm, yanking her out of Reese's closet, and got in her face. "Where is Colette?"

Her mother struggled against his grip. "If you want her, you'll have to pay."

"What have you done with her?" His voice was dead calm, the threat louder than a drum.

"Let's just call her a down payment."

"Oh God. *No.*" Reese grabbed the edge of the dresser to keep from crumpling to the ground.

"She's your *daughter.*" Blaine tightened his grip on her mother's arm, teeth bared, nostrils flaring. "*Who* has her?"

Her mother struggled to break free, clawing at his hand, eyes darting around the room. "My *boyfriend* will make good use of her."

Gutted, "*Ice*" fell from Reese's lips as strangled and tortured as she felt.

"The fuck he will," Blaine seethed through clenched teeth.

Her mother turned a hateful stare on Reese. "What're *you* crying about? She can take care of herself. She always has."

"She's a *child*," Reese bit out, closing in on her. "*I* have taken care of her since the day she was born. How could you do this?"

Blaine shoved her mother backward and grabbed Reese's arm, storming out of the room as he put the phone to his ear. "Cuffs, the mother is at Reese's. Yeah. Ice has Colette. Can you track her phone?"

"She left her phone here," Reese said frantically.

"Forget the phone. I checked the tracker on Ice's vehicle on the way here. It's in Plymouth. I don't know what vehicle we're looking for."

"Oh God." Sobs fell from Reese's lips as Blaine ended the call with Cuffs.

He pulled her against him with one arm and called his father, rallying the Dark Knights.

Chapter Twenty-Nine

REESE PACED BLAINE'S living room, anger and worry driving her every step, tears of frustration burning her eyes. Two policemen were parked out front, and Saint and Tobias were standing sentinel inside, watching over Reese and all the girls Reba had rallied around her. "I was *right there*. I heard shouting, but I thought it was the music. If I'd just checked on her, I could have stopped him from taking her."

"You don't know that," Chloe said.

"He could have had a gun," Sidney added.

"But there would have been *two* of us." Reese's voice escalated as she stalked across the floor. "Lettie wouldn't have been alone. If I'd just been faster, he could have taken me instead."

Reba touched her arm, stopping her from pacing. "Sweetheart, you can't play the if-only game. Life doesn't work that way, and it is *not* your fault this happened. They're going to find Colette, and that horrible man will pay for what he's done."

Madigan handed Reese more tissues. "Colette is strong and smart. She's going to be okay."

"What if she's not?" Pain sliced through her. She swiped angrily at her tears. "It's already been too long. He could have taken her out of state, or raped her, *or*..." She couldn't say her worst fear. She wouldn't survive losing Colette.

"That's *not* going to happen." Reba pulled her into her arms. "We've got more than forty men, plus the police, out there looking for her. There are roadblocks set up, and the club has a network of people from here to the West Coast who have all been alerted. He won't get far."

Reese's hands fisted, her nails digging into her palms. "I swear, if he hurts her, I'll—"

"You won't have to do anything. Blaine will take him out," Tobias said evenly, as if it were an indisputable fact.

For some reason that amped up Reese's fear *and* her fury. She paced again. "Lettie is out there alone with that guy. She's got to be terrified, and it's our mother's fault. I don't understand how she could do this to her own daughter. Lettie's never done *anything* to her."

"My sister is recovering from a drug problem," Steph said. "Addiction is its own type of evil. It's not fair, and I know it feels personal, but it's not about Lettie or you or anyone or anything other than your mother's next fix."

"I don't *care* if it's a disease that's bigger than her," Reese seethed. "I *hate* her, and I know that makes me a horrible person, but I *never* want to see her face again. And if anything more happens to Lettie or Blaine, I will strangle her with my bare hands."

BLAINE SPED DOWN the road, chased by the thunderous roar of the rest of the Dark Knights. The image of Reese falling apart battled with the echo of the asshole he'd just roughed up to find out where Ice was holding Colette—*She won't be able to walk when he's done with her.*

He tightened his grip on the handlebars. Ice wouldn't be breathing when Blaine was done with him. The police had arrested Reese's mother for breaking the court order *and* for human trafficking. They'd probably arrest Blaine by the end of the night for killing Ice, but it would be worth it to get the fucker out of Reese's and Colette's life for good.

At least Reese was safe. He hated leaving her, but he wasn't about to put Colette's life in anyone else's hands.

He flew into the driveway of the house where that asshole had said Ice was holding Colette, the other Knights falling into line by the curb. Blaine dropped his helmet and stormed toward the front door as Preacher directed men to cover the back and sides of the shitty house.

"Blaine, do *not* go in there," Cuffs warned. "Backup is three minutes away."

Blaine heard screams coming from inside. Rage roared through him as he kicked the front door in and tore down the hall in the direction of Colette's screams. He saw Ice turning around seconds before he saw the gun, and a searing pain radiated through his chest, the impact knocking him backward. Colette's bloodcurdling shriek cut through the air. Adrenaline surging, Blaine charged forward. Another shot rang out as Blaine launched himself at Ice, taking him down as the gun went off again.

Blaine's ears were ringing, the metallic taste of blood pooling in his mouth as he dragged himself off Ice, blood drenching his clothes. Pain gripped him as he pulled himself up on the bed, where Colette was cowering, and drew her, sobbing and shaking, into his arms, choking out, *"I've got you,"* just as his vision went black.

REESE COULDN'T BELIEVE she said she'd strangle her own mother, but the hatred she felt was stronger than her good sense.

Reba took Reese's hand. "You've been Colette's protector, mother, *and* sister for fifteen years, and that woman has made it *very* difficult for both of you every step of the way. You're allowed to be furious with her."

A phone rang, and everyone reached for theirs.

"It's Preacher," Reba said.

Reese stilled, heightened panic flaring in her chest as Reba held up a finger and put the phone to her ear.

"Hi, Preach." She paused, relief showing in her eyes. "Thank goodness." Her brows knitted, and her eyes teared up. Reese held her breath as Reba lifted her chin, eyes blinking dry, her expression morphing to one of practiced restraint. "Okay. I understand. Yes. I love you."

"What happened?" Reese asked as she ended the call.

"They've got Colette. She's okay," Reba said, causing a flood of tears and relief as they all talked at once.

Reese choked out, "Thank God. And Blaine?"

Reba reached for her hand. "Honey, Blaine led the charge. He's been shot."

The air rushed from Reese's lungs, her knees buckling as gasps, *No*s and *Ohmygod*s rang out around her. *No. This isn't real. It can't be.*

"Blaine's on his way to the hospital. Colette refused to leave his side and went in the ambulance with him..."

Reba's voice competed with Madigan's sobs and the blood rushing through Reese's ears as she tried to process the horrific news. *"No."* Reese shook her head, tears blurring her vision. *"No.* This *isn't* right. That drugged-out witch can't take him away from us—" A sob stole her voice.

"He *can't* die," Madigan cried, throwing her arms around Tobias.

Ginger put her arm around Reese, she and the other girls talking at once, reassuring Reese that he was going to be okay. Reese's head was spinning with fear for Blaine, relief over Colette, and hatred for her mother.

"Girls," Reba said sternly. "I know this is scary, but we *have* to believe he's going to be okay. We need to pull ourselves together and be strong for each other and for Blaine. Let's get to the hospital."

As Ginger and Reba ushered them out the door, Reese drew upon all her strength, forcing her worst fears down deep. Blaine had been strong for her and Colette since the moment they'd met. Now it was her turn.

Chapter Thirty

BLAINE WAS ANTSY as shit as the nurse bandaged his shoulder, rambling about how lucky he was that the bullet had missed his brachial plexus and subclavian artery. He didn't give a damn what it did or didn't hit. He needed to see Reese and to get Colette home. Colette had gotten hysterical when the hospital staff had started to take him into another room, and he'd demanded they stay together. Given the situation she'd just been through, they'd allowed it and had checked her out while they'd cleaned his wounds. She had a few bruises, but thankfully, she was otherwise physically unharmed. Her emotional state was another story. Now that the shock was wearing off, she looked like she was on the verge of a breakdown, sitting on a chair with her knees pulled up to her chest, arms around them. She'd been through too much, had witnessed a man die, and had held her shit together better than any ten men could. But Blaine wasn't about to let her struggle through that alone. He'd already told Cuffs to reach out to his sister, Tasha. She was a hell of a therapist, and Lord knew Colette and Reese would need help dealing with all this shit so they didn't end up as bottled up as he was.

But first they had to get through giving statements to the

police, and they wouldn't take Colette's statement without Reese present.

The nurse finished bandaging his shoulder and put his arm in a sling. "Okay, that should do it."

"Thank you." He tried to get off the bed, but the nurse stopped him.

"Whoa, big guy. You're not going anywhere."

"What do you mean? The doc said I'm fine."

"*No.* He said you'll *be* fine. You just got shot through the shoulder, and you have a pretty nasty flesh wound on your side from a second bullet. You're here overnight for rest and observation. Doctor's orders."

"I'll rest at home and report back if I have any issues."

"Blaine, can't you just listen to her and do what she said?" Colette asked.

"I want to get you home, Lettie."

"You can't leave yet," the nurse said. "Do I need to get your father back in here to whoop your butt?" His father and Cuffs had just gone to wait for his mother and Reese.

Blaine scoffed.

"You need to listen to her," Colette insisted.

Her shaky voice tugged at him. "Lettie, I'm fine. I promise."

"I know. You're fine. I know." Her lower lip trembled. "But you need to stay in case you're not fine later. There was so much blood." Her voice cracked, and tears spilled down her cheeks.

Blaine's heart tore open. He threw his legs over the side of the bed, despite the nurse's protests, and reached for Colette with his unharmed arm. "Get over here, sweetheart." She went to him, and he pulled her into a one-armed embrace. "I'm okay. I'll *always* be okay. Most of that blood was from Ice, not me."

Cuffs had shot Ice at the same time Blaine had launched himself at the bastard. When they'd hit the floor, Ice's gun had gone off. Thankfully, the bullet had only grazed Blaine's side and not lodged in his gut. Ice had died at the scene, and Blaine's girls were safe.

"I thought you were dead." She shook with sobs.

"I know. I'm sorry." He held her tighter, barbed wire coiling sharp and painful in his chest, as if it were trying to keep his heart from crawling out of him to get to her. "It would take a hell of a lot more than a couple of bullets to take me down."

"Will you *please* stay here until they say you can leave? I don't want anything bad to happen to you." She sounded young and vulnerable—a good reminder that despite her typical bravado, she was just a fragile kid who was holding on to a lifetime of hurt.

"Yes, baby. I'll stay." He'd fucking fly to the moon if she needed him to. He eyed the nurse. "I need you to make sure Reese Wilder gets in here right away, or we're leaving."

"I'll do my best," the nurse said, and left the room.

"I'm staying, baby," he reassured Colette. "It's okay. I'm not going anywhere."

"Thank you," she whispered, hugging him tighter.

Blaine was still holding her when Reese ran through the curtain, her baby blues flooding with tears as she rushed over and threw her arms around both of them. "Ohmygod. You're okay. Thank God you're okay. I was so scared. I love you." She clung to them. "I love you so much."

"I—" A sob burst from Colette's lungs. "I love you."

"I thought I lost you." Reese squeezed them tighter, her fingers digging into his neck. "I love you. God, I love you so much."

Blaine reached between them, shoving off his sling, and put both arms around them, gritting through the pain *and* the tears burning his eyes as the girls volleyed *I love you*s. Their every tear drove the jagged barbs of wire deeper into his heart. He didn't know if they were talking to him or only to each other, but it didn't matter. Everything he never knew he wanted was right there in his grasp, and he was never letting them go.

"I love you so much." Reese's voice was thin and shaky, just above a whisper.

"Me too," Colette said. "I love you."

"*I love you, too*" charged out, the barbed wire in his chest loosening. "Both of you. I love you so damn much."

Two sets of teary eyes gazed back at him.

"You do?" Reese asked carefully, her hopeful baby blues reaching into his soul for the truth.

"Don't ask him that," Colette snapped. "He took bullets for us. Of course he loves us."

"Well, I don't want him to have to say it just because he almost died," Reese said.

"It would take a lot more than a couple of bullets to take him down," Colette insisted. "He's *fine*. He's not leaving us. Not *ever*."

Reese looked at him in that damn hospital gown, fresh tears spilling down her cheeks, eyes brimming with as much pain as relief and an overwhelming amount of love. "Are you really okay?"

"Baby, it would take a fucking machine gun to keep me from my girls."

"He's too possessive to die and leave you up for grabs or leave me alone to start dating before I'm thirty," Colette said with a teary smile.

Their laughter was music to his ears. "You're damn right I am. I'm not taking any more chances. You're moving in with me. I'll pay off your landlord and get the guys to pick up your stuff from your apartment and your mom's house and move you in tonight."

More tears fell down Reese's cheeks. "Are you sure?"

"Reese." Colette glowered at her. "I want to move in with him, and he obviously loves you. He was a pain in the nurse's butt because he wanted to be with you."

"But it's our fault he got hurt," Reese said through more tears.

"No, baby. It's not. Don't ever say that," Blaine bit out. "None of this is either of your faults." It sickened him, thinking about how furious and hurt Colette had been when she'd demanded to know if her mother was behind her abduction. But he wasn't about to let either of them feel guilty about any of this. "This is on your mother and her alone. She's going away for a long time for what she did to Lettie, and if she ever wants to come near either of you again, she's going to have to go through me."

Reese was breathing harder, hands shaking, looking at him like she couldn't believe it, and he knew it wasn't her heart that was disbelieving. It was that broken part of her that her parents had trampled on and other guys had neglected that was afraid to believe. The part he would spend a lifetime healing, nurturing, and loving with everything he had.

He held her gaze, refusing to let go of either of them. "Buttercup, I have been in love with you for weeks, and I fall deeper in love with you every minute of the day. I know I suck at opening up, but if you're patient with me, I will do whatever it takes to be the man you and Lettie need me to be. The man you both deserve and can be so fucking proud of, you'll never doubt my love again."

Reese took his face between her hands, the way he'd done to her nearly every day he'd known her, and gazed deeply into his eyes, lower lip trembling, tears streaking her beautiful cheeks, as she said, "You already are."

Chapter Thirty-One

BLAINE SQUINTED AGAINST the afternoon sun as his brothers and cousins barreled out of the diner behind him. They'd gone for a long ride and had stopped for lunch. Filling his lungs with the crisp October air, he rolled his shoulders back, feeling a tinge of discomfort in his shoulder. *Totally fucking worth it.* It had been four months since all that shit went down and the girls had moved in with him, and he'd never been happier. Even though Ice was dead and his crew had all been arrested, Blaine had arranged a month of extra protection for the girls through the Dark Knights, just in case there were any repercussions.

Their mother would be behind bars for several years, but it wasn't nearly enough. Hell, in Blaine's eyes, even a lifelong sentence wouldn't be enough for what she'd put Reese and Colette through. Grief, fear, guilt, and even relief had come in near-debilitating waves for Reese and Colette the first few weeks after that nightmare. While the move had brought many positive changes for all of them, Colette had endured the added stress of starting at a new school. She and Reese had been seeing Tasha Revere consistently since that awful night. She'd assured them that those feelings were normal and had taught them ways to handle it when they felt overwhelmed. But Blaine had always powered through grief, and he hadn't been sure *he* was handling it in the best way to help them to heal. He'd also been mired down with fury at the people who had hurt them, and after the way he'd screwed up with Madigan, he hadn't wanted to take any chances. He'd started seeing a sharp therapist named Charles who Tasha had referred him to.

Blaine had always thought he was being strong by keeping everything inside and helping others through difficult times, but as Reese and his grandfather had suspected, and Charles had confirmed, he'd also been avoiding his own grief. He would never be the kind of man who talked everything out, but Charles and Tasha were some kind of miracle workers. They'd helped them all find their way, and their relationships were stronger for it. Reese and Colette were continuing to see Tasha, but there was only so much therapy a guy like Blaine could take. He'd stopped going two weeks ago, when he'd been cleared for wind therapy, aka riding his motorcycle. Today was his first long ride, and the open road was doing wonders for his head.

Cuffs sidled up to him. "How's the shoulder?"

"Never better. Listen, man. Did I ever thank you for taking down Ice?"

"Yeah, right after I gave you hell for going rogue when I told you to wait for backup. You had pain meds in your system, and you'd just asked your girls to move in, so you might not remember, but you did."

"Good, because not a day goes by that I don't thank God for your keen marksmanship."

"We're just lucky you're slower than a sloth." Cuffs cocked a grin. "If you were a second faster, that bullet could've taken you out."

Blaine shook his head, giving him a *Yeah, right* look. Cuffs would never have taken that chance. He knew damn well he'd make the shot. "Seriously, Cuffs. Thanks for saving our lives."

"Just doing my job. How'd Reese take the news the other night?"

Reese had decided she wanted to find out if their mother's rapist had ever been caught, but she was still afraid of the truth being too much for Colette to handle. Cuffs had pulled some strings and had a buddy from out of state run Colette's DNA through the national database. Blaine had no idea how the guy had done it under the radar or how he'd convinced the potential match, an inmate serving a life sentence for multiple rapes and one murder, to take a paternity test, and he didn't want to know. He was just glad to learn the identity of Colette's father and know he was off the streets for good.

"She was relieved to know he couldn't hurt anyone else, but I think deep down she was hoping to find out Colette's father wasn't a rapist."

"That's understandable. He's been off the street for twelve years, and he'll never be able to hurt another woman. That's something. Is she going to tell Colette?"

"Eventually," he said as Zander, Zeke, and Baz joined them. Zeke was another miracle worker. He'd helped Colette every step of the way to settle into her new school and get the help she needed for her dyslexia. It really did take a village. "What's up?"

Zander motioned to Zeke. "He's all twisted up because Aria is acting funny."

"Is she okay?" Blaine asked.

"It's hard to tell," Zeke said. "She's acting weird. Secretive."

"Maybe she's seeing someone," Cuffs suggested.

"That's what I said," Zander agreed.

Zeke's jaw tightened.

Blaine recognized that look. *Hello, green-eyed monster.* "Dude, just talk to her."

"Or fucking claim her already," Zander said.

Zeke glowered at him. "I've tried talking to her, but she's not sharing."

"I can give you some tips for getting women to spill their secrets," Baz offered. "I'm kind of a pro at it."

"Nah. I'm good," Zeke said. "I'll figure it out."

"Hey, guys." Maverick sauntered over with a big-ass grin. "Check out my girl's new smile." He held up his phone, showing them a video of his three-and-half-month-old baby girl, Marybelle Whiskey Wicked—named for Maverick's biological mother, Mary, and for Reba, whose maiden name was Whiskey.

"Dude, that's the same smile as the last eight hundred videos you've shown us," Baz said with a laugh.

"No, it's not," Maverick insisted. "Blaine, you see it, don't you? This smile is bigger."

"Yeah, man. I see it. She's even more beautiful than she was twenty minutes ago." Blaine had never seen his brother so happy, and he sure as hell wasn't going to be the one to piss on his parade. Plus, Marybelle was too damn cute, with big blue eyes and a dusting of dark hair. Reese and Colette were as madly in love with her as Blaine and the rest of them were. Colette had called dibs on babysitting their precious daughter the night she was born.

"He's blowing smoke. It's the same damn smile," Zander insisted.

As they argued about Marybelle's smile, Blaine's thoughts returned to Reese. He hated being away from her today. He'd missed so many Sunday rides, he'd gotten used to hanging out with her and Colette. Sundays had become their lazy days. While the girls tried new muffin recipes and binge-watched girlie movies, he taste-tested the treats and caught up on designs for work or whatever else he had going on. He didn't care what he did. He just fucking loved being in the same house with them.

He stepped aside to call Reese and saw Tank and Gunner talking on their phones. They were probably checking in with their loves, too. Not for the first time and certainly not for the last, he was struck by the thought that he was in love. He never thought he'd fall in love, much less live with a woman he adored and her sister, who felt like his own blood. But as Reese's sweet voice came through the phone, he knew she had not only been put on this earth to take care of Colette but also to save him, and there was no one else on earth who could *ever* fill her shoes.

BLAINE OPTED OUT of taking the long way back with the guys and headed home early to surprise Reese. He was puzzled to see his father's truck and trailer and Tobias's truck in his driveway. He climbed off his bike and took off his helmet, wondering what the hell was going on. As he headed up to the door, he heard music coming from the backyard and detoured in that direction.

He strode through the side garden and saw his father's excavator parked in the grass and Reese and Colette dancing beneath the umbrella of a large tree. His father was twirling his mother, and Madigan and Tobias were slow dancing. Woody, the ornery but adorable dog he'd adopted for Colette the week after she'd been kidnapped, ran circles around them, barking up a storm, competing with "Wake Me Up Before You Go-Go" blaring from somewhere.

He didn't know what the hell was going on, but he watched Reese dancing awkwardly as he headed across the yard grinning like a lovesick fool. Even though he and Madigan had dragged her onto the dance floor several times at the Salty Hog, her moves were still anything but smooth. But *damn*, she was beautiful with that radiant smile, shaking her gorgeous booty with her sister, who thankfully had not inherited the same dancing genes.

Woody darted toward him, yapping away. He scooped up the little dog that had pissed on half his furniture and made a world of difference in Colette's life, letting him lick his face as Reese and Colette ran toward him.

"What are you doing here?" Reese asked.

"You're early!" Colette added.

"You Wilders still haven't gotten the hang of making a guy feel welcome, have you?" He leaned in and kissed Reese. "Did I miss an invitation to the party?"

"We wanted to surprise you," Reese exclaimed.

"You damn near screwed it up, son," his father said.

"Screwed what up?" He looked at Madigan, who, like his mother, looked ready to burst with excitement. Tobias's expression wasn't giving anything away.

Reese beamed at him. "You have done so much for me and Colette. We wanted to do something for you."

"She's including me, and I wanted to help, but this was *all* Reese's idea, and she was annoyingly excited about it." Colette rolled her eyes.

"I was not," Reese said.

"Yes, you were." Colette spoke an octave higher. *"Is this boulder too big? What kind of flowers do you think he'll like? Are these too girlie?"*

"Okay, maybe I was a little annoying. But I wanted it to be perfect." Reese laughed, blue eyes sparkling in the sun. "I know how important family is to you, and I know you have the wings on your back for the people you've loved and lost. But you can't see them there. I thought it might be nice to honor them in a way that allowed you space to have a private conversation with them. I know it's a big assumption, and if I've overstepped, Preacher already agreed to take the whole thing away."

He set Woody down. "Baby, I don't understand. What have you done?"

"We made you a memorial garden." She took his hand and led him around the excavator to a gorgeous new garden at the edge of the woods. In the middle of the garden was a boulder with FAMILY inscribed in large letters across the middle and, in smaller letters, HILDA, ASHLEY, and AXEL, just like his tattoo. Below the *F* in FAMILY was a paw print and the name CLOVER. His chest constricted as he took in the beautiful flowers and plants she'd planted around the boulder, perfectly sculpted stone angel wings sprouting from the ground to the left of the rock, and an inviting wooden bench to the right.

Struggling against the emotions swamping him, he thought about what his father had said about strong women needing a soft place to land. He'd been right about Reese, but Blaine never imagined he needed one, too.

"Maverick made the wings and put the words on the boulder, and your dad made the bench. If you don't like it—"

Overcome with emotions, he hauled her into a kiss before he lost his fucking mind.

"I think he likes it," Tobias said, making everyone laugh.

Blaine drew back, but his eyes remained locked on Reese. "I love it, and I love you, buttercup. More than life itself." He kissed her again. Just a quick, tender press of his lips.

"See? I told you they kiss a lot," Colette said, earning more laughter.

Blaine slid his arm around Reese, smiling at Colette. "Sorry, Halfpint. I'll try to watch that from now on."

"It wasn't a complaint." Colette crossed her arms and lifted her chin. "Just don't yell at me when I kiss my boyfriend in front of you."

"Your *what?*" He looked at Reese. "What's she talking about?"

"Don't ask me." Reese's eyes danced with amusement.

"*Lettie...?*" he fumed.

Colette giggled. Madigan and his mother linked their arms through hers like they were the Three Musketeers.

"How about we go have a few of those muffins you girls made?" His mother arched a brow at Tobias and Preacher. "Who else wants some?"

Everyone headed for his house, chuckling, except Blaine and Reese, who was still beaming at him. "Hey, I was talking to Lettie," he called after them.

"You were talking *at* her," Madigan called out. "Take a breather."

"Maybe Lettie going to the same school as Kendra and TJ isn't such a good idea," he said to Reese. "She said she and TJ were just friends."

"They *are* just friends. She just likes to get you riled up, kind of like you like to make me blush." She put her hand on his chest. "But you're going to need to lighten up about her dating, because it's going to happen sooner rather than later."

"Can we pretend it's not?" He was only half teasing. He knew she was right, but he wasn't happy about it.

"Probably not."

"Then I might need a few more sessions with Charles." He raked a hand through his hair. "I think I just went gray. Do you see any gray hair?"

She laughed. "You're a dork."

"I'm not kidding. Opening up a door for some kid to hurt Lettie is not high on my priority list." He wound his arms around her, pulling her closer. "Can't we lock her in the basement until she's thirty?"

"No, but I love how you love her."

"How could I not love her? She's part of you. Hell, she's part of me." He pressed his lips to hers. "I don't know if I'm going to survive her dating."

"You will."

"How do you know?"

"Because you love us too much to leave us."

He brushed his lips over hers. "I do, baby, and I love the memorial garden."

"It's an exit ramp off the highway," she said sweetly.

His mind tiptoed back to their first motorcycle ride. *You don't scare me, Blaine Wicked. But all that heartache trapped inside you does...Your grief is stacked up inside you like cars on a highway with no exit. Maybe we should build some exit ramps and see what happens.*

She touched his cheek, bringing him back to the moment. "Do you think you'll ever use it?"

"I know I will, because that road brings me closer to you."

Chapter Thirty-Two

REESE LAY IN the bath reliving their afternoon. Blaine's parents and Madigan and Tobias had stayed for dinner, and they'd had a great time. The house was quiet now. Colette was spending the night at Kendra's, and Blaine was taking forever to join her in the bath. She'd been in the tub for only ten or fifteen minutes, but she missed him already. How was that possible?

Who was she kidding? She missed him the minute she drove away from the house to go to work every day. The last several months had been an emotional roller coaster, and through it all, Blaine had been their grounding force. He was always there, holding them when they were sad, making them laugh when they were in bad moods, and showering them with unconditional love. Reese was thrilled that he'd loved the memorial garden, and he'd promised to thank her properly tonight. She shuddered just thinking about what he might have in store for them.

"Blaine?" she called out. "Are you coming?"

She waited for him to make a dirty comment. When none came, she called his name again, selfishly hoping he hadn't fallen asleep, though she wouldn't blame him. He was always on the move and never slept more than a few hours. She didn't know how he did it.

She climbed out of the tub and dried off. Wrapping the towel around herself, she went to find him. "Blaine?" she said as she opened the bathroom door.

Her breath caught at the sight of candles on the nightstands and dressers, rose petals strewn across the blanket, and Blaine sitting on the end of the bed in his boxer briefs beside their sexy toy box, holding a silk tie. "What…?"

"This is for you, baby girl." In the space of a few heart-thrumming seconds, he manipulated the silk tie so it had two loops and put one around each wrist. He took one end between his teeth and pulled, binding his wrists like handcuffs. He stepped closer and got down on his knees, holding his hands up in front of him, fists together.

Her heart hammered against her ribs. "What are you doing?"

He opened his left hand, revealing a gorgeous canary diamond ring surrounded by alternating leaves of white gold and diamonds. "Submitting to you, wholly and completely, if you'll have me."

She opened her mouth to say *If?* but her voice was drowning in a well of emotions. She wasn't even sure she was breathing. But as she looked at him, the love in his eyes drew her shaky voice. "If you want it, you have to say it."

His smile told her he knew exactly where she'd borrowed those words from.

"Reese, baby, you've not only changed my world, but you've become my world. I love you now, always, and forever. Will you do me the honor of being my wife, my queen, my every-thing?"

"*Yes!*" she said through tears, and went down on her knees, pressing her lips to his. "Yes! I love you. Yes." Both of them laughed as she kissed him again and again.

"Give me your finger, baby."

"I feel like I should ask where you want it." She held out a shaky hand.

He cocked a brow as he slid the ring on her finger. "Maybe I need to rethink this submission thing."

"Not a chance." As she lowered her lips to his, she whispered, "Time to see if you can handle *my* wicked ways."

Get ready for Baz Wicked in
TALK WICKED TO ME

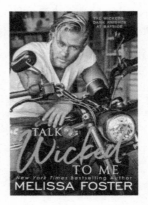

Baxter "Baz" Wicked, the most charming and mysterious of the family, has a career he loves, a brotherhood he trusts, and plans that don't include settling down just yet. Come along for the unexpected, hilarious, and heart-wrenching ride as Baz discovers that life and love can be messy, and carefully crafted plans don't hold a candle to matters of the heart.

Fall in love with Kane Bad and Sable Montgomery
in FALLING FOR MR. BAD

A Bad Boys After Dark crossover novel

She's a badass musician and mechanic given the opportunity of a lifetime, but she has no patience for glitz, glamour, or overinflated egos. He's a billionaire tasked with wrangling her into submission, and he has no time for drama. Going head-to-head has never been so much fun. Especially since neither one is afraid to play dirty.

Have you met
The Whiskeys: Dark Knights at Redemption Ranch?

Sasha Whiskey is done being the good girl. She's ready to wrangle in the one man not looking to be caught and give him a taste of Whiskey. With any luck, one taste won't be nearly enough. Come along for the steamy, emotional ride in A TASTE OF WHISKEY.

Love Melissa's Writing?

Discover more of the magic behind *New York Times* bestselling and award-winning author Melissa Foster. The Wickeds are just one of the many family series in the Love in Bloom big-family romance collection, featuring fiercely loyal heroes, smart, sassy heroines, and stories that go above and beyond your expectations. See the collection here:

www.MelissaFoster.com/love-bloom-series

Free first-in-series ebooks, downloadable series checklists, reading orders, and more can be found on Melissa's Reader Goodies page.

www.MelissaFoster.com/reader-goodies

More Books By Melissa Foster

LOVE IN BLOOM SERIES

SNOW SISTERS
Sisters in Love
Sisters in Bloom
Sisters in White

THE BRADENS at Weston
Lovers at Heart, Reimagined
Destined for Love
Friendship on Fire
Sea of Love
Bursting with Love
Hearts at Play

THE BRADENS at Trusty
Taken by Love
Fated for Love
Romancing My Love
Flirting with Love
Dreaming of Love
Crashing into Love

THE BRADENS at Peaceful Harbor
Healed by Love
Surrender My Love
River of Love
Crushing on Love
Whisper of Love
Thrill of Love

THE BRADENS & MONTGOMERYS at Pleasant Hill – Oak Falls
Embracing Her Heart
Anything for Love

Trails of Love
Wild Crazy Hearts
Making You Mine
Searching for Love
Hot for Love
Sweet Sexy Heart
Then Came Love
Rocked by Love
Falling For Mr. Bad (Previously *Our Wicked Hearts*)
Claiming Her Heart

THE BRADEN NOVELLAS
Promise My Love
Our New Love
Daring Her Love
Story of Love
Love at Last
A Very Braden Christmas

THE REMINGTONS
Game of Love
Stroke of Love
Flames of Love
Slope of Love
Read, Write, Love
Touched by Love

SEASIDE SUMMERS
Seaside Dreams
Seaside Hearts
Seaside Sunsets
Seaside Secrets
Seaside Nights
Seaside Embrace
Seaside Lovers
Seaside Whispers
Seaside Serenade

For the Love of Whiskey
A Taste of Whiskey

SUGAR LAKE
The Real Thing
Only for You
Love Like Ours
Finding My Girl

HARMONY POINTE
Call Her Mine
This is Love
She Loves Me

THE WICKEDS: DARK KNIGHTS AT BAYSIDE
A Little Bit Wicked
The Wicked Aftermath
Crazy, Wicked Love
The Wicked Truth
His Wicked Ways
Talk Wicked to Me

SILVER HARBOR
Maybe We Will
Maybe We Should
Maybe We Won't

WILD BOYS AFTER DARK
Logan
Heath
Jackson
Cooper

BAD BOYS AFTER DARK
Mick
Dylan
Carson
Brett

HARBORSIDE NIGHTS SERIES
Includes characters from the Love in Bloom series
Catching Cassidy
Discovering Delilah
Tempting Tristan

More Books by Melissa
Chasing Amanda (mystery/suspense)
Come Back to Me (mystery/suspense)
Have No Shame (historical fiction/romance)
Love, Lies & Mystery (3-book bundle)
Megan's Way (literary fiction)
Traces of Kara (psychological thriller)
Where Petals Fall (suspense)

Acknowledgments

I hope you enjoyed Blaine and Reese's story. I know there will be readers who want to see the last scene play out, but Reese is such a private person, and she's allowed us into every aspect of her life. The final scene is my gift to her.

If you follow me on social media, you may have seen that I had two friends visiting while I was revising this story. At one point I left the room to take a phone call and my friends jumped in and rewrote a scene. I have received many messages asking to see the scene that left us giggling like children. Below is the unedited clip written in jest by two of my besties, Amy Manemann and Natasha Brown. Go buy their books. I promise they're better than this.

> *Light streamed from his bulging package, and it grew two sizes as he looked at her. His giant jackhammer burst from his pants, putting the Hulk to shame. Her chest heaved and her nipples turned hard as titanium, popping the buttons from her blouse and hitting him in the face. He pulled her against him. His body shook, and he prematurely ejaculated against her leg.*

The Wickeds is just one of the series in the Love in Bloom big-family romance collection. All of my books can be enjoyed as stand-alone novels, without cliffhangers or unresolved issues. Characters in each series appear in other family series, so you never miss an engagement, wedding, or birth. You can find more information about the Love in Bloom series here: www.MelissaFoster.com/melissas-books

I offer several free first-in-series ebooks, which you can find here:
www.MelissaFoster.com/LIBFree

If you'd like a peek into my writing world, I chat with fans often in my fan club on Facebook.
www.Facebook.com/groups/MelissaFosterFans

Follow my social pages for fun giveaways and updates on what's going on in our fictional boyfriends' worlds.
www.Facebook.com/MelissaFosterAuthor
Instagram: @MelissaFoster_Author
TikTok: @MelissaFoster_Author

If you prefer sweet romance, with no explicit scenes or graphic language, please try the Sweet with Heat series written under my pen name, Addison Cole. You'll find many of the same great love stories with toned-down heat levels.

I couldn't get along without my faithful assistants, Sharon Martin and Lisa Filipe, or keep my character sheets up to date lately without the help of Terren Hoeksema. I have loads of gratitude for my incredible editorial team for helping me make my writing shine, Kristen Weber and Penina Lopez, my meticulous proofreaders, Elaini Caruso, Juliette Hill, Lynn Mullan, and Justinn Harrison, and my last set of eyes, Lee Fisher.

As always, heaps of gratitude go out to my family and friends for your endless support and patience.

Meet Melissa

www.MelissaFoster.com

Melissa Foster is a *New York Times, Wall Street Journal*, and *USA Today* bestselling and award-winning author. Her books have been recommended by *USA Today's* book blog, *Hagerstown* magazine, *The Patriot*, and several other print venues.

Visit Melissa on her website or chat with her on social media. Melissa enjoys discussing her books with book clubs and reader groups and welcomes an invitation to your event. Melissa's books are available through most online retailers in paperback and digital formats.

Melissa also writes sweet romance under the pen name Addison Cole.

Made in the USA
Las Vegas, NV
28 December 2023

83658807R00256